Totally Bound Publishing books by Corrine A. Silver:

Wrecked

I0563703

The Blackened Window

WRECKED

CORRINE A. SILVER

Wrecked
ISBN # 978-1-78430-699-1
©Copyright Corrine A. Silver 2015
Cover Art by Posh Gosh ©Copyright August 2015
Interior text design by Claire Siemaszkiewicz
Totally Bound Publishing

Published in 2015 by Totally Bound Publishing, Newland House, The Point, Weaver Road, Lincoln, LN6 3QN, United Kingdom.

WRECKED

Dedication

For David. For always.

Acknowledgements

I wrote this book without any real belief that it would reach anyone other than a few people close to me. I secretly hoped that it would, but knew enough about publishing to know that books don't get published just because the author hopes for it. I wrote it because it made me happy to do it. I enjoyed writing something that explored sex, relationships, sexual politics, BDSM and feminism.

I have to thank the people who have helped me. Very early in my writing I decided that I'd submit short stories because the worst that could happen is that someone would say "No." I started with short story anthologies and I have to thank Rachel Kramer Bussel and Alison Tyler for being the first people to read and accept my work. When I learned about the BDSM Writer's Con Book Contest, I had a similar approach. No one can say "Yes" if I never ask. So I submitted the first iteration of this book, and was selected as a finalist. Dr Charley Ferrer is the powerhouse behind the Con and my gratitude to her and the selection committee is immense. The Con was phenomenal and I got word that the contract with Totally Bound was finalized shortly after I got home.

The people I have worked with at Totally Bound have been nearly supernaturally patient with someone who has never done this before, who didn't know entirely how to use the software correctly at the beginning and certainly didn't know the usual protocols for how to navigate the publication of a book. Thank you to my editor, liaison to publishing and all around possessor of saintly patience, Jenny Douglas. This is most assuredly a better book because of you.

Chapter One

Xander
3OH!3 Double Vision

At the beginning of my second year of medical school, I was ambivalent, at best. Sometimes I felt right on the edge of something amazing, but mostly, it felt like waiting for the real thing to happen. It didn't help that I wasn't hooked in and invested the way most of the Ivy League overachievers were.

My mentor had told me the first year was the most traumatic. He didn't know shit. It was the second year that fucked my world up, and it wasn't school. It wasn't medicine. It was her. She nearly destroyed me.

* * * *

"Hey, Xander! Hold on a second."

I paused, turning to see Dr. Sanderson waving to flag me down before I left for the day. He taught Anatomy to the first years—cadavers, dissection, the whole bit.

9

"Yeah? Hi, Dr. Sanderson." I waited, noticing Stacy waiting down the hall, watching me. The world of history I shared with Stacy flashed through my head and came back to what it always did with her, the way we'd nearly destroyed each other.

She doesn't fucking get it.

Dr. Sanderson shook my hand as he spoke, "Xander, would you be interested in tutoring anatomy? We're short a tutor and you were top of your class. It would really help us and the first years, and we could pay you. I mean, it's just something like nine or ten bucks an hour, but still… Students can usually use it, right?"

I didn't need the money and besides, I had a job at the Window anytime I wanted it. That paid better than ten bucks an hour, and you couldn't beat the perks… Well, actually you could. Literally. But I was bored and needed something more to fill my time. Maybe I'd shake off some ennui if I got a little more involved, met more people. Something other than my simple routine.

"Sure. I could do Tuesday nights." I worked out a few times a week and needed to study some too, I guessed. Tuesdays seemed like as good a night as any.

"Great! I'll find you tomorrow with the paperwork. I usually let them get a little freaked out before having the tutors start. Usually the second week."

"Cool. Just at the library, though. I don't really want to be in the cadaver lab if I don't have to be. I'm still having flashbacks of the smell." I cracked a smile at him. He smiled and slapped me on the back as he turned to his office. I stretched my neck as I turned, knowing Stacy would still be there. I could feel her dark little flame of emptiness trying to pull me into her.

Deep breath.

"Hi, Xander." She said it slow and kind of soft. I don't know if she was trying to be sexy or shy or sweet. But none of it looked right on her, not believable at all.

"Stacy. How was your first day?" I was careful to keep my tone and facial expression neutral. The last thing I wanted or needed was Stacy at my door in the middle of the night. I couldn't risk being even remotely unclear about how things were between us. There were no shades of gray with this girl.

"It was good. Not as bad as I thought. Tough, but I've been through worse." She twitched her lip in the little smirk she knew I hated. It just looked jaded and tainted on her face. She was gorgeous. Textbook pretty, empirically, traditionally, conventionally beautiful. Her hair was a chestnut brown and her eyes were the color of a latte. Tiny little body, made for tossing around and flipping over to fuck anyway you wanted. She had a tan, probably spent the summer somewhere tropical, drinking herself stupid.

Cut that shit out, Stone. You know she's bat-shit crazy. Don't go there again.

She claimed to want me, to love me—still, a decade after what we'd done to each other. She couldn't love anything. At least not anything like me, and I didn't like what I had been like with her.

She stepped close to me, her hand on my chest, smiling up at my face. "Let's get a drink tonight? I want to spend some time with you."

"Can't. I gotta study. And really, so do you."

Her smile broadened as she rocked back on her heels. "There it is. I love that you think you can tell me what to do all the time."

She doesn't get it at all. "I'm not telling you to do shit. Just telling you what I'm gonna do." I sidestepped past her to the main doors out to the parking lot. The parking lot was hot as fuck. Texas could suck sometimes. Not the least of which was when I'd get into the C70—the black C70, with black leather interior. It was a sexy damn car, but I think I'd literally burned my ass a few times.

Even though I didn't want anyone now—and especially not Stacy—I couldn't stop myself from noticing the women around me. Such a range. Black girls, white girls, Hispanic girls, some Native American girls too. Big and small. None of that was all that important to me though—I just really liked women. Their curvy bodies, their softness, their toughness hidden in pliability. Girls I had been with in the past blew my mind. The things I put them through and how they would bend themselves for me. The incredible strength and fearlessness it takes to let someone else play with them that hard. To willingly and repeatedly let themselves be opened up, penetrated, violated. For them to want it as much as I wanted to give it to them. Absolutely breathtaking.

At the beginning of that semester, my mind would wander like that sometimes. Over that summer, I had been the regular Dungeon Master at the Window. It's a kind of cheesy old-school BDSM name for the job of the guy in charge, making sure everyone followed the rules. And the only rules that really mattered to me were consent and relative safety. People call it by a few different names—Risk-Aware Kink, practicing Safe, Sane and Consensual kink—whatever. The key was consent. But all the facets of consent had to be there—the *ability* to consent, *informed* consent, as well as the *actual* consent, because consent from someone who was too incompetent or ignorant didn't mean shit. Informed and enthusiastic consent, that was the key.

Being the DM for the summer let me see everything—all kinds of insanity—but I didn't have to actually take care of anyone. No aftercare, no worrying that I was fucking something up and harming someone rather than just hurting her the way we both wanted. Of course, I got propositioned all the time. But I hadn't actually played at the Window in over a year.

I didn't have anyone I wanted to play with.

* * * *

The week passed in a blur of classes, labs, studying. Stacy kept trying to get me to do something with her. She flirted in that way she thought was sexy and I thought bordered on a caricature of sexiness, like Betty Boop mixed with Jenna Jameson. I blew her off.

On Friday, I saw *her* for the first time in the library, studying late. The girl that was gonna ruin me. I didn't know it then. I just thought she had an ass I wanted to bite. That was the first thing I noticed about her. She had a jiggly ass, and her scrubs were thin enough that I could see how it moved when she walked through the library. Scrubs can be a little deceiving sometimes, but she had a snug T-shirt on and she had a smallish waist that flared out for her hips and a generous ass that I just wanted to put my hands on. She was short—a short, curvy girl was always fun.

She walked across the library and stopped at the desk, turning as she spoke with the clerk. Her hair was twisted up off her neck and as she turned, her profile was visible—smooth skin, a full lower lip, small button nose. But her body looked like sound waves, like some crazy vertical graph from calculus. Her tits balanced out her plump ass and she had the tiniest little tummy her scrubs were hanging low on.

She smiled at the clerk and that was it, I was fucked. Her smile was like getting kicked in the balls. She had that first-year look—vague panic hovering at the edges of all her gestures. But when she smiled, she was fully present in the moment and the panic, the nerves, melted away. Her whole face shifted in a pattern of amusement, and it looked comfortable on her—not contrived, just real. The clerk answered her question, pulling a clipboard over for her to sign. He didn't have a pen and they both looked for one for a few seconds, before she giggled and waved him off as she pulled one from her hair.

Her hair was dark gold with honey and sunlight highlights. *I'm so fucked.* She pulled the pen out and her hair fell down, to the little gap where her T-shirt had pulled up revealing the soft curve of her lower back. The waves of her hair looked a little bit like a shampoo commercial and I wanted to wrap it around my fist, bend her back until tears gathered in her eyes.

Jesus, she's just a girl. Settle down, Stone.

The clerk blatantly stared at her chest while she was writing and the little fucking pervert even started to bite his lip. When she finished writing, she shifted her hips in my direction and I could appreciate why he was drooling—her T-shirt had a low V and her breasts were pretty much phenomenal, but still, he could've had a little class.

Like me right now? Staring at her ass and dreaming of making her yield? Yep. I'm a huge hypocrite.

The clerk watched her walk out, but I watched the naked lust on his face as he pulled the clipboard back to himself. When she was out of the library, he looked

Wrecked

down and grabbed a piece of paper, copying something from the form.

I knew I had no focus left for studying and wanted to punch that fucking guy, so I grabbed my stuff and started to leave. But as I passed the counter, I saw him out of the corner of my eye, adjusting his dick. The dude had wood. Before I thought it through, I turned on my heel and went to the counter.

He was skinny, with stupid thick-rimmed hipster glasses and too-tight jeans. His hair was so intentionally casually bedheaded that I wanted to slap him. He had a tattered messenger bag that he was tucking that piece of paper in and a patched-up Army surplus jacket hung over the back of his chair. The former soldier in me wanted to punch him even harder now.

"Hey, man. I requested a copy of the new edition of Sabiston's. Is it in yet?"

"What's your name?"

"Xander Stone."

He walked to the reserves on the other side of the counter and I leaned forward, grabbing the clipboard and glancing at it. Her name was Leda Collins, and she was signing up for anatomy tutoring. On Thursdays. *Fuck.*

The perv-clerk came back. "Not in yet, man."

"Okay." I started to walk away, but turned back, adding, "Dude, just a word of advice. That chick is beyond you, but even if she wasn't, you were so fucking obvious that *I* felt molested ten feet away. Your need to work on your game."

It wasn't fair and I knew it. I was probably eight to ten years older than him, had half a foot in height and had a military build to his scrawny emo-kid physique. We both knew I could kick the shit out of him, barely trying.

15

He blanched and sputtered. I stood up taller, feeling an awakening in my blood. I smiled as I walked away. These kids who hadn't lived at all were just so ridiculous, and that the girls their age put up with it just reinforced that kind of behavior. Us older dogs had to educate.

I heard him mutter, "Fuck you" as I passed through the door and I chuckled as I reached for the second door of the vestibule. But there she was, kneeling next to a bike, yanking at the lock, which seemed stuck. Each time she yanked back on it, her tits would bounce and it made me smile. I was about to go out and offer to help when she got it and fell back on her ass. She was cute as hell.

She dropped her head in her hands for a second and I thought she was laughing, but when she stood she brushed at her eyes and her lips were pressed in a line. *Shit.* I wanted to go out and make it better somehow, like she was mine. And I laughed at myself, watching her. She was tough, though, grabbing her things and leaving—riding her bike, in the dark, in the borderline shitty neighborhood the school was in. *That shit was gonna change.*

As I pushed through the door finally, I pulled my cell out and dialed.

"Hey, Dr. Sanderson. It's Xander Stone. Just looked at my schedule and I can't tutor on Tuesdays. I actually have Thursdays open."

Chapter Two

Leda
Krewella, Enjoy the Ride

I met Xander in the second week of classes. In retrospect, I was floundering. Classes were overwhelming. I felt lost all the time and I was crying myself to sleep almost every night. But there was Xander, sexy as hell and a lifeline of sorts. He was in the class ahead of mine, at the top of his class—rankings were published—and was a tutor for anatomy. But it was more than his achievement. It was *him*—how he carried himself, how he pulled the world into him, rather than meeting it on its terms. I knew when I met him that he would be a surgeon, the same way I knew I wanted him to touch me. It was in the way he handled things, like they were his, no matter what he was holding.

I was the first of my classmates to arrive to the first tutoring session, but he was there already, sitting at a table in the back of the small medical library, leaning back in his chair with a long piece of black suture tied through his shoelace. He was practicing two-handed tying and his hands moved so smoothly, the knots lining up perfectly on top of each other. As I approached the table, he looked up, but his hands kept going, only faltering slightly when our eyes met.

The thing that drew me to him was intangible. He was attractive, with dark brown hair, cut short, crisp. His eyes, hazel with flecks of orange and gold, were hard, observant, flicking over my face and body as I approached the table. He had a strong angle to his jaw, covered with a day or two of stubble, and his skin didn't have that newness to it that college boys had. He was a little weathered, tan, with a small scar marring his right eyebrow. He had broad shoulders and his faded black concert T-shirt was just shy of being too tight over his chest and shoulders. He had loose jeans on and old Converse. But none of that was *it*. The package was gorgeous, but what was arresting about him wasn't what he looked like. It was how he looked at me. He looked at me the same way he handled the suture—with confidence, unshakable, direct. Almost cocky. We held each other's gaze for a few beats too long to be entirely normal before I found my voice.

"Hi, I'm Leda. Are you the anatomy tutor?" I'd like to say that I said it with confidence to match his, but my voice faltered a bit, thinking about studying bodies with him, his confident hands touching me. I held my breath, waiting for his answer, hoping he'd say yes.

He answered me with a glint in his eyes and a small, suggestive smile on his lips, like he knew where my thoughts had gone. "I'm Xander. Sit down."

It was a command, not an invitation, and I moved immediately to sit. He watched me thoughtfully and raised a single eyebrow as I settled myself across from him. He caught himself, clearing his throat and adding, "A few more of your classmates are joining us still."

I tossed my bag on the table, then got out my textbook and some pens, mainly looking for something to do with my hands and trying to avoid his gaze, because I had this thrill running through me at the way he moved and looked at me and my response. It felt like I couldn't quite take a deep enough breath. It was a heady, almost drunk, feeling after the last few weeks of nonstop, sphincter-tightening anxiety.

"So, Leda, where are you from? What's your story?" He had stopped tying knots and dropped his foot to the floor. He sat leaning toward me with his elbows on the table, and on anyone else it would have seemed friendly. On him, it seemed aggressive, like he was just holding himself back from coming over the table at me. The gold glint in his eyes flickered, despite the banks of harsh lights overhead and I couldn't find my voice for a moment.

"I'm from outside Chicago—grew up there and went to undergrad at the University of Wisconsin." Since the beginning of school it had been one brief introduction after another. It rolled off my tongue with minimal thought once I started speaking.

"More." And I knew that he meant he wanted to know more. He softened the harshness of the single word response with an encouraging smile.

"I'm the youngest in my family. I have an older brother and an older sister. Luke and Julia. They're both doctors too."

"Okay. Family of doctors, check. But tell me a little about *you*." It might have seemed friendly if his tone hadn't been so demanding. He leaned forward, maintaining eye contact while he spoke, almost staring me down while I answered. Maybe his gaze only felt so intense because I was still avoiding it as much as possible. I felt like I was getting off on the wrong foot, making a bad impression, but then a chord of irritation fired through me at his pressure, his pushiness. I almost immediately second guessed myself, unsure if it was his actual behavior or my response to him.

"I don't know." I huffed a sigh of annoyance. "I wasn't intending to go to med school when I started college. I was actually a creative writing major — poetry. Not much of a growth industry. I realized that at best I could get an MFA and teach other people to write angsty poetry, but the reality was that I'd probably be waiting tables at Denny's. Around the same time, I took a women's health course and loved it, so I decided to be a doctor. Of course, my family was thrilled — like you said, family of doctors." It was a quick summary of the last few years, the late night talks with my parents, the shitty conversations with my advisor who didn't think I could handle med school, my sister vaguely warning me off, while she was working hundred hour weeks.

With humor reaching his eyes, he smiled, wide and wild. He opened his mouth to say something else, but the other students started showing up and he cut himself off. I didn't know what to think about him. Something about the way he talked to me irritated me, but also sent a hum zinging through my chest. Everything he did triggered some kind of reaction in me, like my first crush. There was nothing he did that was just neutral — the set of his shoulders, the humor he used to teach, his knowledge base. But by the end of the tutoring session, the constant low grade panic that I had felt since starting the semester had eased a little and did a little more every time his gaze landed on me.

We spent two hours covering the structures of the neck. Xander took his time, walking us through the muscles, making us memorize them before moving deeper to the arteries, veins and nerves. As we reviewed the innervation of the sternocleidomastoid, he'd pause and turn to one of us with a question from something earlier in the session. The first time he did it, my classmate blanched at being called out, but he warned us to get used to getting 'pimped' like that. That our professors and, later Attendings at the hospital, would drop questions on us and expect us to answer, under pressure, with everyone watching us.

His eyes crinkled as he smiled and told us to never give them the satisfaction of stumping us, because, he said, "Fuck them." I liked that about him—the smile and the warning and the 'Don't let them keep you down' attitude.

At ten p.m. when we finished, my own neck ached and I was exhausted. But it was Thursday night. I relished that there was only one more day of classes this week. I could rest over the weekend, but I wasn't planning to leave the library yet because I wanted to pre-read my notes for lectures the next day. So, I didn't pack my things up at the end of the study session, despite my fatigue. The other students all left relatively quickly. I pulled out my notes to review and Xander paused what he was doing. He was much taller than I'd expected once he stood.

"No. You're not staying to study more." His voice sounded too loud in the hush of the nearly empty library. "I can see it in your eyes. You're wrecked. You need to go home and sleep, or at least go home and do something to take your mind off of all this shit for a while."

His bossiness kind of pissed me off a little, but this guy was tutoring me—for free—and I didn't want to be too bitchy, so I schooled my snippy response and smiled. "You know how it is. I just want to get a leg up on lectures tomorrow. Thanks for the help tonight. See you next week."

Clearly dismissing him... Or, not so much. His eyes flashed and his jaw hardened for a moment.

"Leda." His voice was lower, almost growling for a minute. He cleared his throat again and looked up at the ceiling, rubbing the back of his neck. "Leda," he said in a more normal voice, "you cannot spend all day in lecture and all night studying, nonstop, for all of medical school. There are studies that show that after a certain amount of time, usually no more than two hours, your brain needs a break—you stop absorbing the information. So, put your book away and let me walk you to your car."

"I'm all right." *Ease up, dick.*

"No." He leaned over me, a hand on the back of my chair as he crowded into my space and took my book out of my hands, shoved it into my bag, maybe a little more roughly than was necessary. He stood up, picking my bag up with him. "Now." He extended his other hand to me.

And, with the book out of my hand, with the momentary loss of focus, I realized he was right. I didn't really remember much of what I had read, my neck was killing me and I was tired. No, I was exhausted. It was time to go home and sleep. I gave in and took his hand to stand up. His touch was exactly like I'd expected, warm, but solid, strong, not giving at all. He held my fingers tightly and pulled my hand up to him as I stood. I expected him to let go of my hand right away, but he held it for a few seconds longer than was platonic. I pulled it away to grab my bag from him, but he stopped me. "I've got it. I can tell your neck is bothering you."

"Oh, um, thanks. It's my new bed and all this studying. It's killing my neck."

He answered with a flat tone, "You'll adapt."

I repeat... Dick.

He added, "I mean your body becomes accustomed to it. That...or maybe you just stop noticing." He chuckled a bit at the end of his sentence as we left the library. He held the door for me and his soft hand gently ushering me on the small of my back left me with a breathless feeling.

We walked out of the library toward the parking lot and my thoughts started churning with horrible college date-rape stories. *This isn't a date.* "Here I am," I said, as we got to the bike racks.

"Let me drive you home. You can get your bike tomorrow when you'll be leaving campus before dark."

"Hey, man—I appreciate your concern, but I can get myself home." My Windy City toughness, do-not-fucking-try-to-push-me-around attitude surfaced a bit.

"No, Leda. You're going to have to start listening better." He had a matching don't-push-me-back attitude that I appreciated. He was vaguely condescending now, pedantic. When he spoke again, it was a little slower, like he was spelling something out to a child. "I am driving you home. This area of town isn't completely safe for a single woman at night with only a bike to get her out of a bad situation." He paused again, features softening and his voice changed some, became a sexy, hard purr as he looked squarely into my eyes. "Please? I'm gonna worry about you if I don't know you got home safely. I can pick you up in the morning if you want, so you don't have to drive in and deal with getting your bike home."

I had that feeling in my chest again. I looked up at him, feeling like I wasn't breathing right, starting to feel an awareness of my skin, my throat. My mouth was dry and my eyes felt big and wide. I shrank under his gaze. His eyes were warm and hard at the same time. And my mind flashed to fantasy images of him touching me, his skin golden in low light, his hands running over my nakedness, my hips, my mouth open, fingertips at my jaw, stroking down my throat. His hand snaking around to the back of my neck and grasping me there, holding me in place.

"Let's go," he said, pulling me along by my hand again. Of course, he had a cool car, something black, deep tint on the windows, leather seats, but not stupid and flashy. He tossed my bag in the trunk and opened the door for me, offering a hand I didn't take as I got in. When he started the engine, some loud music was blaring, heavy with raw sounding guitar and sexy, drawling vocals. He immediately turned it down, looking almost a little embarrassed. There was an awkward silence for a few seconds.

"So, what's *your* story? I told you all my secrets, now it's your turn." I smiled while saying it, conscious of my not very subtle flirting.

"You hardly told me *secrets*, Leda," he said, a sort of dark mirth coloring his voice as he put the car in gear and backed out. There was a pause in conversation as he navigated through the parking lot and onto the city streets. I watched him as he drove and that steady confidence was there again. He seemed more relaxed and settled into himself.

"Turn left up here on Second Street, and let's start simple. Where are you from?"

"I grew up in Maryland, outside DC. My parents still live there, but I don't really want to talk about my family. Do you want to get a drink before you go home?"

"Weren't you the one just telling me to go home and rest?" I smiled again.

"Well, kinda." He drew the words out, a fake whine. "You need to take a break from studying, fo' sho'." He was actually a little silly for a minute. "Let's get a beer. I know a place."

"Another night, okay? You were right. I'm just really exhausted and want to go home, take a shower and get in bed."

"Oh. Well, I guess we could do that instead." He smiled with a laugh in his eyes.

I just gave him the look, the flirty, I-can't-believe-you-said-that-but-I-kinda-love-that-you-did look and the thought of him in my bed put a flutter in my stomach. I laughed, "Maybe next time, Boss." He stilled for a second and smiled, as I added, "This next building is mine."

He pulled to the curb in front of my building and turned the car off, getting out. As I fumbled in my purse for my keys, he got my bag out of the trunk and came around to my side of the car, holding his hand out for me. I took it this time, but he didn't let go once I was standing and he walked me to my door, holding my hand.

"Thanks for the ride home. I'll see you next week for tutoring," I said, feeling awkward again. I didn't really want to invite him up. It wasn't a date, but it was hanging in the air—the atmosphere of expectation, of more pending, the feeling of 'What's next'? *Will he ask me out?*

"No, you'll see me in the morning for a ride to school." He handed me my bag, and when I took it, he brushed some of my hair out of my eyes. "Your eyes are a perfect steel gray, with bits of white and silver. I've never seen that color before. Very pretty." He wrapped the tendril of my hair around his fingers, with just a touch of tension pulling at my scalp. I stood still under his touch and gaze, holding my breath, aware of his hand, of how close he was. He pulled my hair just a little as it ran through his fingers, letting his fingertips trace my jaw to my chin.

"Thank, um... Thank you," I stammered, as he pulled his hand away. He visibly took a breath and looked down, resolving something for himself.

"See you in the morning," he said, turning on his heel. "Goodnight." And he was walking away.

That was a little abrupt. "Goodnight."

He didn't look back as he walked to his car. Once I was through my entry door, I glanced out one more time and saw him watching me. He held my gaze for a moment before he got in his car and drove away.

He was hard to read. Bossy, but sweet, a little funny, private. I was thinking about him and the strange evening as I got in the shower. He was definitely fun to look at. I couldn't place it, there was something compelling about him, enough that I could shake off how forward he was, or maybe even like it. As the water washed over me, I was aware of my response to him... Something chemical, a hormonal surge of attraction that was most certainly based on something subconscious or pheromonal.

I wanted him to touch me, more than he had. I was vaguely shocked at myself for feeling this strongly after only knowing someone for a few hours. In undergrad, I had dated the same guy for a few years, but there hadn't been very much sexual heat between us. Not like I felt after one night of studying with Xander. I knew it wasn't right, but the thought of any kind of propriety was easily brushed aside. I wanted to kiss him. I wondered what he looked like naked, what his cock was like, how he'd fuck.

The warm, almost hot, water felt great despite the southern heat. Lathering up my hair, I imagined him running his fingers along the back of my neck, standing behind me and pushing into me. His fingertips running under my jaw line with just a little pressure on my throat. *Fuck.* My nipples were getting tight, my breasts felt heavy and my breathing was shallow, thinking of him over me, with water dripping off him.

There was a thrumming through my skin that was gradually concentrating between my thighs. I turned the water off, grabbed a thick white towel and dried off, the rough friction of the towel almost too much. Urgency started to build and I almost giggled, unable to contain the giddy feeling.

Getting into my light nightie, I skipped panties because I knew they'd just get soaked anyway. I felt every muscle fiber as I climbed into bed, imagining him watching me, then on me. My wetness slicked my fingers easily and my puffy lips spread apart with little pressure. Dipping into myself, I started stroking the way I liked it, soft at first but getting harder. I pulled my hair where he had touched it, smelling myself on my skin, a musky, purely female scent. My clit was throbbing and responded to the brushing as I stroked the rest of my pussy. I played with pressure on my clit in circles then directly, harder and harder. My cell phone text message alert chimed, only slightly distracting me as I came, hard, panting, rocking my hips on my hand, wishing it was his body on me.

I panted for a few moments, half-heartedly wishing I was more forward and had invited him up. *How great would it be to be panting with him now, instead of alone?* When my breathing slowed, I got up for some water and to check the text message. A number I didn't recognize.

I'll pick you up at 7:15. Be ready and outside — X

He must have gotten my number off the tutoring sign-up. Maybe it was just the lack of tone in text, but he kind of sounded like a dick. I was still in post-orgasm glow though and didn't want there to be shittiness between us.

Hey — thx again for the ride tonight. If picking me up is a hassle, don't worry about it — L

His response was immediate.

I will pick you up at 7:15. Go to sleep — X

OK, Boss! See you in the morning. Standing outside. Ready to go. Any other instructions tonight? — Leda

Go to sleep, smart ass — X

OK, Boss, night-night — Leda

There was no immediate response, so I wrapped up my bedtime routine. Since moving to Texas, I had been sleeping with my wet hair braided to help stay cool, so it was just brushing teeth, face cream, body cream and checking my locks. My text alert chimed again.

Sweet dreams, little girl – X

That was kind of sweet, but 'little girl'?

Chapter Three

Xander
Metric, Help, I'm Alive

Friday morning, I called Rodriguez, the head of the private security team the senator my dad worked for used.

"Xander, what's up, man?" he answered on the second ring.

"I need a threat assessment on someone down here. Leda Collins. Early to mid twenties. White, brown hair. Wisconsin for undergrad. That's all I've got so far. She's a student at my school." I wasn't going to explain myself, wasn't going to ask for the bullshit teasing that I knew would come if he knew why I wanted the information.

"No problem, you want a full background check, security clearance?"

"You should probably get it, but just hang onto it. I don't want it. Just a threat assessment. I want to learn all the other shit on my own."

There was a pause and I could imagine the slow smile on his face. He was good at his job, good at reading people. And I knew he was putting the pieces together. "Oh...I see how it is, little man. You finally found a girl you might keep."

"She's cute and I'm going to tutor her. I just need to know."

"*Tutor* her, man? That sounds kinky." He laughed. Rodriguez had worked for the senator for at least a decade, and I knew him pretty well. I had shadowed him when I was considering the military. He was former Marines. After the military, I'd worked for him for a while as well. He knew the way I was and knew that tutoring was the least kinky shit in my life. "Maybe I'll see if Mirabella wants to get tutored too?" he added, referring to his wife, who might have been the only person who could possibly kick his ass.

"Okay, dude, come on. Just the threat assessment." I smiled in spite of myself. He didn't give a shit about giving me a hard time, and I liked that about him.

"No problem, man, I'll priority mail to you when I've got it. But, FYI—she's pretty easy to find, and damn. I totally get it." He was already finding her shit. I smiled again, knowing he would get the info.

"Thanks, man." I hung up and shook some tension out of my shoulders. Now, my dad and, therefore, my mom would hear that I was interested in a girl. *That'll be fun.*

I took a quick shower and got dressed. I ate a protein bar as I jogged down to the car. I dropped the top on the C70, and took a moment to just enjoy my life. I had almost everything a guy like me might want. And anticipation was the best part. I liked to drag it out with subs usually, leave them waiting, wondering when it was coming—whatever it was, a slap on the ass, a slap on the face, my cock in her pussy. I liked it when they got to the point that they were practically shivering with how much they wanted it. It was better than the actual sex. It was a serious head trip, taking an otherwise sweet girl and making her beg you for your cock, tears in her eyes.

She lived surprisingly close to me, about a ten minute drive. The devil in my heart smiled at that as I pulled up to her building. She was walking out of the door, right on time. *Points to you, little girl.* I got out of the car, opened the door for her and tossed her bag in the back seat. She gave me an odd look as I helped her into the car, as if she wasn't used to men doing that.

"Good morning, little girl," I said once she was in the seat. I couldn't keep the little smile of glee off my face. Rewards could be as fun to give as punishments.

"Good morning, Boss."

She smiled as I got in and I got a rush at the pet name. Because I was who I was, *what* I was, I would push the 'little girl' title on her till she made it clear she wasn't a little, or didn't want to be *my* little. That Daddy/little girl play hadn't ever been my thing, but she stirred something new in me. Something I didn't want to think about yet.

My playlist advanced to the next song, a band that was relatively new to me, Metric. She smiled big and wide, then began murmuring along with the song. Her little cream-colored sweater, tight Capri pants and stacked shoes had a sexy retro feel that I liked.

I flipped a U-turn and she paused, glancing back the other way.

"Where are you going? I have lecture at eight."

"Little girl, trust me. I'll get you where you need to be, but I want something first." I couldn't help it, couldn't stop myself and I knew it was a little growly.

My blood was pounding through me and I wanted to just pull over and claim her in whatever lawn we stumbled into. But I knew I had to keep it chill. At some point, I'd be able to do that, just stop anywhere and get her on her knees for me. But not yet. I had to earn her total devotion. I knew that.

I pulled into a little mom-and-pop drive-through coffee place I hit up most mornings. I turned and smiled at her. "How about that drink? Cappuccino, iced latte? What's your poison? My treat."

She flushed and, God, it was sexy. "Um, just an iced coffee with a little cream. Thanks." She sounded all small, like she was embarrassed that she drank coffee. I ordered our coffees and the rest of the drive was spent in relative quiet, wind blowing, messing her hair up and it was sexier that way. We got to school sooner than I wanted, but responsibility beckoned.

Before we got out of the car, I asked, "What do you have going on this weekend?"

She answered with a dull tone in her voice, "Studying mostly, some errands and laundry. Nothing exciting."

"I want to take you out tomorrow night. I'll pick you up at eight."

"Sure, we can get that drink." She smiled a little, but her eyes were distant. Working on conditioning, the way I did with all subs, I gave her a smile, and for a moment her face blanked completely. I turned and got out of the car, then came around to get her, but she was already stepping out.

I knew my face was hard, but that shit drives me crazy. Southern girls and all women involved in politics let...*expect*...a man to open the door for them. Yankee girls just don't get it. It's not for *them*. It's for us. I want to protect and provide and that just falls under that category somehow. *We'll have to fix that.*

I felt my face get scowly and turned to walk into school before I commented on it. She at least let me open the door for her and usher her through with my hand on the small of her back.

"Have a good day, Leda." I had to walk away. I wanted to spank her so badly. I shook my head at how fucked up I already was with this little girl—how much all my tight control was already cracking. There was a blaze of trepidation, but I blew it off, wanting there to be someone who could make me lose control, make me feel too much.

Chapter Four

Leda
Lana Del Rey, Ride

While Xander's shifting mood that morning was unsettling, my whole day was actually kind of strange. Other people seemed to be looking at me weirdly, or at least I thought they were. By the end of the day, I was full-on paranoid that people were talking about me. I was in the lab, looking in my microscope, and two bitchy girls from my class approached me. Well, maybe bitchy was a bit harsh. I barely knew either of them, but they were both uber-perky, perfect clothes, pre-Stepford wife kind of girls that just seemed bitchy before you even spoke to them. I sighed, preparing for whatever bullshit they were about to bring into my world.

"Hi, Stacy, Barbie" — those really were their names — "what's up?" I asked distractedly as I identified goblet cells on my slide. But they didn't really say anything, so I looked up and was hit with how much they looked like the stuck up sorority bitches in college.

"Heard you went out with Xander last night," Stacy said with a sickly sweet fake smile on her face. I was genuinely surprised that she knew that anything happened with him and that she cared at all. I was so caught off guard that I didn't even consider my response, but just gave it.

"Oh, it was late and I only had my bike here so he drove me home."

"Did he stay over?"

"Excuse me?" I looked up at her sharply. "No, and not really any of your business."

"Really, why'd he drive you *to* school today then?"

"Not your concern, Stacy. I'm just finishing up here. Do you need this slide set still?" I asked, as I started to pack my stuff. But, I was thinking — *what a stalker!*

"No, Leda, I don't need anything from you," Stacy sneered and walked away, as Barbie trailed her.

Why do bitches always run in packs?

My sour thoughts kept my attention as I left the building. I rode my bike home and the emotional rollercoaster of the day hit me. And all I could think was that I just didn't want any part of any of any stupid drama. School was too important.

Did Xander tell people he stayed over?

What the fuck got up his ass on the drive to the school? I didn't know what had caused the abrupt change in his attitude when we got to school, but I didn't like it. Then there was Stacy and her ridiculous, shitty questions at the end of the day.

Stacy can fuck herself.

I got to my apartment and ran up the stairs, my thoughts still tumbling over each other. I changed into shorts and a T-shirt with my biking shoes and went for a long ride to clear my head. It was hot in September in Texas. Not really a news flash, but back in Chicago, it might have been in the eighties at the worst then an awesome thunderstorm would come through and cool everything down.

The thought of late summer storms set me thinking about a favorite memory. I used to dance in thunderstorms when I was a kid. Right then, I just wanted that feeling of freedom from worrying about other people and what they wanted or thought, so I could just do what felt good to me, what felt pleasant. No matter how hot the weather was before the storm, the rain water was always cool and bracing, almost too cold to breathe through. It took me away from thinking of anything else. There was just the clean feeling of water straight from the sky washing me.

An hour of riding later, I was drenched with sweat and thirsty. My water bottle was empty and I looked around, intending to find somewhere to refill it, and realized that I didn't recognize anything around me.

Shit.

I turned around again. It was an area of businesses and low rent strip malls. I felt my pockets and sickening realization hit me. In my rush out of the apartment, I hadn't grabbed my cell phone.

Fuck.

Who would I have called anyway? I didn't know anyone here other than Xander and I barely knew him Besides, he was too much to deal with—too sexy, too distracting, too moody. Too uncharted. My reaction to him too unexplored. I decided to ride until I saw something I recognized or someone who looked reasonable to ask for directions.

It took me another two hours to get home and, despite stopping to refill my water, I was sick by the time I did.

I got up the stairs and filled a huge glass of water. As I chugged it down, I was shaking and my head was pounding. I immediately vomited it all back up in the sink. I was overheated and dehydrated.

Shit was the only thing I could clearly think, as I stumbled to the bathroom and puked again. The cool tile of the floor felt good on my cheek. *I have no one to help me.* My family was hours away, even by plane. I ran a cool bath and sat in it, letting my body cool down until I started shaking again. I got out of the tub and got some ice in a cup while it drained.

Oh my God, I feel weird and floaty. The ice tastes good. Some juice too. Okay maybe a little better.

I had the presence of mind to get one of my medical texts and look up heat sickness. I didn't have a heat stroke. I drank more ice water and some more juice.

I feel better. Maybe I'm okay. Just a little dehydrated.

I was so wrung out from the day and I was annoyed at myself for getting lost and for not bringing my cell.

What a fucking idiot.

I grabbed my cell out of the bag I had dropped by the door earlier. Three texts. All from Xander.

Little girl, where'd you go so fast this afternoon? I was looking for you. You're in trouble now. X

Little girl? I'm picking you up at 8 tomorrow. Wear a skirt. – X

This fuckin' guy.

Leda – where are you? Respond or I am coming over –X

Well, that text was about forty-five minutes ago.

Was out for a bike ride. Not feeling too good. Will touch base tomorrow – Leda

My doorbell rang shortly after I hit send. I knew it was going to be him, regardless of the text I had just sent. I still felt weak and tired—just completely limp, and I didn't want to talk to him. The doorbell rang again.

Leda — I can see your light on. Open the door. –X

A little stalker-y, no? I grabbed my robe and hit the buzzer for the front door. The building was small with just four units, so I heard the front door open. I opened my door, stepping out onto the small landing at the top of the stairs.

"Hey, Xander. My place is up here. Come on up." I didn't even have it in me to fight him on it, but I was irritated about his behavior that morning and I wasn't in the mood for his bossy bullshit. He was up the flight of stairs in four steps and grabbed me by the shoulders.

"Are you okay? Where have you been? Why didn't you respond to my texts?" He looked me over, then pushed me into my living room. Maybe pushed is too strong of a word—bodily guided me into the room, but not before I registered the relief-tinged anxiety in his features.

Chapter Five

Xander
Depeche Mode, Nothing's Impossible

"I went for a ride and got a little turned around."

I was closing the door, but turned to her as she finished, a look of embarrassment washing her features for a moment. She looked like shit, skin gray, lips dry, eyes sunken.

"And I didn't have...my...phone."

The embarrassment faded and she realized she was alone with me, and got scared. Her eyes widened and she glanced behind me at the door. It wasn't the sexy, fun kind of scared.

"Go put some clothes on." She was wearing a robe and I didn't want her to feel unsafe. Clothing would help. I turned away to give her space. Gave her my back as a sign that I wouldn't hurt her. She wouldn't register it consciously, but the animal brain would be comforted a bit. I watched her from the corner of my eye and she stood considering me for a moment then turned toward the back of the apartment, and her legs started to crumple under her, her face going blank. I lunged for her and caught her shoulders, walking her to the couch. I settled her down next to me. "How long was your ride?" *Little girl, you're gonna be mine and I take care of mine.*

"I don't know, about three hours or so."

What the fuck? She'd said it so nonchalantly. "Three hours, what the fuck, Leda! It was almost a hundred degrees today. Are you trying to die, or some kind of extreme sports freak?"

Her eyes flashed with a touch of temper, despite being washed out and exhausted. "I am going to interpret that like you aren't yelling at me and are, instead, concerned about my well-being."

It was both of those. But I softened my face a little so she knew she wasn't in too much trouble. But it didn't last long. If she was mine, I would have put her over my fucking knee.

"I got lost and couldn't find my way home. It took a while. I think I'm dehydrated, and was actually really sick when I got home, puking and just feeling terrible. I took a cool bath and it seems better. I'm just really cold now and I still feel completely exhausted. I think I'll just have some more juice and go to bed."

"You need more than juice. Your electrolytes are probably all fucked up. You need something like Gatorade, watered down, or I can make you some homemade ORT." I mumbled the last bit, triaging in my mind, if she needed IV fluids or if I should go get her some oral rehydration fluids. She looked confused.

"ORT?"

"I'll tell you all about Wilderness Medicine once you're dressed in more than a robe and have some sodium and potassium working their way back into your system. Do you have anything like Gatorade?" *You give me what I want, and I reward you.*

"No, that stuff is gross." She scrunched up her face and stuck out her tongue.

Such a little. "Okay, how about some salt and honey?" She nodded at me. "Go get dressed and I'll make it." I stood, moving to the kitchen.

I watched her as she went to her room, but she seemed steadier. I got some water boiling, feeding it salt and honey. I could have added some juice, but this wasn't supposed to taste good. My phone buzzed in my pocket.

I pulled it out and answered, "Hi, Mom. How are you?"

"Good lord! You answered. I didn't think you would on a Friday night. Why aren't you out having fun?"

"Who says I'm not? Maybe I just wanted to talk to you." I smiled. As much as my mom could be annoying and pushy, she was a victim of a machine she was dependent on, and I loved her. She had my back, one hundred percent, and I knew it.

"Okay, fair enough. Good son points. I'm calling because we're reserving rooms for the fundraiser already and we'll need to buy our tickets. So, I wanted to know if you were coming or not?"

"Shit—"

"Language, Xander. I'm still a lady."

She was so funny. The drink was done brewing. I filled a cup with ice and poured some of it in the cup.

"No, Mom. I don't know about coming to the fundraiser. Do you even think it would help him? I doubt it."

"*I* want you to come. And I think most people have moved on. It's not like you used a cigar to fuck an intern and got caught then lied, under oath, while in office."

"No." I bit back the laugh in my throat. "I know it has been years, but he's probably still pissed. Look, I have to go. I'll call on Sunday." I hung up as Leda walked into the kitchen. I handed her the drink.

"What was that about with your mom? Fundraiser sounds fancy. And secondly, this is the worst cocktail I've ever had. It's a good thing you're going to be a doctor, because you'd be crap at bartending." She smiled, humor in her eyes and her color returning a little.

"It's not intended to taste all that good, just save your life when you can't get something better. Now you owe me." I smiled and winked at her, liking the playful flirting. I walked toward the couch to draw her to her rest. She sat and a look of relief crossed her face. I sat at the other end of the couch, saying, "Now, you just need to sit and rest. Wanna watch a movie?"

She looked at me, a little confused, but I wasn't about to leave her alone. She responded, "Sure, but I'm pretty tired so I may not last through the whole thing. Really, I am feeling better. You don't have stay here and babysit me."

Tsk, tsk, girlie. Nice try. I picked up the remote and flipped the TV on, found *Ace Ventura: Pet Detective*. It came out when I was in high school and I remember getting stoned with my best friend, Jason, and thinking it was the highest level of comedic genius. After a little while, she stretched out and put her feet up on the couch. I picked them up and sat them in my lap, so I could be touching her. I started rubbing her foot, another little reward.

"You may start getting some muscle cramps." It was true, but probably would have already started if it was going to. She didn't need to know that just then. About an hour into the movie, her eyelids started to droop and she laid her head back. I lightened my touch on her feet, just letting them rest in my lap.

While she slept, I took a visual inventory of her apartment. It was generic, basic—beige carpet, couch and modest TV in the living room. Her little dining nook was co-opted by her computer desk and bookshelves. I respected that. Her kitchen was functional. It was all clearly temporary, the place to stay in until she could leave. *Until she moves in with me, my full-time baby... What the* fuck *am I thinking right now?*

At the end of the movie, I reached for the remote on her coffee table, and she woke.

"Let's get you in bed. It's late, little girl." I placed her feet on the floor and pulled her hands until she stood. I kept my hands near her, but she was steadier now.

"I'll walk you out."

Her voice was weary. There was no way I was leaving. "I'm staying."

Shock crossed her features, followed quickly by wariness. "I'm okay. I'll be fine and just get some rest tonight."

Why do people always fight it when someone else knows what is right for them? God, I'm a cocky dominant motherfucker. I laughed internally, but kept my face stern for her. "No, Leda, you were significantly dehydrated tonight, if not experiencing heat exhaustion. Someone needs to be here in case you need something or you get sick again overnight."

She held her ground for a moment or two, but I could see how much she just wanted to give in. I saw the debate crossing her expression. But I knew she would give in as soon as she didn't immediately deny me.

"Okay, but..."

"I'll sleep on the couch." *Tonight.* "Let's go." I walked her to her bedroom and I understood how uncomfortable it must be. New dude in her room, clearly we had an attraction, but we barely knew each other. I got it, as much as I wanted to snuggle in next to her and stroke her hair till she fell asleep. Not yet.

I settled her into her bed. She had an antique-looking off-white comforter and a wrought iron headboard, painted white. Probably the same stuff she'd had since she was a teenager. *God, a total little.* She sat up and braided her hair, with no explanation, like it was her routine. She looked so young, so soft, so sweet. I just wanted to touch her, and knew if I started, it would be even harder to stop.

"I am sleeping on the couch," I reiterated it more for myself than for her, but, added as I looked back at her, "if you need anything."

I glanced at the clock on her bedside table as I walked out of the room. It was almost midnight. Sometimes, you could tell a lot about someone by what was on their bedside table. She had a glass of water, a novel that I couldn't see the title of, a pack of birth control pills, a few medical text study guides, ear plugs, a few hair ties and a kind of frilly white lamp.

* * * *

In the morning, I left Leda a note and met Jason for our usual Saturday morning sparring session. Jason had been doing MMA for years and had decided to focus on his ground work more right around the time I moved to Texas. Brazilian Jiu Jitsu had become a way that we could get a work out in, catch up, shoot the shit. Whatever.

When I walked in, Jason glanced at me, then did a double take. "You look like shit."

"Thanks, asshole. It's a fucking girl. I just met her and I can't stop thinking about her."

I heard him whoosh a big breath out.

I'd known he'd be surprised, but I didn't want him to start analyzing me. "Let's do some groundwork."

He gave me some side eye. "I don't know, man. You look a little...out of your usual tight-assed control. I don't want a broken face. I'm too pretty."

I laughed. "All right, show me something new so I can practice it, or let's get some gloves and headgear and box."

"I'm not fucking boxing with you until you decompress. Come here."

He stepped onto the mat and I followed. He proceeded to take me through three or four techniques that were new to me. One involved a new way of breaking a guard. I liked it. We went through it a few more times.

Once we settled into a routine, he asked, "So, what's the deal with this girl?"

I tried to explain. "She's a first-year Med student. She's cute as hell. And she's in my tutoring group."

"Okay, that sounds good. Why are you so fucked up about it?"

I felt like a fucking douche bag asshole even as the words came out of my mouth. It was the shit that fake Doms used to isolate new girls in the kink scene. It was how they justified their sexual assaults, their consent violations. "She is a complete sub—a *real* natural submissive. I mean, moves before she consciously registers what I said."

"What the fuck are you having her do?" He smiled, wide and dirty.

"You know, just sit down, come here, whatever. She does it."

"You vet her yet with Rodriguez?"

"Yeah, well…sort of."

He gave me a 'what-the-fuck' look.

"I don't want the whole report. I want to learn her step by step instead of cheating. I have a threat assessment pending and knowing him, I'll get it within the next few days."

He paused, holding a reverse crunch for a moment, thoughtful. "So, what's your plan?"

"I'm gonna take her out tomorrow night."

"You wanna go to the Window tonight? I'm sure someone there would love to have the unattainable Xander treat them."

"No." I rolled my eyes at my own bullshit before I launched into it. "You know how I am, man. Dating? Like, actually *dating* a chick. I just don't do it. It always goes all sideways and shitty."

"Does it?"

We were into the part where he was going to start figuring my shit out, even though he'd do it with leading questions and would never just tell me straight out what he thought.

"With me? Yeah, it does." I'd had enough crappy experiences with women to know I wanted to keep the emotional factor out of my sex life. Jason had been around and seen it.

He scoffed and taunted me with a 'come-at-me-bro' wave. "That's enough of that self-pitying bullshit."

I laughed, but my pride stung some and I stepped toward him, feinting into his reach. When he grabbed the collar of my *gi*, I fired my arm against his wrist, breaking his grasp and pulling him down to the ground.

He landed with a grunt, but aimed his shoulder into me and caught my lip. I tasted my blood almost immediately, but took our momentum and guided him into the mat. I locked his arm up and kept a foot on the back of his neck until he tapped out.

When I released him, he came up laughing, laughing harder when he saw my bloody lip. "Dude, you always make it fun."

Chapter Six

Leda
Justin Timberlake, FutureSex/LoveSound

When I woke in the morning, he was gone. There was a note on the coffee table.

Hey Little Girl
Left at 6. Things to do this morning. Call me if you need anything.
Will pick you up at 8 tonight. Call me if you feel too shitty to go out.
– X

It was almost nine o'clock. I was still feeling a little worn out, but a lot better than the night before. I went to the fridge for some juice and there was the jug of his ORT, with a note telling me to finish it. *Bossy*. I filled up a glass. It still tasted like shit, but I felt better after I drank it.

I camped out on the couch for the day to catch up on studying, breaking a few times to eat, stretch and make some procrastinatory texts, Facebook updates and Twitter checks. Nothing too exciting was happening in my electronic network of acquaintances, friends and family. I kept my snacking light, knowing that I'd probably drink something heavily caloric that night.

Around six-thirty that evening I started to get ready and felt the beginning of a sweet, excited anxiety about seeing him again. I took a shower and went through my usual 'going out' routine. My cell dinged to indicate a text around seven.

Hey Little girl – how are you feeling? Still up for going out tonight? – X

I feel almost 100% back to myself. I must have had a really good doctor taking care of me last night. I'll see you at 8. – Leda.

Good girl. – X

A little rush of pleasure and butterflies ran through me at that text. Good girl. I wanted to hear him say those words to me, wanted to feel his breath on my neck when he whispered them in my ear.

As I finished getting ready, my phone rang. I answered, not looking at the name, expecting it to be him, but smiled when I heard my mom's voice instead.

"Hey, Leeds! How's it going?" She was extra perky.

"Hi, Mom. Good." I paused, the small bubble of Xander-excitement bursting as I thought about the reality of what school was like. My voice fell some when I answered her in full. "I mean, school sucks. It's hard. I'm exhausted and it's too much. But..." I trailed off.

"But?"

I didn't want to tell her about Xander. I wasn't sure why. I told myself it was that it was just a first date and didn't really mean anything yet, but I knew it did. I knew there was something…something spicy, electric, confusing and amazing waiting there. I didn't want her to try to talk me out of it. I didn't want her to know yet. I wanted it to just be mine.

"I think I love it. It's hard, but it's cool. I don't know." I changed the subject, "I went out riding last night and got lost though. Kinda miserable."

I heard her smile in her voice. "Just be careful. Get some rest tonight then."

"I'm actually going out with some people from school."

We spoke for a few more minutes, with her admonishing me not to stay out too late, and me being noncommittal and vague on that subject. It was still great to hear from her and I locked my door with a smile and another blossoming wave of excited nerves when I left.

I was waiting outside, in the balmy fading heat, at eight when he pulled up. When he got out of the car and walked around the front, he looked like something from a magazine, tall, lean and thick all at once, stubble from the day on his face. His broad shoulders just strained his black, slim-fit T-shirt, and his dark jeans fit beautifully. He had some sort of black lace-up boot that disappeared under the perfect break in his jeans. I was distracted by that— *Are his jeans tailored? They just fit too perfectly.*

As he got closer, and his face was better lit by the streetlight, I saw that the left side of his lower lip was raw and bruised, a little swollen. Alarmed, I completely forgot how hot he looked and rushed up to him, stumbling into his chest. He steadied me, a hand on my lower back.

"What happened to your face?" *Shit. Really smooth, Leda.*

He chuckled. "Hi, good to see you too. Glad you're feeling better. You look nice."

That said, I had put in the effort to bring it—hair up in a twist, dangly earrings and a clingy, but not tight, gun-metal gray jersey dress with some strappy heels. The dress stretched across my chest asymmetrically. I had to be careful, with a chest like mine, anything low cut went from sexy to skanky in a half inch of exposed skin.

"I'm sorry! You look great, hi." I stretched up and kissed his right cheek, the one without any bruises. "Seriously, what happened? You were unbruised last night."

"No worries. One of the things I had to do today was my training session. Brazilian Jiu Jitsu. We do a lot of sparring work. You should see the other guy." He smirked at me. "Let's go." He ushered me to the car and tucked me into the passenger seat.

"Where are we going?"

"I'm taking you to a club that I think you'll like, but first a drink and something to eat at my friend's bar." He turned on the radio and drove. We didn't talk too much, just brief inconsequential shit. The bar was clearly in a less savory part of town, not so much unsafe, just a little rougher. He parked behind the building and we went in the back door. He nodded to the bartender, a big burly slab of a man with a shaved head and tattoos down his arms. As I stared back at this behemoth, Xander guided me to a booth, greeting a few other patrons as we passed.

"The owner is my friend, Jason. The bartender is one of the guys I train with."

"Is he the guy that gave you the bruise on your face?" I asked, kind of shocked at the idea of the two of them facing off.

"No, no, he's just beginning. I'm gonna go grab some drinks." He went to the bar and leaned over to talk with this huge man, smiling. He nodded in my direction while saying something and they both laughed a little. The bar had black-washed walls except for one of exposed brick at the back that was covered with the usual liquor and beer signs. It was only slightly crowded, with guys that looked like they worked with their hands and beat their bodies up for a paycheck every week. The few women there had that same toughness to them, with maybe a touch more polish. Xander came back with our drinks, both...lemonade? *That's weird.*

"What's with the drink?"

"We have a long night ahead of us."

Ummmm, what now?

"Frank will bring something else over in a bit."

"Long night? What do you have planned?" I sipped the drink and only when the fresh, cold sweetness washed my throat did I realize how dry it had been.

"I want to watch you dance," he said with a dark, devious twinkle in his eye.

I loved dancing, had loved to go clubbing in Chicago. I loved the press of a roomful of bodies moving to the same loud beat. It could drown out thoughts of anything else and make it so easy to forget whatever was going on in your life, but it wasn't the best first date—too loud to talk. I put on a smile, determined to be game for whatever he threw at me.

"So, thanks for looking after me last night. I just feel so stupid to have gotten lost in a new town." My mood sagged a little thinking about the entire shitstorm that had led up to it. "I had a kind of frustrating day at school that ended on a sour note and I just wanted to forget about it, you know?"

He leaned in. "What happened that was sour? You can't let Dr. Malcom get to you."

He was referring to the histology professor who was notoriously hard to please. My Friday afternoon lab was his class. "No, not Malcom. It's just really different here than it was in college or in Chicago. I'm still working on making friends."

"We're friends." The innocence of the words was completely destroyed by the suggestive cock of his eyebrows, the wicked curve of his lips and the slightly sarcastic, slightly erotic tone of his voice.

I smiled at him, but was a little perplexed. "FYI— friends don't tell each other they want to watch them dance." I said it with a slightly dirty smile back at him.

"Maybe not *your* friends," he answered, mirth and heat dancing in his eyes.

His foot nudged mine under the table. I had my ankles crossed and he pushed my feet apart and put his—huge—boot right between my strappy black heels. And with that small gesture, the slightest of contact, my whole body alerted to him. My breath came quicker, my skin was suddenly too tight, clammy, and I felt a flush creeping up my neck.

Frank came over then, a mountain of a man, lumbering into our little sexual innuendo, ending the moment. He set down a tray with two burgers and new drinks for us. I sucked down the rest of my lemonade, wanting to hang on to my wits as long as possible.

"New house specialty—mojitos," Frank said with a smile.

Up close, he seemed even more massive, and I noticed that he had some random bruises on his neck and arms that almost looked like hickeys. "I've never had a mojito. What's in it? I mean, besides the roofie he told you to put in there."

Frank's mouth worked a bit and he looked obviously uncomfortable. I immediately regretted it and stammered, "I'm kidding! Let me do this like a normal person. Hi, I'm Leda." I put my hand out and Frank glanced at Xander, who wasn't smiling, but wasn't frowning either.

"Leda, this is my friend Frank," Xander introduced him then put my mojito in my outstretched hand. "What do you think of the drink?" he asked, as I took a sip.

It was so refreshing, perfect, crisp and cold. I could easily get really drunk with these.

Frank stood up, glancing back at the bar. "The boss is here."

I looked back, expecting someone much older than me, but the man I assumed was Jason probably wasn't older than thirty, standing behind the bar, popping the tops off some beers for himself and his date. He was scruffy, shaggy hair, short beard. He was wearing jeans and a concert T-shirt that I couldn't read from that distance. His date was stunning. She had big, blonde hair that hung almost to her waist in fat curls, plenty of make-up, with a trim body and great high, small breasts. She was wearing a silver mini-dress with a plunge in front that chesty girls like me look like strippers—at best—in. Even across the bar, she seemed full of life, laughing with a huge smile full of chicklet teeth.

Xander waved them over and they came to sit with us. Introductions revealed that her name was Christy. I kind of expected someone flighty or bitchy, but she was really pleasant.

"So, Leda. Xander tells us you just moved here from Yankee territory? What do you think so far?"

Pause...he was telling his friends about me?

She didn't wait for my answer, continuing, "It's so hard to move to a new place, where you don't know anyone and try to start a new life, but I think you'll love it here, especially this winter when everyone up north is freezing. I went to school in Boston and remember how ridiculous it was there—so cold compared to the south. But I grew up here and had never seen snow in person before I moved there."

And she went on and on. She was one of those people that could carry an entire conversation by herself without making anyone feel weird. It made me smile, made me immediately comfortable because my mom was exactly the same. But after a few minutes, Jason clearly gave her a little look or signal, because, she stopped mid-sentence.

"Oh God! There I go. Clearly I talk for a living, right?"

It hit me. She was the weather girl, just *way* tramped up for a night out. I instantly liked her. Jason smiled at her indulgently and I was impressed that these were the people Xander could call his friends.

"Jason, this place is great—a very chill vibe. How long have you been in business here?"

"We've been open here for about a year and a half. I really like this space a lot, just very chill—that's the exact right word for it, but it's picking up on the weekends in the last few months. Later tonight the crowd will be different—younger."

My hunger hit me with a vengeance as the initial nerves of the date wore off. So as Jason and Xander talked about the bar business, I finished my burger, which was great, and continued sipping my mojito.

In the course of the conversation, I learned that Christy and Jason had been together for five years, since she'd moved back to Texas to do the weekend, late night weather at one of the local television channels. Since then she had been promoted and now did weeknights and clearly loved her job. At one point, Jason leaned across the table and literally shushed her with his fingers over her lips. She sucked his fingers into her mouth with a twinkle in her bright blue eyes, and I got a flush all over. It was over really quickly, but I was kind of turned on by how into each other they were, even after five years.

Xander leaned across the table and grabbed my wrist to get my attention. "Ready to go?"

Christy dropped Jason's fingers and looked over at us. "Where are you going tonight?"

Across the table Jason chuckled and wiped his fingers off on a napkin, but then had to adjust himself under the table.

"We're going to The Nest," Xander told her, his tone heavy with irony or mirth that I didn't totally understand.

"Xander tells me I am going to dance for him," I smirked, getting in on the fun.

He squeezed my wrist. "Not *for* me, little girl. I'm just going to watch."

Christy grabbed Jason's hands. "Let's go too? I haven't been dancing in forever!" I was actually kind of relieved at the possibility of a little buffer to make the whole first date awkwardness easier—and I really liked Christy.

Jason had a little bit of handshaking and owner-stuff to do at the bar, so he and Christy planned to meet us there. We headed to the back of the bar and Xander opened the door for me, grabbing my hand as I walked through and pulling me in close to him as we walked toward his car.

"I'm glad you like Jason and Christy. They're my *best* friends. I've known Jason since high school. He's a great guy, tough but not an asshat, you know? And Christy is perfect for him. Sometimes people miss it, but she is really smart, too. She doesn't talk about it much, but she actually has her PhD in meteorology from MIT. They were one of the factors pulling me here when I was looking at schools. Jason had been down here, promoting clubs and just killing it. He opened his first club about the time he met Christy." He got my door and held my hand as I got settled in my seat.

When he came around and got in, I continued our conversation, "They seem really great and it's nice to meet a woman who is so pleasant. The girls at school can be such bitches."

"Whoa—it's only been a few weeks! Who has already made such a big impression on you?"

"Fuck them. I don't want to talk about them." I could feel my mood starting to deflate even thinking about Stacy and her crappy comments. We got in the car and drove across town. The conversation dropped off a bit until I said, "So wait, you said Jason opened his first club—how many does he own?"

"He's kind of diversified—a club, the bar and a coffee shop. He's looking into opening another club now, but it's a huge investment of time and money. He was talking about not having a good concept yet either. This is where his genius is, you know. I would just convert a warehouse, put in speakers and call it something dumb. He'll have the whole thing worked out, three hundred sixty degrees."

"So are we going to his club tonight?"

"No." He paused. "Nest is another club in town, good for dancing."

"God, now that I know him, I feel like it's kinda rude not to go to his place."

"No, he gets it. It's, well, like I was saying. It has a concept and it is for a specific group of people. He knows I'd never take a first date there. Hell, he doesn't even go that often anymore."

"Why? Is it, like, a total cowboy bar, real country or something else, like real gangster?"

"No it's just…very…intense, like lots of sex in your face."

"A strip club?"

"No." He smiled. "No one is getting paid to get naked, but they might get naked anyway. The rules are very strict, but essentially come down to anything is okay as long as everyone involved is legal and is consenting."

I wasn't really sure what to make of that, but I needed to shift my ass against the seat. "Wait…you wouldn't take a *first* date there? But maybe a second? Do you go there a lot?"

He laughed out loud at that as he pulled up to the valet at a huge club with a line outside. The valet opened the door for me and Xander was there handing off his keys as I stepped out. He took my hand and walked up to the bouncer who smiled and shook his hand, then opened the door for us, letting us skip the line. Apparently, he was well-known here. The unpleasant thought that he must be here often with a lot of dates crossed my mind, but then we were through the second set of doors and the music was loud, so loud that I lost my thoughts and remembered the feeling — the bass shaking my lungs, reverberating within my rib cage, and the only feeling being this moment, the music, the lights and how much I wanted to move.

He still had my hand and was navigating through the crowd to a roped off area in the back. A hostess saw him and smiled broadly, waving us over. She pulled back the rope to the VIP section and they exchanged brief pleasantries that I couldn't hear over the music. We sat on a low, plush couch with a few small side tables arranged around it and she came back with drinks, a mojito for me again, plus a bottle of beer for him.

Once we were settled, he dropped his hand between us and touched my leg, hooking his index and ring fingers under the hem of my dress, not pulling it up or reaching, just lightly stroking my thigh with his fingers. I wanted him to push my skirt up and touch me more, harder. Wanted wasn't even strong enough of a word. It was overwhelming how much I wanted him, but there was something that held me back from taking the next step, from grabbing him and straddling his lap. At the thought of riding him, a small gush of moisture dampened my barely there thong. A beat or two later, I swear he took a deep breath in through his nose, like he could smell me, smell how much I wanted to get fucked tonight.

The DJ started blending the beat into another song and Xander pulled his hand away. He slipped his hand behind me, touching the small of my back. He leaned into me, voice firm, easily heard over the music, "Okay, little girl, get up, get out there. I have been thinking about your body moving in that dress since I picked you up."

"Come with me," I asked him, feeling self-conscious.

He was starting to shake his head, when Christy came up, yelling, "Hey, girl, let's go!" She pulled me up, out of his reach and out to the dance floor.

Chapter Seven

Xander
Far East Project — Featuring Stereotypes, Girls on the Dancefloor

Christy pulled Leda to the dance floor. Despite the crowd, my view of them was fairly unobstructed. I could see them talking a bit as they started dancing, but the music was too loud for conversation and they gradually got lost in movement.

Leda's hips moved, swaying back and forth, slower than the beat of the song. As if she was trying to tempt me, taunt me. But she never looked back at me in challenge like I would have expected if that was really the case. She was just in the moment, dancing for herself, for her own joy in it—and that was sexier than any little tease she could have done.

She and Christy were pressed tight in with everyone else on the dance floor, and periodically one of them would get bumped, but at least initially no one seemed to be bothering them. The music faded between two songs. The bass started pumping, low and aggressive, insistent and Christy grabbed her, spun her and started grinding on her ass. Bending her over. It looked good.

The music stilled for a beat then came back stronger. And it was like the girls lost their minds, jumping up and screaming, laughing. Leda's tits moved like they might bounce out of her dress and her hair was starting to fall out of her clip. She was succulent, something I wanted to have my mouth on.

Jason walked through the club, laughing when he saw them. He grabbed Christy and kissed her, gave Leda a head nod and came up to sit with me. The girls barely paused in their dancing. They were wild, feeding off each other's energy, their tentative movements becoming more abandoned, reckless.

"How's the big first date going?" Jason asked as he sat down, nodding toward the girls and smiling.

"Good. Look at her moving." I didn't look at him because she was more fun to watch. The lights in the place pulsed with the bass and her movements were washed in a red-light strobe effect that seemed like I was tripping. She was looking back at me now and I was starting to twitch my lips in a smile, but Christy grabbed her and pulled her attention away from me.

We watched them dancing, lost in the trace of the music and their movement, barely speaking to each other. But enough time passed and I wanted to touch her.

"Be back in a minute." I got up without looking at Jason. My cock wanted her, wanted her panting at my feet. I walked through the crowd, noticing that I was a good five to seven years older than everyone else in here. Everyone in the club knew it. They responded to that, my size, or just the cocky, alpha fucking way I carried myself. They moved out of my way as I went to get my little girl. Christy was saying something as I walked up behind Leda and pulled her into me.

I wrapped an arm around her like I was taking her hostage, but she didn't seem to mind. I dropped my lips next to her ear, "Little girl, you move so good, but I want you to come drink something and rest for a bit." I held her hip against me and pulsed a little with the music, enjoying her ass against my cock.

Christy smiled because she was just as dirty as me and probably knew what I was thinking. But I felt my cock starting to stiffen and took a step back, pulling Leda backward. After a few steps, we turned around and I guided her to our table.

The waitress had brought another round of drinks, including some bottles of water, which I would have made my little girl drink if she hadn't reached for one first. She was flopped on the couch, sweaty, breathing a little hard. I could imagine that I had just used her, hard and rough. I smiled a little to myself and sat next to her, running my fingers over her back.

The three of us didn't speak, only watched Christy dancing, her shiny silver dress and big blonde hair easy to find in the crowd. And the inevitable dude found her. There's always a dude at the club. Always a dude looking for a girl to grind up on. So here was the one for the night. I was glad it was Christy and not Leda, because I couldn't have been cool about it. My claim wasn't established enough yet to tolerate even a perceived threat. But even if it was…the assumption that any girl is fair game to grind your dick on, just because she's dancing…it just pisses me off.

But Christy and Jason had been through this scenario in so many different permutations that I just sat back to watch. When it was Jason getting hit on, Christy was in there right away, but Jason liked to let it build. Christy glanced over and he gave her the go-ahead. Jason watched her, smiling, but I felt his tension building. He made it through an entire song. The dude tried to say something in Christy's ear, but she just shushed him with her fingers over his lips. And that was it for Jason. He took a deep breath.

"I have to go get her," he muttered, barely audible over the music as he stood up, adjusting his cock, and walked briskly across the floor. Christy didn't notice it yet, but Leda was leaning forward, tense.

Jason approached from the side and the dude noticed him first. Christy opened her eyes and locked her gaze with Jason's. Electricity passed between them and I knew that guy was fucked. Christy moved away from the dude, saying something in his ear as Jason stepped in behind her.

This is when the slacker persona was revealed for an act, because no one looking at Jason would have dismissed the threat in his presence. He ran his hand up Christy's back and coiled his hand in her hair. I moved my hand onto Leda's thigh, her skin a little damp still. I left my fingers light, not flexing. Let her notice whenever she did.

Jason was just fucking with the dude — he pulled Christy tight against him, not letting go of her hair, and slid his other hand up the front of her body till it was wrapped around her throat. The dude started to disengage, realizing there was nothing but a night of trouble for him with the two of them, but Christy felt him moving away and grabbed his shirt.

A small circle was opening up around the three of them. I had to admit it, they were sexy as hell. Three bodies slithering tightly against each other, aggression just below the surface. Jason held the dude's gaze, but licked at Christy's neck and said something in her ear.

Leda noticed my hand, then noticed that she was leaning forward. She took a deep breath and leaned back and I shifted my arm around her shoulders as she moved, tracing designs on her bare shoulder.

"They can be pretty captivating sometimes."

"Yeah. Is that other guy going to be a problem?"

"I doubt it. Christy and Jason both know who she belongs to. It'll only be a problem if that guy doesn't understand that, too." She seemed mollified by that.

"Okay, interesting. Do you want to come dance with me? Maybe I want to see how *you* move, too."

Little vixen. I had to have more of her.

I felt the growl in my chest as I slid my hand into her hair, ruining what was left of her updo. She held her breath, waiting for whatever I wanted to do to her. I knew she'd take it just then. The combination of the music, the bodies, Christy and Jason's chaos, made her easier prey. And, as evil as I was, I knew that's what she was.

She tried to be cool about it and grabbed her waiting mojito, but I saw the slight shakiness in her hand. I took her drink from her and put it back on the table. I knew I was physically towering over her, and I loved it. I picked out an ice cube and lightly tugged her head back by her hair. I held the ice just above her parted lips and let it melt onto her, dripping onto her tongue when she flicked it out at the ice. I rested the ice against her lower lip for a moment. Just as she opened her mouth to take it from me, I traced it down her chin, her neck and across her collar bone.

She closed her eyes and relaxed into me, breathing deep. Her nipples tightened, visible in her dress. I released a bit on her neck just to flex again and a shiver ran over her skin. I knew she'd let me take her home with me, but I knew she wasn't really ready for me. She had no idea how much I would toy with her, couldn't actually consent to me yet, and I knew it. And it sucked. I love anticipation, but patience could suck a dick.

"Hey, y'all!"

Christy smiled like an angel and picked up some water. I knew she knew she'd just interrupted something and shot her a 'what-the-fuck' look. She just splashed water on herself and shouted that she wanted more drinks.

She looked to Leda and said, "Leda, let's go to the ladies' room."

As our girls walked away, Jason waved our hostess, Jenna, down and ordered another round.

"So what happened with that dude?" I shifted to look at Jason.

"He pussed out." Jason shrugged. "But I think Christy wants something rough tonight. Suggestions?"

I gave him a few suggestions of the blindfold and teasing variety, but we stopped when the girls walked back up. Jason grinned then laughed, and I looked at them and saw it, chuckling too. Christy's signature red lipstick was smeared on Leda's lips. *Maybe little girl needs it more than I thought.* Christy was what I liked to call omnisexual. And she'd obviously been kissing my girl in the ladies' room.

The drinks arrived and we sat back, talking. Christy carried the conversation, but she got Leda to open more, asking her about traveling.

"I haven't traveled too much, just a few family trips places. My favorites have been Ireland and Italy. I know, fairly Eurocentric, but I just haven't been too many other places. Mexico for spring break—kind of lame. You know where I want to go that I've never been—New Orleans."

Jason, Christy and I shared a look. Jason and I had met Christy at a kink convention in New Orleans and it was one of our favorite places. We had some serious memories in NOLA. We had been going back to that kink convention every year since.

"Well, that's so close. We'll all have to go one weekend when you two don't have to study so much."

Very good, Christy. She just made us a de facto couple. The psychology of it was brilliant and I shot her a smile. She looked back at me and for a moment there was pure craftiness in her eyes. Then, she slipped up into Jason's lap and they started snuggling.

"Hey, guys, we're going to head over to the Window." He paused and looked from me to Leda. "Do you want to come?"

Do I want to? Yes...but only if I can tie her up. Not yet. "Not tonight, man. Have fun."

We said our goodbyes and a smile lingered on Leda's face after they left. Seeing the tension release from around her eyes was good, gave me a little peace.

"What else do you want to do tonight, little girl?"

"I don't know, I could dance more. I could sit here longer. What is the Window — is it another club? Why don't we go with them?"

"Ah, the Window, actually the Blackened Window. That is...Jason's club. It'll be just really starting to pick up now, but, honey, it's just more than I think you're ready for. In time we can go there, if you want." *When you know what the fuck you're getting into.*

"I'm down. I can handle whatever."

Cute. "First, I doubt you'd be as chill as you think to see someone tied and whipped in front of you or whatever other craziness is happening there tonight, but secondly, and more importantly, I know you can't handle what I would want to do to you once we got there." Her eyes got wide and I imagined her looking up from kneeling in front of me. She shivered like she knew what I wanted to do to her. I rubbed her arms, knowing she wasn't actually cold, but taking the excuse to touch her more. "Let's get out of here."

"Okay, Boss."

So cute. I pinched her lower lip between my thumb and the knuckle of my forefinger, feeling my own lust making my breath tight, as she accepted the little bit of pain.

It was late, but I didn't want to take her home. We could sleep tomorrow. I decided to take her to the Cat's Meow. Something sweet, a little treat.

Chapter Eight

Leda
She Wants Revenge, Tear You Apart

As we left The Nest, he guided me with his hand on the small of my back. The proximity of his hand to my ass and pussy was just about all I could think about, the tight anticipation made me a little breathless. I just wanted him to touch me more, just slide his fingers down, under the short hem of my dress and nestle into my sugar.

We got in the car, and it seemed too quiet after the club. It was nearly two in the morning, the latest I had been up in a while. I was starting to feel it, but I didn't want the night to be over. He looked deep in thought as we drove to another part of town, parking in a garage and walking down the street to a restaurant tucked in between two upscale boutiques. The Cat's Meow was a small diner that was open twenty-four hours a day and, as Xander explained, they had great coffee and desserts. We ordered, coffee and pecan pie for him, decaf and a piece of flourless chocolate torte for me.

"So, tell me what I have to expect in the next year," I said once our orders were in. He gave me a vaguely confused look for a moment, so I quickly added, "At school! What is the first year of medical school like? During orientation my advisor said something about it being traumatic."

"Well, it's intense. There's more to learn than you can understand on this side of it. There are times when all you can do is deal with what you need to learn for the next test, rather than keeping up with everything the whole time. One of my classmates called it pissing on the fire in front of you and moving on."

My heart sank a little. I already felt outclassed and overwhelmed all the time.

He continued, "I know that image is unpleasant, but it's kind of accurate. But you can't get overwhelmed by that—people graduate medical school every year all over the world. It's doable. It's amazing what people can do when they *have* to do it. Look at it like boot camp. You put your head down and get through it, no matter what, and at the end, you can do almost anything!"

"It feels insurmountable, impossible." I took a deep breath and looked up at him, feeling very small in a very big world.

"You're going to do just fine, little girl. Don't let me scare you." His gaze darkened a bit, "Well, not too much anyway. You'll do things you never thought you could or would by the end of this year."

He was simultaneously scaring me, reassuring me and giving me a look like he was thinking of a few things he'd like to get me to do.

"But that brings up a good point, something I should tell you." But he just paused.

"Okay? You can't say something like that and stop."

"I'm just working out how to say it," he said, rubbing the back of his neck. "I like you. I know we just met, but...I...I like you and I'd like to date you, but I am...demanding when I'm dating someone. I want you to think about that. I want you to think about what you can handle with school, because I won't let you fail at school because of me." I got all gooey inside until his voice and face hardened just a bit and he added, "But I won't tolerate not getting what I want out of you if you're mine."

"Uhhmm, I'm not sure what to say to that. Clearly, I like you as well, but I don't know how to respond to that." It was uncomfortable, awkward to be discussing the relationship that we didn't even have yet. I squirmed a little in my seat, hyperaware of the intensity of his gaze.

"I know, little girl," he said sadly. "It isn't really fair for me to take you any further down this road with me without having this conversation though. I just want you to think about it for a bit."

My emotions were all over the place. I was unsettled, feeling like it could be over before it started and who knows what 'it' would have been. And that felt dumb and I got a little angry.

"Wait a minute. This is bullshit, Xander. I don't have any actual information. I am only two weeks into medical school. I don't know what it will be like or what I can handle with it. And what do you even mean about how you are? How am I supposed to know what I should or shouldn't do?"

His tone was conciliatory when he answered, "I know, little girl. Maybe we just take it really slow with each other and you tell me right away if you are getting overwhelmed, if it is too much. Like a safeword."

A what? But I did calm a little. "What's a safeword?"

He groaned with a smile on his face that he tried really hard to hide. "Leda, you don't know what that means?" He looked at me incredulously.

"No, what the fuck?"

"Okay, baby girl — yeah, you might not even know enough to be a 'little' anymore," he said with a smile. "So a safeword is something that people use when they are involved in S&M or really anything sexual that pushes their boundaries."

"Why don't they just say *stop*?" I was confused. "And, pardon me, but did you just say S&M?"

He had the look of someone being diplomatic. "Some people get off on the word stop or no being ignored or pushed past."

"That's rape." I was getting freaked out. *Is this guy telling me he doesn't believe in listening to the word 'no'?*

"No, that's not what I mean. It's just what some people get off on. It's called consensual nonconsent." He was speaking so nonchalantly, as if this was totally normal first date shit. "The key is to have a safeword so that everyone involved knows when the 'stop' is for real. It's like what I was talking about with the Window — everyone has to be legal and consenting. That doesn't mean that you won't hear someone saying no. It's hard to explain, but it is actually pretty simple — you just have to let yourself think past the college 'No means no' rhetoric. I'm not condoning rape or sexual assault or any kind of assault. Sometimes people like to pretend — all kinds of things really, and in any situation. It's really important that everyone communicate openly and have a plan of how to stay safe together. Sometimes it isn't even that. Sometimes it's just overwhelming and you just need to be clear about where the limits are." He trailed off, looking pained, as if I wasn't understanding something that was really important.

"Is this something you're into—this no doesn't actually mean no stuff?" I was a little repulsed and a little intrigued at the same time. But I was hit with a fast rush of shame that it was something that could interest me. Of course, I knew girls in college that got date-raped. It's not particularly uncommon. I did the 'Take Back the Night' marches. But it really didn't sound like he was talking about that.

"I don't ever want to do something with someone, or to someone, if they don't want it. For a while now, my policy has been to check in if there's any question in my mind, make sure that everything I'm doing is wanted. It's really important that you understand that. I will not do something you don't want, but I also want you to consider that you may not know everything you want yet, that there are experiences you haven't even considered yet. Do you understand me, baby girl?" He brushed his fingers across my hand and his touch made me tingle deep inside.

My face flushed and my breath quickened. I nodded to him, wide eyed, not trusting my voice.

"Good girl, let's go. It's past your bedtime." He stood up, extending his hand to me, and left some money on the table.

I felt in a cloud as we walked out. He guided me, his hand pausing on the back of my neck then stroking the length of my spine. As we walked to the car, he continued to stroke my back and the fog of my brain cleared a little to reveal one thought—I wanted him. Then it was all I could think about, leaning my body into him. I wanted him to overwhelm me, to give me a real reason to need a safeword.

We got to the car and he opened the door for me, helping me into my seat and leaning down so his face was level with mine while he buckled my seat belt. He was so close, I could smell his goodness and another wave of lust washed over me. I wanted to lick him. I felt myself take a deep breath and sigh. He looked at me and I think he knew. He had to know. How could he not know? It was overwhelming, so big inside me. He closed my door and my mind cleared a little.

When he got in the driver's side, he turned the radio on and this perfect song was playing. The singer was voicing so many things that I was thinking and at one point, I'm sure that Xander chuckled. When the song ended, he changed the station to something a little mellower, some nineties emo music, The Cure or Depeche Mode. At a red light, he rested his hand around the back of my neck and gave the lightest pressure as the light turned green and he went back to driving.

We got to my apartment, and I stupidly realized that I hadn't said anything since the restaurant. I'd been caught up in my own thoughts.

"Oh God, sorry I've been so quiet! I was just thinking about everything we talked about and I'm so tired all of a sudden. You've been quiet too. Everything okay?"

"I was just watching you. I'll walk you to your door." He got out and came around for me. I was thankful for it because I was suddenly exhausted. He helped me out and walked me to the door, with his hand on my back again.

"Do you want to come up for a drink?" *Isn't that what I'm supposed to say when I'm actually saying I want to screw you?* I fumbled with the keys to open the door. He pulled the door open for me.

"I'll walk you up, but then I'm going."

Crushed! We were up the stairs way too fast. I didn't want the night to be over, but I was stifling a yawn.

"Are you sure you won't come in?"

"Baby girl, it's time for you to sleep. And I was serious about what I said. The first year of medical school is a lot by itself, let alone with a relationship, even if it's only vanilla. And I'm not so simple as vanilla. I want you to really think about what you can handle."

What the fuck does vanilla mean?

"Okay, well, I had a great time. It was... educational." I pushed up to my tiptoes to kiss his cheek, whispering, "Thanks, Xander."

He grabbed me around the waist, holding my body tight to his, one hand snaking up to the back of my neck, turning my head so he could kiss me. He pressed his lips against mine, softly at first, but with more pressure then just the slightest lick against my lips. I felt my body go slack against his, surrendering. I opened my lips and started to kiss him back, reaching up to drape my arms around his neck. I felt more than heard the low growl-groan in his chest as he opened his mouth and kissed me deeply, our tongues meeting and touching. His mouth was just right and he tasted sweet from his pie, but the bitter undertone of coffee was there too. Another low sound from his throat, but this one sounded more like regret and he pulled away from me.

"Goodnight, baby girl." He turned and jogged down the stairs. I watched him, noticing he had a great ass that I hadn't really seen before. At the bottom of the stairs, he turned around and looked back up to me,

"Girl, go put yourself to bed. Now." Even from my distance, I could see twitch in his jaw. I couldn't tell if it was anger or amusement or something else altogether, but whatever it was, it gave me nervous butterflies in my stomach and a smile blossomed on my face.

"Okay, Boss. Goodnight." I blew him a kiss and scurried inside, only catching the faintest glimpse of the smile quirking the corner of his mouth before I turned away.

Once inside my apartment, I couldn't stop thinking of him and what he had said about what dating him is like.

Was he just trying to give me the brush-off, that thing guys do where they make it impossible to date them but won't break up with you, preferring to push you till you do it and then act like it was all you—because he 'didn't want to hurt you'? *Guys are fucking idiots sometimes.*

I didn't think that was what Xander was doing. It didn't fit with the rest of his actions. I ran the night back through my mind while I washed my face and got ready for bed. As I was splashing water on my face and neck, I thought about Christy and Jason and what Xander had told me about the Blackened Window. My skin felt hot and hypersensitive, and I pictured Christy tied to a wall with Jason's fingers in her mouth again. As these thoughts and images started running through my mind, my text message alert chimed.

If you are awake to read this, you are in trouble baby girl — X

Then I'm in trouble. Just getting into bed now. Thanks again for a great night! I had a lot of fun. – L

Yes, you are in trouble. Get in bed. I'll text you in the morning about punishment. And I'm glad you had fun. Watching you dance was…very nice. – X

I started getting all kinds of dirty thoughts about spankings and being tied up like I had just imagined Christy, but exhaustion pulled me to sleep quickly.

* * * *

I slept deeply, but woke with lingering thoughts of kissing him like I had been dreaming of it. It was almost eleven and I had a ton of studying to do, but I also had a killer headache, indicating I'd probably had more alcohol than I thought. I considered a bowl of cereal and my stomach vetoed.

I needed to get into my reading for the week, but I couldn't concentrate between the alcohol hangover and the Xander hangover. I kept thinking of last night, seeing him relaxed when he didn't know I was looking, the feel of his body against mine on the dance floor, the dark thoughts I could see in the depths of his eyes at times and that warning at the end. That he's 'demanding' and won't 'tolerate' not getting what he wants.

Is he a toddler?

I actually laughed out loud at that thought because I couldn't even picture him having a temper tantrum. I couldn't even imagine what it would be like if he didn't get what he wanted.

What does that even mean?

And I knew then, despite his warnings about his needs and the demands of school, I wanted to see where it would go between us, even knowing that I didn't know enough to make an educated, or even very intelligent, decision. I had that feeling of not caring if the decision I was making might be self-destructive, but I knew my mind was already made up.

My plan was to spend the day on the couch, studying—anatomy, physiology, histology, biochemistry. Exciting! My text alert chimed and I silently thanked God.

Baby girl, how did you sleep? – X

Really well, but a little hungover this morning. U? – L

Slept great, feel great. Thinking about you all morning – X

Thinking about U 2. What are U doing 2day? – L

Studying, working out, studying, doling out punishments – X

Long pause. I wasn't sure how to answer that, but I wanted to see him and in my mind punishment was beginning to mean the something akin to sex.

Umm, plural punishments? Do U have other people to punish today or just me multiple times? – L

Oh, baby girl. You are naughty, naughty, naughty. You will clearly need a lot of training. And I am looking forward to every second of it. – X

Training? That response just made me even sassier, but it was kind of hot and I felt like pushing him some—from here, when he was there and any real consequence was theoretical.

XOXOXO bossy — L

7pm — X

7pm what? — L

7pm I will be at your place, ready to give you what you deserve. See you soon, baby girl — X

That felt a little ominous...and presumptuous. Maybe I already had plans. I didn't, but anyway... Seven p.m. I had six hours to study and get myself ready.

OK, should I get something ready? — L

I was trying to get an idea of what this was going to entail or if he was teasing me or what the fuck.

I'll take care of everything, including you. Try not to worry about it too much until then. — X

OK, no worrying about whatever may or may not be happening later for "punishment." I feel like a kid in trouble who's gonna get a spanking. But sure, no worrying today. You got it, Boss. — L

Hmmmm, spanking, really? That's what comes to mind? I like it. — X

What? I don't actually want to be spanked. No, I don't. Wait...but do I? My mind was a jumble of thoughts of being across his knees and my naked ass getting swatted, and I got that feeling like I couldn't quite catch my breath. I was confused with myself—*Do I want to be spanked? I don't even know how to answer that.*

I had planned to spend the day studying and knew I'd be distracted now. I got comfy on the couch and opened a book, not really seeing the words. I was definitely on edge. As the sickly aftermath of the booze faded, it was replaced by a roiling, anxious excitement.

Chapter Nine

Xander
Daughn Gibson, The Sound of Law

I called Jason and woke his sorry ass up. "You're still fucking sleeping? Get up."

"Fuck off, dick." I heard Christy in the background, telling me to fuck off, as well.

"Soooooo, whatcha doing?" I smiled, knowing I was being super-annoying.

"Sleeping, dick. Are you having a crisis?"

"No."

"Good." And he hung up.

I laughed. I gave it twenty minutes and called him back. Christy answered.

"He's in the shower. Are you coming over?"

"Is that cool? Or are you two too wrecked for company?"

"Oh, shut up. You're not company. See you in a bit."

I grabbed my gym bag and left. *Fuck studying today.* The drive to their house took about a half an hour because they lived out in the country a bit, on a fifty acre piece of land. They'd bought it about three years ago and built their home. It was ridiculous, huge.

I pulled into the property and parked in the four car garage, where they kept a spot clear for me because I was there so much. I came in through the garage door, into a kitchen with an informal dining area—

"Hey, shit heads, I'm here. Come solve my problems for me."

Christy stepped out of the pantry with a box of cereal and fixed me with a look. "Shit *heads*? Was that plural?"

I laughed and hugged her, as Jason came in the room. "What's your problem now?"

"So, I told her I was gonna come over and punish her tonight."

"I feel like there's a back story that you skipped. And did you spend the night with her?" Christy fixed me with that look again. I think it's a southern girl thing. "Do you want some cereal?"

"No, I want some lunch though."

"You're welcome to it." She waved at the kitchen, indicating that I could fix it my damn self. "Now, spill it. She would have gone home with you, so what happened?

Jason manned the stove, frying up some bacon and eggs, and I went to the fridge for some bread, cheese and tomatoes to make myself an egg sandwich. "So, we went to the Cat's Meow for some dessert and coffee then I drove her home."

"Dude. Come on. We know there's more to it than that." Jason wasn't wearing a shirt, just low slung sweats. The dude was wiry-ripped.

"All right. I kind of gave her a warning. Kind of said, I'm demanding and require a lot of attention in a relationship, and she should think about that before we go any further. And then, it fucking nearly imploded. I mentioned something about a safeword and she had no idea what I was talking about." They both laughed. "Yeah, fuck you guys. So, I drove her home and was a total gentleman."

They laughed again.

"Seriously! I just kissed her goodnight and told her to go to bed."

"You Dominant-type people are so fucking pushy sometimes." Christy was smiling, but we all knew it was true. They didn't have a Dominant/submissive dynamic to their relationship, except when they chose to play that way. And, being someone who didn't have this need, she just didn't get some of it. She accepted me, even loved me, but didn't get it.

"It's this thing. I tease her and tell her it's her bedtime."

"Is she turning you into a Daddy?" Jason's eyebrows shot up on his face. I'd always been much more of a sadistic, controlling Dom. And while I took care of any subs I had, I wasn't the Daddy-type usually. I just thought I wasn't wired like that, but the more time I spent with Leda, the more I wanted to shelter her and discipline her.

"Maybe." I was still considering it and felt resistant to the label. "Anyway, I texted her when I got home, telling her she was in trouble if she was awake to read it, and she responded. It's like she wants to get punished."

"Wait…gimme your phone. I want to read the whole exchange." Christy held her hand out and I gave it to her. They read it with their heads tilted in together over my phone. "Wellllp. I think she wants to be your sub."

"Right? That response of what should I get ready...for you to come over and *punish* me. No offense, Christy, but she is the perfect woman."

"For you, dude," Jason added with a scowl on his face as he wrapped his arms around Christy. "So, what's the problem?"

"That bit about bringing everything over. I can't really cook anything beyond mac and cheese or a grilled cheese...or something else with cheese." I smirked a bit. Christy hated the way Jason and I ate, but we both worked out enough that it wasn't an issue.

"So take some cheese," she said, with an equally smart ass smirk on her face. "Seriously, take some finger foods — cheese, fruit, chocolate. Make it easy."

"I was thinking about taking some Sangria."

"He can't cook anything, but Sangria he makes." Christy addressed Jason as she turned on their espresso machine.

He shrugged. "Priorities."

"Jace — wanna go work out?"

"I don't really want to drive out to the gym. Let's just spar here." They had kept a good portion of the basement clear of furniture and had put an extra thick pad down when they'd carpeted, knowing that we would likely being practicing here some, too. "But I gotta digest first."

"What was your night like last night after you left the club?"

"The Window was fun." He shot Christy a look. "This one almost got in trouble...forgot to put her clothes on before leaving the back."

I laughed. The Window was like any other club when you first came in. Bar, dance floor, DJ. But there was a second half of the building where all the sexy stuff happened, and there were some rules about where to get naked.

"It was busy though. More so on the dance floor than in back," Jason added.

She put a coffee down in front of him. "Sorry…I was fucked witless."

She brought me a coffee too, for which I thanked her. We sat at their counter, talking and joking. After breakfast, Jason and I sparred. I was distracted enough by thoughts of Leda that I didn't last long.

Once home, I made the Sangria and put it in the fridge to chill while I showered. I tried to distract myself with studying, but she was there at the corners of my thoughts. Eventually, I tossed to book across the room.

I drove to her house, nervous about the open alcohol container in my car, high on knowing that I was going to her house with the intent to fuck with her head…in the best way possible. I didn't know that she was ready for it, but I thought she was.

I waited for her to buzz me in and felt the adrenaline surge a bit. My lips felt tingly and a precursor to pleasure rippled through me. She let me in and met me on the landing and I couldn't stop the silly smile. I was happy to see her, happy she'd let me come back.

"Hey, baby girl. You hungry?" I dropped a soft kiss on her head as I passed her.

"Sure, what did you bring?" She was anxious, but not panicked. It was just there at the edges, a little more pressure in her speech.

"I brought a bunch of finger foods—fruit, cheese, crackers, chocolate. And some Sangria—my mom's recipe, so good. Does a drink sound okay or are you still feeling a little hungover?"

"No, I actually felt better pretty quickly this morning. I'd love to try a glass." We got plates and drinks and sat at her couch, kind of facing each other.

"How was your day, baby girl?" I smiled as I said it, sure she'd spent the day at least half worrying about what might be coming.

She played it cool. "It was good. I got a lot of studying done. How about you?"

"Great! I studied a bunch and sparred with Jason some."

"Tell me more about this martial art you're doing." She sank her teeth into a strawberry, her lips closing down, but wet with juice nonetheless. It was distracting.

"I love it. I bet you would, too." *Look somewhere other than her mouth.* I dropped my eyes and they settled on her cleavage, which looked especially nice in the white, V-neck T-shirt she was wearing. *Focus up, Stone.* "It's a lot of ground work, rather than the standing type of fighting people think of with most martial arts—you know Bruce Lee type of stuff. This is closer to wrestling, but the idea of using your opponent's energy against them is the same. There are some strikes, but mostly submission holds."

I couldn't even say the word submission near her without thinking of her lying at my feet. "When I first started, I just got my ass kicked repeatedly by the guys at my gym, but I've gotten better since then. I still get some bruises, especially if I spar with my instructor." I showed her a new bruise on my chest from Jason today. His heel had caught my pec as he'd figure-foured my neck.

Her eyes bulged a bit. "It sounds rough, but fun."

She said nothing for a few minutes and I didn't feel the need to fill the silence. I wanted her to come to me, in every sense.

She spoke again. "I thought about what you were talking about last night, about balancing school and a possible relationship, and there's no way that I could know the right decision until after the fact. I don't know what school will be like and what I can handle along with it. I really like spending time with you. I don't really want to stop and you'd understand, probably better than most, if I need to pause or spend a bunch of time studying."

I watched her, and only murmured in response, wanting more.

"Now, that said, I don't know what you mean about what you need. You just said you were demanding. What does that mean?" She looked like she knew, but wanted me to say it. I was happy to oblige. She had to accept me just the way I was.

"Well, I want certain things out of a relationship. You've already noticed that I'm *bossy*, as you call it. That's who I am. I want to tell you what to do and I want you to listen and do it." I put my plate on the coffee table then took hers off her knees and put it down, too. I felt the dominance surging through me. "Do you think you can do that?" I leaned into her space, closer and closer until she leaned back. Her eyes were wide again. I shifted past her face and spoke in her ear. "Can you do what you're told, Leda?"

"I think so."

She almost whispered it and I kept moving forward, gently pushing her back on the couch until I was planked over her. I lowered my lips to her neck and clavicle, hooking my finger into the collar of her shirt, pulling it aside so I could get at her skin. She lightly touched my back and breathed a sigh. *That's enough.*

I pulled back. "No, I don't want 'I think so'. I want 'yes' or 'I can learn if you'll teach me'. Until then, I just think it'll be too much for you." I completely retreated from her, sitting back on the couch, knowing that it wasn't fair, but I never said I'd play fair. *There aren't rules, other than the rules I make.* Her face looked a little dejected, like she'd lost her puppy. *Good.* "How about this? Let's just try a little play, a little fun. And then you tell me what you think?"

A flutter of hope in her eyes. "What do you mean?" Her breathing was tense and that sexy flush was back in her cheeks. The way she looked up at me through her lashes, the white shirt — she looked so goddamned innocent and I wanted to strip her down, corrupt her, pervert her. Make her into something that was purely *mine.*

Take a damn breath. Control.

"We can go in small steps. And if it gets to be too much, we pause or stop or switch directions." This was another moment of truth. She'd balk or she'd give. "What do you think? Wanna try?" My palms were wet and I was nervous in a wholly unsexy way. This wasn't the fun part. Yet.

"Okay. Yeah, okay, let's try it."

Thank Christ. I let out a breath I hadn't been aware I was holding.

"Let's say just for tonight and…we'll see." She looked willing to try, but unsure of herself. That was about right.

With the way I had been obsessing over her for the last three days, I knew that this could…change me a little. Make me want it more. Open the fucking floodgates. I'd want it with her, but, I knew in my heart that if she failed me, I'd find someone at the Window to take my need out on.

"So, I have one more warning. If we do this for more than a few nights, you're gonna see parts of me that I don't show people. It might freak you out a little. What I think about doing to you…" The whole world contracted down to that couch, her face, her breath. She had to know that I'd want to fuck with her, but she could trust me. "You must trust that I will not harm you. I may want to hurt you at some point." I already wanted to hurt her. "But no harm will come to you by me or by anyone else. Can you trust me, at least enough to try it out?"

I saw the questions and the fear in her face, and called her on it. "Leda, what are you thinking now? Don't censor yourself—trust me and just say it." She didn't speak. "Now."

She leaned forward and the words rushed off her lips. "I have a million questions and you're scaring me some."

Good.

"But then I think about you being here the other night when I was so sick and, I mean, if you were some fucked up, sadistic bastard…"

That's exactly what I am.

"You could have done anything to me, killed me really, and you didn't. You just took care of me. I think I can trust you enough for one night."

I felt the grin spreading on my lips and it wasn't evil, wasn't depraved. It was just the smile of feeling accepted, the smile of hopes building up. But she had questions. It was important that she felt as prepared as possible before anything happened.

"What are your questions?" I paused, but cut her off before she spoke, changing the subject a little.

"Actually, before we start even talking about things, let's decide on your safeword. Or something to let me know if you're not okay with something that's happening."

She nodded, but her face belied her confusion.

Let's keep it easy. "I think using traffic light colors would be easiest, most straight-forward. Green for 'I'm good. I like this. Let's keep going'. Yellow for 'I'm a little anxious, scared, uncomfortable, overwhelmed. Can we ease up, but not stop'. Red for stop, and everything will stop." I liked that there was a middle ground, and, hopefully, it was easy to remember. "What do you think—green, yellow, red? Will those work for you?"

"Yes." She looked so demure and obedient. Head slightly downcast, looking up through her lashes with big eyes, hands in her lap, voice soft. I wanted to jump on her.

Restraint. I reminded myself I was playing the long game. I wanted more than tonight, wanted to draw it out, so she was my slave in all things, so she was begging me to fuck her, wanted only to be in my bed or anywhere else I told her to be. "Tell me what the safewords are. I want you to tell it back to me so I know we're on the same page." Closed loop communication, less chance for a misunderstanding.

"Green means go—I want more. Yellow means slow—I'm freaked out, but don't stop. And red means stop."

I tried to stop myself from saying 'Good girl'. But it was a perfect answer.

"Okay. Good girl. Now, tell me your questions. I may not answer them completely. Part of how this works is that you don't always have all the information in advance and I make the decisions for you, for what I want for you." The cold heat of control was snaking its way through my body. I felt it in the palms of my hands, in my chest, in the stretch of my neck. I felt solid, in my body, powerful. Her eyes widened as she saw it, then her pupils dilated. *God, she's hardwired for it.*

She spoke softly. "I don't even know what my questions really are. It's just all of it, you know? Like what do you want to do to me? What is the difference between getting hurt and getting harmed? I don't know…so many thoughts are circling in my head that I can't really keep track of them all."

"What I want to do to you…is a very long conversation and truthfully, I don't want to tell you everything yet. I want to make you experience things you haven't experienced before and telling you about them in advance would ruin it." As I spoke, I took our glasses to the kitchen. I had to put a little distance between us before I lost my hold on my control. From the kitchen, I continued, while I refilled our glasses.

"It's essential that you understand the difference between hurt and harm. It's like when I spar with my Jiu Jitsu buddies. I might get hurt, but nothing goes so far to harm me. I may have some bruises, but I'd never get a broken bone, never really have anything bad happen to me. It's the same thing. Some things may happen that are intense sensations, maybe even some pain, but nothing will ever harm you in a way that has lasting effects. In this type of exchange, it's my job to take care of you, even as I push you to your limits. The other side to that, your job, is to remember the safewords and tell me honestly if something is too much, too fucked up for you, too painful, too scary. Whatever."

I sat back down on the couch, a little closer to her, and she asked, "So, are you hinting at wanting to tie me up and whip me or something like that?"

I sighed, internally marveling at her innocence. "Tie you up? Definitely. Whips? I don't know, not tonight at least." Her hands flexed in her lap. That scared her a little. "But there are times that I do want to hurt someone — and that someone would most likely be you. More than anything, I just like to be in control — whether it's physical with some sort of restraint or psychological where I get you to a point where you do something you never thought you would because I want you to do it, because you belong to me and want to make me happy." *I mean, isn't that what every man wants?* I was such an asshole.

I expected her to tell me to fuck off. I had just basically told her I wanted to make her do shit she didn't want to do, that I wanted her so twisted up over me that she'd do what I told her to. Her face was thoughtful, a moment of rejection passed over her features, but it softened and disappeared — and was replaced by peace. *Peace?* Not what I'd expected. "What is it? What is that reaction?"

She didn't pause now, just answered immediately. "My mom is a feminist and I mean like bra-burning, shatter the glass ceiling feminist. I grew up with these messages of 'don't ever let a man control you, control your life. You are in charge of you. You can do anything a man can do, be anything a man can be. Don't ever let yourself feel like less because you're a woman'. And it's a confusing set of feelings to be so intrigued by what you are saying and so interested in giving up control. Does it make me less of a feminist? Or mean that I have less value or something? That seems like bullshit, but I really don't know."

I wasn't really expecting to discuss feminism, and my domlust banked itself in my cock as I tried to answer intelligently. "Well, I can't answer that question for you, but I can tell you three things that may help you decide for yourself. One, none of this lessens your worth in my eyes in any way. Two, I think the submissive person actually has almost all the real control. The dominant person really only has control of the playtime world that both people willingly choose to go together and three, I know a super-feminist woman who is into kink. I'd be glad to introduce you to her. She may have some insights that would help you."

She smiled and took a deep breath. Acceptance.

This was the beginning of her submission, of her learning to belong to me. I savored the moment on the precipice, the anticipation. I wanted to memorize the moment and mentally cataloged the feel of the couch under me, her shallow breaths, the low light in the room, and the red stain on her lips from the Sangria.

Chapter Ten

Leda
The XX, Infinity

He was staring at me intently and I shifted in my seat, ate a chocolate with caramel in it, the caramel squishing out when I bit. I wiped it away with a finger, but then had caramel on my fingers, so I started licking it off—all messy and I felt like an idiot, very uncool—until I looked up at him and the naked hunger in his eyes rocked me back in my seat and stole my breath. He could go from normal to a little scary in a heartbeat, or maybe it was there all the time, in layers or something.

"Stop. Take your fingers out of your mouth."

He said it with such authority that I blindly obeyed him, but the look on his face and the steel in his voice had me on edge, a tickle inside, that breathless feeling again. He took my hand and brought it to his mouth, licking at the caramel. Then scraped it off with his teeth. Not biting me. Not hurting me...just scraping his teeth along the length of my finger. The sensation was intense and different than anything I could remember experiencing with any of my exes.

He paused, taking my fingers out of his mouth. "Green?"

"Green."

He pulled my hand to his mouth again and started biting into the fleshy part of my palm and it didn't hurt exactly, but it was that same type of intense and different. My skin felt hypersensitive. *I* felt hypersensitive. His iron grip wrapped around my wrist and he moved his mouth on me, biting my forearm, the inside of my elbow. His mouth was hot and wet and his teeth scraping me was almost too much, nearly ticklish punctuated with the light sharpness of his bite. My breathing was shallow and quick. I flushed and he pushed me back on the couch again.

"Green?"

"Green."

He pinned my arm above my head and pulled my other arm up to mirror it as he laid his body against mine, letting his weight settle on me, pushing my breath out of my lungs. He watched me closely. With his free hand, he tilted my chin up, scraping his teeth along my jaw and down my neck, to my collarbone. I sighed, stretching and arching into him. He suddenly climbed up me, his knees on either side of my rib cage, his weight exclusively pressing on my chest so I was very aware of each breath. Without letting go of my wrists, or breaking our gaze, he one-handedly took off his belt.

Is he going to pull his cock out right now? I felt the first quake of real fear building in my chest—fear of what sex with him would be like, fear that I truly did not know what to expect next from him. I think he saw it in my eyes, because he changed further, like he was bigger again, stronger, less tentative even. I took a deep breath, saying nothing. But his hand left the fly of his jeans and instead joined the other hand at my wrists, using his belt to start tying them, fastening my wrists together.

"Green?" he asked, his voice soft and tender, even as he tightened his belt on my wrists.

"Green." But my voice was much shakier this time.

"What are your safewords, baby girl?" he asked as he climbed off me, kneeling at the side of the couch.

"Green, yellow, red."

"Are you green?"

"I'm green." I said it with more confidence and he held my gaze for a moment. His eyes held satisfied warmth. He was pleased. I felt embraced in his presence and wanted in a way I had never felt before.

In all my previous relationships, I had felt generically wanted, wanted for my ability to provide a warm, wet place to put a penis. This was different. This was being wanted for all of me, being wanted for my specific body and my specific mind, my specific reactions to what was happening. Even though we'd just met, even though it was all new. I let it ride, let the questions fade away, dropped the worries. I felt hedonistic, slick with wanting, golden and lit from within.

"I'm only going to touch you. I'm not taking any of your clothes off, not trying to push you too much tonight. Just touching you. You will not speak unless it is to say your safeword." As he said it, he pulled my T-shirt up just enough to reveal my abdomen and laid his hand flat across me. It was warm and firm, a hint of some calluses, but most of all it felt big, as if all of my attention was sucked into the sensation of his hand on my skin. He held his hand still for a few beats longer then started gently moving it in small circles on my tummy. The movement against my soft skin created this wonderful dragging friction between us. He held me transfixed and I closed my eyes, laying my head back and willing myself to relax into his touch. His fingers traced circles and lines centering on my navel and the light touch was almost more intense than it would have been if he had grabbed me. Each pass of his hand over my skin felt full of promise, full of risk.

In just a few minutes, I panted under that touch and he climbed back onto the couch, on top of me with his knees on either side of my thighs. He sat back on my legs and continued with both hands on my rib cage, rubbing up and down my sides, coming blissfully close to my breasts without touching them. I was restrained by his body on my legs and his belt lashing my wrists together, and it forced me to focus on what he was doing. His touch, his *nearness* and my agreement not to speak. Without having the distraction of my own wants or my own attempts to do something, my focus was completely undivided.

He traced his hands down to the button on my jeans, fingertips grazing the edge and dipping inside just a bit. I drew a sharp breath. I wanted him to tear my jeans off and plow into me. At the same time, I never wanted him to stop what he was doing. And the stray thought crossed my mind again, that I had only known him for a short time, maybe this was too much too soon. He leaned over and traced the line of my jeans around the sides of my body and under me, rubbing with a deeper pressure into the muscles of my low back.

A low moan slipped past my lips and I dropped any other thought. At my moan, his breathing became more pressured and I glanced at him. His face was set in lines of calm concentration, but when his gaze flicked to mine, it was heated. He brought his hands back around to the front of my body, over my jeans to my hip bones, gripping them and rocking my body side to side slowly. It centered my focus on my pelvis and my wetness grew, the beginning of an electrical awareness of my pussy, just begging to be touched.

I was starting to get impatient and made a little whining sound deep in my throat. He watched me, almost detached, nearly distant, but not gone, not empty. He sensed my impatience and quickly brought his hands up the sides of my body to my shoulders as he lay down across me. He filled my field of vision and it was too intense. I closed my eyes to escape it, but he said, "Open your eyes. I want you right here with me. I want to see every reaction." His voice rolled over me, warm, liquid.

Another moan slipped from my lips. He brought his fingers to my lips and traced them. All the while, I was almost outside myself, fascinated with him, unsure where he was leading me.

"You were supposed to be quiet, but maybe I wasn't completely clear, baby girl. No sounds at all, unless you are using your safewords or responding to me. Do you understand me?"

I nodded my head. *No sounds at all?* Then it was all I could think of, the enormity of this man's presence over me, the heat and electricity of my skin under his touch and not making a sound. Any clinical detachment of my own was gone, and I started moving under him, grinding my hips up into him, trying to get my legs out from under him, without success. He leaned down on me harder and I could feel the rock-hard bulge of his erection against me. I wanted it so bad. He traced his fingers across my collarbone again while nuzzling his scratchy chin into my neck.

I stretched up, attempting to kiss or suck or bite his neck and, without even minimally pausing what he was doing, he brought a hand up to my chest, right over my sternum and pushed me back down, growling into my ear, "Don't move, baby girl."

My reactions to him were so confusing – there was a rush of fear, but the excited fear of a rollercoaster ride, and the intense want for anything he wanted to do to me. This was so unlike the drunken and desperate frat-boy fumblings in college. This was methodical, intentional. He was completely in control of himself despite the hard-on digging into my pelvis. It was as if he had no intention of getting himself off, like he just wasn't worried about his own experience.

The hand on my chest slipped up to my jaw, turning my head to allow him full access to my neck. That hand then traveled up my arms to my bound hands, grabbing the loops of his belt between my wrists and tightening his grip, and consequently, tightening the pressure on my wrists. His other hand continued traveling up and down my curves, light and completely maddening. All I could do was accept – accept all of what he gave me, accept how he played with me. I shuddered another sigh and willed myself to relax into it.

When I thought I was going to lose my mind with how much I wanted him and the sensations all over my body, he sat back up, pulling my tied wrists with him so that I was sitting up as well. Without speaking, he climbed off the couch and pulled me to standing, then turned me so that I was facing the couch.

"Stay right there. Don't move." I felt his absence behind me and a moment later heard him in the kitchen. The refrigerator or freezer opening and closing again. "Mmm, good girl," he said as he came back. I heard something I was sure was ice clink into his glass, now emptied of Sangria. *What is he going to do with* ice?

"Now, for your punishment." He stepped up behind me, his hand on the back of my neck and his lips at my ear, speaking in a growly purr. I couldn't fucking breathe. "You stayed up past your bedtime. You need enough sleep to be healthy and you're going to have to learn to listen."

I started to turn my head to him to let him know what I thought of that, all sexual tension forgotten for a moment, but he caught my jaw in his hand, refusing to let me turn. "No talking, but I think that might be too hard for you. I can help. Open your mouth."

Again, I obeyed him before I even really thought about it. He stepped behind me, left hand still on my jaw and right coming around to put an ice cube in my mouth. Once it was in, he sealed his left hand over my mouth, but left my nose unblocked. I felt myself tense at this next level of intensity, feeling so restrained and confined in him. With his hands on my face, his body was pressed tight against me and it felt like he was surrounding me in every direction. My mouth was so cold and his hand clamped on me kept me from moving. He stepped back to my left side, shifting his left hand on my mouth. His right hand traced over my skin to the back of my neck and started pushing me forward.

"Still green, baby girl? You can nod yes."

I nodded.

"If you need me to stop, you can speak behind my hand or shake your head. Understand?"

I nodded again.

"Good girl. Now, bend over and put your hands on the back of the couch." Once I was positioned, he added, "Don't move until I tell you. I don't want to have to hold you in place for this."

My breathing was more ragged, but he kept going, his right hand caressing down my back, then to my ass, cupping the cheek and squeezing just a bit. He took his hand away and I was sure that a spanking was to follow. I braced for it, but it didn't come, instead I felt the shock of another piece of ice on my back, just above the band of my jeans. He just held it still for a moment, letting me absorb the sensation. Then standing behind me, he kicked my feet apart a little, so there was room for him to stand directly behind me, his hips pushing into my ass, with the length and girth of his cock against the seam of my jeans. I was so wet. My panties felt tight and hot, like they were full of warm pudding, sticking to me, a wild contrast to the ice on my back and in my mouth. He traced the ice up my back, pushing my shirt up and bending to lay his body over mine.

"Still green, baby girl? Nod yes."

I nodded yes and pushed my ass back against him.

He chuckled. "Oh, so you want to play? Are you a bad girl just pretending to be good? Or are you a good girl who slips up some? That didn't seem like a slip to me. Still think you should get a spanking?" His voice was light, teasing.

He continued tracing the ice around my back. It was melting and drops of cold water spilled off my sides and straight down my back into my jeans, some even into my ass crack, chilling me there momentarily.

I shook my head 'No' to the spanking.

He kept speaking, "Has anyone ever spanked you before? Think about the size of my hand on this ass." He paused and grabbed my ass, rougher, nearly savagely. "Think about how hard I could spank you."

My pussy clamped and released involuntarily. The ice on my back finally melted away, draining rivulets of cold water across my ribs and he dropped his right hand to my hip and pulled me back into him. He was so hard, it felt like a slab of granite pressing into my fleshy backside. His hand was still over my mouth but the ice had melted, and my lips and tongue were so cold. Abruptly, he flipped me around and pushed me back on the couch, on my back. He dropped his weight on me and pushed my legs apart, pinning one to the back of the couch, the other falling off the front.

His mouth was on mine almost instantly, and his lips and tongue felt like fire after the ice. He groaned and ground his hips into me in a circular motion so the crotch seam of my jeans dug into my pussy, separating the lips and pressed directly onto my clit. And I couldn't stop myself from moaning into his mouth as I ground my hips back against him.

The hard pressure against me and his body over me and his mouth on mine and the whirlwind of sensations and emotions through the day all came crashing together in my body, tears stung my eyes and my hips snapped against his. It was overwhelming and terrifying and I never wanted it to stop. I felt an orgasm building. I was getting closer and closer and...he just completely stopped moving, lifting his entire body off me in a plank move that I distantly recognized from yoga classes I had taken in the past.

A small but significant whine of frustration slipped past my lips before I could stop myself and he smiled down at me, genuinely amused.

"Baby girl," he said reprovingly, "it seemed like you were having way too much fun for punishment."

And in my mind, I screamed – *Ahhhhh, what the fuck!!!! I need to come, you fucker!* – But, I still had this need to impress him, make him proud of me, so I centered myself, took a deep – albeit shaky – breath and looked directly into his eyes with my eyes still wet, but said nothing. He brushed my hair back from my face gently, such a contrast to how he had been treating me that I was disarmed for a moment. He nuzzled his face into my neck, gently biting my ear lobe. His mouth felt hot and wet and electric. *Amazing.*

"I'll tell you what, you can talk," he growl-whispered into my ear, "but only to beg. Say please."

He lowered his body back onto mine and kept skimming kisses on my neck and collarbone. I slipped my still-bound wrists around his neck and started to breathe heavily again, just starting to lift my hips to meet his, but he dropped the weight of his upper body on my chest and both his hands shot to my hips, slamming into me and pressing me into the couch.

"You're having a hard time controlling yourself, baby girl. I'll help you, but you still haven't said please."

I blushed and felt like he'd just called me a whore who couldn't control herself even for a moment, and really I did kind of feel like I couldn't control myself. Shame welled up in my chest, but he kept me restrained against the couch, licking the front of my throat and slipping his tongue lower onto my chest. Finally, he lifted his head to look at me, a searching look, maybe checking to see if I was okay, but he didn't ask. He started kissing my mouth, like he had all day and no concerns. I wanted to move my body against him, wanted to feel him, wanted him inside me. I wanted him to drive his hips into mine, using his cock to pin me down. I started kissing him back with more heat.

"Just say it, Leda. I know what you want," he murmured between kisses. He breathed out against my skin, "I'll make you feel good."

And it broke me.

"Please," I choked out against his lips. Shame and expectation and lust and panic and urgency all flooded through me. It was overwhelming, but quickly forgotten as he rotated his hips against me again, still kissing me, his hands just lightly tracing over my breasts, brushing my nipples.

"There's my good girl."

His praise undid me, and within seconds an orgasm crashed over me. I felt obliterated and my eyes watered as I quaked in aftershocks. He slowed his motions over me and pulled back to look at me. Surprisingly, he seemed unperturbed by my tears, wiping them away with his fingertips. With his other hand, he released my wrists and I wrapped my arms around him, trying to get control of myself. My breathing was hard and against all reason, I felt myself working up to a real cry. It felt foolish. *Who cries after an orgasm? What kind of weirdo am I? He's gonna think I'm a freak.* I focused on settling myself down, taking deep breaths and slowing my tears.

After a while, he propped himself up over me and smiled softly. "You did so well, Leda. How do you feel?"

I couldn't look him in the eye and a few straggler tears still clung to my lashes. "I...I don't know. I'm shaken? Drained? Like right after a big thunderstorm and everything is wet and soft and clean, like all that tension that was building has crashed over the world and dissipated." I glanced at him, feeling insecure. "Does that even make sense?"

"Yes, it absolutely does." He shifted over me to move back and I was suddenly totally aware that I'd come and he had not. I got this weird 'not-a-good-hostess' feeling that he should have been taken care of as well.

"What about you?" I asked, meaning that I was aware he could end up with blue balls, but he didn't take it that way.

"I feel good. *That* felt good," he replied, the dark gleam still in his eyes. Discretely adjusting his still bulging cock in his jeans and taking our glasses to the kitchen to refill them with fresh Sangria. As he walked back, he said, "So, that is at least a little taste, an *amuse-bouche* if you will, of what I want from you."

Umm, that was 'a little bit'?

"But...what about you? Isn't it uncomfortable not...you know...getting off too?" *Shit – so awkward.*

He smiled, with a little laughter in his eyes. "I'm fine. If you're into this, there'll be plenty of times that I come and you don't, plenty of times for you to reciprocate. And if you aren't really interested in this anymore—well, that's just not my thing. Regardless, I think the best part is the build-up. I don't mind if there's more time until I feel all of you."

He stayed for a while, periodically checking to be sure I was fine...not freaking out. It was sweet, but another huge departure from any other relationship I had ever had. When he left, he offered to drive me to school again in the morning, but I wanted to ride, wanted to have a clear head for classes.

Chapter Eleven

Xander
Jem, Falling For You

She didn't want a ride to school in the morning. So I gave her space, wanted to make her seek me out. But she didn't. She didn't text me or find me during the day. I saw her a few times, studying, ear buds in, world shut out. And I wondered if she was really reading or if she was running through last night—or if I'd completely misread her and she was done with me. Even though I wanted to make her come to me, I wasn't about to neglect her safety for my pride.

I don't want u riding your bike home after dark. If you stay to study, call me and I will pick you up — X

Was planning to study at home 2nite — L

Before I responded with some positive reinforcement, another text came through.

But thank u for looking out for me – L

A wide smiled spread across my face. She was starting to understand.

My pleasure – X

I stayed at the library to study for a few hours, because I knew if I studied at home, I'd just end up jerking off again, thinking about her. I worked on some pathology, knowing it would hold my interest better than any other subject I needed to work on. I had to eat something, but didn't really want to be alone. I texted Jason.

Dude, where you at?

The house. What's up? More women troubles?

What a dick.

No. Fuck you. I don't gots problems. I'm bored and hungry.

What you want to do?

You wanna come into town? Some food then I'll kick your ass a bit?

I'm getting in the car. Might kick your ass first. Then eat. Dick.

Then eat dick? New diet?

Right…fuck you.

I laughed as I gathered my shit and left campus. I stopped by my house and changed into my sparring gear. We met at a taco joint — scummy but yummy. As we were finishing, I got a text from Leda.

Hey, Boss, how was your day? Didn't see u @ school – L

It was a good day. I saw you. What are you doing? – X

When did u see me? Why didn't u say hi? I'm trying to study, but can't focus. – L

I smiled and Jason threw a napkin at me, laughing. I'd had very few actual girlfriends in the past, so I think he was enjoying it almost as much as me. I'm sure it kind of sucked for him and Christy to have me third-wheeling it all the time. I sent a message back.

I saw you a few times. You need space to think about things. Why can't you focus? – X

Just can't. Thinking about a bike ride. What are you doing? – L

No bike ride this late. – X

A thousand warning bells fired off in my mind. *Umm… Hell no, girlie.*

Eating now, but I've been studying, but can't focus either. Going to my gym. Wanna come? – X

Do I want to come? That's hilarious, ☺ but sure – L

Naughty, I like it. I'll be there in 15 minutes – X

"I'm gonna go pick her up and meet you at the gym," I said, getting up and clearing our table.

"I'll call Frank. He'll want to train. You're gonna be too busy thinking of a bunch of different ways to fuck your girl."

"I can mentally fuck her and actually school you at the same time, man."

"Only because I take pity on you." We both laughed, and he got Frank on the phone. He gave me a thumbs-up and I nodded at him as I left.

I was all kinds of stupid-happy, smiling on the drive over to her house. It felt too good and a small shard of doubt pierced me a little. I pushed it away, but knew it was my same old shit. I ruined everything. I'd ruin her too.

When I pulled up to her place, she came out to the car. I got out and helped her into the car, with a kiss as she passed me. She asked about the clothes I had on — the *gi*.

"I'm meeting Jason and Frank there, so we can spar some. You're welcome to watch, or try it out if you'd like. But there are the usual gym things too, if you'd rather." I kept the conversation light, didn't want to push her right now.

"Don't they have to work tonight? Isn't this when the bar gets busy?"

"The bar is closed on Mondays, and Christy does the late news during the week, so Jason is home alone. We usually get together a few times a week to work out."

The drive to the gym was quick. It looked crappy from the outside, but it was an old boxing gym, with newer martial arts stuff. I liked that the people who worked out for show, who went to the gym to be seen rather than actually better themselves, would never be seen there.

We paused near the entrance as she took the space in. Frank came in shortly after us.

"Hey, guys! Xander, thanks for letting me work in with you and Jason. I really like this stuff!"

I smiled and shook his hand.

He turned to Leda, "Hi, Leda." The two of them standing together was hilarious. She looked so tiny next to him.

"Hey, Frank, how are you?" She smiled up at him.

Before he answered, Jason came through the door, loud and stupid like always. "Hey, kids! How's life?" He shot me a look of amused challenge and grabbed Leda in a bear hug, smiling down at her. "Hey, kid, how are you doing? Christy says hi."

Just as my possessiveness began to get wound up, he released her. He was still half-hugging her, but my tension ebbed a little.

"She *really* liked hanging with you this weekend." He looked back at me, laughter in his eyes. He recognized that he was tripping my triggers, which just made him laugh a little more. "Relax, man! Jesus, I'm saying hello. Settle down."

I grabbed her, pulling her away from Jason. I held her to me, facing them, so she couldn't see how much Jason was ticking me off. I dropped my lips to her ear and told her where the machines were. "Why don't you work out for a bit and then come over to the mats and I'll show you some Jiu Jitsu."

Jason and Frank just watched, amused. She nodded and walked toward the treadmills.

As soon as she walked away, I snapped my arm out at Jason, leaving my fingers in a sharp spike as I connect with the soft spot right above his armpit.

"Ouch! Christ, man, settle down. I get it. She's not for sharing. Understood." Frank laughed.

"Damn right, she's not for sharing. Don't fucking test me, man."

Jason put his hands up in mock innocence as we got to the mats. I smirked a smile at him as I rushed him. He anticipated me and grabbed my shirt as he sideswiped my legs and rolled onto his back, taking me down with him. He let our momentum ride and flipped me over. I bridged up to try to drive him off me, but he dropped his weight on my chest. When I grabbed at him, trying to lock him up, he grabbed my arm and pulled it through to flip me onto my stomach, locking me in a rear-naked choke hold. I was fucked. I slapped the mat twice and he let go.

"Can you settle down now?" Jason asked me and it just pissed me off again.

"Fuck you."

"What is the fucking problem, Xander?" He never actually used my name unless he was bothered by something.

I took a deep breath, sitting up on the mat. "Jason." I looked at him, all my anger burned away. "I'm fucked over this girl. And I know I'm gonna fuck it up. I know I'll end up hurting her. But I can't fucking think about anything but her. I just want to be around her."

He looked at me with doubt. "You just want to be *around* her? I doubt that." Even though I smiled a little miserable smile at him, he continued, "Now you know, man. It's a terrifying thing to have what you want. I get you. And if you don't want to fuck it up, don't. Nothing is preordained."

He knew me and knew the right things to say. I took another breath. "All right, sorry about all that." I gestured at the mat and he knew what I meant. "Show me that take down. That was awesome. I was midway in the air wondering what the fuck happened?" I laughed now, stress dissipating.

"It works better with the *gi* on," Jason said and we got our gear on. He was a green belt and I was a yellow belt. We were actually pretty matched — he had more technical skill than me, but I didn't give a shit if I got hurt and would come at him harder than most other people in our class.

Frank and I practiced the take-down. Throwing him was easy once I directed his bulk and each time I came up laughing after he tapped. His throws were clumsier, owing to his beginner, white belt status. After a few turns through the new technique, Frank and I squared off, with Jason coaching him from the side of the mat.

"Frank, wrap him up in an arm-bar." Jason yelled, but I'd already moved. "There, now! Get his lead arm!"

Frank reached for me and I moved, slipping around to his side. When he lurched toward me again, I rolled him and grappled my way to his back, locking him up in the same rear-naked choke that Jason had gotten me with at the beginning of our session.

When we stood, Leda was there at the edge of the mat, face wrinkled in concentration, not really understanding what we were doing. Wet tendrils of hair stuck to her neck and I flashed to licking sweat off her neck in a very different venue.

"Hey, girlie, how was the treadmill?"

"Long and boring, but this looks like fun." She smiled at me.

"Yep, you want to try some?" She nodded and walked over to me. "Okay, lay down on your back. I want to show you something." She laughed and I acknowledged that it sounded dirty, but she lay down and I climbed over her, straddling her abdomen, thinking of last night. "So, in this position, you don't have any control over me, so I want you to get out of this."

She paused then got a look of determination on her face and started squirming, trying to scoot away from me. "No, that won't work, Leda." I just shifted my hips with her gyrations and stayed on her. She flopped down under me. "Here. I want you to plant your feet and rock one way. When you do that, push my knee away with your hand." I guided her hands once and let her try. She must have been a little annoyed because she pushed hard and I fell forward onto her.

She laughed. "I feel like this might not actually be Jiu Jitsu, but some other thing that involves you on top of me."

I smiled at her, but still guided her through the movements. "That's called breaking my guard. Now, get your other leg through."

She did and I was in between her legs. She laughed again, "So, strategically, this doesn't actually seem safer to me."

I smiled and chuckled. "It may not feel safer, but it actually does give you more control. Now, you can control my body, right? Just lock your legs around my hips and see if you can move me."

She had the giggles and didn't get it yet, but she wrapped her legs around my torso. I felt them tighten as she hooked her ankles together and flexed. She started flexing her body, twisting a little from side to side, and I rode it.

She paused and I said, "So, from here, you could flip me and get on top, the position I was in when we started, or you could choke me out."

She stilled and got serious. "Okay, how do I choke you from here? Just with my hands?"

She reached up and I resisted my instinct to grab her and flip her over. Instead, I held her wrists and guided her hand to my arm. "No, I want you to grab one of my arms, pull it close to you. Now, slide your opposite leg up over my shoulder."

She moved according to my directions.

"Now, lock your legs again, shoulder-leg foot hooked under your other knee."

She got herself switched around and flexed her hips, flopping me down, my face on her tummy.

"Harder than that, Leda. You want to choke me, not just grind your pussy into my sternum." It was harsh, but I wanted her to get this.

She flexed much harder and instinctively pulled my arm harder to her. I felt it lock out my shoulder and my air start to get tight. I let her feel it for a moment, then slapped the mat. "Okay—let go, ugh."

She released her legs and I took a beat still resting on her, more because I wanted to be close to her than actually needing it, but sat up shortly.

"You did it. That's how you choke someone who gets on top of you." I winked and added, "If you don't want them there."

Jason and Frank were watching and Jason yelled, "Nice work, kid. Gotta keep this fucker in line."

I laughed and jumped up for some water.

She followed me and took a sip, then said, "I probably need to get home, Xander. Wouldn't want to miss my bedtime." And she stuck her tongue out at me. *Brat.*

I walked closer to her and paused just as I was passing her, resting my hand on her stomach, where I had first touched her last night, and said, "Naughty girl, did you want more punishment? That can be arranged, you know."

She giggled, sexy and cute, then smiled — all innocence. It just made me want to use her. I grabbed our bags and we walked to the car. I held the door so I could watch her ass in her little yoga pants. I was falling for her, falling into her.

The drive was quick and we talked about school some. I didn't want to get anything started since it was late. At her building, she invited me up, but I didn't go. "It's your bedtime and we have school tomorrow, baby girl."

I dropped a kiss on her forehead, soft and sweet. *Fuck this purity shit.* I stepped farther into her space and grabbed the back of her neck, holding there, tilting her head to one side. I leaned over and put my mouth on her neck, right where that sweat had been and, as she sighed into it, I bit down hard. She gasped and, before she could protest, I closed her mouth off with my lips, letting her feel my banked heat, letting her taste her own sweat on my lips. My tongue was in her mouth, tracing her teeth, licking her lips. I pulled away, with no warning.

"Bedtime in forty-five minutes. Get moving." I turned her and smacked her ass as I pushed her through the door. She giggled and jogged up the steps. She was so *good.*

When I got home, there was a note that I had a package waiting for me, that Chen had signed for it. I got down there, just before they were closing the kitchen. We exchanged pleasantries and he gave me a letter-sized package that was sent registered mail. The return address was to Rodriguez at his offices in DC.

Up in my apartment, I sat on the edge of the bed, pausing before opening the Threat Assessment. I knew it wouldn't really matter what it said, that I was already hooked, to the point of being reckless. I opened it and was instantly pissed. There was a cover page with a determination of a negative threat risk, but then there was a folder with her entire security background check. Once I had it, I wasn't going to be able to stop myself from reading it. That was why I hadn't wanted it. It felt like cheating at the game of getting to know her. It felt dishonest—because it was. I opened it anyway and started reading.

I called Jason an hour later, guilt twisting my stomach. "The threat assessment was negative. Minimal risk, but..."

"But, what?"

"Rodriguez still sent the entire background check, even though I asked him not to." I couldn't keep the annoyance out of my voice.

"So what? None of what actually matters would be in there anyway. Just don't read it."

"I already did." The was a pause before he answered.

"Why?"

"Because it was there. I don't know. I just did."

"That's not you, dude. Your whole thing is impulse control. Ever since the shit with Stacy." He sounded worried.

"That's what I'm fucking saying. She fucks me up. I don't feel like I have the best control with her. I mean, I know I'm not gonna lose control if we play together. My head is totally present, attuned to her with that shit. It's just everything else. I was thinking about living with her the other day!" He knew I was talking about Leda and not Stacy.

He blew out a breath. "Shit. What are you gonna do?"

"I don't know."

He changed the subject, and I knew he was trying to distract me from the thing that was stressing me out most. "So, anything interesting in her background check?"

"Not really. Her family lives in the suburbs of Chicago. Mom's a nurse who retired early. Dad's a urologist. Older brother and sister, both in medicine. Both married with kids. They live in the Chicago area, too. Wisconsin for college. Good grades. Long-term boyfriend while she was there, but they broke up before med school. Her parents are centrist democrats and donate a small amount of money to various liberal campaigns and causes. And, well, she's twenty-two."

"Twenty-two. Damn. You better raise her right then, Daddy." He laughed, but immediately got serious again. "So, she's young. You gonna stop seeing her?"

"Hell, no," I answered, surprised.

"Then it doesn't have to mean anything."

Chapter Twelve

Leda
Lenka, Trouble is a Friend

The next morning I woke up with the walk of shame in my brain. As much as I got a thrill out of him, I wondered if it was too fast. I called one of my friends from college during my lunch break at school.

"Heeeeeyyyyyyyy, guuuuurrrllll!" she answered.

"Tiffany...don't you have a job? How is that how you answer your phone?" I asked, laughing.

"Oh, fuck off. I'm a nobody in a cube at an ad agency that promotes cigarettes, booze and porno. No one gives a shit what I say on the phone."

"Fair enough. How's shit? You like this job or what?"

"Yeah. It's good. Milwaukee's fun. Whatevs. How's med school, brainiac?"

Tiffany was *that* friend. That wild one. The one that makes you spend too much money or drink too much or whatever—the girl that says what she thinks and doesn't give a shit if she offends anyone. Every girl should have a friend like her.

I smiled into the phone as I half laughed and answered, "It sucks. It's hard as hell."

"Then why you calling me? Get yo ass in the 'brary!"

"Well…that's the thing…" I trailed off.

"Ooooohhhh! Does he have a big dick?" I heard her put her hand over the phone and say something to someone at her office. "Everyone here wants to know. I'm putting you on speaker. Raul, Jaleesa and Marni are here to help, mama. What's up?"

"Tiffany! Jesus Christ. Are you fucking kidding me right now?"

"No, honey," an affected male voice answered.

I yelped. "Tiffany, I'm not discussing this with your whole office."

"So it is a dude!" she yelled.

I heard her coworkers murmuring. One of the women asked, "Is he more McDreamy or Doogie?"

That caught me in my tracks. "Doogie?"

There was a litany of swearing, then she spoke again, "How about you try to make me feel old? Doogie Howser. Google it. Damn."

"Seriously, Tiff. Come on."

She was sighing as she took me off speaker. "Fine. You know I'm going to tell them anyway though, right?"

It was futile to resist her. "Yeah."

"Okay, so what is it? What happened? You met a guy and…?"

"He's my tutor. And, I don't know. He's totally hot. I mean gorgeous. And I don't know."

"So what's the problem, ho?"

"He's…into some shit."

"Like drugs?" She actually sounded worried.

"No! Kinky shit."

"Whoa. Leda, you've been down there for less than a month. What have you done with my little innocent girl? And does he have a brother in the upper Midwest?" She laughed again. "Seriously, *what* is the problem?"

I leaned the seat back in my car and just let it out. "He thinks I'm submissive and he wants to control me. And it sounds crazy when I say it, but I liked it. It was just a little bit. Just some making out. But, it's like I can't breathe around him. Like he's so overwhelming."

"So, I reiterate. *What is the problem?* He gives you feels in your feelie parts. That sounds great."

"It's just fast. I met him on Thursday. And he's already taken care of me when I got sick, come over and brought dinner and we worked out together last night. I mean… Am I a whore?"

"First of all, I resemble and resent that term. But secondly, none of that sounds all that sexual."

"Yeah… Well, there was some sexual shit too." When she didn't speak, I continued, "He came over and basically dry humped me till I came. Like on day number three of knowing each other." I blew out my breath.

When she responded, her voice was more serious. "What's a slut, Leda? A lady that likes the way she feels when she feels good? That shit doesn't even make sense. Fuck that. The question should be, do you like who you are around him?"

"I don't know. I haven't really hung out with him that much, I guess."

"So, hang out with him some more. See what happens. If you don't feel good about yourself *because of him* — not because of the Catholic school guilt you still have — then that's something to pay attention to.

But if it's just Sister Mary what's-her-fuck that you hear in your mind, tell that bitch to fuck off."

I smiled at the thought. I was Catholic, but hadn't gone to Catholic school. There was no Sister Mary what's-her-fuck in my memories. But I still had a zing of recognition at the truth of her words.

"All right, Beelzebub. You're going to hell, you know."

"Am I? I feeeeeeeellll like I've been there. Yep — it was our shitty dorm freshman year, with the fucked up heater in the frozen tundra of Madison. Never been colder in my life."

"All right. I gotta go back to classes. Talk this weekend?"

"Fine. Go be all smart and shit." Her tone got serious again. "But, Leda, really. Just…send me a picture of his cock. I can let you know if he's worth all this angst."

We were both laughing as we hung up. I loved that girl. The best. I was smiling as I walked back into the school and felt more relaxed, less self-judgmental.

* * * *

Thursday after school, I had another tutoring session and with it another wave a shame-laced shock that so much had happened with Xander in one week. In the tutoring session, I tried to keep it cool, but felt sure that everyone else could tell there was some sort of tension between me and Xander — like a glowing, throbbing neon light pulsed above me, shouting *Skank! Whore! Skank!* But no one said anything or even cast a speculative gaze over me and him.

About twenty minutes before the session ended, Xander got a call and excused himself. As he walked away, he said, "Hi, Mom, I'm still tutoring right now. Let me call you back." That must not have worked because he didn't come back for a few minutes and when he did, he looked annoyed. The group wrapped things up, but I delayed some, intending to check on him.

Before I could ask if he was okay, he picked up my bag, "Come on, baby girl. I saw you rode your bike again. I'm driving you home." He was distant, but a thrill ran through me just the same that he noticed I rode and that he very publically just called me a pet name. So, I just followed him, not even trying to answer.

But once we were in his car, I did ask, "Is everything okay? You seem upset."

"Yeah," he sighed. "Everything's fine. You know how parents can be. There's this fundraiser back in DC that my parents want me to go to, but I just really don't want to do it. I left DC for a reason. Anyway, I don't think it would help with anything anyway." He muttered the last bit.

"What kind of fundraiser is it?"

"A campaign fundraiser. I just hate them. They just seem like total circle jerks and most of the people there annoy the shit out of me."

Apparently, he went to political fundraisers often enough to be jaded about them. I just stayed quiet and waited for him to tell me more.

"My dad is the chief of staff for a senator, and I'm the son with the military service, so it looks good for me to be there, getting pimped out some," he explained, but then carried on, more to himself than to me. "Never mind that I never re-upped my commitment, but left the military for the Bureau for a few years before coming here. And *really* never mind how I left the Bureau then all of Washington to come to med school."

It was more than he had shared about himself before, despite all the time we had been spending together. I had so many questions, but the first thing that came out of my mouth was, "How old *are* you?"

Shit. I was mortified the moment the question passed my lips. *What is wrong with me?* But it snapped him out of his grim thoughts and he laughed for a good twenty seconds, before he glanced back at me.

"I'm thirty-four, *baby* girl. How old are you?"

Oh shit, he was in Junior High when I was born.

"I'm twenty-two," I answered quietly. Trying to move on gracefully and quickly, I added, "A fundraiser sounds fun. And I'd love to hear about your military and Bureau experiences. Is that Bureau as in Federal Bureau of Investigation?"

"Twenty-fucking-two? Jesus. Christ." His expression was hard to read, but he looked a little taken aback. He added, distractedly, "And yes, FBI. Army, then FBI."

The thought of him in fatigues or military dress uniform made my insides quiver a little. He seemed about to say something, but I cut him off, feeling like he was distracted so I could be a little more assertive, up front. I didn't know the word for it, just less submissive.

"How about this? Can I take *you* out this weekend? Whatever night is good for you?" I asked him, smiling. Of course, I didn't know where anything was or anything fun to do here, but I would figure that out later.

He pulled up to my building and turned to me with a smile on his face, "What's this, baby girl? Trying to take charge?" I felt my face betray me for a second and knew that I looked momentarily petrified, because he added, "I'm intrigued. Tomorrow night. What time should I pick you up?"

"No, what time should I pick *you* up? And where do you live?" I asked with a laugh. He gave me his address and we agreed that I'd pick him up at seven. That would give us both a few hours between school and our date to unwind and refresh — or, in my case, scramble to actually get a date together.

Before I got out of the car, I said, "Now, don't worry, you still get to be the Boss and I'm still the baby girl, even though I'm in charge tomorrow night."

He looked at me, smiling wryly, and shook his head. "Honey, you aren't in charge. Ever. But it's cute that you think that." He walked me to the building, pushing through the entrance with me and we made out for a few minutes in front of my door.

He pulled away with a groan and grimace, but before he could say anything, I stepped up, brushed a kiss on his cheek and said, "Okay, go home. It's my bedtime and my Boss gets upset if I stay up too late. Besides, I have plans to put into action for tomorrow night."

He just had a wide happy grin at that response, said goodnight and jogged down the stairs.

I watched him leave and freaked out a bit, because I really had no idea what to plan and I had less than twenty-four hours. In a stroke of inspiration, I got on the computer and found the website for Jason's bar. I called the next day during lunch. Frank answered and we chatted briefly, but he was busy. He gave me Jason's cell phone number and I called him, explaining my situation and asking if he could help me or give me Christy's number so she could help.

Jason conferenced Christy in and I explained the situation again. They both seemed a little giddy at the prospect of me planning a date and I wondered if Xander never dated or if it was really about his control issues. We ultimately decided on early drinks at Jason's bar, dinner at a sushi place they knew Xander loved and we could go from there.

I thanked them for being total lifesavers and asked, for the fourth time, if they wanted to come with. Jason responded, with laughter in his voice, "God, as much as I would love, *love*, to see Xander struggle with giving up some control, I think it would be intrusive for us to be there again. Spend a little time alone and have fun."

That answers that question — he hadn't told them much. Since my internal editing mechanism clearly was broken, I blurted out, "Oh, we've had some time alone."

Jason and Christy cracked up and we wrapped up the conversation, but not before Christy and I made plans for lunch together soon.

Friday afternoon seemed to go quickly, but came to an abrupt halt in my histology lab, when those dumb bitches came over to bother me again. Stacy and Barbie sat at the same lab bench as me, and after a while, Stacy leaned over to me.

"You know, everyone knows what is happening with you and Xander," she said with a sneer.

"I highly, *highly*, doubt that, Stacy. But how about you tell me what 'everyone' thinks is happening, just for shits and giggles." As much as it was bitchy bullshit, I was actually so amused by the thought of what people might think was happening compared with what I knew was actually happening that I wasn't just going to tell her to fuck herself. I wondered what it would be like if everyone really did know what was happening, that he wanted to control me and, to my own shock, I was opening up to the idea and letting him.

"Well, everyone knows you two are sleeping together and you barely know him!"

For the first time, I heard a note of whining in her voice. *Does she want him? Oh that would be too easy.*

"Oh, honey," I said with sugary-sweet sarcastic sympathy in my voice, "I haven't slept with him. He's just friendly. But who knows? Maybe that's the direction we're going in. From our conversations, he doesn't seem *at all* interested in anyone else here."

Her jaw dropped as her eyes hardened.

I added, just for spite, "But hey, thanks for letting me know the way people gossip here. I'll make sure Xander knows how worried you were about our reps."

I was done talking with her, but I refused to flinch so I went back to studying, looking at slides. Out of the corner of my eye, I could see her and Barbie whispering together. Stacy looked furious and worried, even as I heard her mutter 'slut' as she walked by me.

I made a mental note to talk with Xander about her, wondering if he would be as amused as I was, or maybe just pissed off, wondering if he knew her very well.

Chapter Thirteen

Xander
Ladytron, Destroy Everything You Touch

I had looked for Leda all day at school but never found her. I did, however, find Stacy.

"Hi, A—Xander." She saw me start to get totally pissed and watched what she said. She recovered quickly, saying, "Hey, what are you doing tonight? My dad's in town. I'm sure he'd love to see you."

God, this bitch is twisted. Maybe it is time to really put the kibosh on this shit.

"I have a date tonight. With Leda. And are you fucking kidding me right now?" I grabbed her upper arm and pulled her into an empty room. "Stacy, what the fuck is wrong with you? Your dad doesn't ever want to see me again." Tears welled up in her big brown eyes and my anger lost some of its heat. "Why'd you come here for med school, Stacy?"

Her tears stilled, unshed, and she pulled away from me, defiance in the set of her features. "I came here to be a doctor." She dropped her head for a moment. "I came *here* to be with you. We should be together. We're the only ones who know what it was like." She shrugged, the tears now dried, her face blank.

"Stacy. Maybe that's the exact reason we shouldn't be together." My voice was full of pity and not a small amount of regret as I walked out of the room.

I got home about an hour before Leda was supposed to pick me up. Each time I thought of that, the Dom in me kind of growled and I laughed at myself. It was a role reversal, I knew that. But I also knew that I was humoring her. It was only happening because I was allowing it. It wouldn't change the dynamic between us, wouldn't change what I wanted.

She sent me a text at about six forty-five and I made my way downstairs to wait for her. The air was still humid and I rolled my sleeves up while I waited. She pulled up in a white Jetta. Just cuteness.

She got out of the car as I was walking toward her and opened the fucking door for me. *Nope.* I kissed her and said, "You may be planning things tonight, but you're still a lady and I'm still a gentleman." I put my hand on the small of her back and guided her around to the driver's side. She looked sweet in a short, light-weight white summery dress and cute, but excessively tall yellow sandals. Her hair was loose and a little wild. Beautiful.

"*Gentle* man? I don't think that is the right word, but I got it, Boss." The whole 'gentleman who isn't necessarily a gentle man' was an old joke in the BDSM community and I was amused by it all over again, knowing that she had gotten there on her own. But my hope was that maybe she really would understand now. The small things matter. I tucked her into the driver's seat and chuckled to myself, enjoying the moment as I walked around the car.

Once I folded myself in half to get in her car, I asked, "Where are we going tonight, baby girl?" I smiled, but I was ready to be in control again.

She fucking smirked at me and said, "I'm not telling you. You just need to know that we'll have fun. How's that?"

I wanted to tie her up and tickle her till she gave in. *How's that? Not nearly good enough.* "Allll riiiight." I kept my smile on because it was hard to be growly when she was having this much fun.

"We're going to Jason's place first, for a few drinks and just relaxing. Our dinner reservation is at nine."

A late night planned. I liked it. In DC, we often ate really late when Dad would be done at the office. It was a sort of luxury thing to me. No one ever wanted to eat that late with me, but I liked that it felt like you could linger over the meal and not have to worry about getting somewhere else.

We got to the bar and she took my parking spot in back. Inside, it wasn't busy this early, but Frank was behind the bar and I gave him a nod. We sat in the same booth and she wouldn't let me get the drinks. When she got up to get some drinks from the bar, she waved me back toward her as she walked into the little game room. She wanted to play darts.

She was surprisingly competitive, talking a bunch of shit. It was like hanging out with Jason and Christy, plus sexiness. It was a pleasant surprise for those two things to go together. A cat-call whistle across the bar drew our attention and Christy was standing there. She must have had the night off. She laughed as she walked over to us. "You two are having too much fun."

About ten minutes later, Jason joined us, coming out of the office. He looked at Christy with his usual talking—shit smile on his face. "So, has anyone burst into flames?"

Christy shook her head and I thought very seriously about slashing his tires.

He turned to Leda, adding, "I know we said we wouldn't intrude."

They knew about the Sadie-Hawkins date we were having? And didn't tell me. Those little fucks.

"But I just wanted to see this uptight asshole not in complete control of every little thing." He turned to me, a genuine smile on his face, "It looks good on you, man."

I smiled back at him and shook his hand. "What are you two doing tonight?"

He smiled like a total pervert and said, "I don't know, maybe we'll just go home early and entertain ourselves." He goosed Christy and she giggled.

Fucking exhibitionists.

Once we finished our game of darts, we sat at the bar, talking with Jason, Christy and Frank about the stupid inconsequential shit that friends talked about. Leda fit right in and I kept catching myself getting comfortable with her in my world. I loved it and it scared the shit out of me.

Dinner was at Soona Mee, a great upscale Japanese restaurant and I knew that Jason and Christy had given her help. They didn't really like sushi and would have recommended it because I do. I smiled as we sat down.

She ordered a bottle of prosecco, which was a refreshing start to the meal. I asked about her last few days and she asked about mine. And it felt just right, like we had been together for a long time and we still wanted to be together. She looked like she wanted to talk about something, but we were interrupted by a voice I didn't want to hear.

"Xander! Hello."

Stacy was walking across the restaurant. *Did she fucking find out where we were going? Too much of a coincidence.* She leaned across the table, nearly falling out of her dress and air-kissed my cheeks. *I hate that shit and she knows it.*

"Hello, Stacy. How are you? Have you met Leda? She's in your class." Too long in Washington to not know how to surface-fake a greeting while making it clear I was pissed at her.

I knew she knew it, but she ignored it and answered, "Yes, we've met briefly. Leda, how are you?"

Leda didn't know the game and looked at her blankly.

Stacy's lips twitched in triumph as she turned back to me. "Are you going back home for the fundraiser? It's not ideally what I'd like to do on New Year's Eve, but I think I'm gonna go anyway. Maybe we can travel together."

"I don't think I'm going. Focusing on studies and all," I lied to her, just wanting to get her off my scent. And the dismissive way she looked at Leda pissed me off. I looked past her and saw her dad, scowling in my direction. Just to fuck with her, I added, "Is that your dad? How is the Congressman doing?"

She looked sullen and answered, "Oh, he's how he always is." A venomous smile crossed her lips and she grabbed my hand. "You should come say hello."

Strong work calling me out. She knew I had no desire to speak with her dad.

I felt my jaw pop when I clenched my teeth against the desire to slap her face. "Please just give him my regards. Have a nice night." I turned back to Leda, ignoring Stacy, who knew I still saw everything she did as she turned around and walked away, switching her hips in a sexy stomp. Spite driving me, I leaned back to see past her and caught her dad's eye, waving. His face flushed with anger he held in to avoid making a scene. I smiled to myself. Stacy's dad was going to bitch her out when they got to the car.

I snapped back to the moment when Leda snarled, "You know that bitch?"

My eyebrows shot up and I nodded. "Stacy's father is Congressman Jackson. The Senator my father works with is one of his biggest supporters. They've co-authored a few bills together. I've actually known Stacy since we were kids. A few years ago…" *Shut the fuck up! Don't fucking get into that now.*

Leda's face was hard and hurt at the same time. "I'm sorry if you are friends, but she is such a bitch! She's been harassing me about what may or may not be happening between you and me. I thought she probably just had a crush on you. I never would have guessed that you knew her."

I'm gonna fucking kill her. "I will take care of it, but tell me exactly what happened." I had to know what Stacy had already told Leda, but knew it couldn't have been all of it because she was still sitting here with me.

She told me about the frankly childish shit that Stacy had pulled and I could see why Leda thought she was just a bitch with a crush.

"Okay. I'll talk to her, but full disclosure—a few years ago…we hooked up… I mean, we have a bit of history between us." Huge fucking understatement. "But she seemed so young and she is…not my type."

Leda still looked pissed off, maybe more so now after learning that I had had something with Stacy. We still needed to decide on what we going to order and I tried to change the subject to move on to the rest of the night with her. "What should we order?" But Leda didn't respond, didn't even seem to register than I spoken to her. I grabbed her hands on the table and squeezed a little to get her attention.

"I'm sorry. What was that?" She brought herself back to me, but still wasn't completely present and definitely wasn't having a good time.

"Baby girl, is she really that much of a problem?" I made my voice soft when I wanted to yell, because Leda wasn't who I wanted to yell at.

"I don't know. Something about her really bothers me and now... It's just a gross, new level of unpleasantness. I'm sorry, give me a minute and I'll get over it." She took a breath and centered herself. "Let's decide what to order."

We ordered a California roll, salmon roll and some nigiri with some deep-fried edamame, which was a favorite of mine. We shared the meal and talked, but the intimacy was gone. She was distant, instinctively protecting herself, expecting me to hurt her now. She didn't want dessert and I understood. She wanted to get away from me, wanted the night to be over.

The check came and she tried to take it. I grabbed her wrist before she opened it. She held my gaze, but said nothing. I squeezed her wrist and felt her flesh give a little under the pressure. She still didn't give, didn't even flinch. I fell in love with her a little in that moment.

"Baby girl, I let you plan this and my stupid past ruined it. Just let me do this." And, of course, Rodriguez's background check included a credit report and the balances of her accounts as well as her parents' accounts. I had more money than her, thanks to my trust fund and investing in everything Jason did. That and she'd only ever really been a student. She was living on her loan money, like most med students did.

We held each other's gaze in a little stalemate. I kept myself calm, kept my heart rate controlled, but her breath picked up and her pupils dilated. I felt her pulse leap under my fingers. I tightened down more and felt the bones shift, watched her flinch a little. I kissed her fingers then let go, a sick satisfaction in that. I laid my credit card down, feeling victorious.

She sat there, eyes downcast, like a cute little possession, and all my anger at Stacy shunted into lust for her. "Go to the ladies room, freshen up and wait for me back there." While I thought about fucking her in the bathroom, I knew that wasn't going to be the way I first fucked her. She wasn't moving. "Leda, now." My voice was sharp and she snapped out of it and got up.

As she walked away, I pulled my cell out of my pocket and called Jason.

He answered with no hello, just, "Why are you calling me while you're on your date?"

"You haven't spoken to Stacy, have you?"

"Fuck that skank."

"So that's a no."

"Of course, it's a no. You know I hate her. Why?"

"She showed up at the restaurant that Leda made reservations at and I wanted to see if you knew how she would have known."

"Dude, fuck you. Why would I…? Just fuck you."

"I know, man. I'm sorry. But you did help Leda plan this right? Because, there is no way she just picked Soona Mee randomly."

"Yeah we helped." It was Christy. Jason had put me on speaker. "Stacy showed up?"

"Yeah, and it pretty much ruined the night."

"That's 'cause she's a ruiner. Want me to slap her?" Christy was cute when she got pissed.

"No, I handled it. But I think she went to a new psycho low and called places until she found our reservation. She was here with her *dad*."

"Ooh yuck," Christy said at the same time that Jason said, "Shit."

"All right, I'm gonna go try to salvage tonight. Wanna give me a heads up on the rest of the plan?"

"There isn't one."

I took a deep breath. "Okay...cool. I will make it work."

After I hung up with them, I sent Stacy a text.

Leave Leda out of our shit. I'm done with you. Fuck off, or I will find a way to make you realize how much you regret me.

I left a hefty tip to try to clear my conscious a little and got up. I channeled my irritation into my dominance, my lust for Leda and control. Each step across the restaurant brought me more control and I felt my spine straighten and shoulders drop back. I felt the scowl leave my face and the blankness settle there. *Where's my little girl so I can take all this out on her skin?*

She walked out of the ladies room just as I rounded the corner into the long hallway that went along the back of the dining room, next to the kitchen. She met my gaze and her eyes widened. Each time that happened, it sent a thrill through my chest. Her lips parted in a gasp and my cock twitched. My stride lengthened and I met her where she was, sliding my hand into her hair and pulling her head back. I flattened her against the wall with my body.

Smashing our lips together, I refused to let her move. I ran my hand up her flank, my thumb brushing her nipple, as I brought it up to her throat and squeezed. Once I had her secured with that hand, I took my other hand out of her hair and pulled the strap of her dress away from her shoulder. I kissed her skin there but couldn't resist biting her too.

"This dress is delicious, I want to eat you."

She made a soft mewling sound under me.

Jesus Christ, this girl. I had to get her somewhere else. "Let's go, Leda." I let go, fixed her strap, stepped back and grabbed her hand. It was a fast and fluid movement but not so fast that I missed the flush in her cheeks. She was a little unsteady on her feet and stagger-stepped to follow me.

I pulled her to the car and slammed her body against it, pressing against her, my mouth on her again. I knew she felt my hard-on and I didn't care. I wanted her to know how much I wanted her, wanted inside her. But, even as I thought it, I knew it wasn't time yet. She was special and I wanted her to want me as much as I wanted her before I claimed her. *Fuck that*, more than I wanted her. Losing control.

"What's next, Leda?" I whispered into her neck. She didn't answer and I felt my self-control cracking. "Leda, I'm trying." My voice was harsh and a little hoarse. "I'm trying to let you have tonight, but you need to get me to our next thing now, or I am going do some very bad things to you."

I felt her tremble under my hands and I just wanted to feel it again and again. I kept kissing her, waiting, but not waiting for an answer.

"Well," she kind of sputtered against my skin. "Wait, wait. Xander, wait." She was stopping me, pushing my shoulders back a little and for a moment,

I flashed to a take-down fantasy, pushing her into the car and pulling her panties off. I paused, letting all my air out to deflate myself.

I stood up tall, the master of myself again. My voice calmer, I asked, "Okay, baby girl. What's next tonight?" I asked it hoping that she had something, even though Christy and Jason weren't aware of anything else.

"So that's the problem. I only planned this far and was expecting that we could play it by ear from here."

Oh, goddamnit. I wanted her so much. I made myself solid, refusing to let my cock be a weakness.

She went on, "I had a few ideas. Take a walk in the park—"

Too late to be there now.

"Back to Nest—"

Already did that.

"Back to Jason's place—"

Already did that tonight.

"A late movie…"

Too late and I want to see you.

"Do any of those sound good to you?"

No, what sounds good is tying you up and making you suffer a bit. Getting my hands on you. But I couldn't let myself be that much of a dick, so I tried to make my words soft. "Baby girl, I wasn't planning tonight, remember? You're so sweet." I stepped back, brushing the hair away from her face. "I want to go somewhere quiet where we can talk. I want to hear your thoughts about my control issues and your submissive tendencies."

"Well we could go to one of our apartments. Quiet there."

Really, little one? I felt one of my eyebrows cock up.

"No. If we go somewhere private, I'm going to fuck you, and you aren't ready." While it was true, it probably wasn't the right thing to say. She drew a quick breath, scowl marring her face.

"Whoa! Holy shit, buddy! Firstly, *you're* going to fuck *me*? Maybe *I'm* gonna fuck *you*. Maybe neither of us is getting fucked. Jesus, Xander! Secondly, you don't decide when I'm ready. For anything."

She was so cute when she got mad and she didn't get it. Of course I decided all that shit. Of course I would fuck her. In that moment, I made the decision that we wouldn't have sex until she begged me to fuck her, like a good girl. I started laughing. Again probably the wrong response, but it was like a bunny telling a wolf what to do. It was just absurd.

"Okay, baby girl. You're so fucking cute." That mollified her a little. "You know that's not how it is with me. But this is exactly what I want to talk about. Give me the keys."

She gave me the keys and I walked her around the car to the passenger side. I took her to the Cat's Meow.

Chapter Fourteen

Leda
Goldfrapp, Strict Machine

Once we were settled in a booth in the back of the restaurant, Xander took one of my hands and started tracing designs in my palm and over the inside of my wrist. "Tell me what made you so mad back there," he said quietly, without looking up at me.

"I don't know. All of it, I guess. We can't be alone now because you can't control yourself? And I don't get a choice? And you deciding if I am ready for it or not. I mean, that's kind of fucked up, isn't it?"

"I don't think it is, Leda. This is me. This is how I work. This is what I meant by demanding, and we're barely scratching the surface here. What bothers me about this is that I really do think that you are a sub at heart. Tonight just really confirmed it for me. You decide to plan our date, and at least half of the night is left up to what *I* may want to do after the initial things you plan. You adjust your body to me all the time. You give in. You follow my directions. You accept what I tell you is going to happen. You accept the way the I touch you, in fact I think you really like it. You are submissive." He paused, looking up at me.

I felt stripped naked in front of him. Too bare. "Xander, I don't know how to do this. Yes, I like... I like to take you into consideration when I think about things. I want to do things that...please you." I was searching for the words and they sounded all wrong, so stupid, but they were the closest thing to being able to sum up what I was feeling for him. "I don't want you to be disappointed in me or with the things I do."

My eyes watered a little and I felt my face twisting up in the pre-cry panic that always happened. The waiter brought our desserts with a look of concern on his face. He gave Xander a look, and Xander completely turned his body toward the waiter with challenge on his face, but never let go of my hand. They held each other's gaze for a few beats.

"Thanks. She will have another cup of tea in about ten minutes. Otherwise, we're all set." He said it coldly, with some amount of contempt in his voice, and the waiter seemed to shrink in front of him. Xander turned back to me, trusting the waiter to see to the orders. Xander's voice and face were softer for me. "Finish what you need to say, Leda."

"I don't know what else to say, but I'm freaked out by the idea that I wouldn't be in sexual control of myself. But when you said you'd fuck me, I think that would have been okay with me. I think I would have let you."

"Why would you have let me? Because I wanted it or because you wanted it too?"

"I think both, but then I feel like...we've just met! Seriously, we just met! What the fuck am I doing?" My tears had stopped and I pulled my hand away to brush them off my cheeks.

"See, honey girl? This is what I meant. You aren't ready yet." He brushed his fingers across my knuckles and went on, in a rush, "And that's just fine. I love that you want to make me happy. All these things you're talking about are part of your submissive nature. And the part of your brain that rebels against is the part that is trained to believe that men will devalue and degrade a woman who submits completely. And of course there are assholes out there that do that, but I'm not one of them. A sub is a treasure and should be cherished. Leda, I was serious. *No* harm will come to you from me. I may hurt you sometimes, but I think you'll like it."

I got a quick mental flash of him biting my shoulder earlier tonight and felt a self-conscious warmth in my throat and pelvis.

"The hardest thing for most submissives early on, is admitting that they are submissive and really owning it. Reveling in it…and the trust. That's hard too."

The waiter brought more tea for me, but wouldn't make further eye contact with either of us. The dessert was delicious. I had some sort of berry pie with a honey crumble topping and Xander had a fresh-baked chocolate chip cookie, a la mode. We were quiet for a time, just tasting our food and each in our own thoughts. After a few minutes, I spoke up to ask him to tell me more about the military and FBI life he had before medical school, needing to change the subject to something less intense.

"After high school, I went to West Point and straight into the Army after graduation. I did that for a few years and left when my commitment was up. Then I got a job at the FBI for another three or four years. I took some time off before medical school. It really isn't all that interesting."

"Where were you stationed after you left West Point? Were you a medic?"

"Oh, no. I was stationed at the Pentagon as an underling in the Army offices there. I worked in a counter insurgency program, *very much* as an underling—note-taker, coffee lackey kind of position."

"Really, even as an officer?" He murmured assent and I asked him more about his work. "Counter insurgency sounds interesting—kind of scary, actually. I mean, that's like counterterrorism, right?"

"I wasn't really involved in active operations. The commander I worked with was involved in counterintelligence and some preemptive neutralization scenarios. When I moved to the Bureau, I did similar work. Because I had some experience with it."

"Sorry, pretend you are talking to someone who doesn't know what the hell you are talking about. What is preemptive neutralization?"

He looked like his stomach was upset and pulled back from me, draping his arms across the back of the booth. "Basically, we generated ways to fuck with the bad guys and make it less and less worthwhile to oppose American interests."

"Oh. I think I understand. Are you okay? Does it bother you to talk about this?"

He just looked so uncomfortable. "It is…a part of my life that…allowed the darkest parts of my psyche to flourish. It's work that matters and it's good that someone's doing it, but it's the stuff you don't want to actually know about what the military does. Guantanamo Bay was one of the things people found out about. You just don't want to know how those things happen. You know what I mean? It's like hot dogs or plastic surgery—decent end results usually, but you really don't want to know the process." He looked up at me with unreadable eyes. They weren't really haunted looking, but they weren't clear either. "Excuse me," he said and got up for the bathroom.

After a minute or so, the waiter came back to the table, speaking in a hushed tone, "Miss, are you okay? Do you need help?" He paused then added, "Is that man hurting you?"

I was so startled that I was momentarily speechless. "What? No. I'm fine. I'm fine. I don't need help." I laughed uncomfortably and looked up to see Xander standing behind the waiter, anger plain on his face. There was a horrible slowing of time as the waiter turned and nearly walked into Xander, who had clearly heard at least part of the exchange. I held my breath, but Xander smoothly passed the waiter.

"You okay, honey girl?" Xander murmured to me as he sat down.

I grimaced. "Yeah, I'm fine." It was the most uncomfortable I had ever been on a date, but Xander seemed unperturbed.

He smiled at me before he glanced at the waiter. "Thanks, man. We'll just take the check when you have a chance."

The waiter still looked mortified, but he answered, "Sure. My apologies."

Before the waiter could turn away, Xander responded, "None needed. It took courage to ask." Once he was gone, Xander turned back to me, his smile fading from his lips even as his eyes twinkled with some sort of deviant lust. "Now, this is a good chance for a little lesson."

"A lesson?" Was I in trouble? Already?

"Yeah. Because this whole thing touches on consent and the community approach to avoiding consent violations."

I had had it. I was lost. "What the fuck are you talking about right now? That guy thought you were hurting me."

"And someday, I might. But not like he thinks and definitely not if you don't want it. Not if you don't feel taken care of. And it's probably likely that you'll get asked a question like that again. There will be people that don't understand what we're doing. And you'll always be free to answer however you want. But it obviously made you uncomfortable, so I think it would be reasonable to think about how you want to answer questions like that."

I murmured my assent, but had no response.

"Some subs might say something like 'I appreciate your concern, but I'm very happy where I am, with him'. How would that feel for you?"

"Oh, okay. But isn't it kind of… I don't know, weird to have to answer these questions?"

"I don't know. It doesn't matter if it's weird. What if we were some other couple and I was abusing you and that might have been your chance out? I don't want people to think they *shouldn't* ask when they're concerned. But I don't want it to fluster you or ruin your night."

"But aren't you pissed? He thought you were hurting me."

"It's a reminder to me that no one in public consented to be part of my play. But what really matters to me is what *you* think."

The waiter had the manager drop the check off and we had a brief conversation about how good the dessert was. We stopped at the cashier by the door to pay, but Xander turned to me with a couple of twenties in his hand.

"Why don't you go find the waiter and give him his tip? It'll give you a chance to clear the air if you want. I'll wait outside. This is all you, girlie. Whatever you want to say to him."

I took the cash and found the waiter near the back of the restaurant, folding napkins in a booth.

"Hey, thanks again." I handed him the cash and glanced back at Xander, who nodded at me and walked out of the front door.

The waiter looked confused and started to apologize again, but I cut him off. "Look, I really appreciate that you checked with me, but it's good. I'm happy with him. I'm safe."

As the words crossed my lips, the bone-deep truth of them hit me. Xander was so different than anyone I had ever been with. So completely different. It was navigating something new every step of the way with him.

When I found Xander in front of the restaurant, he smiled warmly and pulled me into a hug. "How'd that go?"

I shrugged and smiled as another wave of contentedness washed through me. "It was fine. I don't think he understood, really. But I did."

"Good girl."

A fucking flood in my panties.

We strolled slowly around the block. It was an upscale section of town with high end boutiques and restaurants. There were people, in couples or larger groups, coming and going from various bars and restaurants that we passed. Some had live music that spilled out of the doors, punctuating the evening. As we walked, we continued our earlier conversation about his life before medical school.

"After I left the Army and joined the FBI, I worked in a similar department. Again, I wasn't high up in the department, but I learned a lot."

"What kind of things?"

"The psychology of it, you know? The psychology of crime and terrorism, the psychology and physiology of interrogation."

"Wait." I paused on the sidewalk as a realization hit me, "You have professional, government-level training in mind-fucking people? I mean, that's what you're saying, right?" My stomach did some flip-flops and I felt, more than ever, like a mouse dangling from a cat's paw, so completely overmatched that there was nothing to do but accept what was coming. And I just started giggling.

"Yeah, yeah, I guess you could say that," he answered me, laughing back.

"Weeeelllllp, I'm fucked," I said, throwing my hands up in the air as my giggles settled. Moving on, I asked, "So what happened? Why did you leave the FBI?" I started walking again, trying to regain my composure.

"There were a few reasons. One, I wasn't totally satisfied. I didn't love the work, even though I was pretty good at it. My parents had pulled strings to get me the interview and I never really knew if I got the job on my own merits. Two, I was already feeling like I wanted to learn more about medicine and do something positive with it. I would read about the physiology of sleep deprivation for an assignment or something and would just be way more interested in the science of it than whatever the actual project was. Three, I committed career suicide at one point, so it was easy to leave then." He chuckled as he said that last part.

"What do you mean—career suicide? What did you do?" His story was fascinating.

He cleared his throat and looked kind of bashful, which seemed so out of character for him that I was even more intrigued.

"I fucked the boss's daughter. And we got caught."

My mind flashed back to his conversation with his mom that I had overheard, something about someone still being pissed and it made sense. Xander kept going, "I got caught with the boss's daughter, who was younger than me. And I was fucking her the way I like as she was bound over a desk. Oh God!" He half yelled it at the sky, laughter in his voice. "I can't believe the shit I get myself into!" He seemed so relaxed suddenly, like the tension had drained out of him at his admission.

But I was kind of horrified. "Did your parents hear the details?" The thought of my parents ever hearing anything about me being tied up and fucked like that was horrifying.

"Not the details, thank God. He had the grace to be discrete, but then again, it was his daughter's reputation as well. She was adamant that he keep it quiet too. And anyway, it's Washington DC. There's more fucked up shit going on there sexually than anywhere else in the country. It seems like everyone is a complete freak. Most of them are very, *very* closeted about it, but a few of them are a little less so. My kink was nothing to some of those guys, but it's all about image, you know."

By this time, we were back to my car and it was about midnight. We got in the car, Xander in the driver's seat again, but he didn't start it.

"I don't want to say goodnight yet." I blurted it out before he could say anything.

"I've got just the place."

He drove to the edge of town and turned into a wooded lot with a long, winding dirt and gravel driveway. At the end there was a turn around, but no house, just a drop-off from right beside the road. There were no other cars and he parked in the middle of the round-about. We got out and he led me down the drop-off embankment, steadying me and ultimately lifting me and carrying me down to level ground.

We were on the edge of a small, still lake. The moon and stars gave enough light to see decently well once my eyes adjusted to the dark. We started walking around the edge of the water. The ground was soft but not muddy. My shoes weren't great for the terrain so I took them off anyway. About a quarter of the way around, there was a small row boat on the shore and we got in, but didn't push out into the water—there were no oars and it didn't look particularly seaworthy. It was just a nice place to sit together. I sat in the bottom of the boat leaning back into his legs and we kept talking. I asked him what made him want the things that he does.

"I don't know. I've just always felt like this. I think lots of people think something must have gone wrong in someone's childhood if they get into BDSM. I just know that when I was in high school and at the Academy, I always felt like something was missing in my sex life. I met plenty of girls and had plenty of sex."

Sidebar — don't tell me that shit.

"But there was something flat about it. You know, it was still good, but it never totally satisfied me. I was always hungry for more. It was actually when I got back to DC, one of the guys I worked with at the Pentagon took me to a club where people were doing things I had only read about or seen in porn. I remember feeling like this was a whole new alien world that I couldn't believe existed. My friend was into being tied up and stuff with a dominatrix, and while that was hot and he definitely loved it, it was not for me."

"Wait, I can't imagine you ever being dominated by someone else. It just seems...unnatural." I kind of screwed up my face in a grossed out expression and laughed, glancing at him over my shoulder.

"One time, early on when I was going there, there was a couple playing in a public room. They had a little audience crowded around them and I wanted to see too, and that was it — it was like the world stopped for a beat, and I knew. There was a girl — I mean she was legal, just young — standing in a clearing in the room, with her arms tied and hooked to something coming out of the ceiling. Her man was walking around her, pinching her skin in all different places, whispering in her ears, licking her — and she was in the sweetest, hottest agony — and that was it. I knew what I wanted, I wanted to make a woman squirm in agony because I made her feel something that was overwhelming, and I wanted to know that she was doing it voluntarily, that she wanted it as much as me. There's something about controlling a woman's body that triggers something in me that makes me feel like an animal, something less than and more than human, all at once. I feel my heart beating in my chest and it just inflates me. Do you know what I mean, Leda?"

As he spoke, he was rubbing my shoulders and his hands started to stray into my hair, pulling it. They migrated around to trace the line of my jaw and throat. I sat still, absorbing his words and his touch. The words washed over me, hypnotic, and my heart sped up, my breath came shallow and fast. Slowly, I understood that I was absorbing what he gave me and that was what I wanted to do, that I wanted to give him all of me, to let him do whatever he wanted to do to me. He slipped his fingers into my mouth and I started licking and sucking them. He licked up the back of my neck, but then he paused. My body screamed silently for him to keep going. He left his fingers in my mouth and kept talking, telling me his story.

"I ran into Jason one night when I was out and he started taking me to some private parties—swinger parties, BDSM parties. It's hard to get into those as a single *guy*—a unicock, versus a single girl—a unicorn. But I was lucky and got into a few and eventually started a polyamorous relationship with a couple. The three of us started fucking all the time and I might have fallen in love, but they were older than me and I was never really going to be in control the way I wanted. When I started to feel possessive of her and jealous of him, I knew I had to leave. By that time, Jason had moved down here and had started his promoting. I came to visit him a lot then we opened the Window. Then I was down here every chance I got." He paused and took a breath that I felt brushing against my neck.

"It's just one more criterion to consider when picking a partner, which makes finding the right fit even harder. Sometimes I wonder if one person can really fulfill all of my needs."

My ears perked up at this and jealousy wound up again.

"But then I see Christy and Jason, and it's clear to me that it's possible."

Jealousy abated.

"What about you, baby girl? What do you think of all this?"

He took his fingers out of my mouth and I was surprised by the twinge of regret at losing that bit of him in me, and a more disturbing feeling—I was disappointed that he dried his fingers on his pants because I wished he had wiped them off on my face or in my hair. *What the fuck is this?*

"I'm still working it out, Xander. I think you're super-intense and intimidating, and enthralling and scary. I feel like I'm constantly surprised at myself and what I feel myself wanting from you—wanting you to do to me—but then other things bother me too."

"Like?" He had started rubbing my shoulders again, but then he worked his hands down my arm as I spoke and he started massaging my hand.

"I like the teasing, but I can't actually give you control of my whole life—where I go, what I do. And I'm afraid that's what you want from me. And every once in a while, I just feel like this is ridiculous because we barely know each other and we are talking about this stuff, but...it feels so good when you touch me. I like being near you." His hands were back in my hair and he was kissing the back of my neck, murmuring in response to what I was saying, but he paused to respond to me.

"I hadn't expected to have a relationship in med school. But the reality is that we met and on some primal level, I'm drawn to you and you're drawn to me. You are what I need and I am what you need. I think you're handling me pretty fucking well, Leda. I'm almost always too much for someone sane. You impress the hell out of me with your willingness to explore this. Girls usually kind of freak when I get into this with them. That's why I had to be so up front with you. But I agree, it's happening quickly between us, but it feels so right and normal to me. Natural."

I turned to face him, excitement in my stomach because that was just it. "Exactly! It feels so fast, but so right when we're together. It's just when my brain gets involved that I start to get anxious. When we're together, I forget all that." I was kneeling between his knees and leaned into him, kissing him then, licking at the inside of his mouth, my arms around him. He was momentarily stunned but then kissed me back with the same heat. "God, I want you Xander."

"Mmmm, little girl."

He groaned into my mouth and I thought, *I'm* little girl *again*. A flush of pleasure washed over me.

"I want you too, but not here and not like this. I want you to vibrate with how much you want my cock before I put it in you. I want you near tears with wanting. Fuck, that sounds so good."

Je-sus! It seemed like I was pretty much already there and I didn't want to wait. My body was driving me, not my brain, and my body wanted all kinds of dirtiness.

"I don't want to wait," I whispered with my lips against his earlobe.

His low, bass-filled chuckle sounded so menacing and enticing, and my panties flooded. I continued kissing him, pressing my tits into his chest, wanting to climb on top of him and grind myself till we both came. His hands dropped down to my ass and started kneading my flesh, grabbing a handful of ass cheek and pulling up. He pulled harder on my skin and it started stretching my pussy lips from behind, just making me more aware of how naked and needy it felt, how drenched my panties were and how hot and ready my lips were. He pulled the skirt of my dress up and the relative coolness of the night air drifted across my thighs and ass. His hands were back on my ass, rubbing, squeezing. He reached down low on my ass cheek, where it met my leg, near the middle, almost, but not quite to my pussy, and pinched me, hard.

"Oh!" I yelped in surprise, but he kept kissing me, his other hand clamped behind my head to hold me in place, and the sound was lost in his mouth. The sting of the pinch faded and increased the sweetness of everything else after. I felt my body flushing with lust. I relaxed back into his arms, almost sagging into him.

He pinched me again, in the same spot, but reaching across to the other side this time. He held the pinch longer, maybe a full five seconds, till I just started squirming and whining into his mouth. He kept kissing me, but rubbed at the spot he'd pinched, and it was *so* close to my pussy. It was almost too much. I just wanted him to touch me there and I couldn't stop myself from pushing my hips back and my ass up in the air a little, opening myself for his fingers as much as I could, inviting him, *begging* him to finger-fuck me. I felt his lips smiling against mine.

"Good girl."

Oh my God! Fuck me!

He slipped his fingers under the edge of my panties and I slipped into holding my breath then panting. The world shrank down to his fingers so close to me, at the edge of my core, the coolness of the air against my sticky skin. I felt his hand bulge into a fist around the crotch of my panties and pull. He tugged until they were mid-thigh and left them there, exposing me. My moisture dampened my inner thighs. One of his hands slipped to the back of my neck and he paused, pulling his face back and looking at me intently, as he ran the fingers of his other hand through my wetness without getting between my lips or giving me any satisfaction.

I was panting and felt a pout cross my face. His lips twitched in a little smirk. He pulled himself closer to me and continued teasing my wet pussy, never actually touching deep enough for what I wanted. A full grin blossomed on his face as I started squirming against him, trying to get more contact, something, anything, *something* into me.

"Please," I whimpered as I leaned forward. His hand paused. Moving my lips to his neck, I added, "I want to feel you. Please, Xander?"

He didn't respond, only held his position—maybe waiting for me to make some kind of move. I rubbed my hands into his thighs and I reached between us, but our positions made it difficult to get a good grasp on him. Nonetheless, I started stroking him through his pants, as much, as I could to give him some sort of pleasure because I wanted to make him feel good, but I also wanted him to fucking reciprocate. I wanted him so much that my stomach knotted on itself. I couldn't stand waiting. Taking matters into my own hands—or so I thought—I started unbuckling his belt and he shifted to make it easier for me, but his fingers actually moved away from pussy, back to squeezing my ass and a hand moved around to my breasts, gently stroking them.

I opened his pants and he helped me get his cock out. It was magnificent. It was solid, thick. In this position, I couldn't guess at length, but it was certainly long enough to make me happy whenever I could get it in my pussy. It was big enough to make me nervous that I wouldn't be able to get it all the way in my mouth. We started kissing again, stroking each other. His fingers had moved back to my lips, but never dipped in and my hand was a tight circle stroking him. I was distantly aware that my knees were starting to ache, kneeling in this wooden boat, but I didn't care.

Then he did something different to me and my breathing hitched. He slipped his fingers between my lips, but not into me, and spread them, spread me. He rubbed his fingers forward and back along the length of my lips, keeping my lips spread wide, but never penetrating me, never directly touching my clit. My slickness let him slide across my skin easily, but there was no satisfaction in it for me, just worse teasing and the intense feeling of being open, exposed. His fingers were so close to my clit that they occasionally brushed against it, making me shudder.

Goddamn, this is torture!

At the same time, a drop of pre-cum oozed against my thumb and I spread it around his crown, rubbing especially roughly around the ridge. He tensed, but I didn't pause. The velvet texture of his skin felt delicious. I brushed him roughly again and the liquid that had been there was stickier as it dried. He hissed between his lips and slipped both his hands between my legs. He pinched my lips and rubbed them, alternating between sides. I faltered in handling his cock.

"Say it again."

His voice was gruff and I thought he was close to cracking. But for a moment, I wasn't sure what he meant. But I already knew he liked to make me beg. I considered teasing him and not saying it but, as if sensing my consideration of mischief, he pinched both lips at once, hard and I was lost to him.

"Please, please, I need to feel you!" It came out in a rush. I couldn't register all the sensations at once, but he released the pinching and slammed two fingers into me. I only realized that it was one finger from each hand when he pulled them apart, stretching me open and tight. I gasped at the intensity of it—the exposure, the emptiness, the potentiality of it.

I registered that I was kneeling in an old boat, with my dress flipped up, panties around my knees and my naked ass aimed at anyone who could be looking from across the lake and now he had spread my pussy wide open. And it didn't matter that it was dark and someone else probably couldn't see me, a rush of shame spread through me. As quickly as the shame flooded through me, I released it. The fire of wanting was simply too much to try to stop it. I didn't care about the risks or repercussions. I started circling my hips, trying to get any type of friction so I could have some release. Somewhere in the recesses of my mind, I couldn't believe myself, how dirty and sexy and wonderful I felt.

But he was strict, not letting my gyrations get me anything he wasn't ready to give me. I pressed my hands against his chest, pushing him back and, as he lay back, his fingers slipped from me, smearing my wetness across the back of my thighs. I was momentarily torn between the ache to have that penetration back and the want to have him in my mouth. He leaned back against the side of the boat, with an unreadable expression on his face, at once peaceful and expectant, but something more as well. As I dropped my mouth down on him, that expression burned into my brain.

I hesitated a little and licked around his head. I tasted the sweat from my own hand before it dissipated in my saliva. I opened my mouth wide and tried to take all of him. It was a tight fit and I couldn't get his whole length into me before I felt his head nudge against my throat. I felt a small wave of disappointment that I couldn't take all of him, but there was a secret glee in knowing that as well. I let my mouth get wet, saliva drooling out of my mouth and down his length. I licked and sucked up and down, while I ran my hands up his thighs to his abdomen.

This position was one of supplication, complete worship, and I knew it. I worshiped at the altar of his cock until I felt his muscles start to tense. His hand was in my hair, slowing me and turning my head, so that he could explore all of my mouth with his cock. The head slid against the inside of my cheek on one side then the other. He pulled his dick all the way out of my mouth and just rubbed the head on my lips. I looked up at him with a question, but when I opened my mouth to ask, he slipped it back in and shook his head at me. He slowly guided my mouth on him, just how he wanted it. His hand tightened in my hair and he started to thrust his hips up to meet my face. When he got to the back of my throat, he stayed there for a moment then released. He did this a few more times, until he held me there, with his cock pushing against the back of my mouth.

"Relax the muscles of your throat."

He said it calmly, but pushed his hips against me a little harder. I relaxed as much as I could and felt the head of his cock nudge a little farther into me.

"Mmmmm, good girl. Keep yourself relaxed."

And he started sliding my mouth up and down his cock, but every time now, he pushed to that new depth. I arched my neck to elongate my throat for him. His hips started rocking against my face, thighs tightening. My hands were still on his chest and he grabbed them both at the wrists with his free hand, pulling counter-traction on my arms to pull me into him as his hips rose to meet my face.

He got to that new depth and held me there, and he was too deep for me to breathe through my nose. A little inkling of panic started in the back of my mind, but he relaxed back and I relaxed in turn. But he was at his edge, rocking his hips against me, hand tight in my hair, driving my face up and down his cock. I couldn't control my saliva or catch my breath. I drooled down all over his cock, and he fucked my mouth hard enough that there was a little stretching type of pain every time he hit the back of my throat. It was categorically unlike any blow job I had ever given.

I felt his muscles ripple under my arms with each thrust, as he got more and more insistent. Small whooshes of breath pulsed out of him with each stroke. In his frenzy, he pushed harder, with new intensity, and slid even farther into me, against the spot that triggered my gag reflex, but I pushed it away. My lips were at his base now, my nose nestled in his pubic hair. And he held me there. I was taut, neck stretched, lips stretched, naked ass and pussy in the air. And I loved it. I started to just bob my head a little under his hand, not pulling up, trusting him to pull out enough to let me breathe in just a few more seconds, but wanting to push him like he pushed me.

My head bobbing was his undoing. He released my hands and grabbed my hair, grinding my face down on his dick, then pulled me back. I took a gasping breath and he slammed his cock into my mouth again, holding me tight against him, groaning, and I worked my tongue, mimicking swallowing though I couldn't truly swallow anything, and continued bobbing my head against him. This time he pulled my face up slowly and I could tell he was on the edge. All his muscles tensed and his breathing was ragged.

I sucked hard, hollowing my cheeks, as I slipped up and down and on the third such stroke, he exploded in my mouth with a loud groan of pleasure, punctuated by, "Oh fuuuuuck!"

I swallowed then gently licked at him, because honestly, he was a sloppy mess. Once he was clean and his post-orgasm tremors had subsided, I stopped licking and sat back on my heels. When he sat up, he pulled me up against him and just held me there for a moment. I could feel his heart hammering in his chest and a sense of accomplishment washed over me.

I did this to him. I smiled against his skin, feeling sexy and powerful.

While I felt accomplished, I still had a powerful need to come. As if reading my mind, he brushed his hand through my hair, which was a complete mess now.

"Now, what are we going to do about you? I bet you're all kinds of miserable right now, cause that pussy is soaking wet, isn't it?"

His vaguely didactic, condescending tone had two effects on me — I initially thought *who the fuck does this guy think he is?* But a second thought niggled at the back of my mind…I liked it. But I was embarrassed to confirm for him how much I needed the get off. When I took too long to answer, his hand wound up into my hair, and he pulled my head back. He kissed my mouth and just when I started to respond to his mouth on mine, he stopped.

"Let's try again, little girl. You need to come, don't you?" With his hand in my hair, he nodded my head for me and I felt so small. My pussy started heating up again. He stopped pulling my hair and just stroked it, smoothing it down, almost as if I were a pet.

I became aware of how much I wanted him touching me. It was all I could focus on, more than wanting to come. I could live with the wanting between my legs if I had to, but I just didn't want to break contact with him. I looked up into his face and we had this wonderful moment, where I felt like the world was right and it made sense, and the constant anarchy of stress in my brain settled, then stilled. I took a deep breath and sank into it, sank into him. He saw it and absorbed me.

Then his hands were on me, moving, just where I wanted them to be.

One hand rested on my ass and the other pulled the strap of my dress down and teased my nipple out. He started kissing me again. He laid me back, running his hands over my body, crawling down over me in the hull of the boat. He was tucked back in his pants and looked perfect, stunning in the moonlight as he loomed over me.

"Touch yourself."

Pardon?

He sensed my question. "I want to see you make yourself come for me."

My thoughts raced. I was ashamed and turned on at the thought of him watching me as I got myself off. I was turned on that I was considering something like that, because he told me to — something I never would have even admitted to doing before him, let alone performing in front of another person.

My thoughts spiraled like this and the thought came that I must look like every Lifetime movie of the week date rape victim—cute young girl, in a white sundress, disheveled hair, panties around her knees, dress bunched up around her middle so her snatch and tits were visible to the world. I became so self-conscious—of my nudity, of what a slut I had been, of my behavior and my dirty desires, of the fact that I was in this random boat at random lake. He saw it a beat before I spoke, his expression changing to concern.

"I don't think I can, Xander. Yellow." And I started pulling my dress over myself, awash in shame and self-loathing. He was immediately at my side, helping me dress, whispering to me, as tears welled up in my eyes and I started shaking.

"Okay, honey, you're okay. You're perfect, shhh. I'm right here and nothing bad is going to happen." Once I was dressed, he pulled me into his lap, wrapped me up in his arms and gently rubbed my back until he felt the tension go out of me and my shudders slowed. Then he leaned back, looking into my eyes and brushing my hair back from my face. "Honey girl, are you okay? What was it? Too much?"

He was so sweet and concerned, and I think I fell in love with him a little right then. I took a deep, but shaky breath. At first, I didn't feel like I could tell him. I doubted that he'd understand. I expected that he would think I was some stupid girl, *stupid little girl*. And I couldn't bear to look at him because I was sure I had let him down.

Chapter Fifteen

Xander
John Legend, Made to Love

Fuck. I braced myself, so that I could be strong enough to protect her from what I feared was coming, and I felt like the biggest piece of shit on the planet. I did this to her. *We didn't discuss limits and maybe self-gratification is a limit for her. She is Catholic.* My own thoughts started to spiral in a version of Dom-drop. *This is just like what I did to Stacy.* I flashed back to the waiter earlier in the evening — that had been warning enough that I needed to slow the fuck down and *take care* of her, first and foremost.

I took a deep breath, still rubbing her back. I told myself to shut the fuck up. I was the Dom. I was going to have to suck it up, deal with my own shit later and take care of her now. I wrapped my arms around her, squeezing a little. Her shudders slowed down and I leaned back to get a better look at her face.

She looked at me with her big eyes all liquid but couldn't hold my gaze, her shame was so great. This wasn't just about masturbation. She sucked in a big breath and spewed it all out. "I don't know. It sounds crazy, but it just felt like too much. I mean, I don't know where we are and any crazy nut job could be watching us... Maybe it was just feeling too exposed. Don't get me wrong, it felt great, but then I had a second to think and my brain turned on and it just rebounded back. I'm sorry."

Oh, Jesus, I'm such a goddamn prick. "Oh, Leda. Don't apologize. I'm the asshole. I pushed too hard, too far and definitely too soon. I'm sorry, sweetheart. This property belongs to the senator my dad works with. No one is ever here that I don't know about. I've sort of become the caretaker of the cabin and the property since I live in town. But regardless, let me take you home."

Her eyes flashed a little. I couldn't tell what it was, though. I pulled her up and held her hand as we walked back. She was silent and I gave her space to work through whatever she was feeling.

I got her in the car and started driving back to town. I took it slow, not wanting the speed to frighten her, wanting to keep things mellow. My own thoughts were spinning. *She didn't say red, only yellow. Maybe I should follow-up on that with her tomorrow.*

About halfway home, she got more antsy, until she finally said, "Wait! So that's really how tonight ends? Yuck. I said yellow. I thought that meant hold on, slow down — not stop, get me dressed and take me home."

She pouted and I was proud of her. I smiled, but said nothing, giving her the space to say anything she needed to, but she looked at me and half-yelled, "Wait, what are you smiling about?" Her own lips started to twitch up at the corners.

"You, little girl. You did say yellow. I know what you said. The venue seemed to be the problem, not so much the act. Am I correct?" The smile faded from my voice and a dominant cadence replaced it by the end of my question.

"Yes." It was so quiet that I glanced at her to be sure I wasn't missing a repeat descent into a negative head space. But she just looked like a little, submissive pet, waiting to be taken wherever I wanted to take her.

"Very good. Because as gorgeous as you are in the moonlight, I really want a good view of your face when you come for me. Let's start now. Take your panties off." I didn't think it would be too much, but held my breath until she moved to do it. She held her cute white cotton and lace panties up and I grabbed them out of her hands. I laid them over my opposite knee and ran my thumb across the panel of fabric in the crotch that was damp and sticky. *This is mine.*

"Push your dress up, so I can see you."

She moved immediately and waves of excited energy bubbled off her. She pulled her skirt up to her waist, but her knees were together. *Not good enough.* I reached across and twitched my fingers between her thighs, which were distractingly soft and smooth, and she acquiesced, spreading her thighs wide apart. The street lights washed a softer, yellowish light over her skin intermittently. I slid my fingers up into her center, lightly stroking her clit, just teasing her, but I didn't want her to come in the car. I wanted to see her writhing on my bed when it happened.

She closed her eyes and leaned back against the headrest. She breathed faster, and a soft moan escaped her. I pushed my fingers inside her, my cock rigid again. I swiped my fingers into her a few times, but then we were pulling into my lot.

"Come on. Let's go, little girl." She got a moment to collect herself as I walked around the car, and she waited for me to open the door and get her out, like a good girl. I smiled as I held her hand. At the door to the building, I smacked her ass as she passed me. She giggled and turned back to me. Whatever sassy thing she was planning on saying died on her lips when she saw me.

I knew I was looming, stalking her. I knew my energy was dark and filling the stairwell. "Get your ass up these steps." My voice was exceptionally quiet, but pressured. She bolted up the steps and my instinct was to chase her, but I checked that, letting my tread drop heavy so she could build up the anticipation and confront her flight-or-fight instinct.

At the top of the steps, I turned her toward my door and walked the rest of the way, right behind her. When we got to my door, I kept coming at her and pressed her into it. She turned her face so her cheek was pressed against the door and I could see her huge pupil. I felt the darkness in me devour that.

I dropped my head forward and grabbed her earlobe between my teeth, pressing down until she winced. "Listen to me. I'm not going to fuck you tonight. Not tonight." She kind of deflated a little. She wanted it. I pressed into her, letting her feel me, all of me, my cock pressing against her ass. "Little girl, I would love to punish that pussy all night. You don't know the things I think about doing to you, but I don't want to push you too hard…yet. But don't get it twisted. You *are* going to come for me."

She sucked in a breath and I reached past her to unlock and open the door as I reached my other arm over her front, holding her to me by pressing into her sternum. I stepped forward, forcing her to step forward as well. I threw my keys on the counter and took her purse for the same. She glanced around, taking it in. I thought about my daydream of living with her, and I wanted her to like it at my place, thinking maybe it would be our place at some point.

I guided her through the open-concept apartment, spun her around and started kissing her, pushing her backward, toward my bed. I reached up her back and found her zipper, and pulled it. We bumped the bed and I dropped to my knees and pulled at her dress till it fell. I still had her panties and all she had left were her shoes and a sheer white bra that her dark rose nipples were visible through.

Her breasts were beautiful, big on her little frame. Staying on my knees, I stroked up her body, cupping her breasts and pinching her nipples. I hooked my thumb at her hip and pulled her down to sit on the edge of my bed. She let me do it. She didn't indicate any desire to stop. She let me move her how I wanted her, lying back with her feet still on the floor, ass right at the edge of the bed.

"Green?" I asked as I stood.

Her voice was dreamy when she responded, "Green."

"Okay, little girl. Show me how you make yourself come." I stepped backward until I bumped the soft club chair my mother had insisted I buy. I had hated it until that moment. I knew it was going to become one of my favorite things in the apartment after tonight. I sat back, with one leg over the arm.

She hesitated, but then ran her hands over her body. She pulled her breasts out of her bra, by the nipple, as she started stroking her pussy. It was a cute little thing. And I was gonna ravage it at some point. A smile played over my lips. She worked her slit and started breathing louder.

Then she lifted her legs up, hooking her heels on the edge of the mattress and dropped her knees to the sides. *Goddamn, modesty gone. Fucking beautiful.*

I murmured softly, "God, you are fucking perfect, girlie."

She sighed and I didn't know if she had heard me, but as I watched, she started shifting her hips around and I saw a new glossiness to her lips. She was getting wetter. She moaned and my cock pressed out. I stroked it through my pants. But when I saw the muscles in her ass and pussy start to twitch, I had to be on her. I jumped up and got to the foot of the bed, knelt in front of her and started to stroke her, sliding a finger inside. She started to pull her hand away, automatically making room for me, but I grabbed her hand and pulled it back. I said nothing. She continued to play with her body and her tension ratcheted up a notch. Her strokes were getting more frantic, more pressured, and I pushed three fingers into her pussy, a tight fit. She spasmed and ground her pelvis down on my hands. I got my thumb on her asshole and she didn't balk.

I wanted to taste her before she came, so I nuzzled into her and she withdrew her hand. I licked her with long, broad strokes. She fluttered her fingertips through my hair as I started rolling my tongue over her clit and pumping my fingers inside her. As she started grinding down on me, moaning and breathing harder, I sucked her clit in between my lips. She snapped her hips at me and I felt my teeth scrape into her clit, but she shuddered and moaned louder.

I leaned back, wanting her to make herself come for me. She slammed her fingers back on her clit, pressing it down harder than I would have expected she liked. She arched up, her voice almost singing as she cried out. She was at the peak of her arc when she stopped fluttering her fingers over her clit and started to breathe out, relaxing. *Fuck that.* I pinched her clit and she screamed, snapping her pelvis up off the bed again.

She dropped back to the bed, her breath whooshing out of her. I pulled my fingers from her, smiling. Just watching her breathe like this could become my new favorite hobby.

"Mmm, little girl, you are so delicious. And you come like art in motion. Perfect." I was a little impressed with that line and felt a little cocky as I climbed up the bed to lie next to her. I kissed her a few more times and we snuggled down, under the covers.

We lay together for a few minutes then she sat up and said something about going home and I actually said, "Fuck that, little one. No fucking way. Put your ass right here in this bed with me." She had a sleepy flush and a smile crossed her lips and she moved to me. I gave her a T-shirt to sleep in and got undressed to my boxers.

* * * *

In the morning, she seemed uncomfortable, gathering her things like she was about to do the walk of shame. I laughed at her, asking, "Oh, did you leave the money on the nightstand?"

She paused what she was doing and looked at me blankly for a moment, then laughed. She stopped trying to leave, and I pulled her into the shower with me, promising to keep it professional. But I made myself a liar and spent a while kissing her.

I took her to brunch, sending Jason a text that I wouldn't be meeting them at Cat's Meow. She had her dress and looked completely appropriate. I was the only one who knew that she was still in the same thing as our date last night. It was kind of dirty, so I of course liked it. I wore some shorts and an old shirt. She smiled at me and she was a whole different kind of stunning with no makeup on, just natural.

As we ate, I thought through the night and was hit with a lightning bolt realization. "Hey, I fucked up last night and I'm sorry."

She looked at me in pure confusion, so I leaned forward to speak quietly. "I wanted you too much and it made me act more recklessly than I normally would. But I want you to know that I haven't been with anyone in…shit, over a year, and I get screened every six months. I know I don't have any infections that you should have been aware of before last night."

Her face blanked out, but she tried to smile and answered, "I got tested after I broke up with my ex. Nothing to worry about here either."

"Look, if you want to go get tested together, I'm happy to do that. Whatever you need to feel comfortable. Jesus, I feel like such a fuck-up right now. I mean that's like sex ed one-oh-one, let alone kink one-oh-one."

She left around two to go home and study. I knew it was the right thing to do, but I didn't want her to leave. That said, I called Jason as she drove away, needing to burn off some of the anxious, unspent tension.

He answered, "Dude…no breakfast with us?" His voice was full of excitement. I smiled.

"She spent the night and we went to that new place for brunch."

"Brunch? How late did Mr. Military Man let himself sleep?"

"Whatever—fuck you. Wanna go to the gym this afternoon, since we missed the morning? I gotta burn off some energy so I can settle down enough to study."

He paused. "Wait, what the fuck did you do last night? I mean sex is supposed to cure that whole sexual frustration thing."

"We didn't have sex. It was just late and I didn't want her driving home."

"Right." He sounded doubtful and didn't say anything else.

"Fuck off!" I laughed. "Meet me in an hour?"

* * * *

We spent a few hours sparring then I spent several hours studying. Sunday was another studying day.

We developed a routine over the next few weeks. School was the focus Monday morning through the end of tutoring on Thursday evening. Then the weekend was together. We'd still study some, but mostly fuck around, go out, fuck around some more and sleep. She was getting more and more insistent that we have sex and I kept putting her off.

I wanted it too, but I wanted it my way and no other way. I wanted her bent in half, twisted inside out with how much she wanted to be used, by me and me alone. It was a topic of conversation occasionally, but one Saturday, after we had been together for at least a month and a half, she was particularly vehement. We were hiking the woods at the senator's property, The Retreat. She was behind me, so I had no idea what triggered it, but she just blurted out, "Xander, I'm gonna have to fuck you soon."

I smiled before I turned to her and pinned her to the tree right behind her. Her breathing was immediately ragged, when my fingers closed around her throat, holding her there while I spoke. "I know, but I'm not putting my cock in you until you realize that you want me to fuck you. There's a difference, little girl." I kissed her forehead as I released her neck, knowing I was torturing her, but loving it.

I started to walk away, in the direction we had been going, when she asked, "What's the difference? I want us to have sex."

"You know the difference," I admonished. "I'm not going to let you fuck me." I turned back to her, but she stood her ground. "You don't fuck me. I fuck you and you take what I give you. When you see the difference, really know the difference down in your tissues, to your toes, then I'll fuck you. I'm not worried, Leda, I've got time and I know you're headed there."

She kind of smiled, saying, "Hmm, I don't know about all this." I knew I was pushing her. There was a risk that she would get sick of the game and tell me that I could fuck *myself*. I wanted to push her to right before that point and make her admit how much she wanted it, just so she could see how little shame she really had. A shameless girl is so fucking hot.

She was quiet for the next twenty minutes or so, and I let her think. But we got to a clearing and took a pause. "What are you so deep in thought about, Leda?"

She searched for words for a moment while I took a few sips from our water bottle. "It's just that it isn't really a relationship of equals. I'm always... I don't know how to explain it. I'm just not clear on the inequality of it."

"I see what you mean. We aren't equivalent, but you have to know that I don't think you are 'less than'. It's a different kind of thing. I'm just not measuring us against each other. We aren't equivalent but we do have equal worth. Does that make sense?"

"But that's totally easy for you to say. You have all the control and power."

I handed her the water and she drank deep. "I hear what you're saying. It's just really important to me that you understand that *I* don't think that you are anything other than a treasure. But...I think you should talk with my friend June. I know her from the kink scene in DC. She comes down here sometimes for her work and she usually spends at least a night or two at the Window. Not to disclose her info, I don't think she would care, but she's a sub. I mean like full-on living the life sub, with a Master, the whole deal — twenty-four, seven. But she is really successful professionally, too. She has the best perspective, the most well-articulated thoughts on being a sub. You might find it helpful to talk with her. She may be able to help you with these questions. Because as much as I want to help you with anything you struggle with, this just doesn't make sense to me. Maybe it's my experiences or that I'm not submissive or just that from my perspective, you really do have a *lot* of power. You're outside of the hierarchy to me. You are...a small piece of heaven, all for me. I don't know." I hugged her to me, more easily affectionate than I had ever been with a girl before. "Would you be open to talking with her?"

Her lips said, "Yeah, that sounds great," with a smile. But her body language was less sure.

Chapter Sixteen

Leda
Muse, Madness

As we hiked the rest of the path we had found through the Senator's property, I watched the way Xander moved, the angle of his shoulders and neck. *Am I really just going to wait until he deems me worthy of his cock? Is that really all right with me? What am I then — just a receptacle for his need? A place to drop off sexual frustration, an entity designed for him and his pleasure alone? To be used when he wants? My own desires, needs and fucking frustrations ignored?*

Something about it irked me, in part because it seemed so shitty and unequal, and in part because deep down, in my most secret thoughts, I liked that idea. And in truth, I knew that wasn't really what he was talking about. If he just needed to flush the pipes, he could do it. I was clearly willing. And he was gorgeous. I'm sure women dropped their panties for him left and right.

When I got home there was an email from Tiffany.

Hey Bitch —
Did u fuck him? How's his dick?
T
— sent from my iPad

I laughed out loud at her audacity as I dialed her.

She answered in her typical fashion. "Hey, lady, so text me a dick pic already."

"Damn, Tiffany! I haven't had sex with him yet!"

"Why the hell not? I thought we fixed this already. There is nothing to feel guilty about."

I sighed, totally embarrassed about the words I was about to say. "He won't fuck me." Tears stung my eyes as I admitted it.

There was a pause of silence then she asked, "Really? Does he give you a reason?"

"He says he's dominant and he won't fuck me until I understand the difference between him fucking me and me fucking him."

"Oh." She paused again and her voice was serious when she spoke again. "What do you think about that?"

"I don't know! I mean he... I get it. It's how he is. This is exactly opposite of every guy ever, right? I'm pushing him all the time, bugging him about it. And I just have to make do with getting eaten out, finger-fucked... I want the whole shebang."

She laughed.

I stopped my rant, but added, "Am I being crazy?"

"Hell no! You know what you want. It just happens to be the dick of the only man in Texas who won't just give it to you. Did you tell him that he's being a pain in the ass?"

"He would just laugh. This is fucking nuts, right?"

"I can't say that I have ever experienced anything like this, but I think there are only two things to do. First you decide if you're gonna wait till his little precious self is ready or tell him to hit the bricks."

"I'm not going to break up with him because we aren't having sex. That's..."

She cut me off, "Then you have to decide what kind of vibrator you need to get."

I laughed again, thanked her for listening and hung up the phone.

* * * *

That night we went to Jason's bar. Jason and Xander played pool while Christy and I were sitting off to the side, talking. Jason came over between shots and kissed Christy, tracing his fingers up her leg, between her thighs. He whispered something in her ear and I watched a flush run up her chest and neck. He started to step away and she grabbed his hand, giving him the poutiest look, and he had a stern look I'd never seen on his usually jovial face.

"Yes, Christy," he said it distinctly, clearly. And she dropped her eyes, the picture of submission. But the minute he turned around, her demeanor changed completely. She stuck her tongue out at his back and laughed. She put her arm around my chair and leaned over to me, mischief and laughter in her eyes. He turned back to look as she whispered in my ear.

"Pretend I'm saying something really interesting and funny. I've gotta teach this kid a lesson!"

I smiled and tilted my head toward her. Jason was half smiling and shook his finger at her then turned back around to finish his game with Xander. I looked over his shoulder at Xander, chalking his cue and watching us. He had a smile on his face, devoid of angst or stress. Just happy watching his friends…doing whatever they were doing.

"Come on, Leda. Let's powder our noses." Christy got up and grabbed my hand, pulling me off my stool.

In the bathroom, I asked her, "What was that?"

"Oh, Jason and I have a funny relationship. We're constantly teasing and playing with each other. Sometimes we try to make each other jealous, but mostly we just like fucking with each other." She smiled and finger-combed her hair out.

"How does that work? How do you deal with the sex club stuff? Doesn't it freak you out a little?"

"What, the Window? No, not at all. We have…an open relationship. Maybe that's not the best word for it. We have a fluid definition of monogamy. Sometimes we play with other people." Her answer smacked of diplomacy.

Feeling kind of dense, I asked, "What do you mean?"

"Oh you know, sometimes we mess around with other people, sometimes other people join us when we mess around. There're some things that I want that Jason doesn't like or can't do, some things he wants that I can't, or don't want to, do."

This was just getting more confusing. "Umm, I don't know what you are talking about."

"Sometimes we need extra body parts." She looked at me and my face was blank. She squared her shoulders to me, and spoke in a very simple voice, like she was speaking to a child. "Sometimes I want to get fucked by two dudes at once. Sometimes I don't really want to give him head. Sometimes we like to watch each other with someone else. Sometimes I want to be tied up and that isn't really his thing most of the time.

Though tonight it might be." She added the last part with a wicked smile and her gaze got distant.

"Oh." It sounded so lame as I said it. And with a rush I realized, tying chicks up *was* Xander's thing. A blaze of anger fired through me, in advance of my thoughts. *Has she fucked him...sorry, has he fucked her? Have they shared her – is that what Jason was talking about at the gym a while back, that I wasn't for sharing?* And I wanted to ask her just how well she knew Xander, but I couldn't bring myself to say it. I felt like it would shatter everything.

We wrapped up our ministrations and stepped out of the rest room, but I split off and headed to the bar to get more alcohol. Vodka with cranberry, plus a lemon drop shot. I slammed the shot down and carried my drink with me to the back room. Xander watched me walk back, and I was sure he had seen me take the shot at the bar. He gave me a questioning look, most likely because I had only been sipping at some drinks before then.

I just wanted, but I didn't know what I wanted. I wanted clarity and answers, or maybe just to go home. And some irrational part of me wanted to stake my claim on him, wanted to fuck him so that it was clear to everyone, *especially him,* that he was mine. This surge of emotions, the jealousy... It was all different than what I was used to feeling in relationships, and underneath it I felt some anger and the consistently unsatisfied horniness fueling it all.

I thought maybe I just wanted to fuck him and it hit me – I understood what he was saying earlier when we were hiking, about the difference between me fucking him and him fucking me. Because at that moment, I absolutely did not want him to fuck me. I wanted to get on top of him and fuck him hard, ride him and make him take whatever I wanted to give him, just say *fuck it — fuck you — this is about me getting off and feeling good and you are a means to an end.*

Whoa. What the fuck is this?

I had never felt like this before, about anyone. I didn't know what it was. I took a huge gulp of my drink. It was this intensity of emotion and sex all mixed up in my body. It was a buzzing in my arms and hands.

Christy had been over teasing Jason and I looked up in time to see her flash her ass at him. They were both laughing. Xander was smiling at them, but looked at me, at my mostly gone brand new drink and raised an eyebrow at me. I gave him the finger. And it was worth whatever trouble I had just bought for the look on his face — a flash of complete shock, followed by a growly smirk, but it broke the tension in me. I still wondered if he had messed around with Christy and Jason, but it felt less intimidating.

Xander and Jason took the last few shots of the game and Christy said something to Jason too quietly for me to make out, but probably inappropriate by the look on Jason's face, followed by her laughter. Xander put his cue away and slowly came to me. When he got to me, he kept walking, forcing me to take several steps back until I was against the wall with his body pressed against me.

"What's going on with you? Are you okay?" He brushed my hair away from my face. Regrettably, the influx of alcohol hit me then. I felt vaguely foggy and my thoughts got stupid. The irritation and the frustration and the sexual tension all came to the surface and I felt like a good, old fashioned bitch.

"Oh! I'm fine, just fine. I just had an interesting conversation with Christy about her sex life and then I thought about mine, ours — or lack-there-of. And I get it a little bit now." My voice was thick with booze and attitude. He cocked his head to the side, confusion on his face.

"What do you mean? What did Christy tell you about their sex life?" There was no guilt in his voice, just confusion, curiosity.

"I get it — the whole thing about who is fucking who. And Christy just told me about the 'fluid monogamy' of her relationship. Can we go somewhere else? Private-er."

"Okay, little girl. Where do you want to go? Wanna go get some dessert again?"

"No, umm, no. I want you to take me home and I want to fuck the hell out of you. I'm so fucking sick of you making me wait." I snaked my hands around the back of his neck, wound my fingers into his hair and yanked, pulling his face down to mine. I licked his lips and when he started to kiss me back, I pulled his head back from my lips and whispered, "No, stop it. Just let me kiss you."

I didn't wait for his answer, but pulled him back to me, licking his lips, only the outside of his mouth. His lips parted softly and I started licking around the edges. Somewhere, my inebriated frontal lobe got a nervous feeling that this didn't seem like my Xander, but my reptilian brain stem didn't seem to care.

My right hand stayed in his hair, pulling just a little, and my left dropped down to his chest then back around his neck, slightly inside his collar. I flexed my fingers and my nails dug into his neck. He drew a shaky breath, letting it out in a hiss. He ran his hands up my sides and I paused in kissing him to grab at his hands to stop him from touching me, but he anticipated it, or I was too drunk and slow. Either way, he grabbed my wrists and yanked me forward. He roughly and quickly guided my wrists behind my back and captured them both there with one hand. And just like that, any pretense of sexual dominance on my part was shut down.

"Leda. Little girl. You still don't understand." He spoke softly and traced my lips and earlobe with the forefinger of his free hand. "That's not how this works. You belong to me. Yes, we are leaving and no, you are not going to fuck the hell out of me tonight. I'm going to make you suffer tonight. I think you need it, don't you, little girl?" He whispered in my ear and I could feel the shock cross my face at the complete reversal. He squeezed my wrists and pressed his body into mine, growling, "Don't you?"

"Uh-huh." I felt a weird and sexy wide-eyed terror, centered in my chest and pussy, making me completely breathless.

"Okay. I'm going to pay the tab and get you some water and you are going to sit your fine ass on this bar stool right here. You are going to wait until I come back and then you'll drink the water then we'll leave." He pulled the barstool out with his foot and lifted me onto it in one motion.

After he walked away, I mumbled, "Shit. I think I'm in trouble."

Christy came over to me. "What the fuck was that all about? He looks like he's ready to tear your skin off with his teeth." She cracked a huge smile. "It looks like you're gonna have some fun, lady!"

"What? He's sort of terrifying!" I turned to her, wide-eyed but flushed with excitement.

"You wanna fuck with his head? Keep telling him yes, just let all the fight go out of you. That'd be hilarious. Or call him daddy all night or something like that."

"I don't know, those aren't really... I don't think I'm into the daddy thing."

"Well, you never know till you try it. Or... Oooohh! Or you could act like he's not getting to you at all. Don't let him know how much you want him! Oh God, the Great Xander, taken down a peg. I love it." She was laughing, but I couldn't really take it in because he was back.

He wordlessly handed me some water and left me to it, while he said goodnight to Jason. The lack of eye contact, the lack of any affection – I knew something was coming and it made me anxious – made me feel rowdy and obedient at the same time. I drank my water down quickly, just because it was what he'd told me to do.

When he came back for me, he grabbed me around the waist and threw me over his shoulder. *Thank God I'm wearing jeans tonight.* I waved at Jason and Christy over his back as he carried me out of the bar, like this was a normal way for people to behave. A borderline hysterical giggle bubbled out of me.

Interestingly, no one in the bar even really reacted. His left arm held my legs in place and, when I squirmed, he slapped my ass with his right hand, before we were even through the door. By the time we got to the car, he had spanked me six more times and my ass was starting to burn. Just before we got to the car, he reached his right hand into my crotch and roughly rubbed around my pussy. I flashed to a slapdash fantasy of him dropping me on the hood of his car and fucking me, hard. He unlocked the car remotely and opened the door with his right hand and kneeling, placed me in the passenger seat.

"Sit still and keep your mouth shut." By now the alcohol was in full effect and I felt slightly slack-jawed and dumb, so not talking was probably fine. He turned the music on loud and pulled out of the parking lot.

Chapter Seventeen

Xander
Minstry, Lay Lady Lay

We drove without speaking. I saw the alcohol hit her, the glazed look in her eyes. But I knew I was in trouble.

I took her to her apartment, knowing I wanted to fuck with her, but that she was intoxicated. She couldn't fucking consent right now. I wouldn't leave her alone, but I wouldn't take advantage of that either. I wanted her to have the security that came from being at home.

Once we were inside, I got her another glass of water. "Okay, when you sober up, we'll talk about this shit."

She looked at me with pure surprise on her face. "But... I thought..." She trailed off.

"You thought I'd want to fuck you while you were too drunk to be fully present." I cocked my head to the side. "Umm, no."

She stilled and sadness crossed her features. "Are you mad at me?"

"Not really. No. I'm just frustrated." I sat on the couch and she came to sit next to me. "It isn't easy. Wanting you all the time. And you keep telling me you're ready. I want to be sure. I don't want to mess this up, Leda."

"Look, I'm not that drunk."

I cut her off with a sharp laugh. "Whatever comes after that sentence is going to be a terrible idea."

She chuckled and said, "Let's watch a movie and I'll get clearheaded. Then we fuck!" She was like a human-emoji giant smile and I couldn't stop my laughter as I agreed to the movie, at least.

I made a quick snack while she found something to watch. Once we were settled, we snuggled on the couch under her comforter. It honestly wasn't that late and I held out hope that she would sober up before bed, so we could at least resolve this before sleeping.

It wasn't a very long show but was light and funny and helped adjust the mood. She drank several glasses of water and had a snack, so I felt better that she would at least not have a hangover in the morning, but when the movie ended, she looked at me, completely clear-eyed.

"Hey, I get that you don't want the first time you fuck me to be when I'm drunk, but please don't tell me that you'd never fuck me when I was drunk. Drunk sex is fun!" She was serious, pleading with me to understand.

"Drunk *sex* can be fun...or awful. Drunk BDSM probably shouldn't be legal— Fuck, probably *isn't* legal."

She winced and I added, "How are you feeling now?"

She shrugged. "I'm completely sober. And I still want you to fuck me." She glanced down at her hands in her lap. "Xander, I always want you to fuck me. It never goes away."

"Really?" My cock tightened in my jeans.

"Yeah. How much longer are we going to do this?"

I felt smirky, like a smart ass, ready to test her a little. "Not too much longer. Come on." I stood and offered her my hand. She took it and I walked her back to her bedroom, feeling my own banked need flaring up again.

I stood her at the foot of the bed and pushed her forward, holding her hips so she bent in half.

"Don't move." My voice was harsh, dark with lust.

Jason had called me on my bullshit while we were shooting pool tonight and I knew he was right. It was time to do this. She was ready, beyond ready. I took my shirt off, my skin already feeling too hot. I pushed her little tank top up over her head and threw it behind me. Then I unbuttoned her little skinny jeans, pulling them down to her ankles. She lifted her foot to step out of them. My hand was flying toward her ass before I consciously decided to spank her. "I said, don't fucking move, Leda."

Her ankles were essentially secured, she was hobbled. I stood back, looking at her body. She wore a lacy black bra with matching boy-short panties. While those could be cute and had their uses, it wasn't what I wanted. I wanted her to be wearing a thong. Or nothing at all. I wanted skin on skin when I spanked her ass. I pulled the shorts up, baring her ass for my hand.

"You were a brat tonight. You know that, right?"

She turned her face toward me, eyes shining with excitement as she murmured, "Yes, Boss."

Sexual triumph washed over me. "You get a spanking. Ready?"

She sighed. "Oh, fuck yes."

I actually stepped to the side so I could fully wind up. I was a few slaps in when the stupid panties started to slip.

I muttered, "Goddammit," and grabbed them in the middle, yanking hard. I was rewarded with the satisfying sound of ripping and they sprang free of her body. Her cute little pussy was right there, all wet for me and I slammed my fingers into her. She gasped and moaned a little. I stepped away from her and grabbed her torn panties where I had dropped them.

I leaned across her body and jammed the panties into her mouth, gagging her. "Quiet, little one. If you need me to stop, stomp your foot." I climbed on the bed and dropped my knee between her shoulder blades, but kept the other knee on the bed, so she wasn't bearing my full weight.

I watched her for a moment, knowing this was intense and maybe too much. I was sick of controlling myself. She made me want to lose control. She made me feel alive in a way I hadn't ever felt before. But then it happened, what I had known would happen at some point in our relationship.

She breathed deep through her nose and she relaxed under me. Chills ran across her skin. She arched her back, bending into a bow for me, her ass up in the air. I grabbed her offered up ass, and squeezed down hard. I saw the tears but she didn't seem to be in distress. She moaned, all muffled by the gag. I took her bra off her. Then I waited, watching to see what she would do.

She shifted. Then shifted some more, and I dug my knee into her back and slapped her ass. Her cheeks were getting rosy. She whined against the gag, but stopped moving. I waited to be sure she was going to stay where I put her. When I was convinced she would, I climbed off her and sat on the edge of the bed, next to her. I rested my arm on her low back and just skimmed a touch across her ass.

I stood up and pulled her up, leaning against my chest. "Climb onto the bed." I whispered it in her ear, a promise that something more was coming. She moved, her jeans hampering her some, but it was fun to watch.

She knelt, facing away from me, and I pushed her over. She caught herself like I'd known she would. She stretched out flat and I lay down on top of her, driving the breath from her lungs. I brushed her hair aside, kissing the back of her shoulders. Then threatened her, "Leda, I am going to spend tonight torturing you until you're crying for my cock. And when we're done, we'll deal with whatever your behavior was about at the bar tonight."

Her eyes watered and she subtly shifted her ass up some. She started trembling a little, and I whispered, more for her benefit than mine, "God, I like fucking with you."

I stood up to pull her jeans off her feet and brushed my fingertips along her thighs, noting the sticky dampness with a smile. She pumped her pelvis into the mattress a little. "Turn over." She flipped herself, immediately. I dropped down, my face in hers, and said, "If you keep moving like that, I will completely tie you up."

I ran my fingers over her skin, pausing at her nipples to pinch and pull them. She moaned again and I clamped down harder. She moaned again. I felt my face going blank the way it did when I played hard, much harder than this. I let go of her nipple and ran my hand over her skin, to her pussy. I played with her and pulled at her well-groomed patch of hair a little. She sighed and closed her eyes when my fingers dipped between her lips and started teasing her. Her breath came deeper and I knew she liked it, so I pressed directly into her clit. Her eyes popped open and she screamed into the gag.

Delicious. My psyche was a dark motherfucker.

I watched her reaction as I started finger-fucking her. She was shaking. She wanted to move. Her eyes started to water again and she reached for me. I continued the rhythm in her pussy, but she grabbed at my free arm, begging without words.

I just reached up and grabbed her wrists in one hand and held them. There was no change to what I was doing to her. I wanted to make her crazy. I wanted her panting my name. I wanted her to keep breaking the rules so I could punish her more. I brushed her clit a few times. She moaned harder and shifted her hips. I raised an eyebrow at her, in question. And she moved again, spreading her thighs a little and grinding her hips up into me. *That was it, little one.* I smiled coldly at her.

"On your knees."

She moved as soon as I spoke. She got up on her knees facing me at the foot of the bed.

"Spread your knees."

She moved to obey, completely open to me—some purists call it *nadu*—unable to hide anything in this position.

"Very nice."

I climbed onto the bed behind her and held a hip and the opposite shoulder, bending her forward. "I'm trying to decide what position I like you in best. I think this may be it." I traced her spine from her head to her ass then pulled her asscheeks apart to see her asshole. She was nervous about it and her muscles twitched. Her breathing came deep and shuddery. I touched the core of her shame and she puckered up, perfectly. I got my fingers wet in her pussy, roughly. She gasped a bit at that, but then I turned my attention back to her backside for a moment more, letting her know that I'd use her however I wanted to.

I was on the edge of what I could handle, ready to give in and fuck her despite all my warnings. I grabbed her hips to pull her against me as I pushed back. She could feel my cock against her and she pushed back harder, offering herself to me, then twisting for more friction.

"Really, little girl? You want this?"

She nodded her head hard and moaned.

"Really? Well, not enough." I pulled away from her at the harsh words and slapped her ass again. She dropped to the bed and huffed out a breath. I smacked her ass more lightly this time, saying, "Settle down," dismissively. She repositioned herself how she was supposed to be.

I leaned into her again and pushed against her, relishing her nudity and the next level of degradation it represented. She was exposed and I was still decent—*decent? No.* It was actually a technique I'd learned in the military. Slowly take things away from the prisoner—one thing at time, until they have nothing left. She had no clothes, couldn't move if I didn't want her to, couldn't speak. She had nothing but wanting me.

I snapped at her, "Look at me." She turned her head, her eyes wide and wet. I held her gaze as I unzipped my jeans. Her breathing picked up again, hope in her eyes and she glanced down at my cock as I pulled it out.

Despite not being told to, she shifted, so that her shoulder was turned under and she could twist around to see behind her even better. She pushed her ass against me and I laughed. I stroked my cock in front of her.

Her eyes went wide in disbelief that I wasn't fucking her. "Is this what you want?"

She groaned and nodded again.

I leaned over her and pulled the gag from her mouth. "Tell me you're green and tell me how much you want it."

Chapter Eighteen

Leda
White Lies, To Lose My Life

This is it! Is he going to finally fuck me? I was completely, utterly clearheaded in that moment. I wanted to feel all of it. I felt a fresh surge of liquid weeping from my pussy onto my legs.

"Absolutely green! Please!" I whined at him. "Please fuck me. I want to feel you inside me. Please, Xander. I don't want to wait anymore. God, I want you to *fuck me*." The words were a tumble of desperation and need.

"Good girl."

As he said it, he slid the full length of his cock into me, no pauses, slow and deliberate, staking a claim. He kept his eyes locked on mine as he did it and it undid me. My body started trembling under him. My breathing was gasping sobs, wrenching through my chest. He reached his full depth in me and I felt the pressure in my belly. He just stayed there, buried in me, impaling me and I quivered around and under him, with fresh tears threatening to become uncontrollable.

"No!" I wailed, as the sobs start to take over. "Don't just stop there. Please, Xander, please just fucking fuck me."

He slid his cock in and out of me a few more times, slowly. And it was the most exquisite torture, when all I wanted was for his cock to be slamming into me, grinding me down and filling me up.

Then, he paused again, just holding me there with his cock. My crying settled to tremulous breathing, but I didn't understand why he was doing this to me, especially because his control was cracking, too. Even though his expression was blank, his jaw was locked and his breathing was very deliberate, like he was doing some sort of meditative deep breathing exercise.

We were locked in a stalemate that I didn't understand. I didn't know what to do to break the tension and let us fall into the abyss of each other's bodies on the other side. After a few moments, it hit me. He wanted me to tell him what I wanted. Not just that I wanted him to fuck me, but how much I wanted it and how I would give myself over to what he wanted.

The realization gave me hope again and I began to willingly debase myself, giving him the words for what I wanted, what he had made me realize I wanted.

"Please, Xander, fuck me. I want you inside me, pounding against me, please, just do it. Use me how you want to use me. I want you to use me and…and…and…*please*. I need to know what this feels like and how to be under you. Please?" I was begging and I didn't care. In fact, the begging made it better. He held himself still in me, held his breath, but I could feel his cock twitch every so often in the stillness. His face didn't move—no expression, no response. Just imperious, holding me there, under him.

I was at a loss. "I don't know what else to say to you. I want you to fuck me. I get it now. You're in control and I just want to belong to you, wanna be covered in you. I want you to grind out your need on me and claim me with your cum. I want to be split open for you. Whatever you want."

It was the right thing to say. There was a glint of vicious satisfaction in his eyes as he pulled his cock out and slammed it into me, again and again and again. I couldn't catch my breath until he found a steady but relentless rhythm. He reached up my body and pinched my nipple, then grabbed the flesh of my breast and squeezed down hard, using it to pull counter-traction against his thrusts. The fingers of his other hand dug into my hip and I was sure I would be bruised, but I didn't care. I was lost in him, in his lust overwhelming me and his need driving this exchange of flesh. When I had almost settled into the power of his thrusts, he paused momentarily and flipped me on my back.

He hooked my legs over his shoulders and drove back into me, pressing my body in half to lay his weight on me. Amazingly, I felt fuller. The peak of each thrust pushed the breath out of me. I felt his body tensing and the reality of it hit me. Xander was finally fucking me. I twisted and ground my hips up to him to get more pressure on my clit and felt my climax building. I ground a few more times and the delayed gratification of the night, of the past few months, paid off as I came.

My body felt flattened, as if a small thermonuclear device had detonated within me. My pussy spasmed and gushed fluid around his cock and it sent him over the edge to his orgasm as well. He gave three more punishing thrusts into my cunt and groaned, collapsing his weight onto me.

We lay there together, his softening cock still in me, our sweat mingling, our cum mingling and dripping down my ass to the growing wet spot on the sheet. His breathing slowed and he licked the sweat off my shoulder, to my neck, to my lips.

"Mmm, little girl. Very good." His eyes were at half mast and he moaned the words out between kisses. I kissed him back and a chill ran through me. I started to shiver, then shudder. He lifted his head and looked at me. "You okay?" No alarm in his voice. Just checking in with me, as he brushed some stray hair off my face.

"Just very intense. I think my body is just re-equilibrating."

He slipped, soft, out of me and rolled to the side. He tugged me into his arms and we lay together for a few minutes, not talking. I felt the enormity of having had sex looming over us. It was one weight lifted and another delivered.

"Let's take a shower and go to sleep." He sat up and pulled me up, as well.

Our shower was a lovely post-lude, warm and sensual and intimate. We dried off, and while I braided my hair, he checked the locks and turned off the lights. When he came back to my room, I was sitting up in bed, half covered by my quilt. He smiled at me, a softer smile, genuine, naked. I hadn't seen it before and the beginning of love swelled in my chest. He crawled into the bed and wrapped me up in his arms again. We snuggled into each other. My bed was not as large as his—where we had been having our sleepovers until that night—so we ended up snuggled in closer than usual.

There, tucked in his arms, under the cozy but light down comforter, I was in a cocoon, insulated from the world. The peace of it lulled me to sleep, his arm draped over me, his breath on the back of my neck.

Chapter Nineteen

Xander
Type O Negative, Cinnamon Girl

I woke a little before her, military training still embedded in my brain. I watched her for a bit, but when I shifted to get out of bed, she woke up. Her eyes were still sleepy and she smiled at me as I leaned over and kissed her. "Good morning, little one."

Her eyes sparkled a little at that and her smile broadened. She sat up slowly and winced a little. As the sheet dropped off her, I saw bruises on her neck and breasts. I didn't comment, but I drank in the sight. She noticed them in the bathroom. She had more on her hips in the shape of my fingers. I stood in the hall, watching her reaction as she took an inventory of the wreckage I had left on her body.

I was just getting concerned that she would be upset, when she stood taller, prouder. "Beautiful," I spoke as I walked in, kneeling to kiss each bruise. We dressed quickly after that and went to brunch.

At the restaurant, I held her hand across the table, playing with her fingers. "So, what was that about last night after you talked with Christy?"

"I don't know why I reacted like I did. She was talking about their relationship and how they sometimes have other people in the mix and...then she was talking about wanting to be tied up, and I couldn't stop myself from wondering if *you* had tied her up ever, if you had messed around with them. And then, it snowballed. It doesn't really matter if it was Christy or someone else right? Because you've done this all before. And..."

Was she trying to call me out on my previous experiences? Fuck that. My voice got hard. I wasn't willing to let either of our pasts impact anything between us now. "And what?" I took my sunglasses off so there was nothing between us.

"And well...it's all new to me. I feel like I won't be enough."

I sighed in relief that we didn't have to have the exes conversation.

"But it's more than that too. It gets to me that there have been other women."

"I see where you're coming from. Let's back up a bit. I've never tied Christy up or fucked around with her. Jason and I have shared women before." I waved off her reflex shock at that. "We've been friends for a long time, before Christy, and it was part of us partying back in the day. When he met Christy, he knew that he didn't want his best friend fucking her too. I've never really had a relationship with someone where it was an issue until I met you. I don't want to share you, with anyone." I suppressed a possessive growl and grabbed at her fingers instead. I looked at her, hard. "There is no one for you but me. I will not tolerate anyone else touching you." *Fuck, take it down a notch, Stone.* "You're what I want. It would be very hard for me if you were to fuck around with someone else."

Her face was sweet-soft in concern. "I don't want someone else to touch me the way you do. Xander, please don't even think about that." She squeezed my fingers, mirroring my possessive gesture. "I'm not interested in anyone else. I'm just worried I won't be enough to keep you happy."

Spoken like a true sub. I smiled, but her expression changed to open curiosity, as she added, "Have you seen them have sex?"

"Oh yeah, at the club, in his bar, in the car. At the Window, I've seen them playing with other people. Sometimes Christy likes to get tied up and be tormented. It's not really Jason's go-to move, so he asks me advice sometimes. It's kind of weird I guess. I know a lot about their sex life."

"How detailed are you? Are you there when he does it?" Her mouth was open a little and she was hanging on every word.

"It depends. Sometimes I have been, other times he preemptively asks my advice. Christy is into some wild shit, but she's not my girl and she's not my kind of girl. Do you understand me?" She needed a little reassurance—I could tell—so, I gave it to her. That was my job now. To give her what she needed, what I thought she needed, even if she didn't ask for it.

Her eyes widened, then she dropped her gaze, murmuring, "Yes."

I wished there was a sir tacked on. A surge of lust went through me at her deference.

"Come on. *You* are my girl and my kind of girl and I want to do more things to you." I stood, holding a hand out to her, "Let's go."

* * * *

I made her undress as soon we walked in my apartment, saying, "No clothes for the rest of the day."

There was a little more push in me, and she had more to give. It was perfect. She undressed immediately and I tangled my fingers in her hair, kissed her and stepped around her to push her forward — toward my bed. I drove her until her knees bumped the foot of the bed. Then I bent her over, face on the mattress. I watched her there for the moment it took me to get my cock out.

With no other preamble, I pushed into her. She was wet, but not nearly lubricated enough and the tight dragging sensation was amazing. I fucked her hard and fast, just for me. And she adjusted and absorbed it without complaint. I smiled in satisfaction, and anticipation of possibilities starting to churn in my mind.

I kept her my little pet all day. We snuggled on the couch. I didn't make her sit on the floor, but I thought about it. We watched some movie, but I was much more focused on her naked body curled into mine. I tried to keep my hands to myself as much as I could, to let the anticipation build.

In the early afternoon, I fed her some juicy slices of peach, and the way she moved her mouth and tongue to catch each drop made me hard again. I sent her to bed.

"Kneel in the center of the bed and wait for me." I watched her scamper away, smiling at the jiggle in her ass. She got herself in position as I put dishes in the sink. I made my way to the bed, watching her face. I couldn't decide if I wanted her to wait looking at the floor, like I had most other subs do in the past, or not. I liked the deference of that, but her eyes were such a great barometer of what she was thinking and feeling.

I wanted to do something more intense, now that we had actually slept together. Once she was situated, I stepped past her and got a blindfold and handcuffs from my play drawer and dropped my line from the ceiling to just above her. I climbed up on the bed, behind her and lowered the blindfold over her face. Her breathing picked up again. I crawled in front of her, enjoying that I was taking more away from her. Her clothes, her sight now.

"Put your hands out, little girl." She moved as I told her to and I cuffed her. She was sitting back on her heels, knees slightly spread. If she was self-conscious about her nudity, she didn't show it. I wanted a portrait of this.

She was about a foot behind the line hanging from the ceiling. One of the great things about owning the building and overseeing the remodel was that I'd been able to build with my kink in mind. I had a system of winches, rope and pulleys over my bed, but had had the interior decorator hang long sheets of fabric to frame the bed...and hide the apparatus from plain sight. With no regular play partners for a while, I had considered taking it down over the summer, feeling like it was mocking me. I'd never got around to it and now was happy about that.

I connected the chain between the cuffs to the ring at the end of the rope. I went to the wall and ratcheted the line back up. She gasped at the initial pull on her arms then let it ride. I pulled until her arms were straight overhead, pulling her up on her knees, but not very tight.

"God, you're gorgeous. Stretched and waiting. Wondering what next."

I turned on some music, my Lana Del Rey mix. Leda didn't speak as I climbed back on the bed in front of her and started touching her, knowing how totally vulnerable she felt. I kissed her and she turned her head to kiss me back. I got undressed, hanging on to the nipple clamps I had in my pocket and stood at the foot of the bed, watching her. She almost looked at ease, as if this wasn't new to her. *Time to change that.* I pinched her nipples, preparing them for the clamps. She made soft sounds deep in her throat, but didn't open her mouth to let them out. I clipped the clamps to her nipples, but didn't crank the screws down enough to hurt. The chain between them looked exotic, like she was decorated for me.

I stepped around the end of the bed, looking at her from different angles. "Spread your knees, little girl." She did, a little. "Wider." I pushed against her thighs and she moved. Her body was stretched tighter, taut in her bondage. So sexy.

I dropped onto my back and shimmied under her. I put my mouth on her, enjoying the sensation of her trembling thighs brushing my shoulders. I teased her with my lips and tongue. She held for a few seconds, but then gave in to the urge to roll her pelvis across my face.

I steadied her with a hand on her hip, squeezing her. She knew I wanted her to hold still. I kept licking at her and used my other hand to press fingers into her pussy. She was sopping wet, the moisture easily coating my fingers.

Chapter Twenty

Leda
Lana Del Rey, Cola

He pushed my knees farther apart, and my arms were tighter still. His mouth worked at me between my legs, kissing and licking up my thighs. I couldn't think of anything but him. The burning in my shoulders and nipples didn't matter, just his lips. He sucked at my thighs and licked in the crease where my leg met my lips. He ran his tongue over my lips, playing with me. His mouth and tongue tormented me. With my eyes covered and the music loud enough to obscure most sounds, my whole world contracted down to this man licking and touching me, my helplessness and the smoldering burn in my nipples.

I felt my orgasm looming when he pulled his fingers from me. His tongue continued abusing my clit and his sopping fingers slid around to my ass, pressed against me there. Lubricated with my own juices, his finger pushed in relatively easily. I felt more than heard him when he groaned against my wet skin. His finger pressed farther into my ass, and it was a curious feeling, clearly the same set of nerves that fed my pussy, but so different. The pressure was delicious, the violation intense and the stretchy tightness burned a little, only serving to echo the burning in my nipples. I moaned again as he started sliding his fingers in and out of my ass, distracting me, firing little darts of pleasure and shame through my skin.

My curiosity and shift in focus had delayed my orgasm, but it was still there, building. Once his finger was buried in my asshole, he pressed it in various directions, letting me feel the different types of pressure and stretch. Waves of self-consciousness were quickly dispersed by the assault of pleasure in my body. He began pistoning his finger in and out of my ass with increasing roughness and speed, without slowing his tongue on my pussy and clit. An orgasm built in my pelvis and I shifted my hips over his face, making guttural sounds, like an animal in rut. My shoulders were killing me and my nipples were aching, my ass felt speared, but his hot mouth pushed me harder.

I whimpered, a vague panic at the prospect of an orgasm while completely bound. There was no way to twist away from or into it. His hands were locked on me and I was stretched too tight to get away from him. I quaked and panted, trying to control the rising tsunami tide that was threatening me.

But I couldn't control it. *He* controlled it. I babbled incoherently, begging him to stop, to never stop, to fuck me and destroy me. Anything he wanted.

"Get my face all wet, little girl. Let me feel how hard you come for me." The heat of his breath against my pussy triggered a deluge of sensation.

"Ohfuckohfuckohfuck. I'm gonna come, Xander." My moans increased in intensity and the world narrowed further, to only the sensations of my body. He reached up with his free hand and pulled the chain connecting the nipple clamps. The sting of them coming off so roughly, followed by a rush of pain, crashed into the feel of his mouth and fingers as my orgasm exploded through me. The muscles of my ass spasmed because his finger — fingers — *did he press more in?* — were there, stretching me, prolonging the orgasm. A gush of fluid released from my pussy. I could tell from the shift in his cheeks he was smiling against me. Aftershocks of pleasure ran through me, but only for a few seconds because he was moving — off the bed, fingers and mouth away from me.

I heard a metallic sound, and suddenly there was slack on the binding at my wrists. My arms dropped down and he was behind me, pushing me over. My arms were sore and weak from being stretched and I couldn't catch myself. He grabbed around my waist and lowered my face and chest to the bed, my bound wrists under me.

"There's my pretty girl," he murmured, skimming his fingers over the curves of my hips. He was naked and his cock was rigid against me, but he didn't put it in. Instead, I felt something pushing at my ass. It was wet and cold and rounded smooth. The shock of something cold and liquid on my skin made me jump, but soon there was a new pressure against my ass, which claimed my full attention. He pressed and it slid into me, with that intense burning and stretching like his fingers. It got wider and tighter then *pop!* It was narrow again and in me, stuck. With no waiting, his slipped his cock into my pussy.

Oh fuck, it feels tight and impossible.

I planted my face into the mattress and let my noises go. The pressure and the fullness and the slickness and the tightness were too much. My arms ached and my tender nipples rubbed against the bed as he fucked me. Wetness ran down my legs and the stretching burn in my ass dulled to an almost-but-not-quite unpleasant feeling of being too full. His hands were on my hips, rocking me back and forth on him. In fact, he was barely moving. He was just stroking his dick with my floppy, wrung out, tight, wet body.

He started pulling me a little harder, a little faster, then he shifted his weight so that he was leaning forward, no longer pulling me. He drove his cock into me, hard enough to crumple my body under his a little with each thrust. He was grunting, thrusting with increasing intensity. He pulled out, flipped me over and splattered hot and wet across my tummy, bound wrists and breasts. I was shocked, unprepared. My breath sputtered, but before I could process it completely, he rubbed his cum into my skin and down over my clit. I tried to squirm away from him, the intensity too much, but he grabbed my nipple in his other hand and just tightened his grip when I tried to move.

"Stop it." His tone was harsh, voice raw. And he slapped my pussy. I jumped, startled by the sound and the sting, but I was almost instantly soothed by the warm pleasure that melted through me as the sting abated.

"Open your mouth." He shifted his weight over my body so he straddled my head. I opened my mouth and his semi-soft dick slipped over my parted lips. It was sticky and tasted like me as he dipped into my mouth. His balls rested on the blindfold. I closed my lips and sucked my flavor off him. He kept rubbing at me, playing with my nipples, occasionally slapping my exposed pussy, sending stinging shocks of pain quickly followed by pleasure through my clit. His cock started to stiffen again in my mouth.

Oh, Jesus, he wants more.

"Okay, little girl. Let's take our time now."

I heard the now familiar metallic sound of the winch, pulling my arms up. The mattress moved under me as he guided me to my knees, spread wide for him again. I was a little disoriented with no visual input, but I thought I was turned around from where I'd started.

The bed dipped and shifted as he slid under me. He stayed sitting up, arms around me, and pulled my face down to him for some sweet, soft kisses. It was such an odd juxtaposition — the sweetness and softness of the kissing with the aching stretch in my arms, the continued stretch and fullness in my ass.

I loved kissing him, regardless of the pain. As we kissed and his warm hands stroked my back, a strange sense of power and sensuality and sexiness flowed through me. It didn't matter that I was bound and used like this. I loved it. And my body and sexuality were the conduit to these feelings, to this connection with this man. This man that I lost track of myself with, *he* was stroking me and loving me, using me, pushing me. I knew I was safe with him, but I also knew that my definition of safety was changing. I understood what he had told me at the beginning — he would never *harm* me, but he might *hurt* me. I took a long breath through my nose and felt glorified, practically deified.

He lay back on the bed and guided my hips over his, sliding me down his cock. I started rocking and shifting my body over his, on him. With my arms bound up over my head, it felt awkward and precarious, but his hands were there, guiding me, balancing me. My pussy was tender and sore and incredibly sensitive. The fullness in my ass accentuated the tightness and I could feel each shift, each millimeter as he slid into me. I smiled, lost in the moment, unconscious of my lips moving.

"What are you smiling about, little girl?" His tone was soft and I heard the smile in his voice. He kept rocking his hips into me, guiding my hips on him. I got the impression that this was going to last a long time.

"I understand now. I trust you." Chills ran over my flesh and his hands tightened on my hips. I felt completely freed. I could soar. I could fall. I knew he'd catch me. He gave me a whole separate room in my life, a place where I could just be my most elemental, where I didn't have to manage anything.

"Elaborate." A hand stroked up my abdomen, cupping my breast, teasing the nipple.

"I don't know how to explain it. I am yours. I get it. And, I can just let go. I can stop worrying, because of you. I feel so beautiful. Not how I look, just this beautiful feel, like I'm made of light, subtly powerful, claimed, owned, cherished, relished. I can't explain it. It feels *right*." As I spoke, tears welled in my eyes and started to leak out from under the blindfold, my lips twisting with the unnamable emotion.

"Gorgeous girl, you are relished, cherished, mine." He pushed his hips up into me harder, pulling me onto him harder. Slow, soft tears kept slipping from my eyes, even as my body descended to a new level of relaxation, lulling me to a peaceful mental numbness.

* * * *

Eventually he was done with my body and untied me. He took what I learned was a butt plug out of my ass. I was sore all over, wrung out, aching, exhausted, but I felt completely cleared, washed clean. He helped me into a bath he had run while I was dozing in a post-sex hedonistic haze. He sat on the floor at the side of the tub, sipping a beer and repeatedly prompting me to sip the orange juice he had poured for me. He must have showered already because he was dressed and his hair was wet. When I was done, he helped me dry off, pausing to rub his thumbs over my wrist.

"You'll have to wear long sleeves this week. You bruise easily."

I registered this but didn't respond. The world outside his apartment wasn't registering now. Beside it was mid-October and the weather was cooler. I could wear long sleeves.

Chapter Twenty-One

Xander
Al Green, Love and Happiness

I stared at the endocrinology cascade I was supposed to be studying, but the feel of her small body next to mine, her breathing, her soft little movements were too distracting. She trusted me. She was mine. *Mine.* And it felt different. It felt peaceful to have her here, to have her trust me. I could get lost in her. We could make our own little world where I'd just own her and she'd love it.

The sex had been incredible, ridiculous. She'd dropped into subspace, becoming more pliant, languid and passive, until she'd just hung from the ceiling. She'd felt like warm, wet taffy pulled over and around my dick. The knowledge that she trusted me had been my undoing.

When I'd untied her, she'd flopped into my arms, like a sexy, used up rag doll. It was another favorite in the highlight reel I was building in my mind—all her. She looked too cute in my boxers and T-shirt, but I let her sleep. It was early evening, but I thought she was probably going to just stay the whole night. She woke when I got up for a beer. I brought her a glass of water which she drank then she fell back asleep, quickly and easily.

I studied for a few more hours, periodically watching her and daydreaming ways to torture her. Just when my eyes were starting to feel gritty, I got a text.

We need to talk. – Stacy

Not even in the least, bitch

There was a long pause and I thought she had given up. Of course, I was wrong.

I can still feel you. Let me come over.

Do not come to my home. Ever. I'm so fucking pissed at you. Find someone else to bother.

How about Leda? I could bother her.

There was a brief rush of panic at the threat, but I didn't really believe she would go that far. She and I had a long, sordid history and she had never brought any other girls from my life into it. She was always only interested in fucking with my head. But I was clearheaded in a way that I hadn't been in the past and it allowed me to see through her bullshit.

The threat hung in my mind, but I chose not to respond, at least until I had calmed down enough to be more rational. Leda turned in her sleep next to me, rolling so she was facing away from me. The wall sconce on my side of the bed cast her in a warm, amber light. Her hair was loose, flailed about behind her, the lines of her back soft. I didn't want any of Stacy's bullshit, *my* old bullshit, to touch Leda, never wanted her to even be aware of it.

* * * *

The next few weeks were filled with school, but only as a break from constantly being on her. She knew she was mine, on the surface. She hadn't really learned what that meant yet, but I pushed her, tried to make her understand. She didn't really seem to have limits.

I wanted her to find her limits so I had something to push on, but she tried everything I brought to her. She acquiesced. She adjusted and gave in and allowed. Admittedly, I hadn't pushed as hard as I might have if she hadn't been a kink newborn, but it was like once she'd tasted it, she couldn't stop.

I loved it, of course, but it unnerved me too. Usually, if something seems too good to be true, it is. I tried to nudge up against her limits with some things that didn't seem too rough or fucked up. I repeated the nipple clamps and butt plug. I did want to fuck her ass, and I knew I would at some point, and she seemed completely at ease with that. No reservations.

One Saturday night, I tied her, bent over the back off the couch, and did other shit for an hour or so. She was antsy, but didn't speak as I cleaned some things in the apartment, ordered some food from Chen and went down to grab it. When I came back up, I caught her shifting her weight and thought that she might be getting uncomfortable. She still said nothing, and that got the half-wood to full attention. I dropped the bag of greasy Asian goodness on the counter and unzipped as I walked over to her. She wasn't wet at all, only had the baseline moisture that some females always had, so slipping my cock into her felt rough and tight. She stifled a sob against the upholstery of the couch then moaned deeply as I fucked her. She went liquid over me almost immediately and I came, untied her and snuggled her up into my bed. She just took it all in stride, like it was normal. I knew it wasn't normal.

It was unnerving that she accepted my dominion so easily, wore it with such grace. There had to be a disconnect somewhere. I'd wake in the middle of the night and push her legs apart. As she would just be opening her eyes, I'd start fucking her and she would just lie there, allowing it. Never commenting that she was tired. Never annoyed that I was waking her up. She'd just smile at me and stretch out against me, wrap her legs around my torso and rock into the rhythm of my thrusting, sleepy softness to her features.

After a few weeks like this, I decided I had to push her a little harder. I had gone to Shibaricon a few years back and decided to try some of those techniques. I put on some old R&B that was completely incongruous with having her thighs tied to her ankles so all she could do was kneel at my feet. I box-tied her arms behind her back, with one loop loosely around her neck. Once she was restrained, looking up at me with her big, liquidy, innocent eyes, it was like there was nothing else for me but that room, those eyes, that mouth. I needed her to know that there was nothing for her but that room and me.

Squatting down in front of her, I touched her face with my fingertips and her lashes fluttered closed as she breathed into it and angled her head to the side to push into my hand more. I lightened the pressure of my fingers and traced them down to her collarbone. She slowly opened her eyes and met my gaze, but didn't speak—she had already learned not to speak unless spoken to when we played.

I sat back on my heels and pulled my shirt off. Satisfied, greedy excitement crossed her features and I smiled. *She thinks I'm gonna fuck her soon, that this will be quick.* I laughed to myself. She wanted it and didn't balk at all the shit I did to her because she got off most of the time. She could handle delayed gratification, but could she handle orgasm control, orgasm denial? I decided that she wouldn't come that night, but I would most certainly torture her some. I traced my fingers over her breast, to her nipple and just squeezed lightly. She tensed, expecting harder pressure, but I left it light and moved my hand down to her tummy, then between her legs. She was wet, soft lips parting for my fingers and leaving me sticky.

I stroked over her until her breathing became heavy and pressured. When her hips started rocking against my hands and she was getting wetter, I scooped my fingers across her, collecting what moisture I could, and stood, pulling my cock out. Standing right in front of her, I started stroking my cock with her lube. Her lips parted and she met my gaze, expecting a command, some direction, rough handling or at least use of her mouth.

I didn't slow my strokes and I knew my face was blank. She stretched up toward me as much as she could in her restraints, nonverbally letting me know how much she wanted me to use her...in the particular way that she wanted to be used. That was the lesson—*I use you how I want.*

Confusion and frustration crossed her features when she realized I was fucking with her in a whole new way. Then she looked a little disappointed, sad a bit and my cock swelled in my hand. A drop of pre-cum dampened the head and I felt myself start to tighten.

"Open your mouth, girlie." My voice was tight and strained as I held myself back from ejaculating until her mouth was open. I came hard, splashing in her mouth. When I finished the post-come aftershocks, I tucked back in my pants and walked away.

I smiled at her small sound of disbelief. I got a glass of water and leaned against the counter, watching her. There were a million jumbled thoughts running though my head — the things I wanted to do to her, say to her. How I wanted to make her miserable in a sexy, sensual, degraded way. How some of the most vulgar thoughts went through my mind when I looked at her pretty little self all tied up and confused, my taste in her mouth.

Once I had recovered a bit, I strolled back to her, where she was still silent, waiting. I knelt down on the floor, right behind her and pulled her back to me. She was helpless and spread out in front of me. I traced my hands down her shoulders to her hips, keeping the pressure light. Bringing my hands to her front, I let one rest low on her pelvis, just touching the top border of her cute little thatch of hair. The other hand drifted up her chest, between her breasts until I could wrap my fingers around her neck, just lightly, just letting her know how much worse this could be.

She sighed deeply and dropped her head back against my shoulder. As much as she could let the tension out of her body with all the rope, she did. I traced my fingers over her breasts, lightly still, tracing around her nipples, letting her lean against me. I turned my face into her hair and breathed deeply. She smelled like purity, clean. The sadist in me wanted to make her dirtier. The part of me that was lonely wanted to keep her safe forever.

As I licked her earlobe, I trailed my fingers over her body, slipping one into her mouth. She sucked on it like she was grateful, and my cock started to twitch again. The harder my cock got, the more I wanted to defile her. I took my finger out of her mouth and dropped it down, grasping her pussy, rubbing her clit. As her breathing got heavier, harder, more pressured, I increased the pressure on her clit, just until she started moving her hips a little against me.

I dropped my fingers farther and pressed into her cunt, but just left them there, not moving. She whined a little and rocked her hips as much as she could. *God, such a good little whore.* Her breath came hard and she turned her head away, eyes closed.

"Little girl, what are you doing?" I kept my tone light, but there was a hint of judgment there too. She moaned, knowing she wasn't supposed to talk unless I prompted her for an answer. I flexed my fingers in her pussy. "This is mine. What are you trying to do with it?"

She pushed her hips forward again, begging with her body. I wanted to tell her what a shameless, degraded, depraved little slut she was. I wanted to show her.

"What do you want, little girl?"

She looked at me, eyes wide and imploring. She opened her mouth to answer me, and I pulled my fingers from her cunt and shoved them in her mouth, deep enough to gag her. Her eyes went wide and watered a little against the reflex. My cock was harder again and I started stroking my fingers in and out of her mouth, letting my own tension build.

"All of you is mine, is for me to use however I want to." Her eyes questioned that, and I jammed my fingers further in. She shifted to take them, a little bit of saliva drooling out of her mouth. "Even if that means barely using you at all."

A sad acceptance settled in her eyes, and I pushed her back to her knees, off my chest. I stood, taking my pants off. Her eyes were drawn to my piece. I knew she wanted it, wanted me to fuck her. Instead, I sat on the arm chair a few feet away, just watching her and stroking my cock. Her lips were still wet, and a little drool was on her chin from my fingers as I'd pulled them out. Her chest was flushed and her eyes were wet. A good and proper little slut.

I wanted to tell her all the things I was thinking, like the whole concept of twenty-four-seven service. That she'd be mine to use anytime, anywhere. *Is that what I really want? Is it what* she *wants?*

She moaned a bit, eyes filling with tears and she leaned forward, stretching her back and imploring me all at once. Her eyes were screaming, *please*. And it turned me on all the more. I stood and walked to her and she sat back up straight, hopeful. I touched the side of her face and she pushed into my touch. Her eyes closed. I hooked my thumb into the corner of her mouth and pulled her jaw down, just as I started to come. Into her mouth again. She accepted it.

I untied her and carried her to bed. I put her on her tummy and got some massage oil to give her a good rub down. Being tied up tight like that can be hard on the muscles. She moaned a little into the mattress, and it sounded as sexual as any other sound she had ever made.

"Maybe you just make those sounds for everything? Is that the case, little girl? You can answer me." I smiled as I teased her. She flipped her naked self over with a glint of humor in her eyes.

"Not before you, Boss." She started sitting up, still smiling, and added, "Now, I'm hungry. Do I least get to eat some food, since you're apparently not gonna let me eat any cock?" She laughed hard at the shock that I knew crossed my face.

I stood up, in mock horror. "What's happening to my sweet little girl? Am I ruining her already?"

"Oh, Boss! I think I get nastier the longer I go without an orgasm. Soooooo…if you don't like my nasty talk, you could probably fix it." She little-girl flirted with me, smile on her face, laughter in her eyes.

"Well, can't change the plan once we start. Sorry, little one." I tossed her clothes to her, adding, "Get dressed. Let's get out of here for a bit and get something to eat."

She dressed and we went to the bar for a burger. She seemed on-edge, but not as bad as I would have been if our roles had been reversed. I kept finding myself staring at her, watching her across the bar where she chatted with Christy and Frank while Jason and I played pool. My mind wandered, impressed with her stamina, her willingness and just her capacity for fun and joy. But I couldn't make myself trust it. Couldn't believe that there wouldn't be some fallout, backlash, something. But she kept surprising me. The smallest little bubble of hope took hold on my dark heart, made me think that there could be someone who could take me as I was.

"Dude." Jason nudged me with his pool stick. "I'm fucking talking to you, man."

"What? Shit! Fuck off." I laughed back at him.

"What's going on with you?"

"It's like she has no limits, no push back at all. Everything I do to her, she just takes, with a smile." I was unable to even put it to words how weird it was.

"Do you want her to reject it?" He gave me a look as he set up his shot.

"No, I don't know. It just seems too good to be true. She's damaging my calm." *Firefly* was such an amazing show.

Jason shot back another Jayne quote, "Shiny. Let's be bad guys." We laughed together, but he sobered after a moment and added, "Seriously, why don't you take her to the Window? If that's not too much, you're probably set."

What would she think of the Window? It's so much more. I let the thought of her suspended, bound in rope, float through my mind, loving the image. I had suppressed so much of myself, not wanting to be vulnerable, open to possibly being rejected, or hurt, or left wanting, not to mention the risk of feeling like I couldn't control it, couldn't control myself. Or the fucked ramifications of shit going colossally wrong. I weighed the decision over, going back and forth on how I wanted to approach it.

* * * *

A week later, I still hadn't decided if I should approach it, let alone how.

"Stop being such a pussy." Jason had a talent for summing shit up.

"I'm not being a pussy and fuck you. I don't want to go through all the shit I went through with Stacy again."

He scoffed. "I call bullshit. You're afraid she's gonna freak and you'll lose her."

"Well, is that a stupid thing to worry about? And stop stalling, let's go." I slapped the mat twice to indicate I was ready to start grappling with him. It was a Monday night and Leda was home studying.

He came at me and hooked his foot around the back of my neck. When I took the bait and tried to grab his leg to figure-four him, he shifted and got me into a side guard. We grunted around for a bit trying to submit each other. Ultimately, I broke his guard and locked up his ankle. He tapped.

"Dude," he said as he grabbed some water. "Either you take her and she accepts it, you take her and she freaks, or you never take her. So you pretend to be something you aren't or give her the chance to decide for herself."

I huffed out a breath. He was right. I didn't want him to be, but he was. I didn't know how she would handle the magnitude of difference in what I did to her and what my basic drive wanted.

Chapter Twenty-Two

Leda
The Dandy Worhols, The Last High

School was consistent—more to learn than it felt like I ever could. All the time I wasn't having sex was spent studying or in class, occasionally eating and sleeping. My grades were actually quite good, for how distracted I felt. What I found was that by the end of the week, when we hadn't spent the night together for several nights in a row, my concentration got worse. It was like he purified all the distractions out of me over the weekends and, come Monday morning, I could focus on the task ahead. We were public about our relationship and no one other than Stacy really seemed to care.

At least one night per week, Xander would go to the gym with the guys for Jiu Jitsu. Christy and I would go out sometimes, and she pressed me for details, but I didn't really share anything with her.

Weeks passed like that and I was genuinely happy.

Winter break was coming. Two weeks with no school. It made me think about the possibilities of what two weeks uninterrupted with him would be like. *Maybe even dangerous.* But we both had family obligations. He was going to DC and I was going home to Chicago. Of course I was excited to see my family, but the thought of being apart from Xander was awful. I fluctuated between sadness at that thought and anxiety about finals. All our time together felt pressurized.

A few weeks before finals, we were both feeling edgy, too much pent up energy clawing at the inside of our skin. We were studying together at the library so we weren't tempted to get on each other, but the casual touches were getting more suggestive and my concentration was completely blown.

"Hey, we need to blow off some steam this weekend. Let's go to the Window." He said it so casually, like 'let's go see a movie' — which is what every other boyfriend I had ever had would have suggested to blow off steam. *He's all 'Let's just go to the sex club that our friend owns, where I have publicly tortured and fucked other women'.* It took me by surprise and I delayed answering him.

"A while back you once said something like 'we' opened the Window. Were you involved in its creation?"

He smiled slightly. "Yes, I'm a silent partner. I trust Jason. He's talented at creating fun. When he moved here, he was a club promoter and we started getting capital together. I put a bunch of money I had saved into the club." He sat back in his chair, a satisfied look on his face.

"I see." *My boyfriend owns a sex club.* "What would we do there?"

"We don't *have* to do anything, but…I need to check out of my brain some. I need to hurt someone." A cold gleam tinged with excitement burned in his eyes. "Truthfully, Leda, I want you to see that part of my world, but if you don't want to, I can live with that. But I need to go and I need to know that you're okay with that."

It was at odds with the Xander I knew and understood. He was always in control and never seemed to *need* anything. And I thought he hurt me a fair amount of the time—nipple clamps, spankings. My pride stung that I couldn't satisfy all of his needs.

"Well, I want to go, but I hate the idea of you with someone else. I mean, are you talking about fucking someone else? I can't handle that—hard limit, red." He had been trying to get me to tell him what my *hard* and *soft* limits were for a while, but it seemed like such a weird topic to me. I had no idea what my soft limits were and all the hard ones seemed like they should be obvious.

"I don't want to fuck someone else. Come with me and then you'll know I'm not fucking someone else. I'll save it all up for you." A questioning look crossed his face. "I don't know if you can handle what I'm thinking about doing. I want you to know what I am talking about before we even really consider playing this rough together."

"Okay. I'm intrigued, a little freaked out. But I'm calling Christy so I have someone to talk with when you are…doing whatever you are going to do."

"Perfect. Christy and Jason are good sounding boards." His face brightened. "And June emailed that she'll be around this weekend. I was thinking we could meet her for a drink or lunch, but this is even better."

* * * *

The rest of the week passed in a blur and I was alternately totally focused on studying and completely distracted by anticipation. All week, Xander seemed edgier, something dark in him growing. We decided to go on Saturday night and all night Friday he was antsy and distracted. We had sex, as usual, but I could tell he was holding back. And when he came, he sounded more frustrated than triumphant.

Saturday, I tried to study and couldn't, so I tried a bike ride instead when the rain broke for a while. The air was brisk and my head cleared. I felt more centered, my nerves settled. I got ready, wearing the same gun-metal gray dress I'd worn on our first date, maybe to subconsciously remind him of what we had. He came to pick me up and the tension rolling off him was palpable. He grabbed me, pushed me against his car and started kissing me. All of him was rougher, harder, pushing into me more. He buckled me in the seat, but dropped his face in my lap and bit me, smirking widely at my yelp.

At the bar, I ordered a Lemon Drop again, but he only drank Coke, telling me that he wanted to be completely clear headed. Jason and Christy met up with us there. They were brimming with barely contained excitement, and I felt so out of my element. That was how it had always been though, since I'd started dating Xander. Always off balance, always taken just a little bit further than what was comfortable. This was the first time in a while that I had really had misgivings.

Christy and I hit the ladies room before we left.

"God, girl! I can feel the nervous energy pouring off you! What are you really worried about, deep down?"

"Just the obvious, you know. I'm worried that he's going to remember that I was just a phase, that he's sick of holding back and he'll realize that he has been slummin' it this whole time with me." It came out in a rush and tears sprang to my eyes. She turned to me and hugged me.

"Leda, that boy is devastated by his feelings for you. I mean completely destroyed, wrecked."

Those were a lot of negative sounding adjectives and I wondered if I should be concerned about that.

"I think he can't reconcile being in love with you and what he should do with his basic need for some occasional sadism. He never wants to hurt you like that. You're too precious to him."

She thinks he's in love with me?

She let me go, looking in my eyes, momentarily serious. "Tonight will be a learning experience for both of you." With her eyes trained on mine, she adjusted the neck of my dress, accentuating my cleavage then reached in my bra and pinched my nipples so that they were poking through the fabric, very visible. "That'll get his attention." She smiled devilishly as she nearly skipped out of the restroom. I giggled, letting go of some of my tension as we left.

It did get his attention. When we got back to the table, he grabbed me and pressed the length of his body against me. "Chilly, little girl?"

"No. Christy."

He barked out a laugh, and tension in both of us broke a bit.

* * * *

The Blackened Window was dark and industrial feeling. When we first entered, it was into a large space that wasn't that different from other clubs I had been to. Loud music, central bar, people dancing. The floor and bar were concrete. All the staff wore all black, some with random appearing BDSM accoutrement—a guy with a spiked cuff bracelet, a waitress with a red velvet collar. Jason guided us through the space, greeting patrons and staff alike. We headed up to a second floor open loft overlooking the main party space. A cocktail waitress delivered some drinks and we watched everything spread out below us. Jason's pride was evident in his posture.

Xander exuded dominant glory. He wore all black, leather pants and a cotton V-neck T-shirt that looked expensive. His eyes ate up everything around him, maybe looking for June or someone else he knew, maybe trying to find a play partner, but he never took his hands off me. He guided me around by the small of my back, occasionally tracing his fingers up my spine to the back of my neck. I'd worn my hair down, at his request, and he tangled his fingers in it, pulling my head back for a kiss. And after a few drinks, he told me we were ready to move to more entertaining pursuits and clipped a thin bracelet around my wrist, but when he did, I noticed his matching bracelet—and that Christy and Jason each wore one as well.

"Are you ready, little girl?"

I nodded at him, wide-eyed. He took my hand and guided me through a door at the back of the lofted VIP area we'd been in. Christy came with us, but Jason stayed back to do owner-y things. Xander led the way, down a dark flight of stairs that had occasional bare red bulbs situated in the seam between the ceiling and the walls. Christy was behind me. There was no going back. Deep bass still thumped through the walls, sensuous and relentless.

The stairway opened into an area under the loft. It was like a foyer, an anteroom, of sorts. There was a type of 'coat check', where some people were dropping off or picking up clothes. They were selling a few random items there as well—condoms, lube, zip ties of varying sizes. A chill washed over me. *I am so out of my depth.* Christy was shining in all her bubbly effervescence, but Xander's whole demeanor had changed. He was at once mentally stalking through the room for someone to release all his need on and possessively holding me close to his side, clearly staking a claim.

From the anteroom, there were doorways and passages to other rooms. Christy informed me that these went to the actual play spaces. She wanted to go to the left and take me with her. She pulled my hand and Xander squeezed me tighter, shaking his head at her. She gave him a sweet, innocent, pleading look.

"Just to show her around. Besides it'll give you a few minutes to decide who you want. I won't let anyone touch her."

He relented, roughly kissing my temple as he let me go.

Chapter Twenty-Three

Xander
David Guetta featuring Kid Cudi, Memories

"All right, but seriously, be careful, Christy."

Christy saw the warning in my facial expression and understood that my instinct was not to tolerate Leda being away from me, potentially vulnerable.

Once they walked away, people noticed me. People who were regulars here, long term regulars, who had been around long enough to know me, at least by sight or reputation. The sinews of my muscles felt tight in my back and my face fell into the blanked out expression I wore when I played. I felt powerful, untouchable.

The music faded into another song that reminded me of conquest, conquering, the tremble of a woman's thighs under my teeth. I felt my lips trying to pull back in a snarl, a dark smile, full of menace and soul-deep power opened on my face.

I watched the crowd around me, nodding to a few other Doms I knew, a sign of respect, but not open challenge. There were very few that I counted friends, but many I felt a kinship with. A few that I loathed. My mind flashed through images. The snap of a dragon-tail whip against the back of a creamy thigh, the jolt of her head as I slammed her into a wall, her moan-gasp as I licked her at the corner of her jaw. Interestingly, they were all generic images, no specific woman, not Leda. This wasn't about her. It was about my dominion.

I walked to the door of the true dungeon play space, watching the various debaucheries playing out in there. Submissive-types—and a few Doms—dropped their eyes as I surveyed them. The new DM was actually a Dungeon Mistress—Kyla. She was a previous wrestler, like a real professional. The same height as me, could possibly lift as much as me. Hard, almost masculine angle to her jaw. She was dressing some new dominant-type down. I saw why behind him. A young woman with a bloody mouth, crying. And while some people may get into that intensity, she didn't seem to.

The guy made some smart-ass comment, like a total pussy, to Kyla's back as she started to walk away. She heard him and turned on her heel. Her hand snapped out from her body faster than I could follow. She delivered a strike with extended fingers directly into his trachea, and he dropped, grabbing his neck, choking and hacking, eyes tearing. She stood over him, fingers in his face. I knew what she was doing. She was rescinding his invitation into the club. Essentially, kicking him out, black-listing him in the kink community. There were always a few discrete bouncer types around and two of them appeared at her side, the threat imminent. But the crap 'Dom' got up, hands in the air, spewing some hateful shit, but leaving. The few bystanders who had been watching were nodding their heads, agreeing with Kyla's intervention.

The bouncers escorted him out and Kyla turned to the sub girl, who had stopped crying, but was looking up at her in awe. I smiled, knowing Kyla was a good hire. She escorted the girl out of the dungeon, and I knew she'd be taking her to the recovery room—a quieter space with couches, refreshments, low lighting, blankets and no sex or play allowed. As Kyla and the girl passed me at the door, she met my eyes with a knowing look, raising her eyebrows as if to suggest I could rescue this little one. I subtly shook my head and she kept moving.

There was risk in this type of play, no matter how well partners knew each other. The risk was most assuredly higher when people didn't know their partners well. I suspected that girl didn't know that guy well, and I didn't really want to play with someone I just picked up. It was too much risk. I couldn't even imagine Leda's response if I took a sub too far in front of her. Whatever it was, it wouldn't be good.

I left the dungeon, and went to find my girls. Christy was honorarily mine when Jason was busy here. Not to control or play with, just under my protection. I stood at the door of the sensualism space. Leda and Christy were on the other side of the room, holding hands and whispering to each other. Christy's face lit in lust, while Leda's was full of wonder. As I watched them, Leda's wonder faded a bit, was replaced with heat. Her nipples tightened through her dress and a flush crept up her neck. Her lips were slightly parted and her tongue was just visible at the edge of her lower lip.

Mine.

Like she'd heard me, she looked up at the door, saw me. And her body language answered mine, saying 'yes'. I pointed to the ground in front of me, thinking *Get the fuck within arm's reach of me, now.* She leaned to Christy and kissed her cheek, disengaged and came to me. As soon as I could reach her, I grabbed her hand and pulled her out of the room, pressing her into the wall. I claimed her mouth with mine, laid my body against her, driving the air from her lungs.

"You are mine. Don't forget that tonight," I murmured against her mouth, still tasting her. As I pulled back from her, I saw worry in her eyes. "And I'm yours, little girl. I won't forget." I brushed her hair back from her face, resisting the urge to tangle my fingers on the back of her scalp and bend her in front of me. Instead, I took her hand and pulled her toward the dungeon.

She hesitated on the threshold, intimidated, but I pulled her on, refusing to let her fear stop me now, unless she safeworded. I pulled her through the space, intending to find an area where I could start teasing her a little, teach her what she was now. The low sounds of ecstatic agony washed over me, occasionally punctuated by the crack of a hand or implement on flesh.

I didn't speak to her further. I can admit that I was parading her a little. I pulled her by her hand and she was so overwhelmed that she just followed where I led. *As it should be.* She looked wide-eyed, innocent and young. I knew I looked feral, predatory and menacing. I loved the dichotomy.

I passed a few areas we could have played in, but they weren't right for various reasons—a scene I didn't want to be close to, the wrong implements. We were passing another scene that I didn't look too closely at—a female sub, kneeling in front of a Domme, who was speaking softly to her. As we were about to pass, the Domme stepped back and turned, catching me in her peripheral vision. Mistress Seraphim.

I knew Seraphim from the scene, only knew her scene name. She was my age, maybe a little older, with deep cocoa skin she kept wrapped in leather and latex. She was a bitch of a Domme and was hard on her slaves...and she owned slaves, didn't just have subs. She turned and walked to us, intentionally leaving her slave, making it seem careless, as if she wasn't all that important to her.

"Xander, you brought a fresh one, very fresh by her expression. New slave?" Her voice was thick with disdain. She didn't agree with how lenient I was with subs. She was just into different shit that me. The old BDSM mantra trickled through my mind, *your kink is not my kink.*

"This is Leda. Leda, this is Mistress Seraphim. Say hello." We hadn't even discussed dungeon etiquette. But Leda was such a sub that she just naturally did a pretty good job.

She dropped her eyes, mumbling, "Hello."

Seraphim saw Leda's discomfort and decided to fuck with her, snapping her paddle against her hand with a loud crack. "Little Leda, come watch me train my slave. She has been very defiant. I think you could learn something, maybe your Master here would pick up some techniques." Her face stretched in a devilish smile.

It was perfect. Seraphim was a sadist in all senses of the word and would be open to a new way to fuck with her slave. I thought she might be able to help. I leaned into her space and spoke into her ear. "Leda is *exceptionally* new to this and I want her to see what we do without pushing her too much. Can you help me out?"

As I stood back, the evil in her eyes was awe-inspiring. She turned back to her space, saying, "Come with me."

Her slave still knelt, with her eyes downcast, breathing softly.

Seraphim turned back to me. "This thing is my pet. Why don't you take her tonight, Xander? She'll get the pain she craves. Your Leda will learn something. And I won't wear my arm out. That girl can take a lot." Seraphim rubbed her shoulder as if she remembered some previous play session that had worn her out.

I considered the offer. It was nearly perfect, but all hinged on her slave's honest consent. It felt weird to get that now, when we were practically already in-scene. "Your girl would consent to that?"

"I believe so. She's accustomed to being used by others. She knows what she is, but, for your comfort, let's ask her. Girl-thing, attend." Seraphim's voice wasn't pitched louder than usual, but her girl scurried over and resumed her picture-perfect resting pose at her feet. Seraphim tilted her chin up. Her features had an Asian cast to them and her eyes were a warm chocolate brown. Her hair fell in a loose sheet around her shoulders and she only wore a pair of black panties. "Red. I'm halting our scene for a moment. Understand me?"

The girl's tension dropped even as consternation crossed her features. "What the hell, Sera? Why are you stopping?"

"That fucking mouth." Seraphim smiled, "I'm not displeased with you, but I'd like to alter our plans.

This is Master Xander. He's a friend of mine. He is training a new slave and wants her to see what he likes. I'd like to lend you to him for the night."

A wave of pleasure washed over her features. "If it pleases you, Mistress. I am happy to serve."

Seraphim ruffled her hair. "Of course you are. Because you want to be a good little pet." She turned to me. "Will she do?"

I smiled. "What's your name, girl?"

The slave tensed, but Seraphim stilled her and answered me, "She doesn't use a name when she plays. She goes by girl, or thing, or the letter A. She doesn't want an identity." Seraphim shrugged as if it meant little, but her eyes drilled the message home to me. This was part of this girl's kink.

That set chills trickling over my skin. "I need a safeword and limits."

"Her safewords are Capsize, Red or the house safeword, Cajun. Her limits are fists, kicking, blood play. *My* limits include those, but you also may not fuck my slave without both her and my consent."

A small squeak escaped Leda's lips and I tightened my grip on her hand. "Very good."

Seraphim made a gesture that the slave was all mine, but turned back and added, "You should know she's incredibly defiant. She needs to be torn down, Xander."

I smiled again, reveling in my own wickedness. "Very good."

As Seraphim moved A to a table for me, I found a safe space for Leda, along the wall, outside of anyone's backswing. "Sit down," I said, as I pushed her shoulders down. She sat so cute, like a lady, with her legs folded under her.

I squatted down in front of her and grabbed her jaw to get her full attention. "You will sit here. You will not move. You will not talk with anyone other than me, Mistress Seraphim, Christy or Jason, and only if they seek you out. Anyone else in here tries to talk to you, I want you to immediately come get me. No one should fuck with you, but there are always predators."

She looked at me blankly.

"Little girl, tell me you understand."

Her pupils dilated and her pulse jumped. "I understand, Xander." She smiled, giving me more reassurance than any words could have, but she added, "I'm green, Boss." I kissed her hard and walked away.

I didn't look back, but it took all my discipline. Seraphim's slave was naked and arranged on a table for me. I bent down so my face was in her face and tilted her chin up to force her to look at me. "Tell me your safewords."

"Capsize, Red or Cajun," she said confidently.

"You agree to this?"

She glanced to the side and saw Seraphim stepping away to get her drink, when she looked back at me, she rolled her eyes. "Sure." Her tone was pure brat.

"What are your limits?"

"I doubt it'll matter. You look like a pussy."

I paused, surprised that she'd be so provocative from the start. I glanced at Seraphim chatting with the Dungeon Mistress, Kyla. When I looked back at the girl, challenge was written in her features as she spoke, "My Mistress has earned my respect. You haven't. Give me your worst and we'll see which one of us breaks first."

I had to stop myself from laughing. *This is going to be fun.*

I grabbed her face, squeezing enough to make her lips press open, ugly. I just held her there, staring her down and she met my gaze, daring me to hurt her. I squeezed her face a little harder, and I saw a wash of want go through her eyes, quickly replaced by that challenge again. I felt my lips quirking into a smile, and nodded as I stood. As I turned away, I was aware of Leda, watching, tension visible in her shoulders. She would learn.

Seraphim had laid her toys out on a table to the side. Floggers, paddles, rope, a Wartenberg Pinwheel, a whip, a dragon tail, restraints, gags, clamps and a few candles. I grabbed a flexible, thin cane, knowing it could be too much or just enough.

A was laying face up, legs spread, knees bent over the edge of the table. She was clean shaven, wet, lips plump. Her anticipation was visible in the way she shook a little, breathing quickly.

"Here we go."

She tensed and I waited a few beats. When her tension eased, I snapped the cane across her thighs. Once, twice. Shifting a bit, so the welts bloomed distinct from each other. She held her breath and I gave her a few more.

"Don't hold your breath or you'll pass out. That would be disappointing."

I held her gaze as I dropped a few more swats across her thighs, delivering the last one high enough that it was at the crease of her legs meeting her hips. The cane just caught the bare mound of her pussy. She whined and moaned, starting to squirm.

I stepped closer to her, steadying her, my hand on her tummy. She moaned again and pushed her body into my hand, a fine sheen of sweat already making her skin a little tacky. I bent across her body and picked her head up by her hair.

"Are you going to hold still or do you need to be tied up?" I knew my face was blank and my voice was cold. I didn't care about warm fuzzies right now. I didn't care if she liked me, thought I was a 'good guy'. None of that mattered. All that mattered was that she respected me, feared me.

"Yeah, why don't you tie me up? It'll be fun." Then she fucking winked at me and smiled.

I laughed as I stepped away to grab the rope. I wound it around her body and the table, with a loop around her neck that would be pulled if she moved her limbs too much. I liked the predicament bondage, where moving one thing caused a different problem for a sub. As I stepped back, Seraphim was there, handing me a spreader, nodding toward A's groin. I strapped it between her thighs, locking them open.

"Is she being a brat?" Seraphim smiled. She obviously had expected that her sub would give me shit.

"Just a bit." I stepped to the end of the table.

Seraphim smiled and gestured for me to take the lead.

I leaned to the girl's ear. "Ready to begin?"

She nodded, sucking in a breath and letting it out slowly.

I stood and she was laid out in front of me, a complete offering. I rolled my shoulders back and straightened my neck. I took a moment to savor her anticipation, and checked Leda in my peripheral vision. Her eyes were wide, eyebrows up, biting her lip. *Jesus.*

I snapped the cane down on the inside of A's arm and she twitched. Then I moved to alternating between sides, consistently getting the delicate flesh on the inside of her upper arm, leaving cross-hatching welts. Each strike garnered a jolt, but she was starting to pant and a thicker sweat dampened her hairline.

I grabbed the edge of the table and spun it one hundred and eighty degrees so I stood between her propped open knees, and her pussy looked so inviting, wet and just starting to gap a bit.

I looked at Leda, thinking about being inside her. She was leaning forward, mouth parted, eyes bright. She shifted her hips a little, like she was thinking about sex too. *Is she getting hot watching this?* My cock ached and I felt a growl in my throat. She smiled at me, and the bestial part of me was quelled for a bit.

Her eyes shifted to the slave in front of me and her expression was…envy. Not jealousy, *envy*. She wanted to be there. Maybe not the exact situation, but she wanted to be surrendered, vanquished, ravished. Fucking wrecked.

A took the short break to take a few breaths, and I switched to a flogger, knowing I wanted to hit her more and I'd make her bleed eventually if I kept going with the cane. A small voice deep inside was appalled and disgusted, but this was what I was. I could not — and would not — try to change it. I had been through all that self-loathing, trying to do anything else with myself and my relationships. It didn't work.

The slave-girl had closed her eyes, but tears leaked out at the edges and I smiled at how peaceful her face was otherwise.

"Starting again." I said it as I snapped my wrist, not giving her a moment to prepare. I rolled my wrist around over and over, never pausing. The falls of the flogger snapped against her skin, and I stepped around the table, moving up the side of her body and around her head. I whipped her flanks and her breasts as she shuddered and moaned, shifting her hips. I found that I liked being at her side best, with access to all of her.

After a series of strikes with varying intensity, I held for a moment, then struck her chest repeatedly. As she rode the pain and sensation, I grabbed a nipple, squeezing until she vocalized. The sound of a woman in pain, in the right pain, was perfection. She opened her eyes and looked at me, anger and warning there. She didn't like that shit. But no safeword on her lips.

Mistress Seraphim joined me at the table. Her eyes ate up the markings on her slave and her fingers followed them, lightly. The gentle sensation seemed to make her more miserable than the pain had. She whimpered, tears rushing from her eyes now. Seraphim trailed her fingers to her slave's groin, touching and caressing.

When A started to roll her hips, Seraphim stopped, smearing her own wetness on her face. Fucking degrading. I loved it. Being on the same team with Seraphim was fun. I pinched the girl's inner thigh, while Seraphim stepped away. I watched the slave as her eyes found Seraphim coming back, with a lit candle.

She made a soft mewling sound, almost a whine. I leaned down to speak directly in her ear, made my voice calm, my words distinct. "Shut the fuck up." No mercy. "If you can't shut the fuck up, I'll gag you." She moaned again and that was answer enough for me.

I went to Leda, wanting to engage her, wanting her naked. She watched me, but only moved once I extended a hand to her. She stood, smoothing her dress, confusion in her features. I brushed a loose wisp of hair behind her ear, and knelt, so I could reach under her dress.

I stroked my hands up the back of her thighs, found the edge of her panties, yanked the fuck out of them, and was rewarded with a loud rip as they came free.

"What the fuck?" Leda barked her surprise at me. Seraphim laughed, loudly, knowing where I was going.

I didn't look at Leda, only guided her hips back down to the floor, as I murmured a condescending, "Shhhh," and shook my head. "You're going to help, little girl."

She settled back to the floor, watching me. I breathed deeply and looked back at her, feeling the moisture in her panties against my palm. "You're getting wet watching this, aren't you? Still green?"

Her brow furrowed a little. "Yes, green. But, is she okay? She seems like maybe she wants to stop."

The slave-girl was lost in a sensation haze...maybe to subspace. "She knows her safeword. She has yet to use it." I said it dismissively, then added, "I don't even think I'm pushing her that hard. She seems like a pain slut." I stood up and walked back to the table, without looking back.

I crouched back at A's head and said, "How are you doing? Do you need a break?" She just shook her head, and I added, growling the menace in my chest, "I'm gonna fucking hurt you now. I'm not interested in your whining. You want that gag?"

She nodded, eyes locked with mine, begging me for more. I jammed Leda's panties in her mouth and a little shock then amusement ran through her eyes.

Seraphim joined us, smiling. "Lovely."

"What is her safe sign?" I asked.

"I brought it." She wrapped a small elastic with a bell around her wrist. "She'll ring it if she needs to you stop."

I stepped back and picked up the candle, that now had a nice pool of melted wax. Without preamble, I poured the wax on her, across her body, to her mound. She threw her head back and arced off the table, scream muffled by the gag. *Goddamn, that's nice.*

I was peripherally aware of Christy, mostly naked, sinking to the ground next to Leda. They leaned together, talking. Seraphim reached for her slave's pussy and her moans changed to something tortured and lusty, deep and nearly feline. I switched back to the cane and started pelting her body. She writhed in her restraints, crying and moaning. My focus narrowed to her body moving under my ministrations. Seraphim's laughter, the few people watching us, even Leda—they were all peripheral. It was only this girl and me and her acceptance of my pain.

It was just a moment, but those were the moments that cleansed me. Seraphim's voice brought me back, brought the world back.

"Xander, where have you been?" She said it conversationally, as she pumped her fingers in the slave's pussy.

"You know," I answered, equally nonchalant. "Been busy." I continued caning her body, thinking about Leda so close to me. A moved and moaned, alternately pushing into us and recoiling from us.

Even though Seraphim and I may have looked bored, neither of us was anything other than one hundred percent focused, constantly gauging our shared sub's response to our treatment. I took my lead from Seraphim, but the girl seemed to be on the edge of coming. My mind flashed to Leda's face when she came, eyes closed and head thrown back.

Seraphim's slave snapped her hips, bucking off the table and Seraphim and I both laughed. I asked, waving in the direction of A's pussy, "Want me to take care of that?"

The wicked gleam in Seraphim's eyes made me smile and she stepped away from the table. I caned her pussy three or four times and she screamed.

I shifted around the table so I was at her head, and muttered, "Shut up," as I pressed my dick into her face, while I kept caning her pussy.

Seraphim stood at her knee, laughing, almost bouncing on her toes with pleasure. While I struck, the girl kept screaming, but also pushed her face against me, like a cat looking for a snuggle. In a different situation, I might have thought about unzipping my pants and fucking her face, but I didn't want her. I wanted Leda. I flashed to Leda stretched out in front of me, and it was a jolt. I stopped caning A's pussy.

The moment I stepped back a bit, Seraphim slammed her fingers into her, nearly fisting her. Her cunt left a pool on the leather under her ass. She was getting tighter in her restraints, her neck muscles cording against the binding. She shifted her hips up, moaning hard. Her eyes squeezed tight and she bit down on Leda's panties. Her sounds got less and less human and she moved in rhythm with Seraphim.

Seraphim was focused on her girl, watching for a signal of some sort. When it happened, Seraphim face shifted in malice and she stopped fucking her. She stretched her own body across the girl-thing's tortured form and slapped the fuck out of her face. A's eyes flew open, with a low moan, as if she hadn't expected anything less than that.

Seraphim sneered. "You stupid cunt. You haven't earned it yet. Flip over. We've only gotten the front half of you." She reached under the table and pulled the quick release knot, yanking back so the rope slithered off her body, but she didn't move.

I crouched back at her head. She panted, gaze hazy. I spoke in her ear, "Time to move. I'm not done with you." She didn't move, and I felt the dark surge in me. "Move your ass, cunt." She still hadn't even flinched. "Or not — I don't give a shit how much you make me hurt you."

Chapter Twenty-Four

Leda
The Piano Guys, Moonlight

Everything rushed at me, slow and fast at once. Christy sucked a breath in and grabbed my hand. The degree of change in Xander was shocking. This was so far beyond the little slap-and-tickle games he had been teaching me, and that realization hit me hard, square in the chest. What had been so earth-quaking for me had barely registered on his personal kink Richter scale.

Everything up till now had been his slow way of indoctrinating me into this—to his darkness, the depths of his depravity. Even the first sensual space Christy had taken me to—a room with couches and pillows strewn about, people in varying states of undress mingled together. That had been almost peaceful.

This was not peaceful. This was my *boyfriend* torturing someone in a room full of people torturing other people.

Mistress Seraphim's slave flipped, draping her body on the table, flat on her stomach, face turned so she was looking to the side and her hips bent over edge. She was tear-stained, but not suffering, only acceptant. After a moment of staring directly at me, she registered that she was looking at me, and she took a deep breath, smiling. Her gratitude crossed the space between us.

I contemplated that. Despite what this looked like, she was at peace, grateful even. *What was it like to be so surrendered, to be at peace?*

Jason found us, breaking me out of my contemplation. He squatted and said, with a laugh, "Why the fuck are my peeps sitting on the floor in my club?"

"This is where Xander put me so I'm not moving." I said it with a smile, but I think my unease was palpable. Christy laughed and stood to kiss her boyfriend. She whispered in his ear, likely recounting the recent exchange and they sat back down with me.

"It's been a really long time since he's let himself go like this. I think he thought he could just shut it off in med school or something."

Jason said it as a sort of apology. I was about to respond, but my words were cut off by a loud smack.

Xander was using Mistress Seraphim's paddle on the girl—her ass and the back of her thighs. A single smack echoed through the room and she moaned, the sound half agony, half rapture. But then she wiggled her ass at him and giggled, her body jiggling some with her laugh. *Jesus* Christ, *this girl is taunting him.*

She twisted her neck to look over her shoulder at him. He looked back at her with the same disbelief I felt, but then he laughed. Mistress Seraphim stalked up to the head of the table and yelled at her, while Xander pulled his shirt off. His torso glistened with sweat and his laugh still crinkled around his eyes. Christy and Jason both looked at me to see my reaction, then back to the small show. I knew my face was agape, just shocked. I wondered if it was getting out of control, but... *Xander needs this, right? Does he really need this?*

I took a deep steadying breath and tilted my head back against the wall, closing my eyes for a moment. When I opened my eyes and looked around, a small crowd of people had gathered, a surreal assortment of leather and status.

Xander took a homerun swing at her ass with the paddle and she screamed, loud enough that most of the other noise in the play-space silenced for a moment as people looked to see what was happening. He started fucking with her, varying the speed and intensity of the paddling. He'd start with a medium intensity and pace then occasionally hit her so hard her whole body jerked on the table. After a few moments, he paused and she braced for another, but he just tapped her lightly and laughed.

He rubbed his hand over her ass, squeezing the bruised and welted skin. Her body was completely slack, completely conquered, completely accepting. Mistress Seraphim squatted at her head, speaking to her in a steady stream. I couldn't tell if it was encouragement or invectives at this point. A tried to lift her head and chest off the table and Xander pushed her back down on the table with a hand between her shoulder blades. He leaned over her quaking body, and said something in her ear. She raised her arms up to the top of the table, over her head as he stood and walked away for a moment. Seraphim grabbed them, pulling her tight.

He came back with a flogger and whipped it along her sides, getting the tender skin of her underarm, the sides of her breasts and her waist. She panted and shook. A heavy feeling settled in my stomach.

This may be too much. I don't know if I can do this. I can't do this.

Mistress Seraphim held a hand up to stop Xander, telling her slave to flip. Interestingly, she moved with speed to follow her Mistress's commands now. Seraphim's face melted into a beautiful smile and she murmured something as she yanked my panties out of A's mouth, tossing them aside. She unzipped a hidden zipper in her BDSM-fanstasy get-up. It went from the front to her ass, effectively granting access to her pussy. She climbed on the table and lowered herself onto her slave's face. The girl's jaw and neck flexed as she licked against Seraphim's grinding. The Mistress grabbed the flogger out of Xander's hand and started fucking her girl with the handle. He stepped back, hands in the air, but smiling.

But he didn't move away. He just stood right there, watching them. When the slave started arching her hips up, he pressed his hands on her hips, holding her down so Mistress Seraphim could continue fucking her. The Mistress' breath started coming in pants.

Seraphim came almost silently and slipped her legs back off the table. She stepped to the side of the table, so she could continue fucking her slave and whisper in her ear at the same time. I could see her lips moving in a rushed murmur, telling her to wait, to hold it in, wait, not yet. A's body was shaking and her eyes were closed tight. She panted and murmured back to her Mistress, begging to come. Seraphim smiled and told her slave to come. She immediately obeyed, pussy spasming as Seraphim slapped at her clit a few times for good measure.

Xander stepped back, brushing his damp hair back off his forehead. A took several deep breaths and sat up, waves of pleasure still quaking through her. She was tear-stained, wax cracking over her hatch-marked skin, but still had a dreamy smile on her face.

Seraphim stepped to the table and gently ran her hand up her sub's back to her hair and whispered something in her ear. A gracefully slipped off the edge of the table and crawled to Xander. At his feet, she sat back on her knees and looked up at him, offering herself, the spreader bar still holding her knees apart, her pussy completely visible. The muscles of his torso bulged and tightened, but he only reached out to pet her hair a few times, shaking his head, with a somewhat regretful smile on his face.

Her eyes now downcast, I read her lips as she said, "Thank you, Sir."

As he stepped back, a few of the on-lookers clapped, which sort of took me by surprise. He looked up, smiled and acknowledged the audience for a small moment. Then, he turned his heated gaze on me and crossed the distance between us. He yanked me up, kissing me, flattening me against the wall. He reached under my ass and hitched me up and I wrapped my legs around him. His Dom-adrenaline rippled off him and he seemed almost mindless.

I pushed him back just the slightest amount. "Hey, Boss."

Chapter Twenty-Five

Xander
Maroon 5, Animals

Her voice was soft, sweet, sounded like heaven, and made me need her more. My brain was in overdrive, but the term of endearment she had assigned me was the clearest sign that she still wanted me.

"I need to be in you." My voice was harsh, hoarse and gravelly. I opened my attention to my peripheral vision, focusing on Jason. "Jason. Office keys?" I held my hand out, knowing that Jason knew what I wanted and why. He dropped them in my hand, wordlessly, his face was solemn and I pushed aside the thought that he might not have been pleased with me. Didn't care in that moment.

I dropped Leda's legs to the ground and turned, yanking her with me by her wrist. I didn't care if it hurt a little, didn't care how it looked to anyone else. We crossed the dungeon, through the foyer, up the back steps. She didn't speak, but her breath came fast.

In the loft, I pulled her with me, along the back wall until the office door knob was in my hand.

I opened the door, pulling her in behind me, turning and shoving her down on the couch. The latch of the door clicked and I felt victorious, like I had trapped her. I wanted to be balls deep in her immediately, but loved the anticipation too much to just dive in.

"Come here, little girl." It was a command, only meaning make yourself available and open to me. She was under me on the couch and I couldn't get enough of touching her. I dropped my mouth on her legs, pushing her knees up, bending her in half so I could lick the back of her thighs. I held her in place with my shoulders, stretching back up to kiss her face, bite her neck, as I unzipped my leathers. I pulled my cock out and found her pussy like it was my home. I shifted her legs around me as I entered her. Her gasp was a reward, sending neurotransmitters singing through my brain.

She was soaking wet, so slick and slippery and she shifted her hips, angling to take more of me, to meet my rhythm. I tore at the neckline of her dress, wanting her tits in my hands. Her luscious fucking tits. Her luscious fucking body. *Could I ever tolerate the marks on her that I'd just left all over that girl?*

"God, your body. Fuck, Leda." I wasn't even conscious of what I was saying, mumbling fragments of my thoughts as they went through my consciousness. I needed to fuck her more, harder, deeper. I slammed my hips at her and she only whimpered, gasping against my chest. And the fucking animal I was thrived on it, fed on it, just wanted more. I kept the onslaught, unrelenting, twisting my hips to vary the pressure.

Her breathing came faster, whimpers more frequent. I wanted to cover her with my body, my scent, all of me, mark her mine forever. Claim her in every way that mattered. "God fucking dammit. What are you doing to me? I wanna destroy you, have you forever."

She moaned back at me, wordless, accepting, imploring. I grabbed her shoulders, pulling counterforce to my thrusting. She murmured encouragement of some kind and it was enough.

"You are mine—all mine, no one else, ever again." I squeezed a hand around her throat and she gasped, actual fear in the sound.

It pushed me over the edge and I came, squeezing the breath from her, groaning, getting off on her strangled cries matching mine.

I dropped my weight on her, relaxing my hand on her throat. I was completely spent, drained, emptied. I never wanted to let her move. I wanted her to stay under me, legs wrapped around me. She did. She lightly ran her hands up and down my back. Both our breathing calmed and slowed back to normal as my dick softened.

I brushed the hair out of her face, my worries rushing back at me. Worried that she was terrified of me, that the sex we had just had hadn't been wanted, that I'd misread her. Knowing that I wouldn't blame her if she told me to fuck off. But…if that wasn't what was going to happen, I had to engulf her, let her know she was absolutely safe with me.

"Honey girl, are you okay? Was it too much?" My voice was calmer, but even I heard the anxiety there.

She took a deep breath and I braced myself. "I'm okay, Xander. It may have been too much, but that's what you always give me. Too much, more than I think I can handle. It's one of the things I love about you."

I went still and quiet. *Did she just say she loved me? She could love me?*

Moisture stung my eyes and the most immense sense of acceptance and joy went through me. I smiled, knowing she couldn't see it. It wasn't for her. It was for my pure happiness. "You're amazing, little girl."

Relieved, I sat back, pulled her into my lap to snuggle. I couldn't keep the shit-eating grin off my face. When I had a little more control of myself, I shifted her and stood. "Let's go be social a bit."

"Will you come dance with me some? Please?" She was so sweet and I wasn't in the mood to deny her anything.

We had a few drinks on the couches in the loft. Christy and Jason came and went a few times. But we snuggled into each other like we had a happy secret that was just ours.

"Come on, Boss! I love this song! Come dance with me." She leaped out of my lap, smiling and holding her hands out to me in supplication.

She was so excited and cute. I couldn't say no, even though I disliked dancing. I let her lead me down the steps, a small smile on my lips. On the dance floor, she made it easy for me. I just moved some to the beat and she rubbed up on me. It was actually pretty nice.

As a song faded and another started, I heard a familiar voice, "Xander! Sweetheart!"

I felt her hand on my shoulder, turning me as I was turning to answer her. June.

She was about five foot eight, with silver-streaked red hair. Her face was plain, but her eyes were a gorgeous green and her smile was so pure, so filled with delight that I couldn't help but love her some. I grabbed her, hugging tight and kissed her cheeks. "June! How are you, love?"

She pushed back from me in surprise. I wasn't normally so effusive. A pleased confusion crossed her features. "Did you play already? You're so relaxed."

I introduced Leda and June was cordial, but eyed Leda speculatively. We danced, but couldn't really talk much over the music. After a few songs, I pulled them off the dance floor, to the loft. We had a drink with June, but I could see Leda's eyes drooping. Leda rested her head against me and I explained the night to June, who nodded knowingly.

She was only going to be in town for a few days, so we planned on meeting for brunch in the morning. As we said our goodbyes, June again gave Leda the once-over. Not in a jealous or catty way, just information gathering, recon. I wondered about that.

We found Christy and Jason in the recovery room, sipping drinks with a few leather daddies and their boys and bois. Mistress Seraphim was on another couch with A stretched out, asleep with her head in Seraphim's lap. She was stroking her hair, and I was struck by the beauty of what they shared. I caught her eye and smiled. She waved us over and the woman she had been speaking with left.

I sat in a club chair and pulled Leda into my lap. Seraphim continued stroking her girl's hair and looked up at me, pleasure on her face, relaxed. "Thank you, Xander. That was excellent and exactly what she needed." Her smiled widened as she turned her focus to Leda, "And, Leda, you did better than I expected. You're a good girl for Xander."

Leda blushed and smiled at the praise. I reflexively tightened my arms around her, proud of her, pleased with her. She responded by shifting in my lap to lay her head on my shoulder. She drifted in and out of sleep there as Seraphim and I spoke, rehashed the scene, comparing notes, discussing safety, limits. I was pleased to get to know another Dominant, and could have spent another hour talking with her, but Leda was clearly done.

I carried Leda to the car, her head lolling around. A few people looked askance, but I knew they were newbies and offered each a full smile. She woke a little as we passed through the front because it was so loud. But once I got her into her seat and buckled in, she dozed again. I took her home, smiling the whole way. I got her tucked into bed, in my T-shirt and nothing else — sexy as fuck. She was beautiful as she slept. I took a quick rinse off shower and climbed into bed next to her, feeling like everything was right.

* * * *

In the morning, we had brunch with June at the Cat's Meow. Most of the conversation was June and I catching up, reminiscing. I had met June and her husband and Master, Michael, very early on in my time in the DC scene. Leda sat at my side, quiet and observing. Occasionally, I would catch June with that same speculative look on her face, watching Leda and how we interacted.

I hadn't really had many relationships when Michael had been mentoring me in DC. Certainly, nothing like this. I knew June worried about me. She was my kink-mom, if such a thing could exist. There was nothing sexual there. She was not sexually available to anyone but Michael. She had just watched out for me ever since Michael had put me under his protection and tutelage early on. He's a neurobiologist, so he taught me about the brain chemistry of D/s, subdrop, subspace. I combined that with what I had learned in my working life about interrogation and fear.

As June started to question Leda about her education, in a gentle, getting-to-know you way, I watched the two of them. June was twice Leda's age, but was kind to her, not condescending, as it would have been so easy to be. Leda was open. June asked about Leda's experience of med school thus far, how she liked Texas compared with Chicago. Everything but submission, kink.

As I was getting impatient, I played a game with myself that I always did when I was getting annoyed. I started cataloguing details about the surroundings or the people I was with. Leda was as she always was, soft and fresh-scrubbed, pure, sweet. Her eyes had smudges of exhaustion under them and I filed that away, knowing I needed to get her to bed sooner tonight.

June had a bracelet that I noticed as she gestured. I couldn't place it, not that I kept track of her jewelry, but in the kink world, jewelry had layered meaning. After a few moments, I reached out and grabbed her hand, cutting her off mid sentence. It was forward to touch another Dom's sub, but I knew them. And it wasn't sexual. The bracelet was beautiful, exquisitely made, twining strands of precious metals, with a small, delicate plate of metal — platinum I thought — in the middle, a small diamond accent at the end of the word.

Joujou

"June, what is this? I've never seen you wear it before."

She blushed, smiling widely. "It was an anniversary present from Sir."

Leda's eyes widened at the title, but I spoke too quickly to allow her to question it. "How many years now?"

"Twenty-four since we started dating, twenty-two since we got married." She stroked her finger across the word and my high school French came back to me, slowly. I remembered they were Francophiles. Then the translation clicked.

Toy.

Michael amazed me. He put a fucking collar-substitute on his wife that said *Toy*. The balls that man had. And that June was completely overjoyed to have it, to be marked, claimed…fucking tagged like that. Amazing. I felt the sly smile on my lips.

I'm sure June saw the wheels turning, my envy and the hope that maybe I found something with someone that would make me that happy. She leaned toward me, holding my hand. "Xander, why don't you go away?"

Chapter Twenty-Six

Leda
Brad Sucks, Making Me Nervous

June and I sat together, sipping coffee, neither of us speaking for a few minutes. "So, what questions do you have?" she prompted.

"God...all of it, I guess. Just tell me about how you do it." I didn't even know how to ask the questions.

"I had to search for my Master Right." Amusement crossed her features. "Before him, I'd find someone and think it was going to work and then something wouldn't be right. It can be really easy for subs to get taken advantage of. You have to trust your instincts and listen to your intuition more than you would if you were just vanilla, or even if you were a Dom, I think. It's just how we're wired, I guess. We want to please. We want to trust."

I nodded at her. It made sense, but I felt sure it wouldn't happen to me. Xander wasn't going to hurt me. I trusted him.

She continued speaking, leaning forward to emphasize her point. "What a really good Dom understands is that at the most basic level, a sub actually has as much control as his or her Dom. She, or he — the sub, is the one willingly giving herself, and her permission, her *consent*, is the only thing that allows the scene to continue. If the Dominant doesn't have consent, it's assault or rape. That's why safewords are so important."

"Wait, back up — what's a scene? And then tell me more about safewords. Really any terminology, because I feel a little behind in most conversations."

"Okay — a scene is what defines the boundaries of the power exchange. So, last night, when Xander played with Seraphim's A — did he start after getting her consent and then was there a clear point when it ended?" I thought back to her thanking him, and nodded. "So everything that took place within that boundary of consent was the scene. Sometimes, people have less clearly defined scenes, like my Master and I live like this almost exclusively. When we get home from work until we leave again in the morning, I'm his."

"Jesus — is it all like what Xander was doing last night? I mean he kind of kicked the shit out of her."

"No — there's a lot to explain to you. You're a true neophyte." She sighed like she was starting a big project. "For me, sometimes it's making his dinner and doing his laundry, sometimes it's begging him to use me, and sometimes, when I'm good, I do get used." A pure joy suffused through her at that thought. "But let's back up. Safewords are important because the intensity of the scene can tap into really deep feelings. Some fantasies are about overpowering someone or getting overpowered. Sometimes, when it's really good, it's so psychologically overwhelming that the sub isn't consciously aware of what she, or he, is saying."

"But wait, if they are so overwhelmed that they don't know what they're saying, what if they actually want to stop and can't say it?" *Have I found an inconsistency that may tear the whole thing down?*

"Well, the hope is that if you truly want something to stop, when you start to feel that way, you would have the clarity to safeword—because you'd be focused on not wanting it, not getting lost in it. That's why the best safewords are specific and not something one would usually say in the course of play. But sometimes people get so lost in it that they can't remember, can't bring themselves to stop it. Sometimes the mindfuck of it and the desire to please prevent the sub from safewording when they should. It's hard. It is…a thing that everyone playing should be cognizant of before it starts. And the Dominant is hopefully in tune enough to read the situation well. But we walk on the edge of risk. Everyone should do it as responsibly as possible."

That surprised me. I expected some explanation that would make everything about this seem safe all the time, risk free.

"Xander called that woman a pain slut last night. What's that? And what about her not having a name? Isn't that fucked up?" The questions were starting to pile up in my brain, coming at me out of any logical order.

She smiled. "A pain slut is a specific type of sub who gets off on, who *needs*, the pain to get off, or at least to get lost. It's a type of masochism. I wouldn't actually characterize her as a pain slut. I think she is more of an SAM." At my blank look, she continued, "Smart Ass

Masochist—someone who goads their Top into punishing them. For masochists, SAMs, pain sluts—sometimes it's the pain itself, sometimes it's the degradation, sometimes it's the subspace." She shrugged. "About her name, or lack of one... People are into different things. It's just one way she gets what she wants out of the scene, I guess."

"Can you explain subspace?" It was fascinating, a whole other language.

"Subspace is a place the sub's mind goes during a scene—or after, sometimes. You may have already experienced it. My theory is that the intensity and the endorphins induce a kind of euphoria almost like a high. My Master talks about endorphins, various neurotransmitters and brain chemicals that act like opium. He thinks all that combines to create subspace. Either way, I love it there." She laughed and added, "I may be addicted, because I really get crabby if we don't play often enough."

"Okay...I think I may have experienced something like that. There have been sometimes with Xander where I just feel really peaceful, but it isn't a druggy feeling and it's usually right away in the...scene." I looked at her hesitantly, and flagged down the waiter to order a Bloody Mary.

She nodded. "I think you're talking about a different thing—the shedding of responsibility and burden that comes with accepting your submission and trusting your Dom to take care of you. It's one of the most attractive parts of being a sub, in my opinion. My work is intense and hard. When I come home, my Master gives me a way to take a break from it."

I nodded. It made sense—medical school had felt so overwhelming until Xander.

Her face became serious as she continued, "Has he talked with you about subdrop?"

"No, what's that?"

"Subdrop is probably one of the worst parts of being a sub. I think it is anyway. Subdrop is the emotional and physical hangover that sometimes comes from playing hard." Seeing no recognition on my face, she took a deep breath and continued. "My husband says that it's from all those brain chemicals getting used up. Just like everything else, everyone is unique, but for me, it's a feeling of nothingness in my soul. I cry and feel like I can't get out of bed. Sometimes, I get really angry at Michael, like 'how could you do this to me? What kind of monster are you?' Even though he did it with my consent, usually because I was begging him for it. Does this make any sense?"

"I don't know. Subdrop doesn't make sense to me. I guess there are times that I cried a bunch during sex or felt really emotionally raw. But I don't know... I just thought it was PMS or something."

"You know, I kinda think subdrop feels like really bad PMS. I get really moody, exhausted, sometimes even achy, depending on what we have been up to. So, the important thing then is aftercare."

"And that is?"

She nodded. "Aftercare addresses the fact that we can't play the way we play and then just get dressed and act like nothing happened. Good aftercare can help decrease subdrop too. There's no specific thing for aftercare, but the biggest parts are re-establishing security and safety by attending to one's basic needs. I think it's the responsibility of both partners, but it often falls to the Dom more than the sub. Anyway, a good cuddle, something to drink, a shower, some chocolate, comfy clothes. These are things some people use. For me, one of the most important things is when Michael reminds me that he loves me and tells me what a good girl I am. That praise makes me feel so good.

"The worst though, is when the subdrop hits a few days later. Sometimes I'm getting pissed off at traffic more than usual and crying and wanting to scream at someone. And I have to think through the last few days to see if we had any intense play. More often than not, we did and I realize that I need a little TLC. Now, here is where the aftercare becomes some of the sub's responsibility. I *have* to call Michael and let him know, so he can help me. And then it's my job to find a place and the materials to take care of myself."

"You *have* to call him or what? You get punished?" It irritated me.

"No." He voice hardened. "Can you imagine the mental acrobatics someone has to do to reconcile loving someone and wanting to hurt them? Can you imagine what that's like when she's then begging you to do it? And that you both get off on it? So, then consider what would happen to you if there was true mental, emotional fall-out from you intentionally hurting your most loved one, *and she didn't even tell you, didn't give you the chance to take care of her.* I have to call him because I love him and it's how *I* take care of *him*. Not letting him take care of me afterward is locking him out and I won't do it. We work because we are all access, twenty-four seven."

I took a deep breath, absorbing that information. This was so much more than I expected and June had thought about all this, was living it. Thoughtfully. Intentionally. "Okay, but I have to ask—doesn't it bug you sometimes? To constantly be less than? I don't know how to say it...it's like, don't the bonds ever chafe? Are you subservient to him at all times? Is there ever a break?"

"Obviously, we live in the real world and go to parties and work functions and church, where this relationship would be misunderstood, at best. He's my Michael, my husband, but at the core of both of us, he is my Master. And I belong to him, all the time, but he's pretty lenient, I think."

"What do you tell people about your relationship? I mean...when you do talk about it?"

"Oh, I have a few girlfriends who understand and are fine with it. Some of them are in the lifestyle, too. But mostly I don't try to explain it to others because they don't need to know and I don't care what they think. I don't need their permission or approval, you know?"

"Yeah, I get it." I smiled. I wanted to be as calm and confident as June. She was amazing. "Okay, so go back a little. You said a pain slut is a type of sub. Are there other types?" *Is there an entire taxonomy of kink?*

"Oh, yeah! There are probably tons of types of subs, but another relatively common type I've seen is the brat."

I raised an eyebrow, clearly not understanding.

She smiled and leaned back in her chair. "Okay, actually, let's take another step back. There is a dynamic called Big/little. It is usually Daddy and little girl. But sometimes it is Mommy/little boy or any permutation of those."

"Umm, what? That's sick!" My stomach completely dropped into my ass as I thought of all the times Xander had called me *little girl*.

"No, it isn't about *actual* fantasies of sleeping with one's *actual* relative. It's the dynamic. The Big—Daddy or Mommy—is usually this loving, benevolent, but stern force. They want their littles to be the best version of themselves and train them to this effect. But there is sex usually, too. The little usually thrives with that kind of attention and often has a cute, stereotypically childish thing going on, with an adult's insight and ability to consent. Does that make sense?"

"Hmm, I don't know. It freaks me out a little. Like, Xander calls me Little Girl, all the time. Is he...my Daddy?"

She shrugged. "Not if you don't want him to be. Not if you two haven't negotiated that."

"Negotiated? That doesn't sound sexy."

"Come on, Leda. Consent is sexy. Like that dry mouth, sweaty palm, it can't happen soon enough type of consent. That's sexy as hell." She smiled and took a sip of coffee. "Negotiation helps everyone lay out the boundaries, or limits, early on. But more than limits, it lays out desires, hopes — what you *want*. How many non-kink partners have ever asked about what you wanted in bed, before you got there?"

I'd never had a boyfriend ask me if I *consented* to something he did, never had someone try to find out what my limits were. It had always seemed like consent was assumed and it was my responsibility to let him know *after* he had crossed a line. It was a thunderclap of realization and insight into the absolute bullshit of that. And I thought about Xander pushing off sex in the beginning of our relationship. I thought he just wanted me strung out on him. And maybe it was that, but it was also about real and true consent. He wanted my wholehearted, panting at his feet, tears in my eyes, needy consent. The revelation spread through me and I smiled at June.

"I get it. I think I do anyway. Xander held off on sex with me for a long time. But, that chick last night — she acted so…aloof at first, but I saw her. She loved it and she really didn't want it to stop, right?"

"She is a much more seasoned player than you are. My guess is that she has a degree of clarity that you might not, yet. And she and Seraphim have played together for a long time. Seraphim can read her well." June shrugged and flagged the waiter down for refills of our coffee.

After the break of getting our drinks filled, I started back into the conversation. "This idea of a little, I don't know. If they're in a child's mentality, can they truly consent?"

"Of course they can. They're still adults who can still walk away any time they want. Who can still say this is not what I want. But you're skirting around a really important issue." She raised an eyebrow at me again and I shrugged. "For many subs, there's a risk of wanting to please and submit to someone else, more than wanting to take care of oneself. I don't know very many in the lifestyle who haven't done something that they later wished they hadn't because they were so into the scene that they didn't think through whether they really wanted to do something. It's Risky, with a capital R."

I took a deep breath and weariness washed over me. What was I doing? Was I really exploring the possibility of letting someone else destroy me to build me back up or something like that? But I had regrets in previous relationships too. Was it really all that different? My thoughts were spiraling, so I latched on to the last thing that made real sense to me. "Okay…go back, what is a brat?"

"So, a brat usually has a Daddy type of figure and she acts out to draw his punishment. She'll act bratty to force his hand, so to speak." She smirked at her pun. I heard her words, but it didn't really pull me away from my spiraling thoughts.

My voice got small and I looked down at the table when I asked, "How do you reconcile yourself to submitting to someone else so completely? I mean, not only as one human to another, but also as a woman to a man?"

She drew a deep breath and looked at me. "I wrestled with this for a long time at the beginning. How can I have worth if I let someone else use me? And what's wrong with me that I want this? Am I just twisting the usual male-dominance/female-subservience that has permeated history? How is this not abusive, right? Are these the types of questions way deep inside that are bothering you?"

I looked up at her, shaken at how well she articulated so much of what I felt and nodded.

She continued, "Well, there are two issues. One, I can hopefully clear up for you, the other you have to deal with on your own. The first is that submission is the most extreme form of feminism there is." She put up a hand to forestall me when I balked at that. "I know it sounds crazy. I'll come back to it in a second, but it sort of hinges on the second thing, which is that you have to accept your own desires. If you want to have these things done to you, then you do. It's fine."

"Okay, but I don't see how I can completely accept it without coming to terms with all the other stuff. So, go back to the feminism thing. No offense, but that's kind of fucked up, right? Like almost Stockholm syndrome-y."

"Hear me out. One of my favorite quotes about feminism is that it's the radical notion that women are people. The whole feminist movement fought for women to be able to vote and work and earn the same pay as other people, i.e. men. To be treated as equals, right? The crux of it is that a woman can do and be anything she wants—a politician, a scientist, an athlete, a stay-at-home mom, a priest—whatever, *without her value as a person being diminished*—just like a man. She has an inherent value that should afford her the same opportunities as anyone else. So, who has the right to tell me I can't be a sub, or *shouldn't* be a sub, just because I'm a woman? No one. The idea that somehow being a female sub is playing right into the misogynists' hands is a flawed argument that again takes the individual woman's agency and power away. I think this is the most feminist thing I can do, for this exact reason—it really pushes up against the notion that a woman can be anything she wants. I refuse to let anyone place limits on me based on my gender."

Her voice was fierce, but it softened and kindness crossed her features, as she said, "But the key is to accept that this is what you are—or at least what you want right now—that this is truly what you want—or this whole feminist argument kind of loses steam. I'm sure some of our feminist forebears may cringe at the idea, but if your heart's desire is to submit to Xander, then do it. It doesn't lessen you in any way. In fact, I think you become a more self-actualized person in the acceptance of yourself."

I actually got chills and tears stung my eyes. I hadn't thought this deeply about it before. And I wasn't sure if I was ready to accept it yet.

"But what about the people who will say that you only want this because you have been programmed by a misogynistic society that sexualizes female subservience?" She gave me a surprised look and I responded, "I took some women's studies courses in college."

"That's a good question, but I think it gets kind of dangerous to start to expect people to justify why they are attracted to who and what they're attracted to. I mean, can you imagine someone asking someone why they're sexually attracted to men or women? Or why blondes or why Asians, whatever? Maybe, someone will figure it out, but I guess I don't think it really matters. For me, that argument just doesn't ring true. We sexualize lots of things. Maybe it does sexualize female subservience, but it also kind of turns it on its head because of the insistence on consent and negotiation. It *isn't* something I have no choice about. And, at the end of all the intellectual debate, I'm in love with Michael for more than his ability to dominate me, but I am fulfilled, sexually and otherwise, when he does."

I took another deep breath. "Thank you, June. This was enlightening."

"What do you think? What do you think you want with Xander? I don't mean to pry, but I kind of love that boy a little. I really don't want him to get close to complete happiness and then get his heart broken." She gave me a pointed look, waiting for an answer.

Sub, my ass!

There was nothing to do but tell her the truth. "I think I'm falling in love with him, but it scares me. Last night scared me. I don't think I could handle—no, I *know* I can't handle getting destroyed the way A did last night. And I don't want Xander to settle. I don't want to feel like he's always left wanting."

"When I saw the two of you dancing, he looked relaxed and fulfilled and you looked happy and content. Nothing wrong with that. He doesn't have to get everything from one person, does he? Maybe he trains subs or is just a disciplinarian, but he's your Dom? Could you live with that? It wouldn't be the first time a couple had a relationship like that." She raised a questioning eyebrow.

My gut twisted at the thought. "My knee-jerk reaction is that I don't want to share him."

"Is that your reaction or is that what you think it should be?"

I opened my mouth to respond that it was all me, but before I spoke I caught myself. "Last night was actually a really great night. Don't get me wrong—I wouldn't want to do that every night. There were a few things I didn't love but I have weirdly mixed feelings about it."

"How so?"

"Well, in general, I didn't mind. I really had no problem with him inflicting pain, but at one point he pinched her nipples and at another point he kind of ground his dick into her face. I kind of got jealous. Then, the other side was that, at one specific point, I could hear what he was saying to her, and it scared the shit out of me. But here's the fucked up thing, June, I was *so* turned on watching him. It was like he was just so powerful and, and, and...magnificent."

"Awe. That's the feeling. You were in awe, and then you wanted him between your legs." She said it so matter-of-factly that it felt like an accusation.

I laughed self-consciously. "Well, yes. There were layers, though."

"Tell me—I'm kind of enjoying being the sub-whisperer." She smiled and sipped her coffee.

"I feel like this a lot with him—like I'm flattened, like he is so....so....*him* that I almost can't handle it. I guess its awe, but then there's darkness to it. Like I want him to take me and not like some old school romance novel. Just *take* from me, take me to whatever level he wants to. I want him to smother my existence within him." I knew I wasn't making sense, but she was nodding along with me, eye glittering, like it made perfect sense to her.

"Like you want to get lost in him?"

I nodded my agreement.

"You're his, in your heart. You're his sub. He's your Dom. You guys just have to work out the details."

Chapter Twenty-Seven

Xander
Nine Inch Nails Ringfinger (Twisted Remix)

I had been studying for about two hours when June called.

"Hey, June. How'd it go?"

"Perfect. She's lovely, Xander. She's smart and funny, but she has an independent streak in her too. She's not going to just roll over and take everything you give her."

"Good. I've had doormats. I don't love it."

"Do you love *her*?" Her tone was exacting.

"You don't waste time." I laughed, delaying an answer. She just waited in silence. "I think so. June, it's just crazy. It's like someone built her for me specifically. She responds like I've always wanted a girl to respond to me."

"So, I think she's yours in her heart, but she hasn't accepted it yet. I don't know if she will. Her brain may veto her heart. There are some objections that she hasn't worked through. I hear how happy you are, but you still need to guard your heart."

Her tone was sad, but I knew she was probably right. There was so much of me that Leda had yet to see.

"I know you're right. I don't want you to be." I paused, that crushing feeling back in my chest. "How did you and Michael know?"

"There was a moment for me. He had me bound and blindfolded at a club. He was letting newbies take turns with a flogger, so he could refine their technique. And I was terrified at the public display, being offered up like that, but he talked me through it, right at my ear. And I knew I'd always be safe with him. It was a weird place to have it all click, I guess. There was a moment when the fear just went away. But it was more than that. I don't know if there was one moment for Michael. You could call him. He'd love to hear from you, I'm sure."

"Let's get together for dinner over the holidays. I'll be in DC for about a week and a half."

"Absolutely. Why don't you come to our house? We won't have to keep our voices down while we talk about kinky shit." She half-laughed.

"That's sounds perfect. Let me know when, and I'll be there."

After I hung up with June, I turned back to my books, knowing that Leda needed to study and probably just unwind from last night and me and just all of it. I studied for a few hours before I had to move. I considered the gym, but wasn't ready to deal with whatever had been bugging Jason the night before. I ended up going for a run, just ran till I was sweaty, then turned around and ran home. I made a snack and showered, considered calling Leda, decided against it, and eventually opened my books back up. An hour or so later, when I was just thinking of dinner plans, she texted me.

Hey Boss man – wanna come over? – L

Little girl, how has your day been? And yes. I'll be there in an hour? – X

Good day! June is...smart. ☺ How do you feel about me making you dinner? – L

How do I feel about her making me dinner? Fucking great. Just about perfect. The only thing closer to perfect would be her making me dinner, in my–our–apartment, naked.

That sounds good, little girl. 1 hour. X

Despite my general feeling that she wouldn't be inviting me over if she hated what happened last night, I was still anxious. It was her seeing me, passing judgment on a more naked part of me. But I wouldn't let fear control me, change me.

I threw on some jeans and a T-shirt with my leather jacket over it. On the way to her house, I listened to some old school music to get myself steeled up. I couldn't stop myself, I advanced the tracks to the remix of Ringfinger. Nine Inch Nails. The rest of the drive was spent smiling at the disjointed memories I associated with NIN.

I was on her street sooner that I wanted to be. I was thinking of the feel of her skin under my hands last night, the stickiness on her thighs, her voice as I compressed her throat. *God, I am a fucking monster. And she is inviting me in for more.* All the old dark longings opened in my chest. I wanted to be on top of her, grinding into her until she winced.

Shaking my head and trying to clear my thoughts, I turned the car off, stopping the song. At her door, I stopped, took a breath. Hit the button for her apartment. She buzzed me in without a word. *That shit isn't safe, little one.* She opened the door to her apartment as I mounted the steps.

I waited for her to say something, but she just waited. Standing there, jeans and a long sleeve T-shirt, barefoot. Hair wild. Beautiful. *I'm so fucked.* I grabbed her around the waist and kissed her, deciding I was going to keep going until she gave me any indication that she didn't want it, didn't want me. She tensed at first then leaned into me, relaxed against me.

She smiled as the kiss ended, looking up at me, saying, "I made some lasagna and a salad. Hope that's okay." She gestured toward the couch, as she finished some things in the kitchen.

By all means, girlie. You can wait on me. I smiled, "Perfect. How was talking with June?"

She answered me from the kitchen, "Well, first of all she is a genius and secondly, she loves you."

What the fuck was that? Did she really think that?

"She's married." We were on the cusp of when most girls in my past had gone all sideways, crazy as fuck.

"No! She loves you like a brother. She helped me process some things, but she was also protective of you. She's a good friend. I'm glad you have her in your life."

I was pleased with that, but…process things?

This was what I was worrying about. *Confront it, Stone.* "What did you need to process?"

"A bunch of stuff."

She thought she was cute, thought I couldn't tell that she was trying to fuck with me a bit. *Not happening, little one.* I felt the rumble in my chest before I knew I was making a disapproving sound.

I cut it off and tried to communicate like a human. "Little girl. I want to know. I don't need to know your whole conversation, but I do want to talk about last night. How are you and did talking with her help?"

She disappeared below the counter as she took the lasagna out of the oven. She took too long to answer, and I started to tense my muscles to go get her. But she started speaking and I relaxed back into the couch. "Xander, it helped me fast forward through processing it, but I would have gotten to the same place either way."

And that it is?

"It was incredibly hot."

What? No really… What? "Hot?" My dick twitched a bit.

"Yeah, hot. You…you took my breath away. It was stunning to see you so raw, so pure. It scared me and it turned me on. I mean, you know how wet I was." As she spoke, she put the oven mitts down and came into the living room. She knelt in front of me. *Like she is fucking trained already.* The voice screaming in my head was too loud. I sent a mental Xanax through my muscles. *Slow the fuck down, boyo.*

I kissed her forehead and tipped her head back with my thumb under her chin. "You didn't feel jealous?"

She paused a beat and looked at me, her eyes not hiding anything.. "A little. But, I don't know. I'm the one you fucked."

Jesus Christ — sub jackpot!

"There was something sort of amazing about it. I don't think I could ever handle that kind of thing, though. I'm sorry, I just don't think I want that."

She was apologizing for not wanting to get the shit beat out of her. I knew it was fucked up, but I thought her fucked up parts might match my fucked up parts. "You're not a pain slut. And honestly, I don't think I could do that to you." My thoughts went back to standing over that slave, but seeing Leda, and the feeling that gave me. "A few times, I sort of saw you in her place, and it took me out of the moment."

I leaned forward, kissing her hair and neck, wanting to protect her and knowing that, on some level, I wanted to protect her from me. Love was a serious mindfuck. "Leda." I murmured her name and pulled her into my lap, straddling me so I could see her face. "I was so anxious about last night. What parts did you get jealous about?"

She was uncomfortable. Her gaze slipped away from mine as she answered, voice soft. "Grinding your dick in her face. I mean, it was a little much, right?"

If we were at a limit, I needed to know. But all I had wanted in that moment was to be grinding in *her* face. I let the dominance out a bit, and my voice had an edge when I answered. "Did you wish I was grinding my dick in *your* face, little girl?" I saw that flush in her cheeks and she dropped her gaze completely. Shame. I smiled as she nodded, small and embarrassed. I wanted her to lean into her shame, wanted her to admit that she wanted the things she wanted. "Say it."

"Yes."

"Yes, what?"

"Yes… I wanted your dick in my face." She mumbled it, and looked up at me, probably trying to gauge how much I was judging her. *No, honey. You get good stuff when you debase yourself for me.* My cock surged.

I stood, keeping her wrapped around me. "What else did you wish I was doing to you instead of her?" I carried her into her bedroom and tossed her down on her ridiculous little fairy tale bed, planning to do some evil there. She hadn't answered, and I started pulling off my belt, thinking of wailing on her ass with it.

She knelt in the center of the bed, watching me, pupils widening, nipples just tightening enough to be visible. "Uhh…her nipples. You were pinching her. It seemed too…intimate. And I didn't mind the wax" — her voiced softened with embarrassment — "but I think we could try that sometime, too."

So fucking perfect. "Jesus, little girl. Are you just innocence incarnate?" I asked the air around me, not really expecting her to answer. I opened the fly of my jeans and pulled my cock out. "Get your mouth on my cock."

She looked at me in want and I flexed my muscles, sort of preening, as I reached to pull my shirt over my head. She slipped to the floor and engulfed me in the warm wetness of her mouth. She knelt in front of me, working her throat around me, licking. She didn't seem to ever mind getting drooly and messy when she sucked my cock and the sloppiness just made it hotter.

"Give me your hands." My voice was strained, but she reached up, let me crush her little wrists in my fist. "I didn't tell you to stop." She had paused, waiting to see what I was doing. I pulled her arms against me, and she moved her face down my length, swallowing against any resistance in her throat. "That's my good girl." My voice was soft and she looked up at me, with my cock still half in her mouth.

I swallowed hard against the surge of wickedness that rushed through me at the look in her wide eyes, the shimmer of cock-drool on her chin. This wasn't enough. I wanted her body under me, pressed down tight, I wanted to hold her down and make her take everything I gave her.

I let her work on me a little longer, but as I started to feel the pressure of my orgasm brewing in my balls, I stepped back—simultaneously pulling my cock out of her mouth and pulling her forward by her arms. She was left off balance, mouth wet and gaping. "Get naked."

She regained her balance when I let go of her wrists and she stood, pulling her shirt over her head. Her plump tits bounced in a raw-red lace bra. Her nipples were visible, deep and rosy. She peeled out of her jeans. And was only wearing a tiny g-string, black. One of the super-low ones made for the ridiculous low cut jeans chicks wore now. The string cut into her hips a little as it dropped to the small triangle of fabric covering her.

I nodded at the bed. "Get up there." She scrambled backward as I advanced, and I saw a little fear in her eyes. She knew what I could do...what I did. She knew I would do it. Her nipples tightened more. I shook my head at her. "You're not fucking naked."

Her eyebrows shot up on her face, even as a smile played over her lips. She was having fun. My heavy heart lightened a little. *Could she really be willing to take me as I am?* She reached behind her back and unsnapped her bra, letting it fall away. She held my gaze as she slipped her thumbs under the g-string. But I cut her off, "You took too long, little girl. Leave it."

Confusion crossed her face and she slowly pulled her hands away, let them hang at her sides, as I crawled onto the bed. I pressed her back with a hand on her sternum. She took it, leaning back and maneuvering her legs around so my torso was between her knees.

I reached down and grabbed the wisp of cloth that was supposed to be panties. A resigned expression settled in her features, which was replaced with a little surprise, when I didn't rip it off her. I pulled it aside and yanked up a little, knowing it was pulling tight in her ass and pussy. She gasped and before she recovered from that, I pushed my cock into her. Her gasp became a moan.

After we both came, we took a quick shower to rinse our skin, and went back to the kitchen for dinner. She was getting close to being completely unselfconscious around me. She had just put on a pair of tiny shorts that I hoped to God she only wore to bed and the same T-shirt. Her ass cheeks were visible, jiggling, cute and sexy. I wanted to put a handprint on her so bad.

I smiled at the thought. Smiled at the relative release of pressure from my heart. I knew she was mine.

"What?" She cocked her head to the side, smiling back at me.

"Hmm? Nothing." I held the laugh in, but knew it was reflected in my face. She was fun to tease.

She threw her napkin at me. "Come on! What are you thinking over there?" I didn't answer her, letting her clear the dishes. When she dropped them in the sink, she looked over the counter at me, trying to look hard and failing miserably. "You know what? No dessert till you tell me."

Oh fuck no, girlie. "Number one, you're dessert and I'll have you whenever I want." I smiled, lightening my tone. "Number two, I was thinking about how good I feel after last night. It definitely drained the aggression but…I can't seem to get enough of you now."

She held her breath a moment and her hands must have stilled because the clink of dishes paused before she answered, "What about you? How was it to have me there last night? Was it weird?"

Weird probably isn't the right word. But not usual, I guess. Uncomfortable, yes. A total mindfuck, absolutely. "I was worried you might freak out a little." *Or a lot.* I stood and cleared the rest of the dishes from the coffee table. When I stood behind her at the sink, I pressed my body against hers and put the dishes in the sink. I dropped my face to her neck, breathing her, tasting her again and again. These little shorts were the best and worst thing ever all at once. "But Goddamn, the look on your face and knowing you were there watching me with her—fuck, it got me so hard. I wanted you, on your knees, begging me, big eyes looking up at me."

I skated my fingertips over her hip, under the shirt, felt the stagger in her breath. Digging my fingertips into her skin, I spun her to face me. I crowded her space, face just above hers, my hands gripping the counter on either side of her. "Leda. Can you take it?"

Her face blanked. She opened her lips to say something, but nothing came out. I drove my hand up the front of her body, between her breasts, to her face. I held her toward me, forced her to hold my gaze. "Can. You. Take. It? All of it? All of me?" My breath caught in my throat and a sick knot tightened in my gut.

She trembled, pupils dilating. "Yes." She whispered it, but she didn't look away. It was real.

"I'm going to hurt you. I'm going to fuck you." I grabbed the hair on the back of her head. "I'm going to make you cry. I'm going to put you on your knees." Her tremble was a full shudder now, as I started pulling her to her bedroom. "I'm going to stretch you open. I'm going to tie you down. I'm going to make you scream."

There's a place to grab a scalp that hurts without pulling too much hair out, at the base of the skull. I pulled her along and when we got to her bed, I threw her down. She panted, didn't move otherwise, only waited for me to defile her.

I was absolutely in love with her.

Chapter Twenty-Eight

Leda
Garbage, You Look So Fine

I kept my eyes closed and let myself get lost in it, in him. When he lay down on top of me, I wrapped my arms around him, clutching him to me. Waves and waves of happiness washed through me. He was everything, a whole world unto himself.

He murmured something to me as he ran his hands through my hair. I missed it, but the sweetness in the tone sounded so much like love. I was falling for him, falling into him.

Once we were naked, he pressed his body back down on mine. Our eyes locked in a close gaze. I had my hands resting on his shoulders and angled my legs around him. A look of awe crossed his face, almost incredulous. But whatever the thought was, he didn't voice it. He just slipped into me, holding me. I trapped him against me, locking my ankles together.

Mine.

He shifted within the confines of my legs, no complaint at how tightly I grabbed him. He slid within me. The sensation of him dragging against my skin was overwhelming, distracting, and the joy that I had been feeling since acceptance had washed through me exploded in my chest. My smile cracked wide across my face.

He planted his elbows just above my shoulders and brushed my hair back from my face, smiling at me, kissing me. He pulled back in the midst of kissing me and I followed him up. He took the advantage and slipped his hands under my head, cradling me to him. I mewled a little sound of appreciation, licking his lips and shifting my hips to clench him.

It was a give and take. His move then mine. Then his reaction again. He ground his pelvis into me and the deep pressure made me gasp. I arched against him, pressing my breasts up toward him. I stretched back from him and his eyes glinted with something I couldn't name. He kept at my pussy, stroking harder each time, until I gasped at the apex of each of his thrusts.

My fingers traced up his back, over ridges of the muscles in his arms. I wanted to make it better for him. I wanted to make him feel as good as he made me feel. I closed my eyes for a moment and when I opened them, the cold stare was there. *He* was there. There was a pause, a moment when the world waited. I waited, breath held.

He half-growled and yanked my head back with a hand tangled in my hair. When my throat was bared to him, he dropped his lips on me, his teeth grazing me. Cold electric shocks fired through me and I spasmed involuntarily.

He shifted himself around and pressed his elbow onto the front of my shoulder, holding me down and still keeping a hand wrapped in my hair. With his other hand, he traced over my skin toward my nipple. The intermingled sensations contrasted against each other, overloading me.

My brain wasn't working right. My thoughts piled on each other incoherently. I was just reaction and reaction and reaction to each thing he did. I twisted and twitched away from him, then back toward him. His fingertips traced my nipple. I shivered and arched my back to press into his hands. His made a low chuckle tinged with ownership.

He gave my nipple a small pinch, then brought his fingers to my lips. He watched me, concentrating on my response to him. The pads of his fingers traced over my lips and pushed them apart. I opened my mouth, but not wide enough. He hooked his fingers on my lower teeth and snagged them down, forcing my mouth open to its extreme.

He stroked my tongue before moving his fingertips to my jaw line, just holding my mouth open. "Just like that, little girl." He murmured as he moved his lips over me. Licking my mouth.

And his hips, his cock kept pushing into me. Relentless. He seemed engrossed in my mouth, grazing my lips, watching my tongue struggling to find a place that wasn't so exposed. I shifted and brushed my hand over his shoulder. It snapped him out of his wonderment about my mouth, and a look of pure aggression crossed his face.

He pushed himself up, so he was over me, swiping a hand between us to grab up my wrists. I was drowning in sensation, unable to get away from it, away from him. The impulse was there. It was too much, too intense. He was too close. I was too raw, too vulnerable. But he held my wrists there, pressed into the mattress right above my head. I couldn't go anywhere. I was only where he held me. Kissing me.

I let it happen, didn't even consider safewording. It was terrifying, but I wanted to be pushed wherever he was, wherever he wanted to push me. I wanted all of him. I let myself fall into him and the fear fell away. I stretched back and clamped my legs around him. I opened my eyes and met his gaze, refused the impulse to shrink away from him, away from how scary it was to be this open to someone.

He saw it, right away. He held my gaze, a slight sheen of sweat on his forehead. I wanted to hear him tell me he loved me. I wanted to know that I made him happy. That I was his and special and... I didn't even know the words for it.

He held my gaze and whispered, gentle, soft. "You're perfect, little girl. Everything about you makes me want more of you."

"Then take more of me."

His blank face melted to something warmer and he growled and pounded his hips against me. I moaned, letting my mouth fall open and his eyes dropped to my lips.

"Fuck. The sounds you make, Leda." His breath was a low grunt at each thrust. He released my wrists and slipped his forearms under my shoulders so he could grip the back of my neck, pushing me down to meet him when he pushed into me. Harder, harder, harder.

And it felt so good, the nerves low in my pelvis were smothered in pleasure, no way away from it. Melting over my bones, melting onto him. My breath was ragged and I felt so close to coming, so close to him. My thoughts fired out of order, not making sense. Just flashes always shattered away by him, his overwhelming presence.

I put my fingertips on his chest and traced up to his throat. When he met my gaze again, I whispered, "Please." Not knowing what I was asking for, and holding back against the instinct to call him Daddy.

He saw it there though, saw his little girl, right where she should be, under him, begging quietly. He groaned hard and came, pressing me down into the mattress. He was everything. The *only* thing that mattered to me at that moment.

Chapter Twenty-Nine

Xander
The Rolling Stones, Paint It Black

In the morning, we drove to school together. The air was brisk. Not as bad as DC would be when I went home. Not as cold as she'd be in Chicago. I wanted her to come to DC with me, wanted to take her somewhere else altogether. I resolved to figure out a compromise.

At lunch, I took a quick walk to the C70, mostly for fresh air, to clear my head and checked my phone. A text from Jason.

Dude – call me. J

Whatever had bothered him at the Window needed to be addressed. I called him, expecting to get a dressing down, but not really sure why.

"What's up?"

"Are you okay?" He sounded worried and annoyed at the same time.

I scoffed. "Yeah, why?"

"You didn't look in control the other night at the club. I don't know, man. You seemed a little on the edge."

"What are you talking about? I'm fine." I said it knowing that my brain had been working overtime, working myself over about Leda.

"You aren't acting normal lately."

"I don't know, dude. I'm... I mean what do you want me to say? I'm all kinds of fucked up about this girl. She's too fucking perfect and I don't trust it. I keep waiting for her to realize I'm a monster and tell me to fuck off."

"You're not a monster!" It was Christy's voice, clearly from across the room.

"Dude, fucking speaker phone? What the fuck, man?"

Then, clearly he gave her some non-verbal signal, because she responded, "Jesus, I'm sorry! But you weren't gonna say it. Xander, you need to know that you're not a monster. You are perfectly lovable, kind, caring, protective, loving. *Lovable*. Do you understand me? Lovable."

"Okay, Christy, he gets it. He's loveable." Jason's tone was conciliatory.

"Per your estimation, Christy. Doesn't mean she'll see it that way."

"Just stop doing that. Stop it. Cajun!"

I laughed when she dropped the House safeword from the Window.

"Seriously, give her the chance to surprise you. Did she give you some reason to worry?" Jason added.

"No, none. That's what's so scary." I flashed back to a commanding officer in the Army, talking about intelligence gathering. 'Something that looks too perfect is fake until you see the inconsistency that proves it's human'. My voice was distant when I spoke again. "She's too consistent."

Jason spoke with a more serious, take-no-shit voice. "Well, as your friend, I hope you realize that there's nothing wrong till there's really something wrong. But as your business partner, I'm telling you to get your shit together before you play at the club again. You didn't have the type of control that makes me trust you. I could tell when I was watching you."

I blew out a breath, considering fighting with him about it. *Fuck it.* I swallowed my little bit of pride under some arrogant bravado. "Got ya. Ooorah, sarge." And I hung up on them.

Don't be a bitch.

I didn't respond to his text. I knew I was being a dick and he was just watching out for me and her, and our money, and whoever could be on the receiving end of my hands. I got it. I was just pissed. I was pissed that she made me feel raw, weak. She felt dangerous in the most tricky, covert way. It was just that gut instinct that *something* would go wrong, and soon.

The rest of my afternoon sucked. I was in a shitty mood and wasn't listening well. I waited for her at the end of the day and she must have been held up with something because she didn't come out with the big group of people leaving her class. But Stacy did.

"Hey, Xander." She smiled, kept an appropriate distance. "Going home for Christmas?" She acted like a normal acquaintance, not the other half of the most fucked up relationship of my life.

"Yeah. You?" Cordial, but cold. She knew where she stood with me.

"Yeah, about an hour after my last test. Can't wait to leave. I'll see you at the gala?"

"Presumably."

"Maybe we can get a cup of coffee or something while we're both home." She said it so innocently, it kind of caught me off guard.

But I was in a bad mood and was still pissed off at her...and Jason. "You think your daddy would let you out with me?"

Rage crossed her features. She hated being trapped in a political family as much as I did. Maybe more. She hated that her dad hated me, that he'd never forgiven me, even though he'd never publically censured me either. She opened her mouth, ready to spout off some shit, but I stopped her short, "Fuck off, Stacy."

She raised a hand to slap me, and I caught it easily, stepping into her space. "Is this what you fucking want from me, Stacy? You want to hurt me?" I squeezed down on her wrist, slowly, but without pause when she winced. "You know that would just make me want to hurt you. And you know I can. But I don't *fucking* want you. Is that what you want to be around? You should've put me in prison when you had the chance."

I dropped her arm, walking away from any response she may have had. I went back to the first year lecture hall to find Leda. She was bent over a book with one of the TA's. A British dude, here working on his renal cell cancer research. I actually laughed at how my day had pretty much been a perfect storm of shit fucking with my head when I saw how close he stood to her. She looked up at my laugh and I waved at her. She smiled crookedly, head cocked to the side in question.

The TA took a step back — *yeah motherfucker, you* were *inappropriately close to her just then.*

"Hey, girlie. You good here or should I grab a spot in the library?" She didn't need to know how bad my day had been. She didn't need to know that the TA and I shared a look in which he acknowledged my claim and my alpha status to his beta at best. And that was it. I just needed to alpha the fuck out on a bunch of people. I could have gone to the Window, or the gym, or even to the bar and picked a fight.

But my girl was there, looking at me. She felt like the sun shining on me.

"Nope, I'm all set, honey."

When she turned to get her bag, I shared a look with the TA — *See, motherfucker. Recognize.* It was unnecessary and he dropped his gaze and mumbled his goodbye to Leda.

* * * *

Wednesday night, I still hadn't heard back from Jason and I wanted to spar some.

Hey. Gym? — X

His response was fairly quick. I knew that Christy was at work, so he'd probably be home alone or at the bar.

Yeah. Give me 45 — J

Forty-five minutes later, we were grappling around on the mat, not talking. He figured-foured my wrist the first go-round. In the second round, I broke his guard, flipped him on his back. He broke my guard almost immediately and we broke apart, circling each other. I didn't watch his face as we moved, but kept my eyes trained on the motion in his torso, watching for the little tell of action before he moved.

He grabbed at my leading arm, but I pulled it back and slapped him across me, guiding his body through my space, toward the opposite side. At the same time, I wrapped myself around his back, locking him up in a choke-hold. I knew the slap was more aggressive than how we usually sparred, was harder than sparring should have been.

He dropped an elbow into my gut, and it was enough that I loosened my grip for a moment, but it was all he needed, pushing up against my forearms and twisting away from me. His eyes flashed with anger. "What the fuck, Xander?"

"What the fuck, what? Dick."

"Figure your shit out, asshole." And he came at me again, locked me up and flipped me onto the mat, face down. He could have submitted me, *should* have submitted me, but he moved slower than usual and I took the opportunity. I pressed my body up, carrying him with me. When his weight started to pull him off the side of my back, I dove into it, driving him back against the mat, with my forearm across his throat, until he tapped.

I relaxed, letting him go, but he popped up into my face as I leaned back. "What the *fuck*, man? What is fucking wrong with you?"

I drew a breath to yell back at him, not caring who was watching, and looked down to gather my words, but when I looked back at him, the look on his face stopped me. He wasn't only pissed off at me. He was worried. It made me take the extra beat to think through what I was about to do. This was my oldest friend. The only friend who'd stood by me after Stacy.

I blew out the breath. "Look, man, I don't know. It's all the same shit, but it's been a shite week. Stacy. I'm sick of how dudes look at Leda, and she doesn't fucking notice. I'm all kinds of fucked up about going home for Christmas. I don't want to see my parents."

He sat back on his heels, anger draining from his face. "So, don't go. Fuck them."

"You know what it's like. The shit I would get if I didn't make an appearance, especially on New Year's Eve. I know it's dumb."

"Yeah, it's dumb. You're a grown-ass man." He reached off the mat for water and looked back at me. "Did you ask Leda to come yet?"

I hung my head a little because I had decided to ask her at least a week ago. "No."

"Fucking get to it. Having her there will make it better."

"I doubt it."

Once we had talked a bit more, and were laughing again, we sparred for another hour. Then, we took turns on the heavy bag, holding for each other, laughing between flurries and combinations. It felt good to get the aggression out, but I wasn't completely drained.

* * * *

The next night was the final tutoring session and no one showed up. Leda and I laughed a little and tried to study, but it didn't last long. On the drive back to her house, I found my nuts.

"When are you getting back from Chicago?"

"On the third of January. Why? What are your plans?"

"Well, that fundraiser that my mom's been up my ass about is actually a New Year's Eve party. I was wondering if you'd be interested in flying to DC to go with me. I think it's the only way it'll be bearable."

She smiled and I breathed out, unsure why I was even so fucking neurotic about it. She leaned a little toward me, pulling nearly all my focus to her. "Yeah, let me look into what it would take to change my ticket up."

So, this was where it might get a little weird, and I knew it. "Umm, I already looked into it." A faint look of surprise registered on her face as I kept speaking. "The senator's sister and her family are flying down from a private airfield outside Chicago on their jet on New Year's Eve. You could just fly with them."

She sat back, but didn't share any concerns, if she had them. "Okay. Let me talk with my mom about it, too."

"It kind of sucks that we won't be here. The Window has a really kick ass New Year's Party. Maybe next year, when it's not an election year."

I sent Jason a text the next day.

She's coming to DC. Thanks for calling me on my bullshit and sorry.

Whatever, dick. I told you she couldn't go a full 10 days without your dick. HA!

That's my fucking woman you're talking about, and what about the part we just finished where I wasn't in control? You want to get hurt?

The pseudo-threat. A huge part of guy communication.

Your fucking woman. That's what I said. And I ain't scared of you, douche-bag.

I actually laughed. He just understood when to push, when not to. He sent another text before I responded.

What are you doing next week?

Finals, why?

I need a second opinion on a ring for Christy.

Thursday? I'm done around noon.

Yeah, I'll set it up.

* * * *

Finals were what they always are—figuring out how to be the right kind of dancing monkey for whatever asshole was playing the music. I did well—not because I was smarter than anyone else there, but because I had a different kind of interest in how the body worked. I wanted to learn about how it fit together, so I could know best how to take it apart, how to put it back together when life broke it.

Leda stressed out though. She was up cramming most nights and I had to remind her to go to bed. But she did great and each test was a weight off. Each A was a little buffer to her self-esteem and she seemed happier by the end of the week.

Thursday she had testing all afternoon, and I went to meet Jason. He had arranged an appointment at an exclusive jeweler downtown. When we sat, a small, anemic-looking blonde offered us champagne, which we declined. The manager worked with Jason, going through look-books, getting an idea what he liked. They had to know the kind of money Jason had because they jumped to platinum and huge rocks. He took it in stride and mostly didn't ask my opinion.

While they talked and sketched out a design, I picked up a few other look books and thumbed through them, absentmindedly thinking of picking a ring for Leda someday. At the bottom of the stack of books, there was a book of titanium jewelry. It was mostly geared toward men — more utilitarian, severe looking. But there was a page of necklaces, actually dog tags meant for men to wear and I thought of a collar for Leda, thought of June's bracelet labeling her Michael's toy.

The anemic blonde noticed I was looking, and approached me. "Can I help you pick something out? Are you looking for something for yourself?"

I looked at her, amusement in my eyes. I flicked my eyes to her name tag, strategically over her breast, drawing attention to the low neckline of her blouse. "Tori," I said with a smile, "I'll never put a dog tag on again. No, I was thinking about something for my girlfriend."

She sat on the couch next to me, her knee bumping mine, and started flipping pages. I was amused by the not-so-subtle flirtation in the face of my mention of my girlfriend, wondering if this was how she worked all customers or if there was something specific to me and this situation. "Are you looking for a ring — or something else?"

"Hmm, I'm not sure yet. I don't think a ring. We haven't really been together that long."

She flipped the pages to the back of the book, to more delicate looking chains, with heart-shaped pendants. "Something like this?" She flipped the pages further and the pendants became a little more aggressive looking, heart-shaped locks. My eyebrow quirked up. And on the second to last page there was a small charm necklace with a key, a heart-shaped padlock and a triskelion. It was a symbol of BDSM, had been for years. It kind of looked like a yin-yang with a third part in the mix. *So this store, at least occasionally, catered to wealthy kinksters. Excellent.*

I pointed at that necklace, more to gauge Tori's reaction than a real interest in it. "That one. Tell me about that a little."

She blushed a little. "It is a lovely necklace with several charms. We are able to add others, or substitute some out if you'd like. The last page, here, shows other charms available." She turned the page, tongue to her lip. She knew what the triskelion meant. She was breathing faster, licking her lips nervously, afraid to make eye contact.

I sat back on the couch and just watched her anxiety flurrying through her. She didn't actually play, I decided, based on her reaction. She probably just read about it, fantasized about it. She shifted toward me and closed the book, looking down at it. She folded her hands and looked up at me. "Do you see anything you like?"

The nerves in the question were palpable. She wasn't *really* asking me to play with her, but she liked the idea. I answered her, dominance leaking into my posture and voice. "No."

She drew a quick gasp and her eyes widened. I leaned forward, at little into her space. "Let me correct that. Nothing in the book is quite right. Let's make something, just right, exactly what I want." I let my words flow out slow, enunciated, and watched them roll over her. Her nipples tightened in her shirt and her breath came raggedly. She had a faint tremor when she brushed a lock of hair out of her face.

"Xander! Jesus, man. Come here." Jason's voice snapping at me pulled me out of the little exchange with Tori. I gave her a rueful look and spread my hands in a gesture of innocence at getting pulled away from her. But, as I walked away, I was struck with dissatisfaction. Just fucking with girls wasn't the same kind of fun anymore. I wanted to fuck with Leda, but I knew exactly what she'd do. She'd be perfect.

Jason had created a design with the jeweler and wanted to show it to me. I knew what he really wanted was for me to stop fucking with that girl's head. But it was *so* much fun. A smile still crinkled the corners of my eyes as I sat down next to him.

"I think it's amazing, man. Just like the two of you. It's unique and perfect." It was a huge emerald cut diamond set so the long axis would go across her finger. There were surrounding stones that were irregular and a faint, iridescent blue. "What are those?"

"Raw opal shards."

"Wow." I had a deepening respect for this jeweler.

"We won't have the final design until we pick the stone and the shards. The shards are irregular and we'll make a one-of-a-kind piece with them. I will order the opals and I can pick the best if you'd like, or you can come in and be more hands on if you'd like, Mr. Johns."

"Call me Jason. Yeah, I think I want to come by to work on it, but I want it as soon as possible."

I smiled wide at Jason. Christy was gonna say yes. The ring would be perfect. The wedding would be perfect. They would both be happy. I couldn't want anything more for them, but I wanted more of Leda for me. I wanted to mark her, make a claim on her.

"It's perfect, man."

Jason looked up at me, genuine peace and happiness on his face, and I envied him.

"I think I might get Leda something, too."

He cocked a questioning eyebrow at me as I turned back to Tori, who seemed to have recovered her calm. I smiled to myself about how fun fucking with chicks could be.

"Tori? I need your help."

She looked up at me in surprise. "I doubt that very much, Mr....?"

"Xander Stone." I extended my hand to her. She blushed cute and shook my hand. We sat back on the couch and I explained what I wanted to her. "Is that possible?"

"Of course, Mr. Stone."

"Xander. You should call me Xander." My voice was a heated purr, low enough not to carry across the room to Jason's judgmental ears.

"Very good." She paused. "Xander." She hooked that same errant strand of hair behind her ear again.

"When can you have it for me?" I loved fucking with girls so much, there was something so fun about making someone so slightly uncomfortable.

"It can be ready in one week."

"Oh..." I let my features fall into a semblance of dismay. "That won't work. I'll be in DC."

"Umm, I can see about rushing it?"

I put my hand on hers to calm her, saying, "I don't want to rush this. I want it to be perfect. So, let's do this. Why don't you ship it to me in DC?"

"Very good, sir."

The rush at that was so nice. I clearly needed to play some more. "Thank you for your help, Tori."

Back on the street, walking to the car, Jason punched my arm. "What the fuck was that about?"

"What?" I asked innocently, with a devil smile on my face, knowing exactly what he was talking about.

"What? That *shameless* flirting. What about Leda?"

"Are *you* fucking lecturing me about monogamy right now?" I laughed and he joined me.

"Dude, you just looked like you do when you play. That didn't look like a little innocent fun to me."

I took a deep breath, acknowledging what he was saying. "This is another problem with Leda. Since I started playing with her, it's like it's all I think about. And that little chickie was shameless. You know they sell triskelion pendants there? And she knew what they meant."

"Yeah, that place is a favorite of Kyla's."

* * * *

When finals were over, the relief on my girl was palpable. She needed to burn off some of that anxious energy, but first, some rest and recovery. We stayed at my place Friday night, watched a bunch of silly movies, ate Chinese food from Mr. Chen downstairs. We laid across the couch together, her chest on my abdomen, her head resting on my chest while we watched our movies.

We slept late, but did wake in time for my session with my Brazilian Jiu Jitsu instructor, Guillermo. Jason skipped it and the class was canceled due to the proximity to the holiday, so it was a one-on-one session. I was more focused than I had been recently and Guillermo took advantage of that, working me over, pushing me hard. I came up bloody and bruised. I was getting frustrated with repeatedly getting schooled when Guillermo called me out on it.

He nodded in Leda's direction, saying, "You are worrying your girl. Settle down."

"Yep. I'm good." I looked at Leda and she did looked concerned. The thought that someone like her could care about someone like me, could absorb and want everything I gave her—nothing could seem too bad. I felt the tension drop off my shoulders and smiled at her, waving her over. I thanked Guillermo and we left.

I wanted to take her back to the Window again before we left for break and broached the subject. She agreed easily enough. When I brought up calling Seraphim to see if she and her toy wanted to play again, she seemed less sure. I explained, "I want to try something a little different this time. I want you to play, too."

The shock on her face was priceless. It was quickly replaced by rapid-fire misgivings. "Uhh...I don't know, Xander."

Reassurance now. Consent now. Negotiate now. So later is easier for her. "I'm not saying I want to torture you. I just want you more involved. Not just watching."

It didn't reassure her. I felt the mantle of domination settle over me as I pulled onto a random side street and parked. We turned to face each other and she opened her mouth to say something, but I didn't want to hear it and put my fingers on her lips, shushing her.

My voice came cold, direct. "Let me rephrase, little girl. I will pick you up at eight. Period."

She tried to speak despite my fingers still on her mouth. "Xander." It came out all muffled, questioning, nervous and it made me want to fuck her throat. My lips pressed into a line and I covered her mouth completely with my hand.

"Leda. This is how it is. You always have an out with your safewords. Don't worry about tonight. It'll be a different kind of session. Let's see how it goes."

Her eyes widened, pupils dilating a little. I felt her hot breath against my hand, faster, harder. She nodded and I let go. I was silent for the rest of the drive, waiting to see if she'd push back. When we got to her building and she was quietly smiling next to me, I took a moment to pause, enjoy it, thinking *good girl.*

I walked her into her building and I think she thought I was going to just leave. *Fuck, no, girlie.* I followed, crowding her, letting her know I'd take anything of hers whenever I wanted it, including her personal space. She looked askance at me, but I didn't flinch, only kept driving her forward.

As her apartment door clicked shut behind me, I yanked her back to me by her arm, dropping my mouth to hers and pressing a hard kiss. I grabbed at the back of her neck, the back of her head. She yielded as she always did and I guided her down to her knees, pressuring her shoulders.

She just fucking did it—dropped to her knees in front of me, big eyes looking up at me and waiting. I leaned away from her, resting against the door, and pulled my cock out. I stroked myself hard just looking at her and thinking about all the fucked up shit I wanted to do to her.

"Open your mouth."

She dropped her jaw, holding my gaze. I slipped my dick in her mouth, not caring that I had just worked out and I was sweaty as fuck. She needed to understand that at a very basic level, sometimes I wanted to use her, without regard for her pleasure. She started sucking, sliding her lips across me. *No, no, no, girlie. How I want it.* I tangled my fingers in her hair and stilled her motion. I paused long enough that she looked up toward me, and, as she did, as I held her gaze again, I pushed my cock into her mouth, to her throat. I paused when I felt the muscles of her throat convulse with her gag reflex.

As she breathed thin, raspy breaths through her nose, I turned her head with the hand in her hair, pushing the head of my cock against the roof of her mouth, her cheeks, down on her tongue. "I want you to feel all of it, Leda. Your mouth is mine."

Her eyes held acceptance, acquiescence. I slowly drove my cock back deep in her mouth, to her throat and she gagged a little, but I didn't stop. I loved the look of her eyes watering while she had a mouthful of my cock I was in her throat, past her gag. "Your throat is mine. Do you understand me?"

I waited until she nodded, and when she did, I face-fucked her, not needing much more to come. She couldn't hold it all in and she drooled a little on her chin. I was breathing hard, but it made me smile. I swiped my finger through the mess on her chin, smearing it over her face. My face split in a cold smile and I took my cock out of her mouth, wiping off on her face, in her hair.

And left. Left her there, on her knees, my fluids drying on her face and in her hair. Left her there like a degraded little whore. I smiled as I walked back to the car, tying my gi pants back up. *Let her chew on that all day*. In the car, I sent her a text. No apology, no explanation. Just more instructions, more I-own-you shit.

8. Be ready. Don't make yourself come before then. – X

Ok Boss. Please don't tell me I can't come all night though. Pretty please – L

Just Ok, Boss? *She's amazing. She's perfect.* My thoughts spiraled in this twisted amalgam of lust, love, want, control, evil, menace and purest pleasure at her existence reverberating with the fear that'd it'd all go sideways soon. The drive home was fast and I thought of how I wanted to respond to her. I thought about how much she would really suffer with orgasm denial, orgasm control. Forced orgasms would be amazing.

I texted her back, trying to keep the balance between evil and loving.

Maybe, if you're good, I'll let you come. Later. Much later. See you at 8 – X

I knew I'd let her come. Her face, the hitch in her breathing, the moan in her voice. All that was addictive. I wasn't planning on giving that up, but it was about pushing her. We'd be apart for a week and a half and I wanted her to know, as much as she could, that she belonged to me and that I was mean sometimes.

I took a quick shower and spent some time packing, finalizing plans for the trip, including meeting with

June and Michael. But in the end, I was bored and called Jason. Christy answered.

"Hey, slut." Her voice was a little flat. I couldn't tell if it was a joke.

"Umm, hi, asshole. What are we doing?"

She giggled a little. "I can't stay mad at you."

"Why were you mad at me?" I was baffled by the entire exchange.

"Jason told me about you hitting on that girl. Dude, what about Leda?"

This was fucked up, because I knew he didn't tell her the circumstances that brought us to the jeweler. I voiced the other thing that bothered me about it, "Are you calling me out on something related to *monogamy?*"

She laughed again. "Kinda. You and Leda aren't me and Jason. The only question you need to answer is 'would she have been bothered by your behavior'?"

"If I let that question rule me, I'll go crazy."

"Just come over. I'll try to explain it."

I drove to their house, confusion rushing through my thoughts. When I got there, they were in the great room, like it was an intervention. I walked in with the same trepidation everyone who ever walked into an intervention probably felt. I sat in an oversized arm chair, across from the two of them on the couch.

"So…" Christy started, but I cut her off.

"Is this an intervention?" I laughed. "Because, if so, I need a drink."

They laughed too and some of the tension broke away.

Once we were settled, Jason spoke, his voice uncharacteristically adult and calm. "I'm worried that you aren't in control of yourself. This is different from the domination shit. I don't know what it is, but it looks a lot like when you were with Stacy."

I sucked in a breath. "It's different, man. It just is. Stacy was ten years ago. I was a kid and didn't know what the fuck I wanted."

Christy interrupted me. "You were just about the same age as Leda." She left it at that, not drawing further comparisons and letting me decide what to make of it.

"Seriously, dude, what was that about with the girl at the jeweler?"

I looked at him in surprise that he would bring it up in front of Christy, but he continued, "I mean, we were there to get a necklace for *your girlfriend*. And you start flirting with that chick. That's not you."

"How do you even know? I've never had a relationship like this, barely had relationships at all. Maybe this is me as a boyfriend. Maybe I'm a huge dick. Maybe I can't be monogamous. Can't be faithful. Why do the two of you care so much about this?" There was frustration mounting to venom in my words.

Christy pressed her hand over Jason's when he was going to explode back at me. She spoke instead, "Xander, we love you. And you love her. You will fall apart if you fuck this up. We'll love you no matter what happens with Leda, but we don't want you to have to go through that if you can avoid it."

I couldn't argue with that. I would be a fucking mess if I lost her over something stupid like that. "I don't know what is wrong with me, but I have to push it. I won't go too far."

"Whose definition of too far, Xander?" Christy interrupted softly.

I continued, "I won't go too far, but I have to be right there. I can't be restrained like you're talking about. I didn't touch that girl, just talked to her, just fucked with her head some, but the truth is, it wasn't as fun as I expected it to be." I hung my head. "See, I'm a fucking monster." I stood up, pacing a bit, then walked to the wet bar and poured another drink.

They sat silently. Finally, Jason spoke, saying, "What kind of monster do you want to be?"

Christy and I both looked at him with confusion-laced shock on our faces. Jason added, "If you fucking believe that about yourself, and we can't convince you otherwise, fucking do it intentionally. Decide what you want to do, who you want to be. But you have to talk to Leda. Consent, Xander. She hasn't consented to a poly life, hasn't consented to you fucking other girls, or even picking them up."

He was right. I could try to fool myself, but in another life, I would have taken that girl home from the jewelry store and fucked her senseless. There were D/s relationships like that, where the D-type person could fuck other people. *What would Leda think about that?* I thought of her on her knees in front of me, following orders without complaint. *She might be all right with it.* And a huge realization hit me, that she wasn't a challenge anymore.

I spoke the thought. "She just makes it so easy. I don't have to work at all. She just submits, gives it up."

Both of them looked confused, but Christy spoke, "Isn't that what you want?"

"I don't know. I don't believe it, don't believe it's real. She's not a challenge and..." I trailed off, not sure what I wanted to say. "I don't want to be with anyone else. I just don't know what to do with myself when it works. And that chick was just supposed to be mental masturbation."

They were both silent for a few minutes. Finally, Christy spoke, "Why can't you just enjoy it?" Her face was so sad, so heartbroken for me.

Jason put a hand on her, stopping her from going on. He knew. "Because nothing good lasts, Christy."

She stood and crossed the space to me. She sat in my lap and spoke as she hugged me. "It can't if you don't think it can." She kissed my forehead as she stood, then left the room.

I looked up at Jason. He didn't say anything, but then jumped up and got a drink. As he sat back down, he said, "Is it Stacy or your parents?"

I was over it, exhausted with it, pissed that there was even a possibility that those things could still be impacting my life. I scrubbed my hand over my face. "I don't know and, honestly, I don't want to know. I just want to get fucked up or get lost in fucking someone else up."

"All right, man." He left it alone and I knew he understood. He had been around enough to have seen my parents and was definitely around when shit went down with Stacy. He took a breath and knocked back the rest of his scotch. "Wanna spar?"

"No, Guillermo beat the shit out of me since you weren't there this morning. Anyway, I got some shit to do before we go out tonight."

"What are you doing for the last night in town?"

"The Window."

I didn't miss the look of concern on his face when I said it. I just chose to ignore it.

I called Seraphim on the way home and arranged another play date, discussed a little of what I wanted to do. She was happy to make her slave available to me, laughing at my plans. A small war of warning and pride went off in my brain that she would approve of anything I was planning. I chose to laugh at it, push through until there really was a problem. Christy and Jason meant well, but there wasn't a problem until Leda or I felt there was. *Right?*

Chapter Thirty

Leda
Air, Sexy Boy

Needing to do something with my anxious energy until he came back for me, I called Tiffany.

She answered, a little breathless. "Hey, girl!"

"Ummm, hi? Am I interrupting something?" I laughed.

I heard the smile in her voice. "No, I'm on a treadmill, not a man, unfortunately."

"You want to try to hook up while I'm home?"

"When will you be in Chicago?"

"I get in tomorrow, and I think I'm going to DC for New Years with Xander."

She put on a fake snotty tone. "Ooooohhhhhh — hoooooo. Someone is hot shit."

"Shut up, bitch. I need some girl time. This man is crazy."

"Yeah? Tell me something titillating. My sex life is just about nonexistent right now. This new job is too time consuming."

I paused, not wanting to talk about it, but needing to vent some of the pent up energy his goodbye had left me with. "So, I'm just gonna be blunt, okay?"

"I never want anything else."

"So, he just dirty face-fucked me and left. And...I'm not allowed to get myself off before we go out tonight." There was a pause in which neither of us spoke, so I continued. "I'm sorry. Didn't mean to freak you out."

She cleared her throat. "Oh, girlfriend. I'm not freaked out. That's hot as hell. But only under one condition—he has to let you come sometime tonight. Too much delayed gratification and he just starts to seem ungrateful."

"Yeah...he usually doesn't leave me hanging. But he did it once. Oh *God*, that was the worst night."

Her voice got thick and purred through the phone. "Yeah?

I didn't really want to get into a replay of our various sexual exploits and changed the subject a little. "The thing is, I just want to fuck with him tonight."

We talked for a while more and she helped me formulate a good plan for the night. When we hung up, I had a few hours until he picked me up. I ran to the modestly sized mall in the area to get something fun at the lingerie store. I had almost settled on a very traditional get-up in royal purple—thigh highs with a garter, barely there panties and a demi-cup bra that I nearly spilled out of. But at the last moment I saw something more provocative. If he was going to push me, I was going to push right back.

I settled on a black leather miniskirt, cut like a school girl uniform skirt, with white thigh highs that laced up the back like a corset. On top, a white Oxford shirt, open to just past my plaid striped demi-cup bra. My hair was full and loose, my makeup very light, no jewelry. My shoes were stacked heels in the style of saddle shoes. The overall effect was innocence perverted.

I smiled at myself in the mirror while I got ready, feeling like I looked like someone's dirty fantasy. Smiled wider when I realized it was my own.

Chapter Thirty-One

Xander
Cobra Starship, Good Girls Go Bad

There was a warm spell and the air was brisk but not outright cold. I drove to her building, my mind racing with thoughts of her that tumbled over each other, mixed up with a low level dread I couldn't shake.

She stepped out of her entrance as I parked in front of her building. I saw her but didn't really see her, my mind still focusing on what was wrong. Not looking at what was *right*, right in front of me. I got out of the car and walked around the hood, intentionally clearing my mind to be fully present with her.

Any thoughts that weren't completely cleared disappeared in a heartbeat when I looked up at her. *Oh fuck.*

She wore a school girl outfit, white thigh high tights up to a little leather miniskirt, to a shirt that looked like it could have been her dad's, tied around her waist and unbuttoned, with a peek-a-boo plaid bra. She even had the shoes right.

Oh goddamn it.

I stumbled a bit, my feet not working right, because all the blood in my body was screaming into my cock. She just looked like a little private school rich girl who was mad at her parents and out to make some bad decisions. I could be as bad as she needed me to be.

Mine, fucking mine, minemineminemineminemine.

I grabbed as I reached her, and held her neck still, tilting her head just right. I lowered my mouth to her and claimed her again. Just like earlier. *This is mine, goddammit.* It was primitive. I wanted to brand her, mark her, put a sign on her so everyone knew who she belonged to. I wanted to lock her in my apartment and never let her out again—just keep her there, tied up and waiting for me. I wanted to put a baby in her. I wanted her on a cellular level.

All the insanity of the last week, all my weird insecurities, my fucked up past... All of it burned away in my mind and there was only her and the shape of her ass under my hand, the soft press of her body against mine. Her yielding. And it was all that mattered.

I breathed against her hair for a moment, savoring the scent of her. And newly clean of mind, I let my muscles flex, felt my masculinity wash over me. I felt my need to control her. I wanted to look in her eyes and see it in them, see that she thought I was all-powerful.

I stepped back from her and took a slower look at her. A slow smile spread over my lips. *Point to you, little girl. You want to push me? Okay.* My cock swelled, thinking of her pushing me. My smile grew, earlier worries seeming unfounded now.

"I love this, but…little girl, it makes me want to tear it off you. I want to get your knees all dirty. Let's go." I pulled her along with me to the car.

Jason and Christy were already at the bar and dropped their jaws, faces slack with shock when we walked in. As we passed them, Christy mumbled something and they started laughing. We stopped to grab a drink from Frank, who tried so hard not to react to her attire that I couldn't even get mad at him that he couldn't stop himself from glancing down to her tits every third word.

The early crowd of blue collar regulars lined the walk to our booth. *Fuck, I might murder someone tonight.* I kept a hand on her, but everyone knew anyway. Wasn't a bad idea to make sure there was no mistake.

We spent some time savoring our drinks, talking, trying to ignore the fucking blatantly sexual elephant in the room. Christy and Jason sat with us for a bit, not commenting on her clothes, but the mirth never left their eyes. Jason and I got up for another round and, when I looked back at Leda and Christy, they were laughing like they had been friends forever. And I wanted this forever, hanging with my best friends, my sexy-ass girl there tucked under my arm. I smiled, feeling better than I had all week.

"There it is," Jason said, nudging my shoulder. "A smile."

I smiled wider at him. "Yeah. Here I was thinking she wouldn't push me and this is what I get." I laughed. "Dude, she is so fucking perfect."

"Why do you think she did it?"

"I have an idea. I think I might have left her a little frustrated this morning." I chuckled a bit more, thinking I was going to love denying her orgasms, if this is what happened when I did.

As we walked back with the drinks, the girls erupted in laughter again. Jason sat next to Christy, pushing against her. "What are you two laughing about?"

She answered, "Well, *I* was laughing at how fucked these two are over each other. The funny thing is that Leda knows how fucked she is, but Xander, I don't think you really grasp it yet."

Leda flushed red, and I wondered how Christy could say I didn't know after the conversations of the last week.

Either way, I smiled. "I think I have an idea."

* * * *

When we got to the Window, Leda's eyes shone with excitement and she didn't notice the initial looks of speculation or the way I reacted to each predatory gaze in her direction. I guided her up the stairs to the loft, away from the majority of the crowd. Those people could fuck themselves.

Leda and I snuggled into a couch, across from Christy and Jason, who were doing the same. I leaned back and took some slow breaths. Leda sat next to me quietly. After a few seconds though, we turned toward each other...and said nothing. It was awkward, and I groped around for something to say, but was cut off by Jason's loud crack of laughter.

I looked toward him as he leaned over to me, yelling, "That's just rude, man!" He kept laughing and rested back with Christy, who was wiping a tear out of her eye, a laugh still on her lips. I looked at them, thinking *what the fuck?*

But Leda leaned into me, asking, "Did you ever get in touch with Mistress Seraphim? Are we meeting up with them?" She looked anxious.

I nodded at her, not offering comfort or reassurance at first. "Not till later though." I took a breath and decided that it was my last night with her before break—fuck being the cold-ass Dom the whole time. "Come here, little girl."

She snuggled into my side, under my arm, and I sighed contentedly. I just let myself enjoy her presence, the warm pressure of her against my side, the sweet look of fear mixed with excitement when she spoke to me.

I wanted to feel her skin under my fingers and dropped my hand to trace the bared skin of her back, between her shirt and skirt. She came alert, tension building her muscles, breath coming deeper.

I left it like that, not offering anything more, just to see what she'd do. And my little slut pushed her tits into my side, head tilted up toward me. *She wants it. Good.*

I cocked an eyebrow at her with the look of 'don't fucking test me, little girl'. I set my Coke on the low glass table in front of us and shifted sideways on the couch, looking right at her. I held her chin when she tried to look down because she instinctively knew she was in some trouble.

"Are you getting pushy, little girl?"

She saw the warning in my face when she tried to answer, because the words died on her lips. I nodded her head for her.

"What do you think I do to pushy little girls?" I was struck by how fucking brave she was to sit in front of me, not shrinking, not running away, when I went all cold and evil. I waited for her to answer.

She mumbled, too quiet to hear over the music, but her lips were readable. "I don't know."

"Yes, you do. You saw me take care of A." She paled, eyes wide with fear and I wanted more of it. Her fear slithered over my brain like a drug. I wanted to lick it all up. I dropped my hand from her chin to her throat and pushed her back against the couch. Held her there as I leaned forward, so my lips brushed her ear. "Did you think dressing like this would make me forget who or what I am and who and what you are?"

The gravel-growl in my voice got harder as I spoke and I felt her pulse leap under my fingers. She started to tremble, but didn't pull away. This was teetering on the edge of bad. I knew it and pushed it anyway, lightly shaking her by her neck and raising my voice, "Did you?"

She yelped, "No!" Her breathing was erratic, irregular, and she pushed against my arm, yelling, "I just thought it would be sexy and fun. Fuck, Xander. Yellow!"

I dropped my hand, surprised, but a small voice in the recesses of my mind was not surprised at all. But, she started crying and I hadn't expected that. I leaned over her again, raising my hand to her face and she flinched away. Ice pick in my heart.

That was it, the moment. The thing I needed to see. It was the consequence of how I was treating her. It wasn't anything other than rational on her part. I fucked up and now she didn't want me near her.

She yelled at me, "No! Just give me a fucking minute. I don't know how to be whatever it is you want me to be. I don't want to do this with you if it isn't going to be fun for both of us."

"Shit, me neither, honey." I pulled her next to me. "Come here, little girl. Shhh." I murmured into her hair. "You're perfect. You did exactly what I expect of you."

When she calmed, I went on, "I want you to push back against me. I want you to be you."

Her muscles went tight. This was the mindfuck of it and I knew it. *Be you. Don't change, but I'll punish you for it. Give me a reason to hurt you.* I tried to soften it a little, wanting to protect her. "But, sweetheart, what did you think would happen with this outfit tonight?"

The tension fell away from her and she slackened against me, resting her head on my shoulder. "I didn't think about it." And once she spoke, the words tumbled out of her in a rush. "I didn't have some big plan. I just thought it would be fun, cute, a little sassy or sexy or something. I was teasing you a little, I guess."

I made my voice gentle, but stern. "What did you think other people would think?" I paused to let her answer, but she didn't speak. "Because I think that there are some people here who will take this look as an invitation to spank you like a bad school girl. At a minimum. I'm not saying that dressing like this really *is* an invitation. It isn't, but it *is* provocative. God knows I feel provoked. But I will not be moved or controlled by you. I am what I always am, and you are what you always are. Mine."

She looked up at me, wet wide eyes glittering in the lights from the club. She looked mollified, steady. Her mascara was smudged a little and I liked it. I knew it was fucked up because I wanted her to cry, but never wanted her to feel anything bad, but wanted to cause her pain. It was a fucked up tangle in my head. But one thing made sense. *She was mine.*

I gave her a minute to respond if she wanted to, to pull away if she wanted to. But her features settled into something akin to peace and I leaned forward, slowly, to give her time to retreat if needed. I lightly kissed her lips, slow and soft. She yielded to me and her lips opened, admitting me into her.

Chapter Thirty-Two

Leda
Lindsey Stirling, Anti Gravity

I looked up at him, feeling oddly settled and solid. Deep inside my psyche, there was something reassuring and secure in knowing that he wasn't as reactive as me. He leaned into me, kissing me, slow, his tongue tracing my lips and opening me, stroking into the depths of my mouth. There was nothing like kissing through tears.

The way that he kissed me obliterated the rest of the world from my awareness. He was leaning over me, trapping me against the couch, but he kept his lips soft, his tongue slowly moving over me. He felt like honey.

We took our time getting into our play, first visiting the sensual play room. We settled on a low couch and watched the bodies moving together. I sat on his lap, facing the action in the room, and felt him get hard, pressing into my back. Xander's hand slipped around my waist and up to the swell of my breasts, tracing the curves, while he kissed, sucked and bit at my neck. I turned toward him to tell him I wanted him, but he anticipated me and shifted me over him so that I was straddling his lap, facing him. He slipped his hands up the sides of my thighs, under my skirt, to my hips. When we were kissing again, he made a low frustrated growl when he yanked at my panties. They didn't move because of my position. He gave up trying to pull them off, and instead, traced the crack of my ass under me to my wetness. His fingers teased and tickled me. I could feel his muscles tightening, his sounds growing more frustrated. He stroked up my back, flipping my skirt up as he moved his hand.

"I need to fuck you...soon." He growled into my ear. "But this isn't the right place for what I like."

What we *like*, I thought as he stood up, holding me in position with my legs wrapped around him.

He carried me out of the room, with some amused bystanders watching us. He didn't put me down once we left the room, but continued carrying me to the hidden stairwell that came from the back of the loft. Once tucked into that alcove, he set me down and reached under my skirt, pulling my panties down to my knees. He slipped his fingers into me. I reached for his hardness through his jeans, gripped him and stroked.

We went at each other like there was a deadline, like we were panicked, frenzied for a few minutes, frantically touching, before I unzipped him and pulled his cock out. There was a bead of pre-cum at the tip that I rubbed around with my thumb. He tilted his head up and groaned. I gazed up at him, memorizing the angles of his neck and jaw, how the muscles of his body tightened and arched toward me, seemingly without volition. When he dropped his gaze back down to me, I got a brief glimpse of a feral part of him before he spun me around and pushed my upper back down so I bent in half as he slammed his cock into me, all in one fluid movement. He ground it into me, unrelenting, punishing.

"God, you are so fucking dirty. Panties around your knees, getting fucked in a stairwell."

Oh...why yes, yes I am. I smiled to myself, owning it, reveling in it.

"Just for you." I moaned and he pounded into me harder, a few more times before his muscles tightened and released. He came deep inside me, but I was so wet that it only added to my saturation.

We sat in the stairwell for a few more minutes, laughing, catching our breath. He was so beautiful in these moments when the tension was gone from him, laughter touching his eyes, expression unguarded. But after a few minutes, the hardness returned to his face. He looked at me, softening his expression for a moment, kissing me again, but when he pulled back, his face was hard. The Dominant Xander. The Sadist Xander.

"We're going to find Mistress Seraphim and her slave and I'm going to spend some time training her. I want you involved. Do you have any objections?"

"I don't want to be away from you, but I'm nervous about participating. Can't I watch again? I liked it last time," I whined.

"I'm gonna ask you to trust me. Wait and see if you like it, but give it a little try, at least. Okay?"

I nodded and we stood to leave the alcove. As we walked, he added, "You know what I'm going to be thinking about the whole time?"

I shook my head.

"Your dripping wet pussy."

My jaw dropped at the vulgarity of that.

He paused again, thoughtful, then grabbed my face. "Do you know what this means to me, Leda? That you accept me, and what I need. God, that you are everything I need." His voice sounded pressured, strained.

I stared up into his face, unsure what to say, so I didn't speak. But something about that statement planted itself in the back of my mind, unresolved. This feeling that he thought this was a sacrifice for me.

I knew there was something there to work out, to tease out, but I pushed it away. Gruffly, his kissed me again. "Let's go."

Seraphim and A were just arriving when we stepped out to the foyer-like room. They were checking Seraphim's coat and her slave's clothes. Seraphim's eyes widened a bit at my clothing and A just smirked.

Seraphim air-kissed Xander's cheeks, saying, "Hello, hello. School-girl, Xander? Really?" She smiled and shook her head.

He answered, "I know. I'm not letting her out of my sight tonight. But…how has your pet been since last time?"

"Well…the same as always. I don't know what to do with her." She sounded like some wealthy socialite talking about her lap dog. "She has her moods and gets so defiant. She knows she should be on her knees, but she's still standing."

The woman sneered at us and stood a little taller, jutting her jaw out. Seraphim let out a little disgusted sigh and grabbed the back of her neck. With her other hand, she strapped a collar with attached leash on her. A very intentionally drew her gaze to meet her Mistress' directly. Seraphim's eyes narrowed and she slapped her. Then, the anger seemed to go out of her and she turned back to Xander.

"See what I mean. Just so *bad*. She was a little better after last time, but it was short-lived."

"I guess we'll just have to try harder." Xander's voice was conversational, but his face was a little terrifying—flat, blank with occasional flashes of menace.

The slave-girl turned and looked at him, saying nothing.

Acceptance crossed Xander's face and he turned back to Seraphim. "May I?"

She nodded her assent for the slave to be used. Faster than I expected, he grabbed her hair and pulled her forward and down, at the same time, hooking a foot behind her knee so her legs crumbled. She fell to her hands and knees between them. He hadn't let go of my hand through the whole series of movements.

"Ah, that's better," said Seraphim, yanking at the leash and pulling her pet along to the dungeon.

Xander turned to look at me. "Green?"

"Green." I said with a freaked out smile, but then on an impulse, I stepped close to him, onto my tiptoes and kissed him quick, a big smile flashing across my lips.

He smiled back. "Just for your peace of mind, I spent some time negotiating with them this afternoon. They're good." He followed them, my hand pressed tight in his.

Seraphim led her slave, who was crawling on her hands and knees, on the leash. They were definitely showing off. Xander's demeanor had changed as well, his back straightened and his face closed off, but he never let go of my hand.

I knew what to expect this time, but I still found myself staring around at various scenes playing out in front of me. One Domme had her sub hog-tied on the floor and was fitting some sort of hood or mask over his face. He squirmed against her, shuddering. A few steps away, a group of men were standing around a table, grunting. At first I couldn't make sense of what I was seeing, but as we moved, I was able to see a woman between them on the table, getting filled everywhere and the guys whose dicks she couldn't take were stroking themselves and reaching out to grab and touch and restrain her.

We found a space all the way in the back this time. I had the impression that people watched us as we walked in and I didn't know if it was Seraphim's blood-red leather body suit and Domme-bitch attitude, her slave on the leash, my school-girl get up or if some of them remembered the last time Xander had punished A. Xander was checking some bindings on a grid on the wall, when he turned back to us.

"Okay, girls, let's go."

A sat back on her haunches and looked up at him with a smirk. I was caught off guard by how pretty she was—she had a thin, athletic build and her midnight black hair was swept back off her immaculate face, pulled into a low ponytail. Her makeup made the sneer that blossomed on her face almost beautiful.

Then she said, "Hey, Xander. Fuck you." Her tone was calm, matter-of-fact, but her expression shifted to one of open challenge.

"Fuck me?" He laughed, echoing my thoughts. "Really? After last time?" He shrugged briefly. "All right." He closed the distance between them, grabbed her by the back of her neck and stood her up. He took two steps back and pressed her against the grid of bars, facing the wall. For a moment, he held his body against hers, just breathing her in. She shut her eyes, but he stepped away just as she began to relax back against him.

He said, "Tell me your safeword," as he started strapping her hands and arms to the wall. She didn't answer him, but didn't fight him either. He stepped to her side, where her face was turned. "What is your safeword, cunt?"

She spit in his face. And the world stopped for a moment. I gasped, looking from Xander to Seraphim and back again to see their reactions. The Domme was smiling slightly, pulling some things from her bag. Xander stepped back from the slave, pissed.

"Fuck your safeword, bitch."

A chill ran down my spine at those words and his facial expression as he wiped her spittle off his face and smeared it on hers.

Seraphim stepped up to them with clips in her hands. "Tongue, little bitch. That wasn't nice and you know it." Apparently, this wasn't abnormal behavior for her. She stuck her tongue out and Seraphim placed two clothespins on it. Her eyes closed and she moaned, grinding her hips into the bars in front of her.

"Thanks, I like that." Xander smiled. "Now, cunt, since you can't really talk, safewords don't matter. So a safe sign or gesture."

She moaned a venomous sounding growl and gave him the finger.

"Oh, perfect. There we go. You give me the finger if you want me to stop." He said it with a smile and I could see her thoughts cross her face. She wanted to be able to give him the finger just to piss him off but everything else would stop and she wouldn't really want that.

Point to Sadist Xander.

"Thuck eww," she said, as she drooled. He just laughed at her, then turned to me.

"Little girl, come here." I walked to him, wide eyed. He took my hand, stroking my palm. A watched us closely, trying to figure out what was next.

His voice was calm, soft, purring. Almost coy. "Little girl, she's being bad. Do you think you can help her be better, more like you?" I gave him a completely blank look and his hand slipped to my wrist and pulled me closer. He whispered, lips at my ear, "I want you to feel this. I want to see you squirm. And I want to mind fuck her. I need your help."

I pulled back to look at him. "Xander, I don't know... What...what do I even do? What do you mean?" *He couldn't expect that I was going to whip her or something. Could he?* His face was serene, smiling even.

"You just follow directions like the good girl I know you are. Now, take off that shirt." His hands moved to my shoulder as I automatically started unbuttoning the shirt. Shortly, I was standing in my bra, skirt and stockings. "Now come here." He moved me over to A's side and unstrapped her arm and leg. "Get in there, between her and the wall."

I shot him a look. "What?" I thought maybe I didn't understand what he meant.

His hand was in my hair moving me, as he growled, "Get your ass in there." He slid me in, then paused for a moment to lean his forehead against mine. "Trust me. You'll do just fine. You'll be perfect."

I took a deep breath as he strapped her arm and leg back down. This nameless woman and I were now face-to-face, bodies pressed together. I breathed deeply, smelling her expensive perfume and her body. Her abdomen was pressed to mine, a soft, warm pressure pushing me against the bars. Her legs were spread and my feet were between hers. She still had the clothespins on her tongue and her drool dripped down on my breasts.

Seraphim was on one side of us, smiling as she ran her hand over A's body. She moaned, closing her eyes and dropping her head forward a little. I started at the touch of hands on my ankles, strapping me to the wall. I knew it was Xander, even though I couldn't see him. A moment later his face was opposite of Seraphim's.

"Arms up, little girl."

I shifted around to get my arms up over my head and Xander tied my wrists as well. The binds cinched into my skin and my brain relaxed, giving up worry.

I trust him. Nothing will harm me.

The wave of acceptance washed over me and my fear evaporated. When the first strike came against her body, I heard the smack at the same time that her body jerked against me and she moaned, dripping more drool on me. I knew it was Seraphim hitting her because Xander was still standing with us.

Excitement gleamed in his eyes. "Green?"

He was asking me to trust him, to allow myself to be taken somewhere without knowing the plan. Curiosity and fear churned in my chest. Then, just like that the bewilderment settled and my nerve steeled. I wanted him to be proud of me, here on his turf, in front of everyone. I wanted to please him. I wanted to make his blank face smile.

But more than any of that, *I* wanted to know. I wanted to know what it would be to be in it, in the middle of it. "Green." I smiled at him. He stepped away and my eyes shifted to the more experienced submissive's. She smiled at me, and only looked marginally insane, smiling with her tongue compressed between wooden clothespins.

And the onslaught started.

Seraphim and Xander must have been standing on either side of her because the strokes were coming too fast for it to be just one person punishing her. She braced her body, groaning against the pain. After a handful of strikes, a rhythm evolved — they alternated sides of her body and she rocked against me, side-to-side. We were skin on skin, sharing the same air, her face filling my vision. It was incredibly intimate, being that close to someone as they were punished, beaten. I saw each nuance of her pain, of her evolving lust and pleasure.

It went on for what felt like a long time, but may have only been a few minutes. When they stopped, she was panting and slumped against me. Our breasts pressed together and she dropped her head back, a grin on her face.

Xander was right there, his face next to hers, speaking in her ear, but looking at me. "That was just a warm-up for my arm. Don't tell me you're already tired?"

She turned her head to him, an eyebrow cocked up. "Kith my ath."

"Kiss your ass? With a whip maybe." He stepped away with a sly smile still on his face. I had a wild rush of jealousy that she had made him smile like that.

The room was visible over her shoulder and there was a small crowd watching two subs tormented by two Dominants. Xander and Seraphim were conferring and he stepped back with a strap. It looked like a belt with no buckle. I hissed a breath in and A's eyes whipped to mine a beat before the first crack met her ass. She held my gaze, like she couldn't look away, as nine more strokes fell on her. With each one her eyes would widen for a moment and her body would tense as she sucked in her breath. Her upper lip glistened with a fine sheen of sweat. When the final stroke snapped against her skin, she slumped against me again, this time dropping her head on my shoulder. That gave me a very clear view of the room. There was a handful of people watching, some of whom made eye contact with me, their faces passive or alive with some sort of frenzy in-check.

"Jesus Christ," I muttered. "This is fucking crazy."

I glanced around to find Xander, intending to call *Red* because it was just too much, too ridiculous, just too fucking crazy. But when I found him off to the side at a table with Seraphim, pulling instruments from her assortment, he looked different, vital in a way I hadn't really seen before, relaxed, smiling. He turned, his gaze finding mine, eyes hardening. He squared his shoulders to me and the sharp passion, the power, the fury in him stole my breath, settling over and into me. I didn't want to stop this.

I focused on my own body, my breasts wet with my partner in torment's sweat and saliva, my abdomen pressed tight against her. My pussy clenched in on itself and dampened my thighs, leaving me sticky. I flashed back to our sex in the stairwell and his comment about dripping from me.

Another wave of God-knows-what — submission, endorphins, subspace — whatever — hit in force and the tension dissipated. I didn't care that these people were watching this bizarre degradation. I wanted the intensity. I wanted Xander's fury and power to subsume me. I felt my face flush and my expression changed, tension leaving my neck and jaw. I saw it reflected in him as he stepped toward us. I could tell he knew my fear had dropped away—or at least changed to something exciting and pleasurable. He pressed his body tight against A, who in turn was pressed into me. He grabbed the back of my head and delivered a tight, hard kiss, over her shoulder.

"You know what I just thought about, little girl? How wet I bet you are right now."

I surprised myself by my answer, a bright, "Me too!" And A giggled.

"Don't pretend you're not drenched too, cunt. I see you grinding up on my girl." Xander reached between us and pinched her lower lip until she moaned. And as she whined, he brought his other hand around to my side and traced his fingers over the curves of my hip and waist, his thumb brushing roughly over my breast. Xander's gaze locked on mine, but he leaned toward her ear, his words measured and dripping with malice as he said, "You're such a whore."

He was actually talking to her, but for a moment it felt like he had said it to me and I caught myself getting a rush of sweet-tinged shame.

He stepped away, but it was only a short break before he started in with the flogger. After several strokes on her butt, he started on her legs. She moaned and ground into me. The tendrils of the flogger wrapped around her thigh with each stroke and moved air over my legs too. A few strokes later, whether intentionally or not, he changed his stroke and the tips of the strands clipped my thigh. I jumped. He must have seen my movement, because he paused and appeared at my side.

"You okay? What happened?" He looked worried.

"I'm fine. It just clipped me a little." I shrugged, not wanting to alarm him, but drinking his face and concern in. In truth, the sting was fading to delicious, lovely warmth, making me more aware of the sensations all over my body.

"Yeah?" Seeing that I was just fine, his gaze darkened a bit. "Did you like it?" And before I answered, "Let's try a little more."

He stepped away. Before I was ready, the flogger came down on her again, but a longer portion of the falls hit my inner thigh this time. Before that fully registered, he started raining down blows on us. She was, by far, bearing the brunt of it, but both of us were twitching, hissing and moaning.

After a few more minutes, Seraphim stepped up and removed the clothespins from her tongue. She screamed as the blood rushed back to her tongue. Xander had paused and stepped to our other side, checking in with us. He slid his hand between our bodies, down to the space between our pubic bones, and yanked my skirt up so my upper thighs and panties were bared, visible between her widely spread legs.

I felt an internal echo of an objection, but it was quiet and distant and I didn't want to listen to it. I said nothing and he started in again with the flogger. The ends of the flogger's strands flicked against my bare skin. It stung in a way I hadn't experienced before and it was so close to the line of my panties that I was panting. With each strike, my co-sub now moaned loudly then slumped into me. Xander paused again in his ministrations. While he paused, she looked up at me, fire in her eyes.

"Do you like it?" she whispered. There was sweat running down her cheeks and mascara ran down her face, washed away in her tears.

"Yes," I peeped.

"Me too." She leaned her face forward to mine and laid a soft sweet kiss on my lips. "I like it more, like this, with you." She pressed her body into mine again, free of the pain now. She breathed more quickly and her pubic bone ground against me. Just as I started to grind back into her and craned my neck up to kiss her again, Seraphim's voice shattered the moment.

"I hear you talking, Thing." She smacked her ass. Thing closed her eyes and moaned, biting her lip. "No one wants to hear you. Shut up."

Seraphim started to walk away, but before she was out of earshot, Thing winked at me and said, "Hey, Seraphim, go fuck yourself."

Seraphim stomped back to us and grabbed her by the throat, stretching her back against her restraints. "Gag, plug, clamps, what else are you going to make me do to you?"

When Seraphim released her, her face was red and she gasped. Seraphim stepped away and she leaned forward to kiss me again, her tongue just invading my mouth when Seraphim returned with a ball that she shoved in her mouth. There were straps attached that Seraphim secured behind her head. She grabbed her throat again, pulling her back to place nipple clamps. These were different than other ones I had seen. They screwed down onto her nipples and Seraphim tightened them until the dusky skin blanched. Thing groaned against her gag. Seraphim held a bulbous black rubbery butt plug in front of our faces, pulling a condom on it.

"Leda, open your mouth," she snapped. I obeyed without thinking, because she was a scary bitch. She jammed the plug in my mouth. "Good girl. Thing, you should be taking notes from this little bitch." She swirled the plug around in my mouth and I was vaguely disgusted that anybody's ass toy was in my mouth. At least it had a clean condom on it, but it tasted gross. She pulled it out of my mouth, trailing my saliva down my chin, and pressed it into Thing's ass.

Seraphim was back at our faces. "You know I love you, but I won't tolerate this behavior anymore. Either you belong to me and behave or I'm done with you. I want you to think about that while Xander finishes with you. I'm going out to meet new people."

That threat was a shock and the slave looked frantic. Tears welled in her eyes and she tried to talk through the gag, her voice plaintive. With that, Seraphim stepped away and Xander started back with the strap again. He continued to place strokes in a way that the tip would flick around to my thighs and it hurt so much more.

After a few more strikes, I was starting to squirm and grit my teeth against the pain, and my co-sub was openly screaming into her gag, tears streaming down her face. Xander paused and we slumped against each other, laying our heads on each other's shoulders. I looked up at Xander. He had pulled his shirt off and was conferring with Seraphim, who hadn't actually walked away. She was handing him something and had an expression of complete glee on her face. Xander turned and, seeing me watching, put his finger to his lips as he walked toward us.

"Okay, girl-thing, I can tell you're looking at my girl, looking for sympathy. Not gonna happen. You're all alone and now even Seraphim has left you here — with me. No more looking to Leda for solace." He slipped a blindfold over her eyes and she screamed again into the gag, shaking her head from side to side.

After a few moments, Seraphim walked up to us as well, now barefoot so her boots wouldn't clack against the concrete floor. She had a cane and caned Thing's inner thighs and pussy a handful of times, until she was shaking and crying, screaming almost continuously into her gag. Abruptly Seraphim stopped, dropping the cane.

I immediately felt her fingertips brush against my panties as she started playing with A's pussy. Thing moaned and squirmed against her hand and it was unclear to me if she knew it was Seraphim or thought it was Xander. Then the Mistress paused, giving her a break, but not releasing us. After a few minutes, she was back with a small plastic device that had straps all over it. She held it up next to her slave's ear and flicked a switch that set it buzzing. Her hands were between us, strapping it onto Thing's pussy, presumably directly on her clit by the way she reacted. As she was doing that, Xander came to our other side.

"Little girl, still green?"

"Yeah, but I don't know about her. She's taken a lot tonight."

"Well, Thing? Gonna give up yet? Flick me off if you want me to stop." He paused, looking at her hands, to see if she was giving him the finger, but her hands were knotted into tight balls. "All right, well, Leda was telling me that she might be interested in wax play, so I have a few candles lit over here. Ready to start again, girls?" She nodded weakly, breathing raggedly through her nose. I looked at him, eyes wide, my own breathing shaky. "Let's switch things up a bit."

He reached up and untied her hands, but left my hands and both of our feet tied. He strapped a restraint around her waist, attaching it to the wall on either side, so she could only bend backward, but couldn't actually get too far. She stretched out while she had the chance, inadvertently grinding her vibrating pussy against mine and I gasped in surprise. She heard me, paused then started grinding on me, trying to get me off with her. She stood and laid her head on my shoulder, unable to kiss me with the gag in, but her hands started roaming over my breasts, lightly at first.

Xander stood back, watching this, and I met his eyes. He gestured as if to say, *please go ahead.* So, while holding his gaze, I dropped my mouth down to her neck and started kissing and licking her. She moaned hard, arched up against me and squeezed my nipple between her fingers. I shut down all doubtful thoughts and started grinding with her, our moans mingling. Her excitement was building, and she whipped her hips at me, harder now, grunting. Xander slowly walked to us, holding a pillar candle and my gaze. He approached, directly behind her.

"God, you have *no shame.* Fucking grinding on my girl like some bitch in heat. So fucking dirty."

She moaned at his voice and leaned her body back against him.

His free hand slipped around to her throat, but he still held my gaze. "I don't want either of you to come until I allow it. Do you both understand?"

She nodded but was shaking and whimpering.

It was too much and I looked up at Xander, gasping, "Soon please?"

The flash of emotions across his face was too fast to read, but I saw softness, pleasure, pride, joy then sternness again. He flexed his hand on her throat and pulled her backward, taking an entire step back, so she bent completely backward. This drove the little vibrator on her clit against my pussy as well. I involuntarily arched my hips to maximize the pressure and started grinding into her. Xander nudged his knee up against her butt, pressing on her welts and the butt plug but also driving us together harder. I let out a loud cry and he started pulsing his knee against her.

"Please, *Xander!* I'm gonna come soon. I can't stop it! *Please!*" The last was nearly a scream of panic. I didn't care where I was, who was watching. I didn't care about anything but him, his lips and waiting for the words. My brain was foggy and I didn't need to think. It was beautiful.

He smiled and proceeded to pour hot wax over both our chests, saying, "Now."

We came, screaming. The wax was hot and intense and my orgasm rocked me so hard my eyes watered.

The crowd around us had swelled to probably about thirty people and several of them started clapping. I'm sure it wasn't my tears specifically that made them clap, but the timing was suspicious and there were a few surly-looking Dom-types, who did seem to be particularly amused by my crying. I shuddered, too wrung out to really care why anyone around me was doing anything.

Chapter Thirty-Three

Xander
Temper Trap, Sweet Disposition

I stood, holding another Dominant's sub as she shuddered, watching Leda sob, wanting nothing more than to wrap my girl up in my arms. Seraphim knew I wanted to attend to my own sub, just as she wanted to attend to her girl. She released the knots and turned off the vibrator.

I distantly registered Seraphim taking Thing down, getting her wrapped up in a blanket.

But Leda was all that mattered for me right then. "Hey, honey girl. Green?" I untied her, kissing her lips softly, kissing the inside of her wrists over the redness left by the rope.

Her eyebrows lifted, worry in her voice. "More?"

"Maybe. Are you okay after that?" My voice was low, letting the loving boyfriend speak more than the stern Dominant. I untied her ankles and she stepped a little away from the wall.

"Okay?" Her voice held disbelief, a little laughter. "Yes. That was insane." She was a little breathless. She pulled her skirt back to see her very small welts and bruises. They looked delicious. I lowered myself to my knees and licked and kissed her skin.

Some would say kneeling in front of my sub wasn't domly, worshiping her bruised body wasn't hardcore. They could fuck themselves. Nothing was more dominant that doing whatever I wanted to with her.

I stood up and wrapped my arms around her, pressing into her. I took her in, her smeared makeup, her fading perfume mixed with the clean smell of her sweat, her soft breath against my chest. "You smell so good and look so wrecked. It's amazing. I want to fuck you. Now. Green?"

She looked at me with doubt. "I don't know."

I had to be in her and if she wanted me to take her somewhere else I would, but I didn't want to. I wanted to plant myself in her in front of everyone. I wanted them to know she was mine, in every sense of the word. I wanted her to know it. I wanted to show it off. I wanted to revel in her submission. "I'm not asking permission, Leda. We're beyond that."

Her eyes widened and her breathing picked up speed as her body tensed in my arms. After only a few moments, the worry left her eyes and she melted into me. Soft, pliable in my arms. *Fuck yes.*

I waited a few beats longer to be sure. It was the tricky thing about BDSM. Her consent was key, but it was true — I wasn't going to ask permission.

When she only leaned into me more, her breath catching at the touch of my fingers, I hitched her up by her ass and wrapped her legs around me. We matched up well, my restrained cock pressed against her panties. I wedged her against the wall so I could free a hand to get my cock out. As I did, I brushed against her soaking wet panties. I grabbed that wet little bit of cloth and yanked it aside—slipped deep into her. I stayed still, watching her face, watching to see if this would be too much. Watching to see if I was miscalculating and fucking everything up.

"If you don't want this, give me your safeword." My voice was hard, strained with how much I wanted to be bouncing her on my dick, but I waited for her assent. She said nothing, just left her forehead against my shoulder. "Then I'm assuming you are green."

She lifted her head—shy look on her face—and nodded. She flushed hard and I saw it. She was mortified, but turned on. I had to push her, make her give up her shame. Even as she nodded, the walls of her pussy rippled against me.

"Fucking say it, Leda."

"Green." She gasped it out and dropped her gaze in shame.

I rolled my hips, sliding against her slickness. I felt her hot wet tears splashing against my chest. The world stopped a bit, my mouth went dry. "Look at me."

She lifted her head, eyes all big and liquid, mascara running down her cheeks anew. She was right there with me, in the moment, no fear or evolving trauma in her features. It was indescribably sexy. "When you cry, I want to fuck you so hard."

I slammed into her, pushing her against the rigging on the wall. It was hard and she absorbed it, accepted it, but sobbed and her tears nearly undid my control. She shifted, changing the angle of our connection.

"Oh Jesus!" She moaned the words out and closed her eyes.

Nope, you are right here, with me. "Don't close your eyes. Look at me."

She opened her eyes and looked at me, but I shifted her around so I could grab her chin and force her to hold my gaze. She wound her arms around my neck and her tears stilled. The sleepy look she got in subspace washed over her face, her body slackening in my arms.

She sighed. "Thank you, Xander."

Her eyes were on mine, so close I could see the flecks of white and cool gray in them. *Thank me? Jeeeezus. I love her.*

"Say it again." I pounded my cock into her over and over, pounded her back into the bars on the wall.

She whispered right against my lips, "Thank you."

I growled some obscenity and came, grinding into her as hard as physics and our respective anatomies would allow.

For a moment, I just rested there, holding her up, my forehead against her shoulder. She dropped her head and nuzzled under my chin, all wrapped around me. After a few beats to catch my breath, I carried her to the back wall of the dungeon space. A couch was tucked into a little alcove there and a few people were sitting on it when I approached. They all got up at the look on my face. They had just watched our scene and knew what we had just been through. They knew we needed a place to rest.

Leda naturally moved her legs around as I sat down, so she knelt around me, straddling me. I reached under her, to put my cock away and let her have a little modesty back, but she jolted up, hands on my chest, eyes pleading.

"No! Don't, not yet." Now she cried again, losing it and dropping back onto me, clinging to me. It killed me to see her falling apart. I wanted to be her glue and put everything back together again.

I kissed her hair, stroking her back. "Little girl, what is it?"

She spoke, her voice thick with her tears. "I don't know. It was intense and sex in public and I just... I don't know. And I'm upset about being apart for a week and a half. I just don't want to lose you sooner than I have to."

She cried harder and I held her. At one point, Jason and Christy approached, serious wariness in their expressions. I waved them off and they left again, but concern was etched in their features. They didn't understand. They weren't D/s. They were just kinky.

But I knew what she was feeling. Knew isn't the right word. I *understood* what happened to a sub, the mental rollercoaster of playing like this. It was fun. It was torture. It was sexy and it was scary. And she'd be feeling wiped out, exhausted, maybe guilty, maybe angry. She'd need me and hate me and love me all at once.

She needed safety, security, softness, tenderness. I had all of those for her. "Okay, honey girl. I've got you." I shushed into her hair, rubbing her back. "We'll just stay right here as long as you want."

All the fear and fight went out of her and she cried until she stopped on her own. It seemed like forever because I couldn't make it stop, because I had done this to her. Certainly with her consent, but I had caused it, nonetheless.

As she rested, melting into my chest, my own thoughts spiraled. I felt like the biggest fucking monster in the world. *I fucking love this girl and I want to destroy her like this. I want it. I want her tears and her wails and her blood and her bruises. What is wrong with me?*

I generally didn't get Dom-drop, but I was sure this was it. That war in my mind knowing that I would want to do this again, despite what it did to her. Knowing what it did to both of us. I was fucked up enough to keep wanting it. Twisted because I liked that it hurt and we had to recover from playing so hard.

My mind flashed to some vanilla sex and watching some TV afterward. It was so goddamned bland that I couldn't ever imagine wanting that. *So I'm a monster. I am what I am and I don't want to change.* My acceptance of myself settled me. I needed to know she didn't hate me, but only when she was ready. Once I had that, I'd be fine.

Her breathing had evened out and I brushed her hair away from her face. She was fighting to keep her eyes open. I shushed her again. "I've got you, little girl. You're okay now."

Her eyes fluttered shut and I saw how bruised they looked, small burst blood vessels from how hard she had cried. I took a deep breath and shifted to fix our clothes, put my dick away. I dropped my head back on the back of the couch, just stared at the ceiling. Relishing the weight of her on me that I felt her with each breath. The tickle of her hair against my ribs.

Sometime later, as I sat there, Seraphim brought our things to us. Her eyes were full of concern and she sat next to me, her girl-slave on her leash at her feet.

"Are you well, Xander?"

I cleared my throat. "Yeah, I'm all right." My voice was tired, but I tried to play it off.

"It's okay to be a little heartsick at how she falls apart. You're only a shitty person if you destroy her and walk away, leave her a mess when she really needs you."

I glanced at her. Her eyes were full of the knowledge of how much this could hurt. She rubbed her girl's hair, pulling her face against her leg.

Seraphim always came across as one seriously vicious and evil bitch. I didn't know much about their relationship outside of the D/s dynamic. I didn't know if they were together or if they only played together.

"Can I give you some advice?" She leaned toward me a little. I nodded. "I'd get her out of this space. When she wakes up, she's not gonna want to be right here, close to where all this shit happened." She stood up, gently pulling at the leash. She looked back at me. "All this"—she waved at me and Leda, vaguely indicating our situation—"only means you love her."

I stammered, trying to respond, not really ready to have anyone make that kind of declaration for me, but she only scoffed at me and walked away, smiling.

I took her advice and carried Leda up to the VIP lounge. I sat on the couch and laid her out with her upper body resting against me. One of the cocktail servers, a super-androgynous person named Slick, brought some water.

Jason and Christy found me again and asked how it went. I was noncommittal about the experience. I was still working through my own weird, mixed response to it. They didn't push it. Ultimately, Leda woke, looking around, all sleepy-eyed and sweet.

She asked to leave and I was happy to take her home, but wanted her to rehydrate before we left. She took a tentative sip of water then gulped the remainder down.

I would have carried her out to the car, but she nudged me a bit to get her feet on the ground. I still kept my hands on her until I had her seat belted in the car.

I took her back to her apartment, half carried her up the stairs, tucked her into her bed. I took a short shower, needing a little space from her for a few minutes. In the shower, I rested my head against the wall—wanting and not wanting this—for the rest of my life.

"Jesus Christ, Stone. Get it together," I muttered to myself as I got out of the shower. I dried off, pulled on some shorts I had left at her place a few weeks ago. She had washed them and set them out, on top of her dresser, like she wasn't sure what to do with my stuff in her space.

In her bed, I wrapped myself around her. I told myself it was to help her feel safe, even in her sleep, but I knew I lied, at least a bit. I did it for me, because I loved the feeling of her in my arms. Her breath expanding against me, pressing into me. I tried to stay awake and savor her, but fatigue pulled me into sleep, sooner than I wanted.

* * * *

The next morning, I ran my hand over her hip, pulling her against me and she woke, smiling softly over her shoulder at me. Her face was a wreck. Makeup smudged and smeared all over, hair a mess. But her smile was perfect. Serene, content.

"Let's take a shower, Boss."

She ran the water, superhot the way she liked it. I stood back watching her get clean, all pure again.

Renewed. The water on her body sparkled and her skin got rosy from the heat.

All I could think about was being away from her, and how much I didn't want it to be happening. A higher order, more rational part of my brain was telling me to grow the fuck up, but this was different and she was different and I didn't want to lose my new toy. Even I knew I was being a total chump, knew it was bullshit to just call her *my toy*. I loved her. I knew I loved her, but it felt cheap to say it, right before we got on planes going to different destinations.

We ate breakfast in near silence. Just some eggs and fruit she needed to use before she left for the break. I watched her eating, her eyes faraway. It was the worst kind of anticipation.

When she stood to clear the dishes, I pulled her into my lap and rested my lips against her damp hair. She smelled like everything I wanted, everything I never really thought I could have. She shifted a little and looked at me with concern.

"Mmmm. I'm gonna miss you." There. I had said it, at least that I'd miss her.

"Yeah. I hate this. Wait here, just a minute." She smiled as she walked to her bedroom.

When she came back, she was fighting a big smile and had something hidden behind her back. When she got to me, she handed me a small present, wrapped in silver paper. There was a small tag— *Yours, anytime.*

There was a flash of a smile as I read that, thinking, *I know.* She settled at my feet like she knew just where she should be, and I opened the package. "What's this, little girl?"

She had such a big, beautiful smile on her face, it stole my breath. "Merry Christmas, Boss."

The box was small, looked like jewelry and I had a moment of thinking how very funny it would have been if we'd shopped at the same store. I opened the lid and it was a key, with a stylized heart-shaped keychain. I smiled at her, pulling her toward me for a kiss, but she forestalled me with her fingers on my lips.

She knelt, directly in front of me, face angled toward the floor, looking at me through her lashes. "So, I want you to have this." She paused and I waited. There was more. "So you have access to me, anytime you want me."

I couldn't fucking breathe. She knew exactly what she was giving me with this. She was giving me permission to invade her space whenever I wanted to. She knew it was another level of submission to me. That she would never be unavailable. Never be off limits. And when I could breathe again, I smiled and pulled her into my lap. "Girlie, you are just about perfect, you know that?"

I kissed her for a few minutes, wanting for all the world to just get inside her again. But we had shit to do, flights to catch. So, I ran home to get my things while she packed. When I came back, she met me at the curb and we went to the airport together, somber again, still nearly silent. Once we were checked in and seated in her gate, it almost got awkward.

She huffed a big sigh and I glanced at her. She had a bizarre, but huge, smile on her face. Forced. "Okay, this is silly. It's only ten days! Why are we acting like this?" She turned toward me more. "You doing anything exciting with your family?"

I smiled at her. She was good for me, keeping me from the shittiness in my own head. "Not really, other than the fundraiser." I paused, then added, "Well, every year on Christmas Eve, my dad rents the ice rink and we have a fun, low key hockey game and then just skate for a few hours. We get a pretty big group of the Senator's staff and their families. It's a nice change from the political bullshit they're always doing. Next year, you should come." I smiled wider. Her ploy had worked and my mood had lifted.

"That would be great." She smiled again, this time genuinely.

"What about you. Any plans?" We had already talked about all this, but it filled the time and I liked how happy she got when she talked about her family.

"Just a few dates."

What the what?

"I'm just kidding, killer! No, we don't really have a lot of specific plans. My siblings have kids now, so it kind of changes things. Before we had the little ones in the family, we used to do an afternoon movie on Christmas Eve, then Mass at midnight. Then, Christmas morning in PJs and a big breakfast. Now, the family is getting too big to stay in one house and the kids are too little for midnight Mass. Soooo, who knows?"

"Well, I kind of can't wait to meet all of them." The stories of her family sounded too perfect to be real—not unlike herself. Of course I thought about my parents. How they only had the thinnest veil over their hate for each other. How they were still married because they couldn't afford how ugly their divorce would get. How they both cheated and that it wasn't really even cheating anymore.

She must have sensed that my thoughts were going dark again because she leaned into me, a little mischief in her eyes. "Yeah…yeah. I really miss them. I'm excited to get home and see them, but I'm really going to miss you. Even though it's only a few days.

However, maybe it will give me a little break to recover some because you, sir, are a little demanding."

I smiled, liking the sound of the word 'sir' on her lips. "Hey, I warned you. But, are you okay? Last night was intense."

"I think so. I'll keep you posted if it changes though."

I smiled wider. *What a good girl.*

She added, "Thank the sub whisperer. She told me about aftercare and how it goes both ways."

Her flight was called and cut off whatever conversation that might have triggered. I leaned into her, a low, dark croon in my voice as I remembered her tied and screaming for her release. "But, I think you loved it, didn't you?"

She held my gaze and her pupils dilated, lips parting.

"Didn't you, Leda?"

A soft blush colored her cheeks and she whispered, "Yes."

I held her face and kissed her. "I'm gonna miss you, too, little girl. Text me when you get there." I stood and pulled her up with me, gave her a big hug and turned her to the door.

As she waited, she turned back to me, bratty-cute little smile on her lips and mischief in her eyes. "Bye-bye, Boss."

Chapter Thirty-Four

Leda
Coldplay, Always In My Head

It was relaxing to be at home, but predictably, my family wanted all the details about my first semester.

"School's great. I even made the Dean's list. I hated histology, but I really liked anatomy." I flushed thinking about Xander tutoring me and my sister caught it.

"What was that? Who is he?" Her eyes sparkled and she grabbed her husband Evan's hand across the table.

"Yeah. I met a guy—Xander." They all leaned in, expectant. "Sheesh, all right! He was my anatomy tutor. He's a second year."

I laughed when they hit me with the predictable barrage of interrogation.

Mom asked, "What's he like, honey?"

Dad asked, "How long has this been going on?"

Luke's wife, Angie, leaned in, "How serious is it?"

My sister, Julia, echoed my mom, "What's he like?"

Her husband, Evan, murmured, "Where'd he go to undergrad?"

But everyone hushed at Luke's question. "What's his specialty going to be?"

As if that was the most important thing about him.

"Something surgical, I think. But he's planning to wait a bit, do some rotations before he really settles on something. But, I mean," I gushed, "his ties are so perfect. I can't imagine him doing anything else."

Evan, who was a general surgeon, and Dad both offered to have Xander come rotate with them, though only Evan looked excited. Dad's face was a bit stormier, like he'd fix this somehow by making Xander operate on kidneys and balls.

I answered, noncommittally, "I'll let him know you offered."

My sister interrupted me, "Enough about that crap," earning her an exasperated look from Dad and Mom. "Give us the details, Leeds."

"Well, he went to West Point for undergrad. He served in the Army and worked in intelligence." Scoffs and jokes about military intelligence being an oxymoron. "His dad is the chief of staff for Senator Noe."

Julia's head snapped up. "The guy who actively tries to get Planned Parenthood shut down. The guy who's against contraception and abortion, even in the case of incest! That fu..." My mom shot her a look. "That fricking guy?"

"Ummm. We don't spend a lot of time discussing his father's boss's politics, so I don't specifically know his platform." I tried to answer diplomatically, but was a little alarmed at what she was saying.

My mom gave her a look of 'tone-it-down', and said, "Sorry, Leeds, tell us more about Xander. What's he like?"

"He is, well…he's intense. He studies hard, is doing really well in school, at the top of his class. He's learning Brazilian Jiu Jitsu and has shown me some of it. He has a friend from high school that lives down there too, Jason. Jason owns a few places—a coffee shop, a bar and a night club. And has been dating Christy for a long time. She's a meteorologist. And, like, the funniest person I have met in a long time."

Evan made a mock sad face and pouted a little. Jules interceded, "Yes, honey, you're very funny. You were saying, Leeds?"

"I don't know. What else do you guys want to know?"

My dad, leaning back in his chair, asked, a little sternly, "How long have you been dating him?"

I felt like I was in trouble. "Well, I guess he asked me out after the first tutoring session, so…pretty much the whole semester. It doesn't hurt to have the tutor studying at the same table as me, pretty much every night," I added smiling, trying to alleviate his concerns.

"Every night, Leda? Really?" His face was a cross between pissed and worried.

My mom interceded again, smoothly carrying the conversation on, "So, he went to West Point, and then served in the Army before med school."

My dad's head snapped up again. "How old is he, Leda?"

I had hoped to avoid this.

"He's thirty-four, dad. He left the Army after his first tour and then transferred to FBI and worked at the Pentagon for a few years before deciding to go to medical school." Everyone tried to cover their shock at least a little. "What? It's not a big deal."

My mom looked at me with compassion on her face. "But, Leeds, don't you think he might be looking for something a little different than you? I mean, he's probably ready to settle down and start a family. You don't want all that pressure, do you?"

"Umm, why not? Jules and Evan met in med school. Lukie met Angie at his friend's wedding, *during med school*. Lots of people get married in med school. Hell, Jules, you had a baby at the end of med school! Why would it be any different for me? Maybe I do want to marry him!" The room went silent and my interior voice was screaming at me. *Shut the fuck up, Leda! Don't go down this road with them, and… Did I just say something about marrying him?*

Angie saved me. "Well, it sounds like you have made a great connection with him. I'm glad you're happy, sweetie. Too bad he lives far away. Would've been fun to meet him."

Luke laughed at that and turned to her. "Honey, you are so sweet, but that guy's gonna be in trouble when we meet him, don't you think? Listen to how overprotective we all are of our little Leeds." He smooched her cheek as he got up to check on the kids, who had started to get a little rowdy in the play room, and my interrogation session was over. *Thank Christ.*

* * * *

As much as I enjoyed being with my family, in the back of my mind, I was counting down the time until I would see Xander again. I was scheduled to leave on New Year's Eve and needed to get some things together, a dress at least.

I had already told my parents about the fundraiser and that I would be leaving a few days early. They didn't mind at all. Jules and Lukie and their families were leaving before New Year's as well, so my parents were planning to go to a party with friends and had thought I'd have to tag along. They may have even been relieved.

Tiffany and I were going to go to the Magnificent Mile to look for a dress. My mom, Jules and Angie all decided to come with us and it turned into a full girl's day, while the men took the kids to the children's museum. I got the dress from an emerging designer that Tiffany loved, who had an edgy new store in the Garment District. It was a deep midnight blue, almost black, draped in a Grecian style but with accents of bare metal, studs and a bare zipper. It grazed the floor and left most of my back exposed, begging the question of undergarments.

My mom had been going to hospital and charity fundraisers long enough that she had a bra shop she loved, where we found a functional, beautiful bustier. I bought the matching thong and thigh high stockings that attached to the clips on the bustier, which earned me a saucy thumbs up from Tiffany.

Fortunately, the bruising from my last night with Xander was well-healed so no one asked any uncomfortable questions. *That seems super-fucked up.*

Angie loved the Christian Louboutin collection and insisted that she help me find the 'right' shoes. She found an amazing pair, dark silver with studding all over and a solid metallic stiletto. I had to practice walking in them, but I loved the whole look.

Once we finished shopping, my mom, sister and sister-in-law went back to the house with my purchases. Tiffany and I stayed downtown to have a night out. After the rest of them left, Tiffany grilled me about Xander.

"Listen, bitch. I love your family, but I did *not* just endure a day of shopping with them for zero reward. Help me out here. I need something for the spank bank. Because, I will note, you still have not sent me a dick-pic."

I barked out a laugh. "I can't even imagine having that conversation with him. I'd be all, 'hey, honey, *lemme take a selfie* with your junk'." I fell to giggles and after a minute of trying to keep a serious face, Tiffany joined me.

"All right, how about a regular picture?"

I pulled out my phone and showed her a few pictures of him that I had taken over the last few months. When she looked up at me with a smile, I just shrugged.

"So, do you love him?"

"Yeah, I think I do. Shit, I think I could marry him. Is that crazy?"

"Well, yeah. But only because marriage in general is crazy. Like, I'm in my twenties and don't know shit about life. How about I promise to love someone forever. Seems legit."

I laughed again. "I'm really happy though. I just feel like everything is easy with him."

She cocked her head to the side. "Really? Because I seem to remember some phone calls about feeling slutty."

"But you were right! Why shouldn't I enjoy my sex life? Seriously, what a fucked up question." I dropped my voice to a more hushed tone. "And the kinky stuff is just fun. Maybe that's not right. It's intense and wild. And *so* much better than sex in college. I mean, an entirely different universe. Can't even explain it."

"Well, try."

I changed the subject with an apologetic, but pointed glance around the diner at the other patrons. "What else should we do tonight? Wanna hit Boys' town?"

"Honey, I don't look nearly good enough for Boys' town." She laughed. That said, we were both in jeans and sweaters. Not exactly clubbing clothes. We made kind of a funny pair. She was *much* taller than me, nearly six feet tall. Her hair had been various shades of red in the time I had known her, but since graduating college, she had gone a dark, reddish blond and it suited her well. It brought out her green eyes and the dusting of freckles across her nose. She had a straight up and down body—not thin or heavy really, just in the middle.

"Well, what then? A bar?"

"No." She looked bored at the thought. "How about Second City? I can't remember the last time I went there."

I got my phone out to check show times on their website. There was an eleven o'clock show, which gave us time to get there and have a drink before it started.

As we walked on Halsted looking for a cab, I started back into talking about Xander.

"Tiffany, it's like he's this force of nature and I can't... I can't even describe it. It's overwhelming." I got a little glow of joy that these were the kinds of 'problems' I had.

"So the kinky shit doesn't bother you? Because you seemed a little concerned at the beginning."

"You know, I don't know. It just seems kind of normal now." I caught myself as the words came out of my mouth. "Check that—the kink when it's just the two of us, seems normal."

"What?" She interrupted, grabbing me and pulling me into a doorway alcove. "You're having group sex? Cause, bravo. And I'm more than a little jealous now."

I laughed again. "No, not group sex. Just...don't judge, okay?" She nodded with a scowl of disbelief on her face. "So he and his friend own a nightclub that is kink friendly and has some play spaces."

Tiffany screamed into her hands a little with a look of pure ecstasy on her face. "Tell me *everything!*"

"Oh my God, Tiffany—people are staring at us." I laughed and pulled her back to the flow of pedestrians. "So, I mean, it's a regular club and bar in front. Super fun, great music. And you have to have a special wrist band or something to get in back. But back there, it's wild. There's all kinds of BDSM stuff going on. But there are other areas too. You come visit and we'll go."

"Holy shit! I just can't believe this is your life. No offense, you just weren't the wild one in college. But, hell yes, I'll come visit, but I need a hook-up while I'm there."

She flagged down a passing taxi and we toned the conversation down for the drive. Second City was hilarious as always. She kept glancing at me and laughing, eventually drawing the attention of the improv team, who pulled her onto stage and asked her what was so funny. She gave it back as good as them though. Ultimately they invited her to stay on stage for a skit and act as the referee and prompter. She immediately prompted *ball gags.*

* * * *

Christmas morning the adults of my family watched the children tear apart the packages. We drank copious amounts of coffee since the kids woke at five a.m., demanding that it was Christmas morning and we had to wake up. My dad and I took the kids sledding that afternoon, to give everyone else a break.

"Leeds, I missed you. I didn't expect Texas to feel so far away." He drew me into a hug.

"Yeah, I missed you too. But I guess that's the bonus of being so busy with school. I don't even have to feel my emotions. I didn't realize how homesick I was until we were at the airport."

"We? Did you fly with this Xander?"

"I rode with him to the airport. Our flights were at the same time-ish." I looked up at my dad. "I really like this guy, Dad. Something about him seems to fit really well. And school has actually felt more manageable since we started dating, not less."

Surprise crossed his face. "Just don't make it harder on yourself. Who knows where you'll end up for residency and where he'll be. And it's almost certain that you'll have some time apart from each other with rotations and residency."

"Dad, it'll be fine." My tone was snippy.

"Leeds, stand down. I just don't want you to get your heart broken and then end up having a hard time with school. This guy may be great, but he's hasn't earned a right to impact your future yet." He pulled me into a hug and brushed his hand over my hair. I inhaled that scent that was just my dad, iced over with the cold air.

Chapter Thirty-Five

Xander
Mazzy Star, Fade Into You

I passed my time at home with studying as much as I could. With my dad at work all the time and my mom always doing something, it was quiet. I did get a package from the jeweler with Leda's necklace and it was perfect. Exactly what I wanted. I had also ordered some things for my parents and they were in the box as well.

I visited June and Michael in their gorgeous Brownstone in a fashionable, hip part of the city.

June's eyes sparkled as she ushered me inside. "Hi, Xander!"

"Hi, sweetheart," I said as I kissed her cheek.

"Sir is in the den. Would you like a drink?" She was in full-on submission and I had forgotten what it felt like to be in the middle of that.

"Whatever he's drinking. Thanks."

In the den, Michael stood as I came in. "Xander, hey, man. Good to see you!" He gave me the man half-hug, half-slap on the back.

"Michael." I smiled back at him. "How are you?"

Michael paused to watch June as she handed me a glass of wine. Then turned to me with a devious smile on his face. "I'm well. You?"

"I'm good."

June had settled herself on the floor at Michael's feet, arranging her skirt around her, neatly. But she made whatever signal that let Michael know she wanted to say something and he inclined his head at her. She spoke, "Really? Something doesn't seem right. What's happening with Leda?"

I laughed. "Shit, June. You're too perceptive."

Michael chuckled, too. Then he did something that surprised me. "June, honey. I'd like to drop the protocol for tonight. Xander is our friend and I'd like both of us to just enjoy our time with him."

She smiled up at him like he had created the sun. "Yes, Sir. I have to go check on dinner, but we're gonna figure this out, Xander." She went to the kitchen and I could hear her humming to herself as she clanged and clattered pans and whatever else. I smiled at how they had taken something really complicated and made it simple.

"How's school going?"

"Really well. I like it and I just finished the first half of the year-long neurology course. It's intense, man."

"Well, yeah. That's why I like it. Have you gotten into brain chemistry yet?"

"No, it was all peripheral nervous system and spinal column for first semester. Next semester is brain and brainstem."

"You'll like it. You just have to make concrete connections to real life."

June walked out from the kitchen and interrupted us. "Stop talking about work and school. What's happening with your little sub-morsel? I was impressed with her when I met her."

"June." There was a warning in Michael's tone at her interruption and general bossiness. She held his gaze for just a beat and dropped her eyes with a small bob of her head. I waited until Michael turned back to me, asking, "So, what's happening with this girl?"

"I'm so glad you're both here. I'm fucking freaking out over her. I'm in love with her, want to collar her, shit...want to marry her."

"Why?"

It was a simple question and Michael's calm but strong voice cut through my anxious, pressured speech. I looked at him, mouth half-open, not sure what to say.

He elaborated, "I've known you for years and you have *never* been particularly serious about a girl. Why this one?"

June settled on his lap, smiling.

"She's smart and kind and funny and a smart-ass. But she gets it and accepts me the way I am. You know how shit-Doms are always telling the newbies that they're 'natural submissives'?" I waited for his nod, then added, "She actually is."

"How so?" He leaned forward a bit, shifting June in his lap.

"She just accepts anything I give her. She...so here, like this— When we were first talking, I joked with her about being in trouble and punishing her and she flirted back. But then, when I promised to come over the next day to deliver said punishment, *she asked what she could do to prepare.*" He nodded in appreciation. "I mean, she didn't even know what a safeword was. And she has instincts. She stands so still when I touch her, like she's been trained for inspection."

"And tell him about playing with Seraphim," June prompted me, smiling.

"So this is where it starts to get weird and, June, you haven't heard this part yet." As I spoke, she stood and directed us into the dining room, where she served us, plating her meal last. As we ate, I filled them in on what had happened with her, how she seemed too perfect to be real, how she pushed me just right, how she tried everything I brought to her. How much it freaked me out.

"Well, she sounds perfect. What's the problem?" Michael made it sound so simple.

"We played again the night before we came up here and I put her in there with the other girl. Again, she didn't even really balk. And then when it was over, I fucked her in the dungeon, in front of everyone, and she thanked me, Mike. She fucking thanked me." Incredulity laced my words.

"Again, what's the problem?" His voice was stern, but kind.

"I don't know. I don't know how to explain it. It's like I don't believe her. And I'm sure I'm gonna fuck it up somehow. And then…" I paused, sipping the wine. "I don't want to hurt her, but I do. I want to let all this out on her, but I never want her to feel the remotest pain. Does that make sense?"

Michael smiled, and held June's hand on the table. "Yes, I completely understand. The loving Dom's dilemma."

"So…what do I do?"

"What do you want to do?"

"I think I want to marry her. But I'm constantly running this shitty monologue in my head. And after that play a few nights ago, I think I had Dom-drop — and that shit sucks."

"Hmm, yeah. Yeah it does." He dropped his gaze to his plate for a minute and I saw a memory running through him. "Yeah, it's awful. But you know what it is. It's the backlash of using up the neurotransmitters, the backlash of doing what we do."

Some slow and sweet love song was playing and I felt incredibly sad, missing Leda, wanting her with me always. Michael pulled June back into his lap and she laughed and threw her arms around him. She spoke, "Xander, we love you. And that girl loves you too. Why can't you just accept it and enjoy it?"

"I don't know."

* * * *

There was a car I didn't recognize in the driveway when I got back. Before I was through the door, I knew it was going to be bad. The only light on was my parents' bedroom.

"Fuck," I muttered as I came through the door, slamming it behind me so that whoever wasn't one of my parents — most likely whoever wasn't my dad — up there knew that the house wasn't empty anymore. I heard a muted yelp and feet moving around a bunch.

I got some water, trying to waste time downstairs because I was going to choose where I confronted whatever asshole my mom was fucking now. I sat at the table, waiting. Predictably, my mom came down first. In her fucking robe. Some guy who was not my dad, by a long shot, sort of scuttled by in her shadow. I had fucking had it.

"Man, if you're gonna fuck my mom, who is another man's *wife*, be a fucking man about it and stand up straight, head high when you walk out." My voice was arctic cold and my mom gasped a little.

"Xander! That's enough." She admonished me, attempting to find some purchase on a moral high ground and failing, epically.

I just scoffed at her and stood. I walked to the man and extended my hand. "I'm Xander, her son. And don't act so awkward. You're not the first one I've found her with." After I shook his hand, I turned to my mother, who was absolutely beet red. "Goodnight, Mother."

I walked away, up to my room. I heard them murmuring, both apologizing, which just made me angrier. If you're doing something you need to apologize for, you're not doing it right. Do what you can live with. I heard the door close and my mom's steps as she came up the stairs.

She opened my door, ready to yell, but I cut her off. "What the hell, Mom? What if I had been jerking off? You gotta knock. I'm thirty-fucking-four."

She drew a breath, about to blow up, but instead she started laughing. "Well, I'm fifty-fucking-seven and I'll sleep with whomever I'd like. You don't get a say, son." She held her head up, holier-than-thou. It was hilarious and my anger cracked as I started laughing.

She sat on the end of my bed, both of us laughing, until we had to wipe our eyes. She leaned toward me. "Jerking off, Alex? Jesus Christ. I *am* still your mother."

"Shit, Mom, with everything we've been through. It would be great if me spanking it was the worst, right?" We both started laughing again.

As much as my mom had faults, she had always stood by me, even when shit blew up with Stacy and my life fell apart. It didn't really matter that I had found her with various men, more than a few times. She always had my back, and I'd always have hers—which was part of what bugged me about that guy. "Who the hell was that, anyway? He was seriously skulking. It was shady, Mom."

"That was Tim, the new tennis pro at the club. I don't know. Go to bed. I don't want to talk about this. Wanna go Christmas shopping tomorrow?"

"Tomorrow is Christmas Eve. Shopping would suck and we have ice skating."

"Oh, all right. I guess I don't really have anything else to get, anyway."

My family kept Christmas pretty minimal. One present each. I had gotten my mom some earrings and my dad some cuff links and a tie clip.

My dad came home with us after the skating party and we actually had dinner together. I tried to keep the conversation light, talking about school, tutoring and inevitably, Leda.

"Oh…this is the one Rodriguez told me about, right?" Dad was conversational, like he wasn't talking about the total invasion of my privacy, that was. *Right…invasion of privacy when they only know about her because I got a fucking background check on her. Hypocrite.*

"I guess so, but remind me to slap him."

He scoffed, "Like you could land one on him."

Mom cleared her throat, and said, "So, you tell us about her. All we know is the background check stuff. She's very cute."

I smiled, because it was true. "She's smart, funny. I like her a lot. She's easy to be around—like it's not complicated unless I make it complicated."

A knowing look passed around the table, but no one said anything, and I was suddenly weary, annoyed at the whole situation. I stood, clearing my dishes. "You'll get to meet her for yourself. She'll be at the gala."

* * * *

Christmas with my parents was peaceful, better than I expected. We were scheduled to attend the Senator's formal Christmas dinner that night and, even though I had done it practically every year, I still dreaded it.

It was excess and luxury, exactly as one would expect when being completely cynical about Washington. The meal was amazing, but it sort of had to be. Stacy was there with her family, but they were seated at the other end of the table. *Someone still remembers.*

She caught my eye a few times, sometimes smiling, sometimes rolling her eyes at the BS flying around the room. After the meal ended, the guests were invited to the various common rooms of the home. Most of the men went to the den to play snooker because Billings was a pretentious fuck who couldn't play pool like the unwashed masses. I groaned inwardly and went the other way, to the bar between the den and the formal living room.

The bartender poured me a neat Macallan 25, and when I turned, Stacy was there. She wore a long red dress with gold threading that was a mix of sexy and festive. She smiled at me, but leaned past me to order the same drink. As I tried to walk away, she grabbed my hand, subtly, almost covertly.

I looked at her in surprise. Absolutely everyone at this party knew what had happened between us. Well, not everything that happened, but they did all know about her father finding us fucking — with what I now knew was questionable consent — in my office at the Pentagon, about him punching me in the face, about her absolute refusal to press charges against me even though she could have and would have won in court.

We were supposed to be personae non-grata to each other. Once she had her drink, she pulled my hand and tugged me out a wide French door to the patio. It was warmed with braziers so guests could smoke or get fresh air without freezing.

"Hello."

She said it sweetly, kind of soft, like we were intimate. But we weren't. Not anymore.

I responded, gruffly, taking a step back from her. "Hi, Stacy. Merry Christmas."

She pressed forward to kiss my cheeks. "Merry Christmas." Her voice was breathy, and she lent the words a dark, lusty tone that hinted at how merry she wanted to make my Christmas.

I held her shoulders and disengaged her from my space. Firmly, so it was clear that there wasn't going to be any merrymaking between us, this Christmas or any other.

Her shoulders slumped and her face fell. "How long are you going to keep punishing me, Xander?" Her voice was actually forlorn.

Empathy colored my response. "Stacy, I'm not punishing you. There's nothing to punish you for. But we don't belong together. You were an important part of my life for a long time, but things changed between us. You have to move on." My last words were more emphatic.

She got a determined set to her jaw that I recognized. She was going to do something stupid and self-destructive, under the guise of refusing to let me tell her what to do. "There's nowhere for me to move on to. No one else I can even think of trying to build a life with. There's just you. You're the only one who knows."

She ran her hand through her hair and I distractedly thought that I would have wanted her to wear it up. She had a beautiful neck. My thoughts flashed to the memory of my mouth on her throat and the sounds she would make underneath me. She spoke again, pulling me back to the moment.

"What can she possibly know about all this? How will she survive this?"

I didn't answer her because I didn't have an answer. I didn't know how Leda would navigate the world I came from. It was full of lying, promises in exchange for favors, fine print fuckovers, ruthless people doing what they thought they had to, to survive. Leda was too damn *good* to know how to deal with this. Finally, I looked at Stacy and just said, "I don't know."

I was too sick of the game with her to keep playing, and she misunderstood, thinking she had a small victory, so I added, "But I'm not discussing it here, with you."

She flashed a megawatt smile and slammed her scotch. "All right, big man. I'll leave you to figure it out on your own. We'll see if you come up with the same answer I did." She walked back into the house and I sat in an Adirondack chair under the brazier, sipping my scotch, savoring it.

I checked the time on my phone, and saw a text message from Leda. It was a few hours old and so sweet and pure that it just twisted in my gut as it nearly proved everything Stacy had been talking about.

Hey Boss man! How RU? Merry Christmas. Miss you.
XXOO – L

I responded, but refused to let my fucked up life touch her in anyway, if I could help it.

Little girl...I miss you too, so much. I'm bored without you. But on the plus side, daydreaming of what I'm going to do to you when I see you. Merry Xmas XXOOFFFFFFF – X

She responded quickly and we had a flirty text exchange that did more to cheer me up than anything anyone currently in DC could have.

What is FFFFFF? ☺ – L

What do you think an F might be? – X

Well, then that was a lot of F'ing. A little pent up, are we? – L

"Alex? What are you doing out here?" My mom was at the doors, beckoning me in. "Come inside. We're leaving and you need to thank our hosts." But I was already moving toward her. I left my empty glass on the bar with a tip and we wound our way through the house to the foyer.

Senator and Mrs. Noe were at the door, saying goodbyes – gracious smiles, glad-handing. He was about the same height as me, a full head of gray hair and some loose wrinkles in his face. She was significantly younger than him, but still older than me. She had a deep strawberry blonde hair color that didn't seem entirely feasible on her tanned, almost swarthy, skin tone.

We said our goodbyes, barely keeping eye contact long enough to avoid being rude. In the car, my mother turned to me.

"What were you doing talking to Stacy outside?" Her voice was worried, more than angry.

"Exactly that. Talking to Stacy, outside."

She just held my gaze, face implacable.

I relented. They knew everything already anyway. "She wants to get back together. She's actually wanted to for a while. It's why she came to Texas for med school. She could have gone anywhere with her letter of rec from the Surgeon General. I mean...done and done. Welcome to med school. She came down there to follow me, try to get back together with me."

There were a few beats of silence then my mom and dad spoke at that same time.

"Maybe you should give it another try. It'd piss her dad off plenty." Dad laughed at that.

"You have to stay away from her, son." My mother's voice carried some alarm.

I responded to both of them. "Or, you can let me handle my own shit."

My mom turned back to the front and asked my dad, "Why would you even *suggest* that, Denny? That little fuck up nearly ruined all of us." Her voice was whip-crack sharp, but Dad was unimpressed.

"Because Jackson is being a fucking idiot lately. He voted against a bill we sponsored and he's been courting that jackass, Rusty Weintraub. You know, the Jew from California."

Jesus, this the gene pool I was created from. God damn it. I'm not coming back here again. I was silent for the rest of the drive, plotting how I'd take Leda somewhere, anywhere, else.

* * * *

The next morning I called Leda, but she didn't answer her phone. I tried her parents' home number. Her mom answered and informed me that she and her siblings had taken the kids out. I asked to leave a message, and once I told her my name, we had a short conversation.

"Oh! Xander! Hi, Merry Christmas! How is your vacation going?"

"Hi, Mrs. Collins. Vacation is very quiet, relaxing. Honestly, kind of boring." I chuckled a little.

"Oh, gosh! With all these little ones underfoot — and really the big ones too — it's never boring around here."

"Well, Merry Christmas to you, too. Could you just let Leda know I called to give her the flight information?"

"Oh, sure. Do you want to give it to me and I can pass it on? Let me just grab something to write with."

I heard her setting the phone down before I answered. I smiled, hearing some of Leda's kindness in her mom's voice. I heard a sound of victory and she picked the phone back up.

"Okay, I'm ready now! I mean, it's really like I can't ever find anything when I need it, but when I go to clean things up later today, I'll find seven pens." She laughed.

"I hate that too!" I let my smile into my voice.

"Ready. Give me the flight info."

"The plane is going to come up on the thirtieth and there'll be a two p.m. departure on the thirty-first, from the private air field near O'Hare. She'll need ID at the driveway. I can text her the exact address. I don't have it right now. She is going to fly with the Senator's sister and her husband. Bitsy and John Ivory."

She had been murmuring along with me, letting me know she has heard me. But she paused there, and I knew it was because of the name. To her credit, she held her tongue. Her voice was a little softer when she spoke again. "Okay, Xander. We will drop her off. Why don't you touch base with Leda before then, just to let her know who to look for?"

"Oh, she'll *know*. They'll have their whole retinue with them and the private airfield there is small. She just needs to ask for the Ivory plane. And people will be falling all over themselves to help her." I laughed and her mom echoed me, but quieter.

She then asked, curious about the multibillionaire business mogul no doubt. "Are they only coming up for one night?"

"No, they're already in Chicago, spending the holidays with their kids and their families. The plane is just based out of DC, so when they are somewhere for a prolonged time, the plane usually needs to be used by someone else in the company. I think it's supposed to save some money somehow. Not sure. Because it is *their* plane. The company has others."

"So, now they have to fly an empty plane up? Why don't they just take a commercial flight or something?"

I smiled, because that was a completely rational question and Bitsy and John weren't rational. "Welllll," I drew the word out, not wanting to sound like a snob, or make them sound snobby, even though they were. "They like to have their space. The amenities of flying their own plane."

She laughed a bit. "Well, I guess if it was an option for me, I would too. So, what have you been doing with your break? Having some fun and relaxing, I hope."

"Oh, you know. Some time with my parents. Saw a few old friends. I'm mostly just bored. Leda was teasing because I've been studying."

"Well, yeah! Why are you studying on your break?"

"Not much else to do. Most of my old friends grew up and moved away and government doesn't really take a break."

"Why don't you just come up with the plane and meet our family? We'd love to have you, Xander."

The invitation surprised me, but also made me smile. She was kind, and talking with her felt like talking to someone who was just *good*. Who authentically wanted the best for everyone around her. "I don't want to impose on your family time, Mrs. Collins."

"Well, now we have a few things to fix, Xander."

Uh-oh. Did I say something wrong?

"First, please call me Kathy. Secondly, we have always been an open house. Everyone is welcome, son. You can most certainly come and absolutely would not be intruding. Besides, Leda is missing you a lot, I think. She'd be so happy to see you."

Her words just fucking flooded me with warmth. "Well, why don't I talk with Leda and make sure she's fine with it. I feel bad springing something on her like that."

"No! Let's surprise her. You just come up and then come on over. We'll play it by ear from there. What do you think?"

"Umm, I don't know. I'd love to meet your family and I do really miss her. Yeah, okay. Let's do it." I smiled, feeling a little excited. "I'll look into the planned flight time to be sure I will be there at a decent hour."

"Sure, we usually eat dinner around six. Why don't I give you my cell number and you can text me when you have the info?" Her voice held a little sneaky-sounding glee.

"Well, now you have to wait for *me* to find a pen. Be right back." I heard her laughter as I set the phone down for a moment, even though I had a pen and paper on my old desk, right next to me.

We finished the phone call and I got to work making the arrangements. The first step was getting permission from the Ivorys—I wasn't at all worried that they might say no, but I wouldn't get anywhere else without their clearance.

Bitsy chided me when I spoke to her about it. "Of course it's fine. Let me have my assistant deal with it. Kelsey!" She put Kelsey on the phone with me and we discussed the details. The plane was scheduled to fly up fairly late, when air traffic is sparser, but she told me she'd fix it, asking when I wanted to arrive.

"Probably around four-thirty. Dinner at her parents' home at six."

"Very good, sir. Any requirements for your car? Liveried, I'm assuming."

"No, I'll drive myself. Whatever kind of car is fine."

"Very good. Shall I arrange a bottle of wine to take to dinner?"

Jesus, I need a personal assistant. She is on top of shit. "Um, no. I don't know their preferences. How about some flowers?"

"Very good, sir. They will be in your car. The car will be waiting at the airport for you. Anything else? A hotel room or will you be staying with them? If so, you need something more than flowers."

"No, a hotel, please."

"Very good. Downtown or near them?"

"Near them."

"All right, Westin or Hilton?"

"Westin."

"Yes, sir. The arrangements will be made before the end of business today. Shall I email you your itinerary?"

"Yes, please. Thank you so much, Kelsey."

"Of course, Mr. Stone."

And just like that, plans were made. Bitsy was a board member of Ivory Industries, but I had always assumed that was a way to ensure votes for John. I hadn't really ever thought she actually *did* anything. Certainly, nothing so taxing that she needed an assistant. But, I saw the benefit after that exchange.

I got the itinerary later that day and sent Leda's mom a text with the details. She texted back a smiley-face emoticon. *This woman is already the cutest ever and I haven't even met her yet.*

I told my parents my plans via text, since they were both gone for the evening. Neither seemed particularly concerned or interested really. I called Jason to tell him what I was doing and he just told me he thought it was a good idea. *No one* seemed at all concerned about this — but me.

It would be good. I had to tell myself that a few more times before I believed it. I didn't consider changing the plans. I missed her too much and wanted to see her. Then, time seemed to move so slowly.

Eventually, I was getting on the plane and the flight attendant was waiting, took my jacket, handing me a scotch. I got buckled in, sipping the drink. It was peaty, smoky. Laphroaig, I thought. I allowed myself to doze as we flew.

In Chicago, there was a Lexus waiting for me. I smiled as I got in. It was silly. I wasn't that into spending money just to show off that you had it. That said, the car was already warm, the heated seat was on, the heated steering wheel was warm. It was lovely. The flower arrangement across the front seat was perfect. Not too big, a really nice bouquet, mostly whites and reds, with some holly and ivy thrown in. Very festive, without being hokey. Kelsey deserved a raise, whatever she was making.

Leda's parents' address was already programmed into the GPS. Kelsey deserved a big raise and a bonus, probably a vacation, too.

Chapter Thirty Six

Leda
Angus and Julia Stone, Big Jet Plane

The night before I was going to DC, everyone was acting weird. Angie wanted to do my hair for me, because, as she said, it was long I-don't-have-kids hair. She created a beautiful up-do with tendrils of hair falling down around my face and I planned to try to recreate it for the fundraiser. My mom was weird too. She kept ducking out of rooms, smiling to herself. The unfortunate thought went through my head that maybe she'd had some great sex with dad last night. *Puke*.

Right before dinner, Angie decided she absolutely had to have some cantaloupe and chicken soup. *Pregnant people are weird*. So, she asked me to drive her to the store. When we came back, everyone seemed on edge, expectant. Finally, I couldn't stand it anymore.

"What is going on? Why are you all being so weird?" Most of them smirked. My dad and Luke scowled a bit. "Seriously, guys!" The doorbell rang and everyone's eyes snapped to the front hall. "Who the hell is this now?"

I got up to get the door, but Mom was already in motion. I heard her greeting whoever was there, then heard Xander's familiar voice. I had a moment of confusion and complete disconnect in my brain. *That voice doesn't belong here.*

"What the fuuu..." I held my tongue at my dad's expression and ran to the front hall.

Xander stood, framed in the doorway. The door where every guy I had dated had stood to gain entry into my life. My family followed me to the door, but his eyes, beautiful, flashing all kinds of emotions, met mine, which were straight shocked and wide.

"Hi, sweetheart." His voice was low and mellow. "Surprise."

"Hi and what the hell?" I turned on my family. "Did you all know about this? That goes for all of you then too. What the hell?" I was smiling and laughing, but I was impressed. In a family our size, it's hard to surprise anyone. There are too many mouths that might let something slip.

My mom answered and I saw that she was holding a bouquet of flowers that Xander must have brought her. "Xander called the other day to talk with you while you and Jules had taken the kids to the bouncy house place, and we got to talking."

Everyone groaned and sighed. My mom could literally strike up a conversation with anyone at any time. It was one of her gifts. "Anyway," she said over the susurrus, "he was calling to let you know your flight time and one thing led to another and we decided he should come up with the plane."

"Oh...okay. Well, come in," I said backing up a bit.

I turned to step back and Lukie and Angie, Jules and Evan, my dad, the kids were all piled up behind me. "Guys, come on!"

My mom, being who she is, intervened. "Xander, please come in. Let me introduce our family. This is Leda's older brother Luke, his wife Angie. Those two small fries by them are Kevin and Liliana. This is Leda's sister Julia and her husband Evan, their son Gussy."

"Mom, his name is Gus," Jules interrupted.

Mom carried on like she'd said nothing, "And my husband, Jim."

Xander stepped in, first to my father, and extended his hand, "Sir." It was the first time that I had seen the military bearing in him. It was interesting and odd to see him formal and slightly deferential.

Oh, God, this is all so weird. My dominating, sadistic boyfriend, bringing my mom flowers, shaking my dad's hand, and meeting my whole family, the *whole* family. I knew he would have met them eventually, but I had expected to be prepared.

After he'd shaken everyone's hands and my mom had taken his coat, and the kids had all inspected him, everyone started to move back to the kitchen for dinner. He grabbed my hand and held me back.

"I hope this is okay. I just missed you so much and, well, it was kind of your mom's idea." He smiled a little sheepishly and it was honestly cute. He pulled me into a hug, resting his chin on top of my head. I pushed back a bit to look up at him.

"Yeah, of course it's okay. I missed you too." I stood to my tiptoes and kissed him.

From the other room, my mom yelled, "Anyone who wants to eat dinner, get to washing up."

She had been saying that to announce dinner since I was a kid and I smiled at the sound of the kids running through the house. I grabbed Xander's hand, pulled him into the kitchen, and noticed there was an extra place set. No wonder Angie had 'needed' melon and soup. They'd had to get me out of the house. I couldn't have gotten the grin off my face if someone had paid me.

Mom was arranging the flowers in a vase and I went to the kitchen sink to wash up. Gus, who really was rapidly becoming known as Gussy, came up.

"Auntie Weedie, I need hewp." Gus reached up to me. I picked him up and tried to hold him to the sink, but, he was getting too big for the one-handed pick up now. Xander was there, smiling warmly at Gus.

"Hi, Gus, can I help?"

Gus nodded, enjoying being addressed and treated like more of a big kid. Xander picked Gus up under the arms, and I helped him wash his hands.

"Thanks, Weedie, and...you."

Xander and I giggled at that.

As Xander washed his hands, he glanced at me, "Auntie Weedie?" He scrubbed like a surgeon, even when he wasn't really paying attention to it.

"Oh crap. So my nickname has always—"

"Leeds!" yelled Luke. "We've called her Leeds since she was little and the kids can't really say the L's, so she became Aunt Weeds, then Auntie Weedie."

"Leeds, huh?" Xander smiled at me. "I kinda like it."

To my family's credit, they didn't interrogate him too much, but I think they were all dying to ask questions. My sister avoided bringing up Senator Noe's politics, but I knew she wanted to.

After dinner, the kids all had bath time and Xander and I slipped out under the guise of taking out the trash.

"I can't believe you surprised me! You're crafty."

"Yep. It really was your mom's idea though. I couldn't say no." He smiled and pulled me into a kiss. My mouth softened from my smile into his kiss as his tongue swept against my lips and tongue, soft, patient, not demanding anything. He moved his hands to my face. He pulled his lips back and rested his forehead on mine, "I missed you so much, Leda. I've never felt like this before. You terrify me." The last was a whisper.

I kissed him again, a little choked up at that. *How could I terrify him?*

"I got you a Christmas present." He held out a small box.

I opened it and noted the name of a prominent jeweler in Texas on the box. It was too big to be a ring box, but I still got a flutter in my stomach. Opening it, I found a gorgeous long chain-link necklace with a heart-shaped padlock on it and a small square disc with the word *HIS* on one side and an *X* on the other. It was a darker silvery metal I didn't recognize.

"Titanium and platinum, honey. It should be just long enough to hang in your cleavage...where I want to be all the time." He smiled and kissed my forehead.

I looked up at him, smiling. "I love this, but it's too much, Boss-man."

He shook his head. "Little girlie, you don't get to say anything I give you is too much."

I smiled again at that and felt a familiar pull in my pelvis. I handed him the box as I turned around. "Here, you put it on me the first time."

He put his hands on my shoulders and turned me back to him. "I don't think you want to explain this to your family tonight. Let's save it, love."

Love? I flushed a little and tried to suppress the grin that pulled at my cheeks. *Could he love me? I want him to love me.* It was a whole different kind of breathless. It was more than sex and kink and getting tied up and pushed hard.

I pressed myself against him, suddenly shy. He kissed my forehead again and ran his hands over my back. But I shifted to look up at him and heard the deep rumble of an I-want-you purr in his chest as he pulled my hair to fully tilt my face toward him. His mouth settled on mine.

But the garage was cold and we had to go back inside after a few minutes. Mom and Dad were sitting in the living room, Mom drinking tea, Dad drinking scotch.

"Xander, would you like some tea?" My mom asked.

"Or scotch?" My dad added.

He smiled at them, something polite and detached. "No, thank you. I still need to drive to my hotel and get checked in. And I'm not much of a tea drinker. Leda must have gotten her tea habit from you, Mrs. Collins."

Jesus, he saw everything. Both my parents looked pleased with his response, though I suspected for different reasons. We sat with them, chatting about the plan for tomorrow, while my sister and brother, and their spouses, tucked their kids into bed. After a while, the adults were all in the room.

"So, are we playing this game or not?" Julia asked, pointing at the Trivial Pursuit game that we had set up earlier.

"I don't know. What about something more like Charades or Pictionary? Something with teams? It might be a good idea to ease Xander into this family's competitiveness." My mother was such an excellent hostess.

Xander glanced at me, eyebrows raised at that. Ultimately, we agreed on Pictionary and split boys against girls.

"It's finally even! And it's good to have one more person diluting the Collins intensity," Angie laughed. "And I need some cookies. Honey?"

"Really, Ange? You've been eating all day." Luke answered her. Julia and Mom groaned and threw pillows at him.

"I'll get you some cookies, sweetie. Milk, too?" My mom stood and Angie nodded to that. "And Lukie, this is your third time through a pregnancy. Don't you know to keep a lid on that kind of stuff? Anyone else?" Everyone wanted cookies and I went with to help my mom.

We loaded a tray with the ridiculous amount cookies she had made with the kids this week. Chocolate chip, peanut butter, cut outs with icing, oatmeal raisin, gingerbread and chocolate covered peanut butter balls called Buckeyes.

"He's awfully good looking, Leda. And he's clearly falling for you hard. He can't keep his eyes off of you." My mom prattled on as she filled a pitcher with milk and I got glasses down for everyone.

"He's great, Mom. I think I'm falling in love with him." I thought of how safe I felt with him, and how totally on edge, too. It was perfect, and I had to stop myself from gushing.

"As long as he isn't a complete waste of time." We turned together and both stopped short, at Xander just stepping into the room.

"I came to see if you needed an extra set of hands for carrying things?"

A flush of embarrassment ran through me, worried that he heard our conversation.

"Yes, thank you, Xander. Can you take this pitcher?" Mom handed him the pitcher and picked up the tray of cookies. I carried the glasses, a new little swarm of nerves in my tummy. He acted completely normal, as if he hadn't heard anything, but I didn't believe that for a second.

The game went well. The guys won, but only because they kept getting sports-related clues. Angie ate seven cookies and had two glasses of milk. But Xander wasn't too far behind, four cookies and an extra large glass of milk. Admittedly, they were awesome cookies.

We were up late, talking and laughing. Everyone was trying to give us advice on specialties and how to study for boards, except Angie, who just ate. She was in her second trimester and finally past the morning sickness, so she was making up for how terrible she had felt for the last few months. She had even skipped Thanksgiving altogether.

It was almost midnight when Xander left, shaking everyone's hands, thanking my mom and dad for their hospitality. Thanking my mom for suggesting that he come up and meet them. I walked him to his rental car and kissed him goodnight.

"Our flight is at two. I will be here at noon to get you. Be ready."

"Of course, Boss. Anything else?" I felt vaguely secretarial saying that and a whole new set of fantasies began to take hold in the back of my mind.

"Yeah, I want you to get yourself off tonight, thinking about me getting myself off in my hotel room, thinking of you."

I drew a sharp breath at the unexpected instructions, but then mentally chastised myself. *Why would that be unexpected?* It wouldn't even be unexpected for him to tell me to get on my knees in the snow and suck him off. *Well, maybe not in my parent's driveway.*

"Little girl, did you hear me?" He tipped my chin up to him.

"Yeah." My voice cracked, throat dry. I swallowed and tried again, "Yes, heard you. I'm to make myself come, thinking of you making yourself come, thinking of me." I pressed myself into his chest. "But, Xander…"

"*But*? How does that usually end, little girl?" The menace was delicious and sent chills up my spine. I tilted my head back to look in his eyes as I lifted to my toes and licked his lips.

I whispered against his mouth, "But all week, I've touched myself to fantasies of you over me, pounding me into the bed, fucking me so hard, so good." I ran my fingers over his neck, into his hair. "I miss you inside me."

"Little girl," his growl was a warning.

"I want you in my mouth so hard and so long that you leave me with chapped lips." I pulled back again, looking into his eyes. "Will you fuck my mouth like that?"

"Fuck, Leda. You're killing me."

"You're on my home turf tonight. I'll be on yours tomorrow." I kissed him softly, one more time before turning to head back inside. "Goodnight, Boss."

His goodnight was just a deep groan, but I got a text message before I made it to my bedroom.

You're going to pay for that. You know that right? – X

Yeah? Well, that might have been my goal…XXOOFFFFF – L

There was a long delay before his reply and I thought I was in trouble.

I'm checked in at the Westin, if you need anything tonight. – X

Really? That's it? And btw…there's a whole bunch I need tonight. We just covered that – L

Yes we did. You're working on some punishment and we have a lot of time together in the next few days. You know what I want you to do tonight. I'm getting started now. – X

One-handed texting now. – L

I'm thinking of your skin under my hands, your mouth on me. – X

I'm thinking of being tied on your bed, stretched out tight, ice cubes in my mouth – L

I'm thinking of fucking your ass in front of a mirror so I can see your face when you stretch out to take me – X

My fingers traced my skin, so wet, spreading my lips apart and pressing into my clitoris. The thought of his cock in my ass was mouth-watering and terrifying at the same time.

Well, now I'm thinking of that too. So tight and full.

I'm thinking of tying you up and cutting your clothes off you. Spanking your ass, my hands on your throat.

I pressed into myself, harder, more insistent. It was such a poor substitute for being with him, but I was getting close.

I'm so close. I want you, on me, in my mouth. Please 2moro?

Yes. So good, little girl

I came at yes. Thanks. :) L

Me, too. –X

There was a pause for a few minutes before I got one more text from him.

I'm thinking of you trusting me. – X

I do trust you. – L

I wanted to say 'I love you', 'I always want to be near you' and all the other crushy things people say when they're enthralled with someone. And dammit, I was so enthralled, taken over, subsumed. In love with him.

* * * *

He picked me up at noon, on the dot. Once through to the gate, we were able to immediately board and wait for our flight on the supremely comfortable plane. We waited for less than twenty minutes for the Senator's sister. She flowed onto the plane, processed, coifed blonde hair, oversized sunglasses and a fur wrap. I immediately felt like a complete slob in my leggings, boots and oversized sweater

Xander stood and smiled. "Mrs. Ivory. Thank you for allowing us to hitch a ride."

A young woman trailed after her, carrying lots of things and behaving deferentially. I assumed an assistant. Then a gentleman, there is no other word for a man in his sixties, fit, dressed in an immaculately tailored suit. He brushed past Mrs. Ivory, his hand grazing her butt, which triggered a slight smirk from her.

"Oh, Alex! Why are you so formal? I've known you forever. Of course, you can fly with us. Now introduce me to Leda." *First, Alex? Second, she knew my name?* I would be revisiting all of this at a later time with Alex...Xander...*Alexander?*

He had the grace to grimace slightly, knowing that I would have questions for him. "Mrs. Bitsy Ivory, please meet Leda Collins. Leda, this is Mrs. Ivory, Senator Noe's sister."

She was thin, but her presence was huge. She took her sunglasses off and she had clearly been Botoxed and lifted and stretched, but not ridiculously so.

"Leda, a pleasure to meet you. I'm not sure how Alex roped you into this."

Literally, Bitsy. He literally roped me at one point.

She continued, "We *have* to go, family support and all that. I've taken a few Xanax to get through the flight. Do either of you need one?"

Weirdly hospitable. "Nice to meet you and thank you again. I appreciate being included, because he did kind of rope me in." There was a seriously bleak moment when she looked at me blankly, and I heard a small croak from Xander, before she laughed and I laughed with her, adding, "I know it's routine for you, but I'm excited. I haven't been to DC since my eighth grade class trip."

She smiled at us, turning to Xander. "She's sweet, Alex. A little young, but then again, I'm fifteen years younger than John. Either way, don't fuck this one up." On the tail of that jarring statement, she turned from us, calling, "John, come be pleasant and say hello to Alex. You should meet Leda."

Mr. Ivory looked up and nodded, giving the *one second* finger gesture, as he finished a phone call. A few moments later he joined us, shaking Xander's hand.

"Mr. Ivory, this is my girlfriend, Leda Collins. Leda this is Mr. John Ivory."

We shook hands, and his gaze lingered on my chest. I thought, *oh, so you're an old perv, whose wife is rapidly becoming more sedated.* Bitsy was indeed looking droopy. He handed her a crystal highball with amber liquid that I assumed was scotch and she gulped it down.

Smiling again, though with lids at half-mast, she answered my unspoken concern, "I have a terrible fear of flying, Leda. Just hate it. And I figure, there are two doctors on the plane." Her tongue was starting to sound a little thick, and John guided her farther back in the plane by her elbow. She took off her fur and gave it to the assistant. She was painfully thin underneath, far more so than I had thought when she still had the bulky wrap on. I was concerned on a whole new level about the Xanax and alcohol.

Once we were in the air, Xander turned to me. "So…about my name. It's actually Alexander. I have gone by Xander since I was fourteen." He cringed a moment. "Sorry I didn't tell you that."

"Anything else I should know?" I took a deep breath. "I mean it *is* really weird to have had you…in me, and just now find out that I haven't actually known your name."

He shrank a moment then, he changed. The Dom Xander looked back at me, hard eyes, set jaw, but he said nothing for a long moment.

"Do you regret it?" His voice was cold, flat.

"Christ, no, Xander. I just feel a little kept in the dark with you sometimes."

"You like being in the dark with me." His voice shifted to the low purr that I loved, but I wasn't gonna bite.

"So, can I call you Alexander now? It's so upper crust sounding. Like where's your yacht, *Alexander?* Where are you summering this year, *Alexander*, Europe or the Cape?" I put on affected voice that was truly very similar to Bitsy's. His face blanked with surprise at my sass and I dissolved into giggles. "Xander, I don't really care, I guess. It's not like you know everything about me." I stood, intending to find the restroom, but he grabbed my wrist.

"Where are you going?"

It wasn't like him to be anxious like that. "The bathroom. Where else could I go?"

"Be careful." There was a distracted, kind of stormy look on his face.

Trying to figure that out distracted me as I walked back to the rear of the plane. I noticed Bitsy draped over a long couch, asleep. And I walked directly into something, tall and firm, smelling expensive and male. I snapped my head around and was looking into John Ivory's buttons. I looked up at his face and he smiled down at me, but didn't step back. Something about it was a little charming, but he was older than my dad and his wife was unconscious a few feet from us and my boyfriend was here too. And it got gross in a hurry.

"Excuse me, Leda." He brushed past me, a little closer than necessary. But then I was past him, walking again, eyes on my path now.

When I stepped out of the bathroom, Xander was there, waiting for me. There was no way he'd missed the close call with Ivory. With a forced calm to his voice, he suggested, "Let's get a drink."

There was a small galley kitchen stocked with refreshments. I decided on water. I wanted all my faculties. There were some weird vibes on this plane. I flashed to a mental image of Samuel L Jackson shouting, "There are some weird motherfucking vibes on this weird motherfucking plane" and cracked a smile.

One eyebrow cocked, Xander asked, "Something funny, Leeds?"

"Hard to explain, the inner monologue is hilarious sometimes. And more to the point, who said you get to call me Leeds, *Alex*?" I answered with a laugh.

He released a little tension from his shoulders and brushed a kiss across my temple as he took my elbow to lead me back to our seats. It was exactly the same gesture that John had used with Bitsy earlier. I allowed myself to be guided and found that I liked it. He felt like an anchor in the best sense of the word.

Once we were seated, I asked, "Why did Bitsy know my name before you introduced us?"

"Security protocols. The Senator gets a lot of death threats, so everyone getting close to him or his family has to be cleared by their private security team. There was an actual foiled assassination attempt few years ago. Someone got a package though security to his office, back when all those white powder anthrax threats were being made by mail. So, that freaked everyone out a bunch."

"Naturally. Was anyone hurt?" This is what his world has always been.

"No, fortunately. But what these shitheads don't get is that it was the lowliest assistant opening the mail and sorting it for the office. She's the one who would have died. Dumb fucks."

Our conversation meandered from there for the rest of the flight, which was relatively uneventful. We arrived in DC and thanked the Ivory's again as we deplaned, promising to see them at the fundraiser. They got into a waiting limo. Bitsy was a little unsteady, but still breathing, so I counted that a plus.

Chapter Thirty Seven

Xander
The Glitch Mob, Animus Vox

Once we were through the airport parking, out on the road, I started heading toward my parents' house, on the far side of DC. I was still pissed about John's behavior. He was disgusting, a sick pervert. And I wanted to protect Leda from that. Forever. And what was I doing? I was taking her right into the middle of it.

"What's up with you right now?"

I glanced at her when her question pulled me from my thoughts.

"You've been really quiet."

I answered, trying to keep the banked anger from my tone. "My mind is just rehashing things. John is such a fucked-up old pervert. I saw him staring at your chest and your ass. He just pissed me off. As much as Bitsy is a lushy old MILF, she deserves more respect than he gives her and, well, clearly you're mine." *For fuck's sake.* "It just pissed me off, but he's a billionaire, married to my dad's boss's sister and the biggest campaign supporter Noe has." I paused, but she didn't respond, so I kept going. "Truthfully, I don't really want to be here. I want to be holed up somewhere, just you and me."

"Oh."

There was a pause. What could she really even say to all that? She wasn't prepared for what we were walking into. Stacy was right. And, that...that more than anything, pissed me off. But Leda kept talking, a smile on her face, despite all that shit.

"My family loved you, you know. They all thought you were great."

I smiled, but didn't answer. Perhaps sensing how tense I was about this situation, she asked me to prep her some. I explained about my Dad's career, how he'd become Noe's right hand man. How it had destroyed what was probably a loving relationship between my parents. And I finished by explaining how things were now between them. I wanted to be open with her, wanted her to know everything about me, even knowing I'd never tell her *everything*.

She responded with a comment about my mother possibly being fulfilled by her relationship with my dad, comparing it to our kink. "Maybe they worked it out. To each their own, right? I'm sure some of my girlfriends from college would be appalled at the shit I let you do to me, but—"

I cut her off. "*Let* me do to you? Try again." The frustration and fear churning in me funneled into the words and I wanted her. I wanted her on her knees, taking whatever I gave her. There was no *let* about it.

She sucked her fat lower lip into her mouth and started to fidget. Her breathing was shallower and her voice quiet when she answered. "Okay, Boss. If my friends knew about all my new experiences with you and that I *want* it to happen, again and again, they'd probably think I was crazy. But the point is they can't judge me—or us—because they aren't living our lives."

As much as she was probably making a valid and important point, I could only focus on one part of what she said. "You want it to happen, *again and again*?" S

he nodded, that sexy apprehension making her eyes go wide.

"Mmm, good. Because you need more." I grabbed my cell off the dash and one-touch dialed my mom.

"Hiya, sweetheart! Already landed?"

"Hi, Mom. Yep, we just landed."

"How was the flight? Was Bitsy drunk? How about John? Was it very bad?"

"Of course, Bitsy was drunk. And, yes, John was inappropriate, as always."

She made a small sound of annoyance before saying, "How did your Leda do? Didn't scare her off too much, did it?"

"Not too bad. I kept a close eye on her."

"Well, I hope that's all you kept on her in the plane. You young people and your mile-high business. Anyway, I can't wait to meet her. Are you taking her out to dinner first?"

"Yeah, at eight. You should come too."

"Oh! Honey, that's so sweet. I'd love to. Where should I meet you?"

"The Club. I'm going to go get us checked in first. Meet us for dinner?"

"Okay, hun. I'll see you there."

"Okay, Mom. We'll see you then."

"Tell Leda I'm excited to meet her."

"I'll tell her. Love you. Bye."

I dropped my phone and took the next exit to flip a shitty back onto the highway, heading back into town.

Leda looked around in confusion. "Xander, what was all that about? Hotel? I thought we were staying with your parents."

"It's been too long since I've been inside you." My mood was lifting as I thought about what I wanted to do to her, and the depravity reached my face in a smile I knew probably scared her a little.

* * * *

The check-in process was smooth and we were walking into our room within moments. It still wasn't soon enough. I ushered her in front of me, just to watch her walk across the space. I started to walk toward her before the door closed and when it slammed home, she startled, but I was right there, on her. I pushed her down on the bed, loving that I took her by surprise. I lay down on her back and stopped her when she tried to turn over.

Everything in me changed. I felt feral, animal. I wanted to tear her apart, just to be able to lick every part of her. I wanted to watch her take everything I had.

"Don't move, until and unless I tell you to. Ten days, Leda. It's too long. Never again." I wasn't in the same kind of control I usually was. I was on the verge of out of control and it felt so goddamned good. I wanted to let it all go. She must have felt the difference in me, because she was panting, eyes wide, lips parted just a bit.

The fear looked so good on her. "I think I like it when you're a little scared of me. I think you like it too." But she was smart and didn't take the bait.

She didn't move, except her panting breaths, as I pushed up off her. I wanted to see her ass and found the waistband of her yoga pants. I yanked them down and they got hung up on her hips and ass. *What a beautiful fucking thing that is.* I pulled harder, until the material gave with a ripping sound. I just pulled them far enough to expose her sexy ass.

I stood back and just looked at her plumpness, her heart-shaped loveliness. "Wiggle your ass for me, little girl." The words felt sick and wrong on my lips and it got me hard. She shifted back and forth a bit. "Faster. That's not wiggling." I gave her a little swat.

Something in her gave. She let out a puff of air and gave up her reluctance. She shook it, getting the right rhythm for a perfect jiggle.

"Good girl, very nice. I love your ass. You know that, right? It was the very first thing I noticed about you." She shifted a little to try to look at me and I put my hand on her ass cheek, squeezing till her flesh bulged between my fingers. A warning and she knew it. "It was before we met, before tutoring. You walked across the library, and your scrubs were thin enough that I could see the perfection. Then you turned and the rest of your body looked so just fucking edible. But, you turned a little more and I could see your face. That was it. I was done. Had to have you."

I rubbed my hand slowly over her ass and onto her thigh, remembering that first day in the library, changing the group I tutored. *And now she's mine.* The possessiveness washed through me like liquor. "How ready are you for me?"

I pushed my hand between her thighs. She was wet. Not sopping—I'd seen her like that before. This was the 'just starting' wet, damp, ready for me. I buried my fingers in her, a claim, but inside she was even hotter. The wet heat of her was intoxicating and I wanted more. But wanted all of her, wanted to remind her that I owned all of her.

When my fingers were plenty wet, I stroked back over her ass and pushed a finger in, without much warning or prep.

She simultaneously snapped her hips back to make it easier for me to get in and squeezed down in surprise. "Xanderrrr! Mmmmmmmm, Jesus!" She muffled her words into the bed, but the pouty, whininess was still easy to hear. I smiled and pulled out then pushed a second finger back into her.

Her breath came in waves of pants. I rubbed her back with my other hand and, after a few minutes, felt her consciously relax her ass for me. "Good girl. I'm going to grab the plug. You focus on keeping your ass relaxed for me."

When I stepped away from her, I backed out of her line of sight, waiting to see what she did. As I opened the bag and started fishing for the plug, she predictably turned her head, trying to see what was coming.

"I told you not to move, little girl." I couldn't help but smile. I wanted a reason to punish her. I took it, spanking her a few more times. She moaned and arched back some. I held the plug at her anus, dripping some lube on her. She paused and her breathing slowed as she focused on taking it in. Once it was in though, she was a wanton thing, panting and flushed.

"Get on your knees, on the floor, right here in front of me." She started to move, cautiously. Too slowly. "Now." My voice was hard, but didn't raise it at all. I didn't need to. She jumped and moved. Once she knelt in front of me, I told her to take her sweater off.

She had a simple black bra that was pushed up high. Lovely. I took just a moment or two to watch her. And while I did, her pupils went wide, her face slackened, tension left her shoulders. Her eyelids dropped a little and she started to sway.

I shifted a bit and it grabbed her attention. She looked up at me. And it was like the library all over again. Like a million other moments with her. I was decimated by her. Struck down, weakened and strengthened all at once.

I held her gaze, loving her in my dark, sadistic way, as I unbuckled my belt, opened the fly of my jeans and pulled my cock out. I was hard, rigid, ready to be inside her.

"Open your mouth, girl."

She focused in a little, her eyes darting to my dick in front of her face. She opened her mouth, wide.

But I added, "When I tell you to open for me, I want your tongue out. A welcome mat for my cock. Do you understand me?"

She didn't speak, only opened her mouth wider, laying her welcome mat tongue out for me as she nodded her assent. Then the little vixen, looked right up at me.

"Very good." I smiled at her and watched the pleasure in her eyes. The pleasure in knowing that she was pleasing. I stroked the hair that had fallen over the side of her face, and she pushed into my hand, like a kitty. But I coiled my hand, knotting in her hair and she immediately stilled.

She hadn't closed her mouth and her tongue still waited for me. So good. I pushed my cock into her mouth, felt her shift to accommodate me. As I edged toward the back of her throat, I used the hand in her hair to hold her in place and pushed farther.

Her eyes fluttered closed, allowing me to take what I wanted from her, enjoying that I did. I loved her. I knew it. I had to tell her. After a few more moments of my length in her throat, blocking her from breathing, her eyes flashed open and up at me, a note of panic present in the way they darted. I waited another moment, when I felt her throat convulse around the head of my dick as she involuntarily tried to breathe or scream. Just as her hand came up to push at me, I pulled out.

"Breathe, Leda." It was fucked up, but I kind of loved the idea that I could even control the essential functions for her life. Her breathing was mine. "Open."

She dropped her jaw, her tongue out, even as she still gasped. "Very nice, little one."

I pushed back into her mouth, sliding in with ease as she re-acclimated to feeling me push on her throat. I found a rhythm and fucked her throat. For a while, she tried to lick and suck, to add to my pleasure, slobbering after me, but she couldn't keep up with my pace and gave up. She accepted it and I felt invincible.

For a few moments, I leaned back, pulling her with me, and looked up at the ceiling. But my balls started to tighten and the pleasure of her hot, wet mouth, that felt so different from her pussy, the light scrape of her teeth, the way she let me do anything I wanted to her, with her. It all came crashing at me. I looked down at her and her face was covered with saliva that had drooled out around my cock, and that was it.

My orgasm hit like thunder, almost crippling me in its intensity. I pulled back to come on her, rather than in her. She startled as it hit her cheeks and lips, but it looked fucking amazing. She was an all new kind of wrecked. Wrecked for me. Marked in me. Mine.

She looked up at me, eyes widening for a moment. She looked so good, and I wished I had ever talked to her about taking pictures, but I knew that was too shitty and manipulative to try to bring new elements of play in the middle of play. Even though she made me so much more of myself, made me harder than I had ever been, even though I was sure she'd accept anything from me, would let me photograph her like this, I loved her and couldn't betray her trust like that. Instead, I murmured, "I just want to memorize you just like this."

Chapter Thirty Eight

Leda
She Wants Revenge, Sister

He pulled me up, hands steadying me. I still wavered as I stood. I held onto his shoulders when he kneeled to take off my boots, leggings and panties. He guided me to the bed and laid me down on my back.

"Don't move. I want to savor the way you look right now. Eyes with that sleepy sub look, half-lidded, begging me to do anything I want to you. My cum all over you." He stood at the edge of the bed and undressed. His cock was still semi-erect and he slipped into my soaking wet pussy when he lay down. He leaned on his left elbow and reached between us with his right hand to start playing with my clit. As he did, he swiped at my face, catching a dollop that was slipping down my jaw line. He scooped it up and deposited it in my mouth. I licked his finger off, and felt his cock getting firmer inside me. He rubbed his fingers over my face, getting me all sticky.

"You're so fucking dirty, Leda."

"*You* make me dirty, *Alex*." I said the last with a note of challenge, which earned me a raised eyebrow and his hand over my mouth.

"No more talking for you."

I sighed at the feeling of being restrained and tormented and owned. He started fucking me harder and pinching my clit. As he fucked me, he kept up a running monologue of his thoughts, his lips next to my ear.

"I will fucking *break* you, Leda. Tear you apart. You make me want the darkest things. You're mine. All of you, especially that fucking mouth, that feels so good on me — that spouts off and gets you in trouble. Smart ass mouth."

He kept smashing into my clit, hard. It was intense, too much pleasure, to the point of pain. A surge of sexual fear rushed through me, and I wrapped my legs around him, rocking my hips into him.

He completely stopped. "Are you *fucking kidding me*?" He bit the words off, a look of actual disappointed surprise on his face. He took a breath, his hand still on my face. "I told you not to move. Are you trying to make punish you? Is that what you want? Because I can make that happen, with a quickness, little girl."

I dropped my legs immediately, my eyes wide with combined fear and lust, my brain a little foggy still, but rapidly clearing.

Without moving, without breaking eye contact, he spoke, quietly now. "Leda, we just went to the Window a few times. Having you and having that part of myself out and accepted, I'm all in now. All in with you. And then it just grows and I want more. And then ten fucking days with nothing. No beating the shit out of someone at the club. No fucking you all tied up. Nothing for ten days, except being back here, with all the time in the world to fantasize about how to torment you, how to challenge you."

My body broke into chills.

"Look. I can shut it down completely, suppress it and be nothing of this, or I have to be all of it. I don't think there is in between for me anymore. It frees me and gives me peace. You give me peace when you submit to me and trust me to take you to the edge of what you can handle, beyond what you *think* you can handle—to take you where I want you and you making yourself handle it because it's where I want you."

Tears welled in my eyes, but I didn't know what to say to him. His hand was still over my mouth and I could feel his breath across my face where it was still damp and sticky.

"Now," he said, voice still quiet. "I'm going to torture you a little bit. Do you understand me?"

I nodded, breaths coming rapidly, raggedly from my chest.

"Do you need to tell me your safeword?"

I shook my head. Maybe it was curiosity, a morbid fascination with wanting to see the darkness in him come completely to light, maybe I wanted to ease his temper, ease his need. I think it was all of those things, but more than any of that, I wanted to be pushed. I wanted to go closer to the edge. Maybe over the edge.

"No moving now."

He pulled out of me and pulled me to the edge of the bed. The covers rumpled and caught at the butt plug, jolting it in me. My ass was at the edge of the bed, and he kneeled down so my legs hooked over his shoulders. And he just looked at my pussy. So close, I could feel his warm breath. He just looked and, the longer he looked, the more self conscious I got. *I mean pussies and dicks aren't the prettiest things in the world. There's a reason Tiffany referred to sex as 'bumping uglies'.*

He pinched my thigh. "Get out of your head."

How could he know that?

"I know when your mind wanders while we play. Sometimes I wait to see what will happen, but not today. Today you're all mine, including your brain." With that, he smoothed his palm down my torso to my scant hair.

He wrapped both arms around my thighs, so his fingers just came to my pussy, and pulled the lips apart, exposing me even further. Then he started licking. *Oh my God!* It was perfect. His soft, hot, wet tongue flattened and took broad strokes over my opening up to my clit. He started slowly, methodically. After a few minutes of this, he pulled my lips farther apart, pulling until there was tension, but still his tongue didn't change pace. The pulling transformed into pinching as he started squeezing my lips between his thumb and the knuckle of his index finger. Squeezing down tighter and tighter. And still his tongue continued the languid strokes from bottom to top. I was moaning, starting to writhe around on the bed, but trying so hard to respect his mandate not to move. *And, sidebar, best fucking torture ever.*

After one particularly vehement jerk of my hips, he paused, abruptly letting go of my lips. I moaned, low and guttural, as the blood rushed back into them. One hand came down softly but with increasing pressure on my pelvis, just above my pubic bone. His other hand went to my ass and, after a few quick pinches, started pulling the plug out a little, until I stretched a bit, then pushing it back in. But he said nothing and went back to licking me. I felt myself going liquid under his tongue. A sweet pressure slowly building, deep and low in my body.

That feeling suffused through me, the muscles of my pussy starting to clench and unclench, in rhythm with his licking. He slipped two fingers into me and just held them there, triggering a whole new sensation of being occupied, filled without being fucked. He concentrated his licking solely on my clit and a new cascade of pleasure washed through me. I felt my orgasm building, a small tempest of heat deep inside me. It was so close, so close.

And he stopped. He leaned back, completely stopped touching me.

"Uhhh, what the fuck, Xander? Fuck! I'm so close! Why'd you stop?" I was shaking with the strength of the orgasm pushing against me but not releasing. *Oh God, this is terrible.*

"Torture." He slid back farther, settling my feet down on the floor, and pushed my knees together. He climbed back over me, his knees on either side of my hips. "Now we wait until you settle down. And then we do it all over again." He said the words into my ear, but in his normal voice. No whispers, no real menace even. Just matter-of-factly.

"Xander, wait...no that's just too cruel. You're at least going to let me come next time right?" I wondered at how quickly I accepted what was happening and that it would again, because he said that was what was happening.

"Probably not, little girl." He sat back on his heels. I tried to subtly grind my pubic bone into his ass to get some friction, but he only laughed and raised himself a little off my body.

"You know, sometimes I think you need a little more pain than I give you. You're not convincing me otherwise right now. Take your bra off."

I moved to obey him, a defeated acceptance seeping into my thoughts. As it did, I was able to let go. I accepted it. I was frustrated, sad, burning with need, but I accepted it. Because I was in the moment, because it was Xander with me, pushing me. I couldn't explain it, but there it was, acceptance, growing in me. Tranquility followed. I felt my facial features soften and relax as his hands engulfed my breasts, stroking them, kneading them, squeezing them, pinching all around them. Then rolling my nipples between his fingers. Pinching down. I gasped as he squeezed hard enough to make them blanch. The haze, that wonderful, opiate haze slathered over my consciousness and my muscles relaxed again, accepting him, welcoming him. My breathing came slower, steadier.

"That's it, little girl."

He stroked his hand over my face. His cum was dry and sticky now. Him on me. And I wanted him everywhere. My mouth slackened. With my eyes half-lidded, I looked up into his face. His anger had faded and he was completely focused on me. I held his gaze as he continued stroking my face and hair, until he wrapped a few tendrils of hair up in his fingers and mirrored the action with the other hand, and pulled me to sitting up. He swung his legs back off me and stood, pulling me to standing. My legs felt wobbly, but I trusted him to catch me if I fell. He pulled me to a full length mirror just outside the bathroom.

"Look at yourself," he said, positioning himself behind me, one hand still in my hair.

I looked. My body didn't look any different, but my face looked so different. Unrecognizable, almost expressionless, eyes half lidded, pupils huge. Mascara smudged on my cheeks. My mouth slack, no smart-ass smirk or comment on my lips. I looked drugged.

"This is you, submitting to me. Right now. Deep down. On a cellular level." He let that sink in before he continued, "You belong to me, don't you?"

"Yes."

"You want me to take you, don't you?"

"Yes."

"You want me to use you."

"Yes." I shivered again, and my body's movement pulled at my hair in his hand. The pain anchored me in my body.

"You want me to hurt you."

"Yes." As soon as the word formed on my lips, his free hand came around to my throat. A fine sheen of sweat glistened on his skin. My body felt heavy and I leaned into him, the movement pulling my hair tighter, pushing myself down on his hand around my throat.

"You're my good girl, aren't you?"

I just nodded, words escaping me now. He pulled me back to the bed, again balancing my ass right at the edge, and pulled the plug out. He grabbed some lube and coated us. He watched my ass, pressing my legs back and rolling my hips up, as he positioned his cock and pressed in. He pushed and slid in so easily after the stretching of the plug. He sucked a breath in as he pressed into me in one long stroke. It was a different feeling than the plug in my ass, different than the feel of something inanimate. The slip and stretch of it was heavy feeling, tight, the last violation left between us.

I was just starting to think that it wasn't really torture when he slipped his thumb into my pussy and got it wet to stroke it over my clit, tracing circles, pressing in on me. My muscles spasmed, tightening around his cock, and he let out a low chuckle, but didn't stop. As he played with my clit, he slid in and out of my ass, slick and smooth.

I was floating in the haze of sensation, anchored to the world only through him and his presence. The stretching created a dull, warm ache that seeped into all the tissues in my pelvis. I closed my eyes, breathing heavily, my body slack across the bed. With his free hand, he pinched down on my nipple, shocking me back into my body, eyes flying open. He released my nipple and reached over the other one. I sucked in a breath and looked at him. He was fully present in the moment. His expression was an amalgam of amusement, heat, that Dom-fury I had seen before. There was a hint of ownership there, too. He was more mine than ever in that look. It drove my sensation up another ten notches.

I moaned, writhing into him. His eyebrow came up in that sexy, Dom, what-the-fuck-are-you-doing way.

"I can't help it, Xander. It's too much! I need to move. It's too hard to hold still here while you do all this," I whined.

"That's exactly why you'll do it. Because it's hard and I want you to. Stop moving." He paused to apply more lube to us, and got some extra on his fingers to brush over my clit. "Stay still and take it."

He pressed his thumb into my clit and just held it there for a moment. Then faintly started pulsing his thumb across it, so fast. I tightened my muscles to hold still, but it was so fucking hard. I felt the seed of pleasure building up again, and I was surprisingly aware of my empty pussy. But that seed built and built, becoming a core of cold fire. Twisting in on itself and expanding. My breathing became more ragged. Panting, begging him silently. My pussy spasmed and I felt myself tighten around his cock. Shards of pleasure stabbed through my pelvis and my eyes rolled back with a moan. I wanted to come so badly. I tried to hold it off, took a shuddering breath, swallowing down on the curse in my mouth. But he saw it anyway and he pulled out of me, literally taking a giant step backward, dropping my legs. My body bounced on the edge of the bed as my orgasm faltered and failed, never happened.

"*No!*" I wailed, tears of frustration welling in my eyes. "Xander, please I can't... I can't."

"Yes, you can, because I say you can." His voice was solid, holding no strain whatsoever. Matter-of-fact.

The female equivalent of blue balls...blue ovaries...sad ovaries...sad clit syndrome. *Yep, I've got a terrible case of SCS.* It ached and I felt almost queasy. His cock was still hard. And the bastard started stroking it, two steps away from me. *That motherfucker! Well, if he could take matters into his own hands, so could I.* I got a nervous flutter in my stomach as I moved my hand to touch myself, maintaining our stand-off eye contact the whole time.

He paused in his self-pleasure, wry smile on his face. "Really, Leda?"

I nodded at him. "Yep and fuck you. You're mean."

Chapter Thirty Nine

Xander
Sir Sly, Where I'm Going

Do not laugh. You will lose all Dom-cred if you laugh. But, holy shit…what a little.

She expected me to physically stop her from trying to get off, but I stepped away, over to my bag of tricks. Out of the corner of my eye, I saw her dip her fingers into her pussy and rub her clit. She didn't even falter when I stalked back to the bed, even as I climbed onto the bed next to her. She stared at the things I carried. She had only ever seen the spreader when I used one on Seraphim's slave.

"This is a spreader bar, designed to keep you wide open for me."

She gasped, still stroking herself. She rocked her hips against her hand, threw her head back, trying to get off before I stopped her. But I pulled her hands away from her body and tied them up as she cried and whined. "*No, Xander!* I can't. I can't. I can't."

She was desperate and it was so incredibly hot. That she forgot herself, forgot the whole world, everything but me and what I wouldn't let her have. She closed her legs all tight and started grinding her hips. I just watched her for a second and climbed on her, dropping my weight on her hips so she couldn't move.

She fucking lost her shit, sobbing, bawling. Her makeup was fucked. She was my dirty Miss America, crying and grimacing — but not safewording. She was my fucked up little slut, dying to come. She was my favorite toy.

She kept crying but happened to see how hard I was, which honestly, she probably couldn't have missed. It was pretty much right in her face. But seeing how completely hard she made me, gave her a moment of pause.

"Do you like seeing me cry?" Her voice held a tremor of shock. My cock twitched again as if nodding yes to answer for me.

I leaned down over her, running my fingers over her tits. *All mine.* I crooned in her ear, "Like this? Fuck yes, little girl."

She gasped and I ran my hand up her sternum around her throat. With my other hand, I shushed her. "Shhh. Now, or I'll gag you next."

When she stilled, I moved off her to secure the spreader between her knees. I just traced her curves for a moment and she moaned a little. I could see the wetness dripping from her pussy, pooling on the comforter under her ass. "God, you're so wet. You love this, don't you?"

She looked at me in confusion, but didn't speak. *Good girl.* Then she nodded *Yes*, followed by a quick and much more vehement *No*. I stood over her, surveying her. And it was a power-up. I was more than I was. I was stronger, meaner, better, sharper. Everything.

I grabbed the spreader bar and did a curl with it, rotating her hips up off the bed so I could bend forward and lick her pussy. Knowing I was claiming it. It was my pussy. No one else could ever have it. I licked her again. She melted and all the resistance, all the fired up bitchy heat went out of her. I grabbed the lube I had dropped off to the side. I got us all slick and fucked her ass again. She was still greasy and loose and it felt fucking fantastic.

I petted her pussy, stroked her clit. And when she moaned and squirmed, I slapped her there. Her eyes opened and she yelped. All her muscles snapped tight around me and it felt incredible. I switched my grip to hold her hips around the front and it gave me complete control over her body. I was pounding her ass, punishing it. Hard and harder. And she took it. I looked at her and she was watching me, her face a sexy, twisted misery. And it was good. It was better than good. It was what I wanted, what I needed. I felt my orgasm tightening in my balls and I squeezed my fingers on her fleshy hips, loving the feel of her. She moaned all sick sexy pain and lust mixed up together. It triggered me.

I groaned out an obscenity and pulled my cock out to come all over her pussy. I released the spreader but told her to leave her legs open for me. "You're beautiful and I want to remember this all night tonight."

She held still and I flopped down on the bed next to her. I reached to the quick release on the knots I had used to tie her wrists. "You're amazing, Leda. You did so well." I brushed her hair out of her face. "You always do. Such a good girl"

She held still, waiting for whatever was next. But we were done because I was torturing her. *Time to drop that bomb.* "I'm going to go run us a shower. We have to leave in about an hour to make our reservation and then get back here for the party."

She looked at me in confusion, the sub brain drugs clearing. Then the 'what the fuck' registered. "Really, Xander? All done?" Her anger faded to a whine.

"Yep, baby. Not for the whole night, but for now. And I know you're thinking that you could just finger the bean a bit and get off real quick." She flushed with guilt—*ha*. "I don't want you to do that. I don't want you to come tonight, until you come on my cock, when I say you can. I know that you could easily slip away and finish up sometime tonight without me. But that would disappoint me, and I'd want to do *something* with that disappointment. I want you to do this for me."

Anger, then sadness, then resignation, then true acceptance. "I don't want to come by myself. I've missed you too much. I want you to make me come. But please, *please*, don't make me wait too long."

Her pupils were still wide and her lips still puffy when we left. She was beautiful—her gown was a deep blue and draped over her body elegantly, but still sexy as fuck. It was low in the back and had an exposed shiny silver zipper that played against some subtle silver studs scattered over her. But her shoes were superhigh, too high. I put the necklace, which I knew was really a collar, on her before we left and it fell right where I wanted it to.

We took a car service to the club to meet my mom for dinner. Belatedly, I thought about how it may have been poor planning to play with her that hard right before meeting my parents, but we had both needed it,

I thought. My mother was waiting for us. She stood as we approached the table. She kissed my cheek, ever aware of all the eyes around us.

"Alex, honey." She turned to Leda, who was still flushed from sex and a hot shower, followed by the brisk DC winter air. "And the famous Leda! He was so mopey for Christmas without you."

Cut that shit out, Mom. "Mom, this is Leda Collins. Leda, this is my mother, Nancy Stone."

They shook hands, but my mom pulled her into a hug, air-kissing her cheeks. This was much more effusive than my WASPy mom ever was. I filed that mental note as we sat down. Leda smiled at the warm reception.

The meal was a set New Year's menu, reflecting the chef's French training. It was excellent as always. The conversation was light, because anyone could overhear us. The dining room was packed with all kinds of Washingtonians. Lobbyists, staff members for various public officials and politicians, society types. The upper echelon of the Beltway. Everyone in the room noticed everyone else.

I was raised with it and knew how to play the part. I hadn't given Leda any kind of warning, but she was doing well. She listened with interest to the conversation, laughing at the right times, not too loud, but clearly visible to anyone watching. It was completely unaffected, because it was real. I noticed the leeches watching us, wondering who she was. As much as everyone involved in the scandal with Stacy tried to keep it quiet, there is no place on Earth that likes a scandal as much as Washington, and most people knew something weird, something sexual had happened between me and someone. The stories I had heard were all over the place, from as relatively tame as a three-way to as fucked up as bestiality. So, any woman with me was at least a little bit interesting. And Leda was stunning and young. It made it that much more titillating and I knew it.

My mom knew it too, and took pains to mention Leda's name, often and loudly, intending to be overheard. The context left no doubt she was my date, and clearly more than a onetime only date. People around town would hear about her tomorrow. There was nothing to do except fuck with people — that, or roll over and take it.

When we left, I offered them each an arm with a wide smile on my face, but after a few steps, I moved my hand to Leda's elbow, then to the small of her back and just as we crossed the threshold out of the dining room, to her ass. Let them talk about that shit. I had a reputation for having a robust, nearly animal sexual appetite. *Why stop the rumor now?*

We all rode back in the town car and kept the conversation light, but I felt myself pulling in. I hated these things. Hated all the memories they brought back to me. Hated the weird repressed sexual energy that kept people staring at me for the first half of the night, then invariably led to cougar-wannabes coming on to me later, when they were a few drinks into their liquid courage. They all hoped I'd bring my magic cock and make it all feel good again. It was different than fucking with the anonymous public at the club because these people thought they could use my sexuality to control me, to influence my dad or the Senator.

My mom knew how I felt. Hell, half her friends had tried to fuck me. As we pulled into the line of cars at the hotel, she tapped my foot with hers and I glanced up at her. She smiled at me, glanced at Leda and raised her eyebrows, then winked. She approved.

In the ballroom, my mom pointed my dad out easily but quickly went to the bar. She hated these as much as I did, but mostly because he'd brazenly hit on anything female under thirty and it was embarrassing for her. And living up to his rep, he was dancing with some slut in a skintight, silver floor length gown. The song stopped and it was fucking Stacy that he stepped away from. Of course it was.

I spared Stacy a smile, but she knew the coldness in my eyes and slipped away. "Dad, I want you to meet someone."

My dad came over to us, and the bastard looked my girl over from head to toe, lingering briefly on her breasts. I wanted to punch his stupid face. But, it was quick and I hoped that she hadn't noticed or at least wasn't too offended.

He extended his hand to her. "Leda, hello. Pleased to meet you."

"Dad, this is my girlfriend, Leda Collins. Leda, this is my dad, Denny Stone."

She shook his hand, "Nice to meet you Mr. Stone."

"Did you bring your mother?"

I nodded as he found her in the crowd, but I was ready to move on to anything else. "Well, Happy New Year's, Dad. I think I'm going to take Leda for a drink. See you later." I started pulling her away, but she spoke over her shoulder.

"Nice to meet you, sir. Happy New Year."

Oh, no, little one. You shouldn't call anyone but me sir, but especially not that dick head.

She looked up at me and I must have been clenching her elbow because a little crease of pain cleared from her eyes when I intentionally loosened my grip.

"You okay, Boss?"

I wasn't paying very close attention to her as she spoke, but answered anyway. "What? Oh. My dad is a dick. He cheats. And don't call him sir. I don't ever want to hear that word coming out of your mouth for anyone other than me."

She pressed her body into mine and smiled at me. "Okay, honey. Let's go get that drink."

The party was more of the same. People working the room, false laughter, just falsity in general. I only left her side a few times, mostly when one or both of us needed to refresh ourselves. Every so often, I'd slip her into some hidden corner and we'd kiss some, I'd threaten her and she'd flush. I had left her seriously wanting and it showed.

But I was distracted by all the ghosts of my life, by all the BS I wanted no part of now. Leda took it in her stride. She was a champ, charming and coy. Demurring away from dancing with the old men who hit on her when I wasn't at her side. We danced a few times and she didn't really know how to do it. We'd need to take some dancing lessons together sometime when med school was done.

At midnight, Noe made his speech, asking for money, condemning the Left and trying to be charming all at once. When we counted down, I turned to Leda to kiss her and she looked...troubled. But it was a moment, just a passing thing that she hid from me as soon as I looked at her. I let it go, toasted the New Year and kissed her. As I deepened the kiss, I heard my name being called, a voice I didn't want to hear, but would know anywhere.

"Xander!" I turned to see Stacy, a big smile painting her face.

"Hi, Stacy. Happy New Year." I kissed her cheek, kind of amazed that she was braving her dad's wrath in a room full of people who all thought they knew what happened between us. Her cheek was hot under my lips and, as I pulled away, I saw the flush there. The excitement in her eyes, the way she used to get when we were kids—when we got high and fucked.

"Guess who's here, Xander." She was nearly bouncing on her toes and her excitement was a little infectious. Even though I didn't want to encourage her, I couldn't help but smile. No matter how excited she was, I couldn't be disrespectful to Leda. I pulled her toward me and tucked her under my arm.

"You remember Leda."

She barely registered that Leda was there. "Seriously, Xander! The Nymphos are staying here!"

In just the briefest blink of an eye, a flash of images rioted through my brain. Some chick's tits in my face, licking up the last bit of coke after snorting most of it off her. Stacy with some guy eating her pussy while she tipped back a huge bottle of Jack Daniels. The flash of a hand slapping an ass. A handful of pills. The hard-on that wouldn't go away, no matter how many girls I fucked that night. Licking Stacy's sweat off her back. Laughing when we couldn't walk. Falling asleep on the tour bus and laughing more when we realized we were in North Carolina.

And even though it was part and parcel of my shit with her, it was still one of the best weekends of my life. A once in a lifetime thing. Wildness beyond measure, loss of control, complete hedonism. "Seriously? Why?" I hadn't heard of them in a good five years and had assumed that one of them had died or they'd broken up or something.

"Yeah. They're staying here while they play a few shows downtown. Do you remember when we went to that show?"

Of course I do.

"Jesus, I got so fucked up!" She laughed and I laughed a little with her.

Then I laughed harder, remembering how innocently the night had started. Me and her and a few of her friends. They'd all left when we'd started drinking and it was clear I couldn't drive. "Yeah, I remember thinking I was going to get arrested for plying minors with alcohol if we got pulled over. That was what, ten years ago?"

Her face stilled. "Jesus, yes. Just about ten fucking years ago. I'm gonna try to track them down. You wanna come?"

It surprised me again. She cared less and less about her dad's image and I liked it. I liked that she was thinking for herself. I smiled, but surprise colored my voice. "Aren't you worried about pissing your dad off?"

"Not really. Seriously, fuck him. This is bullshit. Now I get why you went so far away for med school. Come on. Leda can come too." She smiled, glancing at Leda as an afterthought. I knew her and knew she didn't really mean the insult. But it was an insult nonetheless.

"Ohhh, no, I don't think so." It seemed like a terrible idea. As much as part of me wanted to relive my blatantly self-destructive phase, even if just for one night. "But text me if you do find them. I want to hear if they remember you as well as you remember them." I couldn't help but laugh again, remembering her legs all akimbo when she'd passed out in the tub and one of the groupies turning the water on to wake her up.

And Stacy punching her and kicking her off the bus at a truck stop somewhere.

Stacy stood on her tip toes to kiss my cheek, but said goodbye to Leda. I watched her walking away, seeing the woman she had become and feeling nostalgic.

Leda pulled me toward her, saying, "If you want to go with her, you can...or we can. I want to hear this story of an apparently epic night. I never knew you two did stuff like that." She smiled and fuck, she was being so polite and kind. Not nearly as fiery as she had been when we'd gone for sushi and run into Stacy.

I was torn. Stacy was my past. Leda was my future. "We grew up together. I remember her playing with Barbies in the yard at parties with our families. It was a different part of my life. My parents were happy, well...happier. They're good memories. By the time she was graduating high school and I was in college, we were really close, like brother and sister." I felt like a dick. Why hadn't I ever told her any of this? "We saw the Nymphos one summer while I was home and...it was just crazy."

"Really, Xander. If you want to go with her, that's fine."

I was observant enough to know that was a lie, but it was a kind lie. "No, Leda. I don't think that's a good idea. In fact, I think we should leave pretty soon. Let's start making the rounds to say goodnight." I took her hand and led her around the room, saying brief goodnights and wishing people a good new year as we went.

We found my mother at the First—and only—Wives Table. It was all political wives that would never be left. They were all older, had some reason that their husbands would never leave—fear of scandal, lack of a prenup, or a prenup where all the money came from her side. But all their husbands cheated, some of them with men. It was a sad fact of the political world, especially the Religious Right, the Moral Majority. They cheated as much as any other group in the US — maybe more. There were a bunch of loosely closeted, self-loathing gays in the party too. I don't know why that bothered me more.

Stacy popped up at my side as we got to the First Wives Table. "Ahhhh! I found them! They're playing some show tonight, but should be back soon. Check it, they still have the same manager. Butch remembered us... Well, mostly me because...you know."

"You threatened to cut his dick off. With your broken bottle of Jack. I think I remember that you did actually cut him, right? Did he tell you to fuck off?" I laughed again and couldn't even remember why she was gonna castrate him, or how he'd ended up naked with her when she had a broken bottle in her hand.

"No! We...uh...we made up later that weekend."

Oh Jesus, who didn't she fuck?

"Anyway, I'm going to meet their bus when they get back. Probably in a few hours. Then try to hit up the afterparty with them. You should come too."

"Stacy —"

She cut me off. "Please come meet me. It's been a long time and things have changed, Alex. I miss you."

I didn't answer her, just hugged her — and she walked away, without looking back at me. And I knew it was right, but it still hurt a little. I forced myself to smile as I turned to Leda. I needed to feel her close to me and pulled her into a hug, breathing in her scent and relishing the peace the settled in my heart with it. She shifted a little in my arms and her breasts pressed into my torso.

It was enough. I wanted her again. I pulled her back from me to look in her eyes. "Let's go, little girl. I think I owe you something." I leaned past her to say goodnight to my mom, offering to walk her up. She declined, citing Bitsy's current tirade against John as reason enough to stay up. But as I nodded and turned away, she grabbed my shoulder and pulled me down into a hug, so she could whisper in my ear.

"Do *not* fucking get involved with Stacy again. Leda seems like a nice enough girl and I hope it works, but if she isn't enough for you, don't tumble back into that hell hole with Stacy."

"For fuck's sake, Mom. I'm not gonna fuck Stacy tonight. In fact, I'm gonna go fuck Leda. Right now. For the third time today. She's enough for me."

"You looked awfully chummy with Stacy. How do you think Leda feels about that? How do you think Stacy's father feels about that?" She dug her nails into the back of my neck, and didn't even seem to care about my vulgarity about sex with Leda. *Shoulda known. Nothing changes.*

"Okay, Mom. That's enough." I let the Dom voice out a bit and she retracted her claws from my neck, shrank a bit in my arms. I pulled away, a warning in my eyes.

She smiled and touched my cheek, ever the performer. "Just be careful, sweetheart. I love you."

"Love you, too, Mom." I kissed her cheek, for the show more than any true affection I was feeling at that moment.

She and Leda exchanged hugs and air kisses and Happy New Years'. Bitsy laughingly asked Leda how bad the rope was chafing after spending the evening at the party. *Jesus Christ. Time to go.*

In the elevator, I held Leda in front of me, leaning back on me, with the excuse of rubbing her shoulders. I really just needed a few minutes to clear my head before being back with her. I tried to let go of the swirl of shit that party had put in my mind, but couldn't. And Leda's skin was there in front of me, looking so delectable, creamy, lickable.

Before I really decided to start fucking with her in the elevator, my hand was climbing into her hair, grasping her, arching her back toward me. I tilted her head back and up to get easy access to her the warm, soft spot just below her ear. I licked a few times then bit. She tensed then softened into me.

The tension of the night melted out of me, morphed into something else. Something potent, virile, taut and tight. I felt mindlessly possessive of her. She was mine, to do with as I wanted. And I wanted to scare her.

Chapter Forty

Leda
Rammstein, Stripped

"Okay, Boss." That got his attention as we entered our room. "What now?"

He turned toward me, unbuttoning his collar and his cuff links. *Damn, that's sexy.*

"What now, she wants to know? When do I ever tell you what's coming?" His veil of domliness descended over him and his tension faded. Whatever there was with his parents and Stacy and just about everyone else here, he let it go. He held me close to him, running his fingers up and down my nearly bare back, tracing the curve of my ass.

"This dress is nice, little girl. But the heels were too high." He found my side zipper and pulled it down, sliding it off my shoulders, over my hips. He knelt to help me step out of it. I was left in the fancy midnight blue corseted style bra with garters attaching to my thigh high stockings. My panties were a matching g-string.

"Mmmmm, this is sexy, Leda." He leaned against me, face against my abdomen. His breath was a warm rush across my skin.

"I thought so." I ran my fingers through his hair. He stood slowly and my hand fell away.

He dropped his head down to kiss me. It was almost chaste. But after a few moments, his lips started moving, his tongue slipped out and traced the curve of my lips. I opened my lips, letting him in, and I was lost to the sensation of him. His body pressed against me, fully dressed against my lace and satin. He slipped his hands down under my ass and lifted me. I wrapped my legs around him and the shifting reignited the fire that had been banked away for the duration of the party. All the want and need and frustration of our earlier play came throbbing back through my body. I whimpered against his lips and my kisses became more impatient.

He placed his knee on the bed and leaned forward, laying me down under him. But just kept kissing me, stroking his fingertips over my jawline, my collarbone. He wasn't acting like himself. Usually by now, I was stripped, at least of torn panties.

He would usually be growling something vaguely terrifying and simultaneously thrilling in my ear. But he was so gentle now. I squirmed under him, hoping to remind him how much he liked using my whole body, or at least to get a small bit of friction.

"Xander," I breathed into his mouth. "Please, I need you."

He kissed my cheek, then down to my neck, and under my ear. "You *need* me? For what, little girl?" he whispered, almost to the point of being inaudible.

"I need to feel you. I'm dying here. Please, stop..."

He stilled his mouth and hands on me. "Stop?" He propped up on one elbow to see my face.

"No! Not stop. I mean stop this…this…this…" I trailed off, not sure I could finish the sentence.

He smiled, knowingly. He knew I wanted more intensity, rougher sex. He raised an eyebrow. He wanted me to say it.

"I want more," I started, then faltered. I gathered my I-don't-give-a-fuck-if-you-think-I'm-a-whore courage and said, "I want you to fuck me like you usually do, rougher, harder. You're being so gentle. I don't even know what to do with myself."

A grin spread across his face, and it gradually become more and more evil and depraved looking. A chill ran through me, lingering between my shoulder blades. He just watched me a moment more. Then, he pulled a switchblade from his pocket and opened it in front of my face. I gasped, all my sexual excitement rapidly cooling to plain fear.

He saw the glimmer of true fear in my eyes and hummed appreciatively. "That looks good on you."

My thoughts ran in circles.

A fucking knife? Oh my God!

Xander would never actually hurt me.

But…a fucking knife.

He could have killed me a bunch of times, really.

Past non-psycho behavior does not preclude the possibility of current psycho behavior, especially because… A fucking knife!

Yellowyellowyellowyelllow!

I know he saw the fear rushing through me as he dropped the tip of the blade between my breasts and started tracing it down toward my pussy.

As he moved it, not pressing, just scraping, he said, "I've gotten sick of wrestling with your clothes and tearing off your panties. I decided to start cutting them off you now." The tip of the knife was at my pelvis and shifted to the side, under the thin strap and slipped right through it. He did the same on the other side, grabbed the middle of my panties and yanked them out from under me. He then, very deliberately, placed the ruined panties and the knife on the bedside table. I released my breath.

"You scared me," I said, my voice a little shaky.

"Did I, pet?" He murmured as he situated himself over me again. "I meant to scare you a little. Such a good girl, but that fear in your eyes gets me so hard." He ground his rock-hard business into my pubic bone. And just like that, the need slammed back into me, weaving with the fear and adrenaline, triggering a mental overload.

"Oh fuck, Xander. Please fuck me, or let me fuck myself for you. I need to come. It's too much. I need it, please?"

He dropped his head into the crook of my neck and licked and bit me. His fingers spread my lips open and stroked into my wetness. As I started gyrating my hips around with the rhythm of his movements, he propped up on his other elbow and looked at my face, just watching me as my fire built up. He smiled as he slowed his movements. I could feel the wetness and the tightness in my pussy. I looked at him with mutiny in mind.

"Call me Sir. No one else but me, ever."

I hesitated. It felt weird. Like one more degree of we-are-not-equals, but...well, we weren't really, at least during sex. He led. I followed. Or perhaps more accurately, he guided me where he wanted me to be.

"Just ask me pretty, Leda, and I'll make you feel good."

My eyes wide, I whispered, "Please, Sir. Please fuck me."

He smiled a dirty smile, a smile that said 'I just accomplished one more level of dominating you, degrading you, owning you'. That look alone made me feel small and anchored and real. He knelt up on the bed and unbuttoned his shirt, pulling it and his undershirt off. His body was perfect. Fit, tight, but not overly muscled.

"Say it again, little girl."

My eyes glazed slightly with tears of mortification. My voice quavered a bit, but I did it. "Please, Sir. I need you."

He unbuckled his belt and laid it next to me as he stood and finished getting undressed.

"Flip over and put your hands behind your back." His voice was hard, solid, unflinching.

I twisted and flipped and, before I was settled, he had a hold of my wrists. He pulled my arms farther back, stretching my shoulders. He gripped my arms and wrapped his belt around me, just above the elbows. He tightened it down hard till it pinched my skin. As he tightened it, I felt the tip of his cock brush against my ass, and knowing that he was so close to fucking me made my pussy quiver and tighten. He reached under me, and pulled me up so that I was balanced on my knees, face, chest and shoulders.

"Turn toward me, sweetheart. I want to see your face."

I turned and saw that he had a riding crop. Another flurry of fear ran through me, even as my pussy spasmed down again.

"Yep," he said, almost to himself. "That was the look I wanted to see." And he snapped it against my ass. It was sharp and stinging, but not horrible. As the sting faded, gooey warmth spread around from the site of impact. I moaned, closing my eyes.

He snapped it against me a few more times, less than ten but more than five. I lost the singular sensation of each strike and the warmth and sting and burn all started to run together. When he stopped, I was moaning and tears ran from my eyes.

"Please, Xander." I looked back over him, just in time to catch him pulling his arm back to spank me. The impact of the smack over the warm stinging sensation of the crop, it was too much. I let out a sob.

"What are you calling me now?"

"Sir. Sir. I'm sorry," I choked it out. His face reflected satisfaction, accomplishment, and hunger as he shifted behind me and slammed his cock into me. I turned my face slightly and screamed into the mattress.

He pounded at me, pulling at the angle of my hips as I moaned and screamed into the blankets. As I settled into the rhythm and the force, he shifted forward and grabbed his belt between my elbows. He pulled back, lifting my upper body off the mattress. It was sort of terrifying, feeling suspended in space, knowing that he could drop me at any time, even if it would only be a short fall into a soft mattress. My shoulders pulling back and the resultant shift in my torso made my breath feel tighter. Each breath was raspy and fast. My eyes settled on the charm of the necklace he had given me, where it rested on the mattress below me.

I watched it, knowing it marked me as his, as surely as his cock inside me did. And it was everything I wanted in the moment. I felt myself, my very sense of self, melting away, just a puddle of girl under him. It felt amazing. It felt like what I suspected heaven would feel like, like peace, better than peace—contentment and absolute understanding of my place in the world, of my meaning and purpose.

After what felt like a very short time, he flipped me onto my back, my arms under me, making me lean to one side. He barely broke his rhythm and was pounding back into me again, looking at me. Watching me. He scowled a tight grimace, almost like pain. He pushed my knees up, his hands hooked behind my knees and pressing me in half. But he still kept pounding into me. My pussy was wet, but was starting to get sore as well. It was certainly getting roughly used.

He brought my knees closer together and switched his hands around so that his left hand pressed against the back of my left thigh and his elbow crossed to press into my right thigh. He squeezed his right hand between us and started thumbing my clit. I bucked against him, involuntarily, gasping.

"Fucking take it, Leda." He growled. I couldn't see his face, but even his voice seemed different. Tighter, rawer.

"Yes, Sir. Please, just more. More please." My words tumbled from my mouth, nearly incoherent.

Pressing my legs again, he leaned back and spit onto his fingertips, dripping it down onto my open pussy. More lube for us. He rubbed his wet fingers over my clit more. The rush of sensations was a staggered assault to my brain. It was too much and exactly perfect, at the same time. My world was him—the ache in my arms, the aching pleasure of getting fucked like this, the shards of it shooting from my clit, his rasping breath. I moaned again and it lingered, almost one continuous moan for the next few minutes.

"That's a good little fucktoy. My good little girl."

Oh, Jesus.

A knot of tightening pleasure choked out all thought. My sounds became more frantic and he leaned forward, still pressing my clit, but holding my legs back with his body. He brought his now-freed left hand out and held it over my mouth.

"Come for me, right now, but don't make a fucking sound."

My wide eyes locked with his, but I held my breath as his next pulsation on my clit sent me over the edge into swirling, mind-rending pleasure, obliterated to everything but him. A few seconds later, he grunted and ground his hips down into my pelvis, flattening into my clit again, triggering more shards of the sweetest agony to shoot through me.

I panted against him, hard to breathe being bent in half with his weight pushing down on me and his hand pressing over my mouth. I turned my head and he moved his hand, but nothing else. Gasping shudders rippled through my body. He levered his body off me, slipping out of me wetly, and flopped down on the mattress beside me. We both panted for a few minutes, recovering.

After a brief rest, he efficiently untied me and we both got ready for bed. He made sure I had some sips of water and offered to help me get snuggled into a new, surprise set of pajamas — thick, satiny drawstring pants and a gauzy camisole, in a lovely slate gray that he said matched my eyes. But I didn't want to be clothed. I wanted my skin on his skin, even in my sleep. I wanted to have my flesh there for him, even when we slept. He smiled and kissed me, telling me that I was a miracle, as I settled into the bed. I fell asleep almost immediately, nestled into his side, as he fiddled with his smartphone next to me in the dark.

Chapter Forty-One

Xander
Client, Here and Now

Leda dropped into sleep quickly, but I was too wound up, jacked up from that kind of fuck. My tension and anger at my family, my life in DC, all of it, was gone. It was just gone. She took all of me and took it all away. I loved her and resolved to tell her in the morning.

I knew I wasn't going to sleep and started thumbing through websites on my phone. After a few minutes, that bored me and I sent a text to both Christy and Jason's phones.

Hey kids! Happy New Year! – X

Back at ya. How's it going up there? Did the party suck? – Christy

Of course it sucked, but Leda is amazing. I'm fucking all in. – X

Yeah. We know. – C + J

Single sign off now? – X

Yep…we're getting married! – C

Congrats!!!!!!! Finally. – X

Fuck you dude. –J

All right, we're gonna celebrate when we get back. – X

Shit yeah…but I'm gonna go bed my future wife. 'nite – J

Before I answered that, another text came through and I laughed.

Yep…I just got slapped a little for that one. LOL – J

Night guys. Love you – X

It was a long time before sleep pulled at the edges of my consciousness, but it did and I let myself go down, content for the first time in a long, long time.

The buzzing of my phone on the bedside table woke me. I thought I had forgotten my alarm or something and swore under my breath as I reached for it. But it wasn't my alarm and it wasn't morning. It was only three a.m.. *What the fuck?*

It was Stacy.

I wasn't going to answer. I sent it to voicemail. But it started buzzing again before I even put it back down. I knew she'd keep it up all night and eventually it would wake Leda.

I swiped my finger to answer and spoke, barely above a whisper. "What the *fuck* do you want?"

"I found them!" Her voice was loud, full of laughter, didn't care that I was pissed. "I found them and they totally remember that weekend. Remember things that I don't. You have to come have a drink with us. Just come up to the suite and say hello!" Her words were a little slurred, but she was so happy. So excited.

"I can't, Stacy. I'm fucking sleeping."

"Whatever, pussy. What…are you Coast Guard or something?" She referenced an old military joke.

I sat up, half laughing, "No…and fuck you."

"I'm serious. Come up and hang out for a bit. Bring Leda if you want. If you want her to know, that is."

"Leda is sleeping, right next to me. I'm not leaving her."

"Let me come down to you so you aren't worrying about waking her up. You're in room seven twenty seven, right?"

How does she fucking know that? "Jesus, Stacy. Not now, all right?"

"Yeah…I'll be right down. You can be waiting or I'll just pound on the door." She was laughing as she hung up. She was fucked up and I believed her that she would do that.

I muttered, "Goddamn it" as I got out of bed and went to the closet for a robe. I wasn't getting dressed for this shit. She'd just take it as a sign that I wanted to go with her. I took a leak and unlocked the door, knowing she'd be there shortly.

After a minute or two more, I opened the door and stepped outside, leaving my fingers on the doorjamb to keep it from closing all the way. I heard the elevator ding at the other end of the hall and Stacy stumbled out, her hair and makeup a little ruined from the party. Her clothes were completely different—a little sparkly tank top and a pair of super short shorts that I'm sure part of her perfectly tanned ass was hanging out of. She had a bottle in her hand and was smiling and laughing as she stumbled toward me.

I gestured for her to quiet down. She laughed again but caught herself with her hand over her mouth, eyes wide but full of mischief. When she got to me, she smelled of liquor. Not even a specific kind...just drunkenness.

"Hey, daddy," she slurred, trying to sound sexy. She leaned into me and kissed my cheek.

"What the hell, Stacy? It's the middle of the night and you're not a teenager anymore."

"Oooohh. Now you really sound like my daddy." She drunk-flirted with me, even as I pushed her away from me.

"Look, I'm only out here because I didn't want you to wake up Leda, and probably half the floor too. Go back to wherever you want to be. It should be your bed."

"Not till you fucking listen to me, Alex" she said impetuously.

My voice was flat when I answered her, "Fine. What?"

"You don't have to be a dick about it. Damn."

I just gave her the look, and all I wanted was to get back to bed with Leda. When I didn't answer her, or apologize, she went on.

"Look, we've been through a lot and I love you." She waved me off when I would have interjected something to stop her. "Whatever... You don't think I can love you, but you don't really get to make that decision. I love you. That's it. No one in the world knows what makes you tick better than me. No one in the world gets what your life is all about more than I do. We grew up in the same shit storm."

She put her hand on my chest as tears welled in her eyes. "You were the only thing that saved me. You were the lifeboat. I can't stand not being with you."

My heart broke a little for her. Regardless of what we had been through, she was right. We did grow up in a very specific version of hell together. I had seen her missing her front teeth when she was little. I had teased her about her stuffed animals. I had lusted after her when she'd started turning into a woman, in her little cheerleader skirt and ponytail. I had nearly loved her when we were together in our twenties.

My voice softened. "I know. I know. But it's different now. Look, you're drunk. Let's talk later."

She shook her head and stepped closer to me and, when she looked up at me, her tears broke over her cheeks.

She was angry, broken hearted. Her voice cracked, "Alex*ander*. I'm sorry! I'm so fucking sorry that it happened the way it did and you had to leave. But I never forgot what you did to me and how *intense* it was. I want more. I wanted more then."

We had never talked about it after that day. I never knew. I had thought it was all about pissing her dad off—and fucking with me. But it wasn't only those things. My brain didn't even register the most important part of what she said. I just knew it didn't matter, I still didn't want her. "Stacy, that door is closed now."

She got a sly look on her face and leaned into me, looking up at me. Her mascara was smudged under her eyes and her hair fell around her face in a halo. She purred up at me, "I don't think it is. I think there is something left between us. I still wonder, every night, what you would have done to me if my dad hadn't found us. No one else measures up. No one else excites me, twists in me the way you did."

I gripped her shoulders to push her back from me. "Stacy, I'm falling in love with Leda. Our time passed."

She turned her shoulders and twisted out of my grip, but then lunged back at me, wrapping her arms around my neck. Her surprise weight pulled me down and she kissed me. Her lips were soft and wet and insistent, her tongue darting out to lick my lips, still slack in shock.

She breathed a moan out on my mouth and that was it. I was fucking done. I went cold, pissed off that she wasn't listening to me. The irony wasn't lost on me. "You could barely handle me then. I'm just more of a bastard now. There is *nothing* left between us."

I pushed her back, but she kept her arms wound around my neck. "I've changed too, Xander. I think you'd be surprised. And I never thought you were a bastard." She leaned forward on me again. "And tell me, does Leda really know all of it? Does she really know you? The way I do. Does anyone know you the way I do, Xander?"

I pushed her back from me harder this time and she stumbled drunkenly, laughing. I couldn't stop myself from raising my voice, "No, Stacy. Do *not* fuck with this thing I have with Leda."

"Oh…" she mocked me. "Does it feel bad to have someone ignore you saying no?" She paused, letting that hit home, the bitch. "Shouldn't I at least warn her? Have you shown her the dark yet? The sadism, the true deep sadistic shit you love. The blood. Does she know, Xander?"

I looked down, the guilt of what had happened with her all those years ago rising up in my chest, mingling with my feelings for Leda, reinforcing the belief that I was going to hurt her in some way that couldn't be undone. Stacy read it all on my face.

"That's what I thought. She's innocent and I know…I know you're working on corrupting her and making her what you want, but you will destroy her. I'm already broken inside." She was pleading now. "You were the witness to it. You were the fucking trigger, Xander. You know me. I know you!"

I turned away. Sick of the conversation, knowing she was never going to hear me. She grabbed my arm. "Xander, wait!"

I let my arm go limp and slip through her hands as I pushed the door back open. The light from the hall illuminated a swath of carpet in front of me…that had feet standing in it. I looked up and Leda was standing at the edge of the light, still naked, face white, drawn. Eyes filled with tears.

I hadn't wanted any of that shit with Stacy to touch her and I was pissed that Stacy's bullshit had invaded the little cocoon I had with Leda. I displaced my anger and kicked the door shut behind me. Knowing that the shit was just starting. Now, I had to spend the next however long soothing Leda, fixing this. As tired as I was, Leda was everything and I would do anything for her. Anything for her happiness.

I crossed the space to her without hesitation and grabbed her around the waist. "How much of that did you hear?"

She pushed away from me, the opposite of Stacy, echoing my way of pushing Stacy away from me. Her voice was tight, and cold, like I had never heard it before. "Enough to know there's a lot you haven't told me." I tried to hug her close to me, but she resisted and pulled away violently, yelling, "You lied to me! You ask me to trust you with my body, my submission and you *lie to me!*"

Ah fuck. Goddamn it. She turned away from me, looking around for something.

"Wait, Leda, it's not like that. Just wait. Let me explain." I turned on the light, so I could see her face. She was looking for something, picking up pieces of clothes and throwing them away.

She walked past me toward the closet that held our bags and I grabbed her hand, but she yanked it back with a shocked hiss.

"Fucking stop it, Xander. *Red,* goddammit! Red. Stop fucking touching me!"

Holy shit. I was confused by the strength of her reaction. It seemed like too much. "Jesus Christ, Leda, you're overreacting a bit, don't you think?"

She had found her leggings and was sitting on the floor pulling them on. She looked up at me like she might stab me in my sleep. I sat on the edge of the bed, trying to give her space. Trying to understand what the fuck what happening.

She moved to the arm chair across the room and spoke. "You have no idea what I'm thinking right now, so you really don't know if I'm overreacting, first of all."

Oh shit, a first of all. This is gonna suck.

"Number two, I cannot believe you didn't tell me you had a relationship with Stacy. She was the one you lost your Pentagon job over, wasn't she? What am I supposed to think now? And what the hell is she talking about that you haven't shown me yet? What more is there, Xander? I mean, fuck, I didn't even know your real name until this trip. I can't even look at you right now." Her face crumpled and she dropped her head into her hands for a moment, until she gathered herself. Then she looked back at me with such malevolence in that I recoiled, but held her gaze.

The tears built and dropped again. She devolved into sobs. I went to her, knelt in front of her. I lifted her chin and brushed her tears off her cheeks. "Leda," my voice failed me and I whispered. "I'm sorry. I'm so sorry." I said it even though I didn't know exactly what had hurt her. It didn't matter. She was hurting. And I was sorry that she felt any pain at all. "What can I do?"

She didn't answer me and I leaned into her, resting my lips on her soft mouth. She held still for a moment and a fresh waves of tears hit. I spoke against her lips, over her crying. "I love kissing you. Kissing you through your tears. Oh, fuck it. Leda, I love you. I love you, and your tender, kind heart. I love that you're nothing like her, nothing like any of these people here."

Chapter Forty-Two

Leda
Bjork, Army of Me

He loves me?

"Yeah, I know. I heard you tell Stacy before you even told me. And how can you say that but mislead me and lie to me? You don't trust me at all, do you?"

He looked surprised. "Leda, of course I trust you. But there are things about me, my past, my family, my life, that are ugly and I don't want you to see them. I don't want you to know about them."

"You don't trust that I would still accept you. So, either you don't believe in me or there is some seriously dark shit I have the right to know about. Either way, you don't trust me." I felt energy coiling in my chest and needed to move. It was a sickening combination of adrenaline and anger, burning through fatigue that made my arms and back ache. I just wanted to get away from him.

I had misgivings, wondered at my response. Maybe it *was* too much. I had only been with him for a few months. Was it really reasonable to think I would know everything about him, that there'd be no surprises anymore? That was ridiculous. Was this some sort of subdrop?

I argued back with myself. This wasn't like not knowing the name of his childhood pet. This was the fucking bitch that had been making me hate med school, the relationship that had ruined his career. This wasn't a minor omission. And the inevitable question went through my mind. *What else has he omitted? What will he omit in the future?*

I glanced at him. He looked lost, his shoulders sloping down, defeated. It was something I hadn't ever seen in him before. He was always the big, bad scary Dom-Man. This degree of vulnerability was disconcerting and he was diminished in my eyes. He was no longer the infallible conqueror of my bedroom, taking me places I had never been. Taking me beyond the confines of my imagination.

He was just a man, as fragile as me. And I could see in his face that he knew it. He had known it all along. He had asked me to lay myself down for him. He had led me deeper into him, into his darkness, knowing he was faulted the whole time. And recognition flooded through me that this was part of what I was angry about. Not that I was in a relationship with him and there were secrets that I hadn't learned yet. It was that this relationship was different. *He* was supposed to be different. He was supposed to be solid, strength, security. He was supposed to be my safety, but now that was broken. He wasn't any stronger than me, wasn't any more capable of keeping me safe. He wasn't different than every other guy I knew.

I wanted to get away from him to think about it. My thoughts felt too fast and sluggish at the same time. It was more than fatigue. It was too much to muddle through then.

"Look, we're both exhausted. Let's just try to sleep a bit and we can talk about this tomorrow or something." I sighed, stretched and stood.

He looked up at me, through his lashes, doubt on his face. "Okay, sweetheart." As I climbed into the bed, he pulled me to him, so I was sitting in his lap, my back to his chest. He dropped his forehead onto my shoulder. "I'm sorry. I'm so sorry, Leda. I didn't mean to hurt you." He pressed a kiss onto the slope of my shoulder and shifted me into the bed.

As I pulled the covers over me, he stood, saying, "I'm just gonna splash some water on my face and take some ibuprofen. Do you need anything?" When I shook my head, he added, "Be right back, honey."

It felt like goodbye, but I murmured my understanding and rolled over. I waited for the sound of the water and let my tears out a little. I had a fast, furious cry and was wrung out when it ended, whimpering against the wet pillow, as fatigue, both physical and emotional, claimed me.

* * * *

My sleep was fitful and I didn't feel rested when I woke up. Xander was gone, not in the bed with me where I expected him to be. I couldn't hear water running in the bathroom. Sitting up in the bed, the slurry of emotions running through me was too much to analyze or even recognize. The end result was a vague disgust peppered with a touch of relief that I didn't have to immediately confront him, followed quickly by fear that he had left in the night without me.

But, his things were still scattered around the room, and when I finally convinced myself to be a grown up and get the fuck out of bed and confront my problems, I noticed the note he left on the dresser.

L —
Working out, be back soon.
Take a shower, we can get breakfast when I get back.
— X

Was this guy still telling me what to do? I chuckled in disbelief at that, even as I walked to the bathroom and started the shower. Letting the water rush over me didn't clear my head as much as I had hoped it would.

I was just pulling a sweater over my head when he came back. His hair was soaked and his T-shirt clung to him, saturated with his sweat. I was distracted by the movement of his wet shirt over his torso as he entered and the twist of his body when he closed the door. It was as if, after last night and the thought that whatever we had might be in jeopardy, I was re-noticing the way he moved, the shape of him — remembering the ripple of his muscles under my fingers, the expanse of his shoulders, the way he could wrap his body around mine and how it used to feel like the only safe place in the world.

"Good workout?" It was too uncomfortable to just stand here, looking at him.

"Yeah, just ran some, lifted some weights." He looked like he had worked harder than that. "Are you hungry? We can get room service, go downstairs or go somewhere else. What are you in the mood for?"

"Ummm, I don't know what I want." Truer words never spoken. "Why don't you shower and we'll figure it out?"

"'Kay." He paused before turning to the bathroom, his eyes searching mine. I lifted my chin, challenging him to bring it up. He dropped his gaze and stepped away. The shower turned on shortly after.

We settled on breakfast at a small café a few blocks away recommended by the concierge. We walked in silence, the air brisk around us. We sat in the back of the restaurant and didn't speak until we ordered.

"You okay?" he finally asked.

A smile quirked at my lips. "Well, no, not really. Do you really want to talk about this here and now?"

"I can't *not* talk about it at this point." He looked down again, but when he looked back up at me, his eyes held a mix of anguish and anger.

"Okay…so talk." It was perhaps unnecessarily bitchy, but I was still pissed.

"What can I even say, Leda? Of course I had relationships before you. Of course there is more to me than you know about yet. I don't really even know what you're upset about." He cut himself off when the waitress brought our coffees.

Once she walked away, I answered him, "Xander. Alexander. I don't know how to explain it. I'm an open book for you. So open that it feels raw and dangerous. And, you're hidden from me. Your name isn't even really your name."

"I haven't hidden things from you. We just haven't gotten there yet."

"I call bullshit on that! You hid your real name from me. You hid your relationship with Stacy from me. And that's enough for me to question my trust in you. But that isn't even it, right? I mean, what was Stacy talking about that I don't know about—what else is there, Xander?"

"Leda, I never lied to you."

I cut him off, "No, you just never let me see the truth."

We held a tense silence as the waitress delivered our food. It was good hangover breakfast—greasy eggs and potatoes, covered in cheesy goodness, thick, rich coffee and, on the waitress's recommendation, we had ordered a gooey cinnamon roll to split. The food was great, but it was only secondary in my focus. Even after she walked away, we still sat in silence. After what felt like several hours, he responded.

"Okay, what truth do you want from me?"

"I don't fucking know. If I knew, it wouldn't be an issue, right?" My tone was heavy with sarcasm, clearly implying he was an idiot.

His expression darkened to something I had never seen in all our sex-play. This was true anger. He was actually getting pissed off at me. "I'm trying to be open here, Leda. Don't fucking punish me right when you're getting what you say you want."

Jesus, that stung, but my pride wouldn't let me answer in kindness. I just waited, gritting my jaw.

He sensed that he had an edge and leaned into it. "What do you want to know?"

I concentrated on cutting up something on my plate, until he reached across the table and tilted my chin up to look at him.

"Last time I'm asking. What do you want to know about me?" The words were measured and deliberately well-enunciated.

I took a deep breath. "I don't know, Xander. I don't know. What was Stacy talking about? Tell me about your relationship with her, because I think she is a big, bitchy cunt of a person and I can't see how you could see anything redeeming in her." I knew I was displacing some of my anger on her, but I couldn't stop myself. In a sick way, I wanted to see if he defended her.

A quick smirk tugged at his lips before he answered, but when he did, he was serious. "Like I said, I grew up with her. She was there when my parents changed and started to hate each other. She was young and silly, a perfect distraction. She was like a sister. My parents' relationship was why I went into the military—I had to get away from them. My dad was fucking half the interns who came through Noe's office, but then he'd be weirdly possessive of my mom. Stacy was there and we had a bond that I can't really explain to someone who wasn't there.

"When I went to the Academy, she was still in high school. The Army was all-consuming, and got me away from the DC bullshit. But she had to stay back and she was alone. I swear, she was so sweet then. I came home for a long visit one summer and she was just different. Grown up, sexual, beautiful—and aggressive. We started…something. I don't really know what it was. She was beyond my girlfriends. She was just…her. It wasn't really a relationship, but it was.

"Anyway, the next summer, we went to the Nymphos show and, it was a crazy. We met the band and they invited us on the tour bus. And then we just… She was wild." He shrugged.

After a moment, I shrugged back at him and he continued, "We were gone partying and fucking and being crazy for four days. Our parents were freaking out, but no one had cell phones yet and we just didn't go home. They didn't want to make a *scandal,* so they didn't do anything. She felt like her parents didn't care that she disappeared. After that, she just got more self-destructive—more drugs, more sex. I don't know—that's when things changed. There's a black hole in me that she has seen. I mean, she's fucking been in it. And there's a deep part of her that's angry and mighty. There was huge fallout when we came back... And we stood by each other through it."

His ode to Stacy's dark and fucked up beauty was beginning to piss me off. "Okay, so you're both beautifully damaged. What the fuck have you been doing with me for the past few months?"

He blanched at my tone, realizing that my patience was waning. "Let me finish the story. It was one thing for me to be doing all that shit at twenty-two. It was still fucked up, but not so much outside of the normal wild oat sowing of the early twenties, especially for guys in the military. She was only eighteen. It was different for her. She was actively rebelling and she tied all that to me, switched all her weird dependence on her parents to me. We tried to be together, but she was too fucked up and I didn't want to be tied down to one person and she wasn't submissive at all. It evolved into a love-hate thing. We'd fight then fuck. Fuck then fight. When I went overseas, she tried to fuck Jason."

I started at that, not realizing they knew each other or even had a history, but it made sense. "Does she ever go to the Window?"

"I don't know, Leda. I don't have any kind of relationship with her anymore. But I think Christy would let her know how it is if she ever tried to get after Jason again. It's not really an issue, because he really slammed the door on that. He never liked her. He likes happy girls, like Christy. It's why he likes you." He glanced up at me, gauging my reaction to his subtle flattery.

"Finish your story and get to the point that explains why you lied to me, and why you were in the hall with her, in a bathrobe and nothing else, *kissing her*, in the middle of the night when you were supposed to be in bed with me." He gave me a wry glance, implying that I was being ridiculous, so I added, "Reverse the roles for a minute. What if my close friend from childhood, who I apparently had fucked like crazy showed up in the middle of the night and you woke to find *me* in the hall, talking with him, in nothing, *nothing*, but a robe, and you were sure that he kissed me? How would that sit?"

His eyes hardened and the muscle in his jaw twitched. "Okay. I get it. Because I might kill a motherfucker."

"Okay. So stop implying that I'm overreacting." My voice was hard.

"All right, killer." He thought he was funny, but I wanted to slap him. "Ultimately, I was discharged from the Army and got my job at the Pentagon. Her dad was on the Congressional Defense committee. He helped me get the job. When I moved back to DC, she was in undergrad at Georgetown, so we started hanging out again. And then we started having sex again. And she wanted to try to be submissive again. So we started slow, like you and I did."

Oh, what an asshole.

"And she was doing great. So one night, she was at the Pentagon, visiting her dad or something. She stopped to see me because I was working late. At this point, I had started visiting dungeons and play parties and I knew more about what I wanted. She agreed to try…more."

I took a deep breath. Did I really want to hear about this anymore? My stomach was in knots and I stopped eating.

"Are you sure you want to hear this, Leda?"

I laughed as another wave of dread-tinged nausea washed over me. "No. I don't *want* to hear it. I don't want it to exist. I don't want there to be a problem between us. I don't want to think about you touching someone the way you touch me. I don't want to think about you being in love with someone else." My voice cracked.

"I wasn't in love with her. She was like a sister, and—"

"She was like your sister so you had sex with her intermittently, *for several years.* Thank God you don't have any biological sisters." I paused to control myself. I could feel the rising emotions getting out of control. "No. I want to know what happened that changed the course of your life."

"Okay, stop me if it's too much." The irony of that statement stung a little. "You have to understand, we would come together, try to figure out how to be together and then it would implode. We just cycled like that, over and over."

I nodded my understanding, but didn't speak.

He continued, "The night that she was talking about, the night that got me fired, was when I was at the Pentagon. She came to my workroom and told me she wanted to try again, that I was the only person she could ever submit to." His eyes glazed a bit. "I told her it was all or nothing. I didn't want to just dabble in controlling her. She agreed, and I grabbed her. No discussion of limits or safewords. I realize now how absolutely terrible that was, but I was relatively new to BDSM then. I remember pulling her head back by her hair and asking her if she was sure. She said she was and that was it. I turned her around and flattened her across my boss's desk, and secured her hands to the drawer pull with my belt."

Why would I have thought that was a new trick just for me? It's probably the only reason he wears a belt. Dick. Why am I listening to this? Maybe I was more of a masochist than I knew.

"I tied one ankle to the leg of the desk with my tie, and pushed her skirt up. I used some scissors to cut her underwear off and, I went after it." He stopped, as if that was the full story. I waited, but he said nothing.

"Keep going, Xander. I want all the details."

"Why?"

"I don't know. Because I heard her last night. I heard her say that she knew your darkness and she had something to match. I want to know what this cosmic *fucked-upness* is that you two share. I want to know how real it is. Have you just been playing at something approaching normal for me? Was it a game? I have to know."

"Leda, I don't want to tell you this. It's the past and a lot has changed since then."

"The fuck it has. She's at your door in the middle of the night and you just waxed nostalgic about your *whatever* the fuck it was with her. Your shit with her is not resolved. Now I understand why she has been such a bitch to me, at least."

"Leda, let's just let it go and work on moving past this."

"There is no consideration of 'past this' until and unless you tell me the truth. Now." I knew it was irrational. I didn't care. I knew I would probably regret it. I didn't care. I could see something unresolved between them. I had to know before I could decide what to do next.

"Okay. But remember, when you hate me, when you're disgusted with me—you fucking asked for this."

Chapter Forty-Three

Xander
The Neighbourhood, Afraid

When I opened my mouth to tell Leda the truth—the deeply sick shit from my past, I couldn't speak. I had run into Stacy's father that morning and his words echoed in my mind, forecasting what Leda was going to *know* about me as soon as I spoke the words.

I had seen Jackson in the lobby as he'd been coming off the elevator. I'd thought he was going to completely snub me, but as he'd passed me, he'd stopped, pushing his face into mine.

"I don't know what really happened between you and Stacy, but she followed you to Texas. She never said a word against you, even though I saw... I saw what you were doing to her. She never said anything about it, just begged me to leave it alone. As far as I'm concerned, you're a rapist, sick as fuck and should be in prison. She saved you from that. You owe her, you piece of shit."

Leda cleared her throat in an impatient sound.

I swallowed against a wave of nausea and continued, "I had her tied down, with one free leg, so I could move her around however I wanted." I got a reckless feeling, a feeling of fuck it. If it was gonna be destroyed with her, it just proved I really was a monster and I was gonna lean the fuck into it.

"I started behind her, licking her. She wanted it so bad I remember laughing at that. She got offended and said something smartassed. I slapped her ass, hard enough to see the creases from my palm in the handprint on her ass. When she began to protest, I started playing with her, until she forgot she was upset. I got her close to coming and stopped before she could. Just to fuck with her, for no other reason at all. I knew she was afraid of anal sex and I wanted to scare her, so I started fingering her ass. She was so wet that I didn't need lube. I know I was running my mouth the whole time, just spouting off the foulest, dirtiest, most depraved shit I could think of. I was testing her."

I paused to take a breath, looking at Leda to see her reaction. Her face was a blank mask, so I continued, "Mostly I wanted her to prove to me that she would really submit, so I gave her the worst of me. I know at some point, I called her a cunt and she got really mad, and tried to turn over some to yell at me, and I slammed her down on the desk."

In the years since it happened, when I looked back at that day, I knew...I should have been better. Should have been sure she was into it. Should have given her a safeword. A million *should haves*..

"Looking back, I think I knocked the wind out of her, because she stopped talking. This is how bad of a Dom I was then— Fuck! I can't even call myself a *Dom*. I was a stupid kid, trying to be something that I had no idea about." I took a deep breath and continued when Leda gestured at me impatiently. "I thought she was submitting, but she was shutting down. And remember, we had no safeword, hadn't discussed limits. And I don't really know, maybe she was dropping into a crap version of subspace, because she got really limp. I stood behind her and fucked her, still running my mouth about what a whore she was and whatever else."

My brain was a fucking mess. Because this was what I had believed about myself for the last ten years and Stacy had turned it all on its head last night. And now, as I tried to explain it to Leda, I realized I had been replaying all the same shit with her, trying to do it right, but still trying to find a way to be with a girl that I could completely defile. I wanted to be able to love her and hurt her. It wasn't a real thing. It couldn't be a real thing. I had already done all these things with Stacy. My mind reeled in a torrent of self-recriminations. Leda was talking, telling me to keep going, not seeing that I was realizing how much I had been mindfucking myself this whole time.

I looked up at her, wishing she could save me, but knowing that she couldn't. *Ah, fucking hell. It's gonna fall the fuck apart. And then I'm gonna fall the fuck apart.* I kept talking, because it was the only thing to do now. The end was inevitable. I just had to play my part out.

"I grabbed the scissors and told her I wanted to cut her. She started squirming and crying and then she screamed. I cut her off with my hand over her mouth. And here's how totally sick I am, just the thought of her bleeding almost made me come. And then it was all I could think of. I wanted to make her bleed. I wanted to taste her blood. I kept fucking her and after a moment, she started talking against my hand.

Pleading for more, for something different. She was all over the place. I told her I'd let her talk as long as she didn't make a lot of noise, but first to hold her tongue out. She obeyed me, and I flicked the blade of the scissors over her tongue and cut her. Just to taste it."

Jesus Christ, I'm a monster. I'm a monster. Then it just kept running through my head. *I'm a monster, I'm a monster, I'm a monster, I'm a monster.* The realization came that I had to get Leda away from me. She couldn't be with me. I had been worrying that I might harm her in some way. Of course I would. I already was. I wasn't capable of anything else. She was too good. I had to get her away. I let her have the last of my deepest shame, the worst thing I had ever done.

"She started crying and the blood coated her lips. I flipped her over and licked the blood from her tongue as I fucked her, as she cried and whimpered against my mouth, telling me to stop. But you have to understand—she liked to play games like that. Liked to tell me no, just to make me make her. It was so fucked up, I can't even explain it. But it... It wasn't that abnormal for her to say something like that."

There it was. I was as naked as I could ever be in front of her now. She could see the rottenness in me, the wrongness in me. She didn't say anything but her face was pale. I finished the story, to get it over with. "Her dad walked in shortly thereafter. Her *dad*, my boss's boss. It was awful. It's a blur, but I remember him pulling me off her and punching me, while my dick was still out. I was done at the Pentagon. The only reason he didn't press charges or make a huge spectacle about it was that she defended me and wouldn't make any kind of statement accusing me. She saved me from a lot of shit—prison, ruining my dad's life."

And since that day, I had thought I had raped her, even though I hadn't intended to, even though it had been a horrible miscommunication. That I thought she wanted what I had, but the way it ended...I was sure I was the worst person ever. But last night, she had told me she wanted it then and still wanted it now. It was fucking with my head. What I thought was true about that night wasn't.

Leda's voice interrupted my circular logic. "So what did you do then? Because that was a few years ago."

"I took six months off and Jason and I went to Europe. When we came back, I worked for a private intelligence firm, basically mercenary intelligence stuff. I did data analysis and some interrogation shit. The medicine of it was still the most interesting part, so ultimately, I applied to med school. That's the whole story." I waited a few beats. "Well, do you hate me?"

"No. I don't hate you, but...Xander. I, I...I just need to think about all of this. I don't really know what my reaction is. Let's get through this visit and when we get back to school, I just need some space to figure it out."

Yep...that's about the best I could hope for. "Okay. We should get back to the hotel. I think my mom was actually expecting to meet us for brunch. Just promise me you won't make any major decisions about us until we can talk more."

"I won't. Let's go."

The walk back to the hotel was brisk, cold in every sense of the word. I wanted to be holding her hand, have a territorial arm around her. But she kept a solid distance between us, about two steps to the side and one step behind me. Her face was closed off. The crinkle between her eyebrows told me she was thinking.

My mom was waiting in the lobby when we walked back in. She was hungover. I could tell from across the wide space. She could tell before we got close. She got the steel in her spine that meant I was probably going to get yelled at. She kept her cards close to the chest though, let it play out.

"Hiya, kids! Already been out this morning? You're doing better than me! Ready for brunch?"

I was about to decline and get us out of it, but Leda spoke, "I'm not doing much better, Nancy. I think I'm going to lay back down for a bit. But you two should spend some time together." She smiled and played it off, but I knew what she was doing. She was getting away from me.

"Are you sure, Leda?" I asked.

She nodded and walked away.

She wasn't even at the elevator doors before my mom started. "Alex, what did you do?" She was as soft as she could be, but she was angry too.

I scrubbed my hair and rubbed my neck, the need to move overwhelming. "Stacy came to our room in the middle of the night and it woke Leda up."

"That girl is so fucking crazy now." She pulled me into the elevator and hit the button for the top floor. She had apparently chosen to treat herself to a suite. "Come on. We'll eat in my room for some privacy."

Once we were settled and had ordered, she asked again. "So what happened?"

"Stacy called a few times after we went to sleep and it woke me up. I answered and told her to fuck off, but she was drunk and told me she was going to come down and wake the whole floor up."

"She'd probably have done it too. At least you avoided a huge incident."

I closed my eyes for a moment. That was the least of my concerns. "Anyway, I waited in the hall for her, so she didn't knock."

My mom nodded. She understood.

The room service arrived and she answered the door to take care of it. After the waiter was gone, we continued. "So, what did she want?"

"She wants to get back together. She wants me to know that no one other than her really understands me. That I'm the only one for her. But she did it the way she does things, convoluted, twisted. And Leda woke up, heard at least some of it."

"So...why is that so bad? So someone else wants you. She better get used to that."

"No, that's not it. She didn't know about anything between me and Stacy. And Stacy's been a real bitch to her at school. And Stacy kissed me. She heard it all."

"Alex, why didn't you tell her that you had a history with Stacy?"

"Mom, what would I have said? 'That girl that's so shitty to you? I used to fuck her and I think I accidentally raped her?' How does that conversation end?"

"How did the conversation this morning end?" She raised a snarky eyebrow at me, over the rim of her drink.

"Touché, goddammit. Give me some of that," I said, grabbing at her Bloody Mary. She just switched to the screwdriver she had also ordered. Nice.

"But, here's the thing that's really fucking me up the most. Stacy told me that she wanted it that night. That she wants it again, for good." I stood up and started pacing. My mom blew her breath out on a curse against Stacy. "All these years, I've been destroying myself, afraid to let myself have a relationship because I didn't know what the fuck I was doing, because I was sure I had hurt her. Shit." I crumpled onto the couch and my eyes watered at the enormity of how that girl had fucking destroyed me.

I had spent the years since that night convinced that I was morally flawed, one of the things I found most repugnant in the world, and she'd let me feel it. She'd let the rumors her father spread about me go uncorrected. She had seen me, called me enough times to have told me that I wasn't the monster who had ruined her life—and she never had.

Until now. When I was on the verge of being happy, when I had fallen in love with someone else.

My mom came and sat next to me, rubbing my back. "I love you, son. I've never thought you were the monster you thought you were. As much as I want to slap that little bitch, at least she gave that to you. You aren't tainted. You aren't flawed."

My body racked against sobs I tried to hold in and I turned to her. She opened her arms and pulled me into her, the way that no one other than a mom can do.

And it didn't matter that I was thirty-four, that I outweighed her by a good seventy pounds, that I was half a foot taller than her. I was her little boy again. She guided me to rest against her and she kept rubbing my arm, murmuring to me all the things I hadn't let myself believe. My heart was cracking open to even consider loving myself again.

After I had quieted down, and we had both finished our drinks, she said, "So. Now. How are you going to figure it out with Leda?"

"I don't know. What should I do?"

"Well, how much did you tell her?"

"All of it."

"Oh, honey. Shit." She just took a few deep breaths, then added, "Well, you've got your work cut out for you. But I saw her last night. She watched you and nothing else mattered to her in that party. She only wanted to be near you, lived and died by your smile." Further knife wounds in my heart. "So the first thing is, Stacy has to go, completely. You can't have anything to do with her now."

"Done."

"And you have to make sure Leda knows it. You have to remind her what she loves about you."

That seemed like the harder part.

When I got back to the room, Leda was asleep. I made a point to be quiet as I got into a pair of sweats and climbed into bed next to her. I resisted the urge to pull her into my arms, turn her toward me and press her into the mattress with my body, lavishing her with kisses even as I held her in place. I started to get an erection thinking about it. But I didn't do anything with it. I deserved to suffer. I wanted to be near her, even like this.

I fell asleep quickly, which wasn't surprising since I had been awake since Stacy had called in the middle of the night.

Chapter Forty-Four

Leda
John Newman, Love Me Again

When I'd gotten back to the room, I had thrown up the greasy breakfast and cried until I fell asleep. But when I woke again, Xander was there, sleeping next to me. Naked torso and loose, low-slung sweats hanging off his hips. I just watched him for a while. The tight weave of his abdominal muscles and the way they moved as he breathed, the softness around his eyes, his perfectly masculine lips just slightly parted, his rugged hands and wrists. His body was beautiful, sexy beyond reasoning. He turned in his sleep and murmured a sound of sensual appreciation. As I watched, he got hard, but didn't wake.

His virility was like gravity. I felt it pulling me toward him, felt myself getting heated and slick just imagining what he was dreaming up. Recalling the feel of those hands on me, those lips whispering obscenities in my ear, that torso between my thighs.

"Goddammit. I gotta leave," I muttered to myself as I grabbed my purse and keycard.

I got a coffee from the small shop in the lobby. I sat back in one of the wide, cushy arm chairs off to the side behind a wall of ferns, letting my brain rest, spacing out and people watching. Refusing to try to dissect the current bullshit any further.

When my coffee had gone cold, I stood, intending to get rid of it, but I saw Stacy across the lobby. The Bell Captain was coordinating managing her bags for her. She didn't see me so I dropped back down, wanting to avoid her, but shifting in my seat so I could watch her.

"Stacy! Wait for a moment, dear." Xander's mother was crossing the lobby, heels clicking, smile on her face. Stacy turned with a smile. They went together, were cut from the same cloth, but it was another wave of repulsion—his mother was friendly with this girl that had fucked up his life, that he had harmed. *Who the fuck are these people?*

They were close enough that I could hear the beginning of their conversation as Nancy walked Stacy out the door. Nancy was smiling and said, "So, my dear. Safe travels. Xander told me what happened last night."

"Oh? And what did he say?"

"Oh, Stacy. What happened to you?" Her sweet pretension was gone. It was honest sadness and disappointment in her tone now.

"Um, *he* did, Nancy. You know that."

"No, I don't." She cocked her head to the side in concern that didn't reach her voice at all. "Why are you pursuing him if he hurt you so badly? I don't think he really hurt you. I think you couldn't face your father and you just let him assume the worst. I think that you allowed my son's life to be ruined instead of being an adult and taking some ownership of your actions."

Stacy sputtered. "Nancy, we were all drinking last night... I don't know what Xander told you, but maybe he's not remembering it correctly."

They passed through the doors, but I watched them through the window and moved to a different seat to get a better view. Nancy was vehemently gesturing. Stacy stood tall, holding Nancy's gaze. The Bell Captain interrupted them with an apologetic look on his face and Stacy snapped at him. She and Nancy came back inside again.

"Yes, Nancy. I love him. I'm always going to love him. Don't you want him with someone who's his equal? Imagine the life we'd make together."

Now Nancy sputtered. "I don't even know where to start with your delusions. You aren't his equal. And besides that, your father would never condone a relationship, let alone a *marriage* with my son after the lies you told. But most importantly, *he doesn't love you.* In fact, he doesn't even like you anymore. Stacy, you can't ruin lives with impunity and think you can still get what you want."

"Nancy, come on. I always get what I want." She scoffed.

Nancy leaned into Stacy's space, an ice-cold smile on her lips. "You *will not* harm my son ever again, you little bitch. How dare you even talk to me about marrying him? You nearly destroyed him."

"Then we're even, aren't we?"

Nancy raised her voice in exasperated anger. "He didn't harm you! You asked him to do what he did. That's what you told him last night when he was completely sober and *you* were drunk."

Stacy blanched, her face slackened. It was the look of being caught in a terrible lie. *Did she let Xander think he had violated her consent for all those years, when she had consented to it?*

I was going to vomit again. When Nancy and Stacy went back outside, I went to the lobby restroom and wet down a paper towel with some cool water. I rubbed it across my face and the back of my neck.

The longer I looked at myself, the more I felt like *I* had fucked up. Xander was so overwhelming and powerful, I had forgotten my own power, forgotten to take care of myself. I'd let myself get lost in him, let myself become all his. Nothing leftover.

"Fuck that," I said to my reflection and threw out the towel. As I left the restroom, I heard the deep, rich tone of Xander's voice in the lobby, in conversation with his mother.

"No, no note. Nothing. I just woke up and she was gone." He sounded pissed and worried.

"Son, if her stuff's still there, she didn't leave. Probably just went for a walk."

"She doesn't go anywhere without me." His voice was a growl, rough with possessiveness, willing it to be true just with his vehemence.

"Calm down. That isn't going to bring her back to you." Her voice faded as they walked away and I couldn't hear his response.

I knew he was going to be pissed when I got back up there, so I went across the street for another coffee before heading back up to the room.

He was waiting when I got back, sitting in the chair, still in the sweats, with only an A-frame undershirt on top. He looked goddamned delicious. His head was dropped and he lifted it slowly as I came through the door. His face registered relief then pain, then stormy anger.

"If we weren't all fucked up right now, I'd put you over my fucking knee, little girl." His voice was low, restrained but pressured nonetheless.

It pissed me off even as I flushed with some vague sense of wanting. Anger won. "Well, shit isn't fine between us."

His eyes flared. "Where have you been?"

I held my coffee cup up, saying, "I needed a coffee. Didn't want to wake you."

"You should have left a note."

He was right and I knew it. I relented a little. "Sorry you worried. I really thought I'd be right back, but I almost ran into Stacy and I just didn't want to talk to her."

His hands fisted in his lap, tension evident in the set of his shoulders. We held each other's gaze for a span of moments that felt fraught with meaning, anticipation. But neither of us caved. Neither of us reached out.

"I'm taking a shower. What's the plan for the rest of the day?" I asked, my tone cordial, but cold.

"We're leaving."

"Pardon?" I turned back from the bathroom.

"Yeah, I know you don't want to be around me anymore and I don't want to fucking be here, so I took care of it. Just waiting for the details about the time."

I sputtered a little, pissed that he made such a big change of plans without discussing it with me first, but he was right. I needed some space from him. "Okay. I'm assuming that I have time for a shower."

"Yeah. Even if we didn't, they'd wait for us."

"All right." I turned and went to the bathroom. I ran the water to cover my sounds as I felt the tears welling up again. He seemed so distant, so cold, and now, he just wanted to get away from me.

We grabbed a quick dinner at a bistro down the street from the hotel, joined by his mother. It was so fucking uncomfortable. Interestingly, Xander's mother seemed to be a little cold to him and I wondered what he had told her. She was perfectly cordial to me, though.

She drove us to the airport in his car, planning to take it back out to her house where he stored it. Before we boarded, she pulled me aside. "Leda, you have to understand, Alex had a terrible role model of how to be a man."

Umm, whoa. That was out of the blue. "I'm sorry, Nancy. I don't follow. What are you talking about?"

"His father was never home. It was a sacrifice we made because Denny is the Senator's right-hand man. But it meant that I pretty much raised Alex by myself. He does stupid things. You just have to be patient with him."

"Nancy." I cringed. *How do you tell someone her son is twisted? And you don't think you can love him? And really he should be with Stacy because they are each other's brand of fucked up?* "I see the relationship and love between you two. But I don't know what will happen between me and Xander... I mean Alex. I mean, I didn't know his real name until this trip."

"And there's Stacy, who seems like she knows so much about him, has all this shared history." She just stated it, a knowing look on her face.

"Well, yeah. And, honestly, she'd such a...we're just so different. It doesn't make sense that he could have had a relationship with her and then have one with me."

"You just didn't know her when she was younger. She's broken. I don't think he really even knows her anymore. I thought when she went down there for school, they'd reconnect. But...he kept his distance. But, listen to me, Leda, what Xander and Stacy had... It was a lie they told themselves for a while."

As we walked toward the gate, she held my hand, genuine sadness in her eyes. "Let me say two more things. Xander is the only name he has recognized for himself for twenty years now, so I don't think he was trying to hide anything from you." She paused, giving my hand a little squeeze as she breathed deeply. "And, he made a terrible mistake. No one but Stacy and him really know what really happened, but he has paid for it, over and over. He lost his career, the majority of his social network and was shunned by the people he considered an extended family. Jason and I were the only ones who completely stuck with him. It's the moment that has completely defined him since and he hates it. I don't know where you are in your thoughts about him, but just consider that he has already borne an awful consequence and, for better or worse, the decision to go to Texas for med school was to get away from all that and it led him to you."

She pulled me into hug. "I hope I see you again, Leda."

The lump in my throat threatened to choke me and tears welled up in my eyes. "Bye, Nancy."

I walked onto the plane, leaving Xander to say his goodbyes with her in private. I nestled into a window seat and looked out at the night, while a few tears spilled over my lashes.

When he boarded the plane, he sat next to me. I tried to make small talk as we taxied and took off, asking why the Ivorys weren't with us. When he explained that it was Jason's plane, I gaped at one more thing I didn't know about. After a few minutes of obviously wrestling with something, he turned to me and took my hand. "Do you still think you need space from me?"

I gently pulled my hand away from him. "Yeah. I don't know what to say to you right now. I feel like everything about us is built on falsehood. I don't know who you are and I don't know who I am with you. I barely recognize myself anymore."

"Leda." The anguish in his voice, the pain...almost made me reconsider. "Don't do this."

His face was desolate. And I simultaneously felt so sad to see him hurting and so goddamned angry that he brought it on himself, that he set us on this fucked up path when we met.

"Look, you gotta leave me alone about it because you're starting to piss me off even more. Did I fall in love with you? Yes, of course I did. But it all feels like a lie. I don't know what I fell in love with." My tears spilled over again and I wanted to ignore all the shitty stuff. I wanted to climb in his lap, snuggle into him, and lose everything in kissing him.

After a moment of silence, he stood, walked to the back of the plane, to the bar. I sat in my seat, stunned that he was that cold, that dismissive. That he could just turn it off and walk away from me like that. I shifted in my seat to look back at him. He was facing away from me, arms stretched to the sides, resting his hands on the bar, head hanging.

The expanse of his back rippled under his shirt when he moved to pour himself a drink. The flight attendant approached him, but he snapped something at her and she walked away, a look of shock on her face.

He sat on the low couch beside the bar, legs wide, resting his elbows on his knees. He looked up, held my gaze for a moment, face unreadable, hard, distant. Then he stretched out on the couch, glass of scotch balanced on his chest, staring at the ceiling.

I pulled my knees up to my chest and the flight attendant brought me a blanket. She was cool, but deferential. I rested my head against the window and watched the lights of cities pass under us. I faded into a dozy sleep, but woke a while later when we hit some turbulence.

I got up to use the lavatory, and Xander was waiting when I came out. I tried to shimmy past him, but I couldn't get around the bulk of his body. And he didn't shift to let me through. I put my hand on his chest and he sucked a breath in. I could smell the scotch on his breath. *Has he been drinking this whole flight?* When I tried to push past him, he grabbed my wrist and pulled me into him, securing my neck with his other hand.

I gasped and tried to push back, but he spoke and his voice was calm. "Little one, you are asking me to do something that feels wrong on every level. It's my instinct to fight for you, even if it means fighting *with* you. I don't know how to let you go. But I swear to God, I will *never* hurt you and if you tell me to go when we land, I will. But please…*please* consider that there is more to be said between us. *Please* admit that there is still a chance to work this out."

I couldn't speak. The pressure of his body against mine incinerated any thought I may have had. He turned a little, pressing me against the wall.

"I don't know how to give you what you want and if space is what you need, I don't want to fucking give it to you."

The rumble in his voice left me breathless. I felt how I felt the first night he drove me home. A little flustered, a little breathless. His lips were next to my ear and he crooned again..

"You don't really want it either. I can feel the way you react to me."

It was true and I moaned, dropping my forehead against his chest, but his words sank in. *No. That isn't what I want.* It took all my willpower, but I pushed him back again.

My voice was a whisper when I answered him. "Please, Xander. Please listen to me. You have to take your hands off me because I can't fucking think when you touch me. And I need to be able to think right now."

He dropped his hands from me with a curse, but kept his face right in front of mine. "All right, little girl. I'll give you space. You're fucking wrecking me. Every instinct I have says to claim you even more, but I'll give you what you want—because I love you. Take the rest of the flight and when we land, we decide some shit."

I gasped and dashed passed him. He was putting a time limit on how long I could think about all this. *How can he even do that? Does that mean we'll break up if I don't have an answer he likes when we land?* For the rest of the flight, my mind raced through scenarios and memories. Tried to analyze our relationship so I could predict something about the future.

We were back on the ground too quickly. Once we had our bags, he just looked at me expectantly. "Well? What's it gonna be, Leda? Am I driving you to your place or mine?"

"I can just take a cab."

He just laughed and grabbed my luggage, but his laugh was bitter, derisive. He tossed our bags in the back of his car, but he saw when I opened the passenger door.

"Goddamn it, Leda! What are you doing?"

I looked up at him like he was crazy. "I'm getting in the fucking car."

"No! All I want to do is take care of you. All I ever want is to make sure you're safe and happy. Why are you making it so hard?" When I didn't respond, he walked over to the passenger side door and closed it. His voice was calmer. "I want to take care of you. I may want to do a million fucked up things in bed with you, but I never want you to have a moment of true pain or unhappiness. And I know it may seem silly, but the car door is just one of those things. It's like it...just represents...something—fuck, I don't know. Just...I don't want you to open the car door, any door, for yourself when I'm around. I just want you to let me fucking take care of you."

His voice had faltered at the end of his tirade and he looked down at the ground, his chest heaving, and I had a flash of understanding. He wanted me, wanted to cherish me. He may have wanted to destroy me in bed, but only if I liked it too. And everywhere else he wanted to adore me.

June's warnings about the mental acrobatics of Domination and submission flickered in my thoughts and my thoughts came too fast. Flashing back to the memory of the first time he drove me to school, how pissed he was when I got out of the car by myself. All the little moments of his quietly doting on me. Protecting me from everything—from riding my bike home from school late at night, or holding off on sex, and later when we started the kink, easing me into it. Helping with studying for school.

All the lies and half-truths, the omissions, were part of it, part of protecting me. But from himself too. He thought some part of him would hurt me, taint me somehow. He was human, not Superman, even though he wanted to be. He wanted me to see him like some hero. That fractured need for me to love him melted my heart.

He had spent the last few days walking me through his personal hell and it had turned into exactly what he had feared it would. And, instead of raging at me or the world or even Stacy, he was here, laying himself bare to me, trying to make me understand, even while he believed I was going to leave him anyway.

I just barely touched his arm, my voice a whisper. "Okay. You get the door. I get it, Xander. I love you."

He looked up at me sharply, his face set in lines of disbelief. But when he saw my small smile and the tears brimming over my lashes, his incredulity shifted to the purest, most open happiness. He grabbed me around the waist as a low, joyful laugh erupted from his chest. "Oh, thank God!" And he plastered my face with kisses. "Oh my God, Leda, I love you. So much. Thought my world was about to end."

Between kisses, I murmured, "Okay, Boss?"

He answered with a gruff, "Yeah."

"Then why don't you take me home. No one is expecting us until tomorrow. That's barely enough time to make up properly, but I bet you'll make it work."

Epilogue

Xander
Tom Petty, You Wreck Me

All I wanted that night was to be next to her, to feel the sweet curve of her body shimmied up against me. She loved me. Even after hearing all the trash, all the shit I carried around inside me, she fucking *loved* me. There'd be days and days ahead for training her, tormenting her — teasing myself with her body.

As I watched her sleeping, I considered all the ways I wanted to make her yield and cry and scream. And it was all perfect. I thought about a life with her — quick fucks between calls in residency, vacations with no one but us, massaging her leg cramps away when she got pregnant, calling her Mommy for the first time, hearing our kids calling her Mommy for the first time. The million little moments that would make up a life together. I was in love with her, obliterated by her. Wrecked.

About the Author

Corrine A. Silver has been writing stories and poems as long as she can remember. In college, she turned her fantasy life into a degree in Creative Writing, but took a detour into health care for ten years before getting up the nerve to try to publish anything again. She writes stories of BDSM erotic fiction, exploring themes of enthusiastic consent, power exchange and Domination/submission. Whenever her curiosity is piqued by a new kink, she writes a story about it.

She lives in the Midwest with her husband, two kids and zero pets. She continues to (attempt to) balance family, working at her day job and writing. She remembers what not being busy felt like, but is grateful for all the things that fill up her days.

Corrine A. Silver loves to hear from readers. You can find her contact information, website and author biography at http://www.totallybound.com.

Home of Erotic Romance